THE DAY THE WORLD BURNED

Kristina Shuey

Published by Kristina Shuey, Pine City, MN.
www.kristinashuey.wordpress.com
authorkristinashuey@gmail.com

ISBN-13: 979-8-9914132-0-6 (digital)
ISBN-13: 979-8-9914132-1-3 (paperback)

Library of Congress Control Number: 2024918857

Edited by Diane Engelstad
Cover design by Haley McMillan
Maps by Andrea Borich

For my grandparents—Patrick "Papa" Borich, Elizabeth Borich, and Judy Miranda—and for my husband's grandparents, Robert Wiseman Shuey and Lola Virginia Shuey, thank you for always telling me stories.

Author's Note

In Hinckley, Minnesota, on September 1, 1894, the sky itself was on fire. This is not an exaggeration. The fire was so large and consumed oxygen so quickly that unburned carbon and gases from the flames rose up into the air, lingering until encountering enough oxygen again for combustion. This unique trait characterizes an uncommon phenomenon classified as a *mass fire*, also known as a firestorm or conflagration.

Mass fires have tall flaming fronts, reaching heights of one to two hundred feet above the ground. They can remain stationary or move swiftly, reaching speeds of up to fifteen miles per hour. Additionally, these fires release enormous amounts of thermal energy. What distinguishes mass fires from traditional wildfires is their ability to generate hurricane-speed winds and fire tornadoes known as 'fire whirls.'

The mass fire that occurred in Hinckley, one hundred and thirty years ago, began as two separate fires. The first started three days earlier in a farmer's field five miles southwest from the settlement of Pokegama (now called Brook Park). The second likely originated from a spark emitted by a locomotive alongside the train tracks in the switching yard at Mission Creek. These two fires eventually merged in Hinckley, creating what we now refer to as the Great Hinckley Fire.

If you grew up in east central Minnesota, like I did, you have heard of the Great Hinckley Fire. Although it was mentioned during my elementary school years, I had no true understanding of its historical significance. The economic trajectory of the county can be measured in terms of 'before' and 'after' the Great Hinckley Fire.

Before the fire, Hinckley was a rough and tumble logging town and, at the same time, a thriving community. It was the most populated village in the county with over 600 residents, three churches, four hotels, a two-story brick schoolhouse with over 150 students, and several restaurants and saloons. It was also a hub of rail transportation. Both the St. Paul & Duluth Railway (which later became the Northern Pacific Company) and the Eastern Minnesota Railway, a division of James J. Hill's Great Northern system, crossed through the town.

Of course, Hinckley's largest employer and the reason for the town's existence, was the Brennan Lumber Company which operated a mercantile store and sawmill. Each year, beginning in April, after the spring log drive, the shanty boys, (before the term "lumberjack" became popular) would return from their logging camps, and the sawmill would employ over two hundred men. This is when, as Angus Hay, editor of the town's newspaper, *The Hinckley Enterprise*, wrote "the coin of the realm" would begin circulating through the shops and saloons of Hinckley.

But all that changed in the span of five hours. Within this time frame the fire destroyed 480 square miles which is more than twice the size of Chicago. Besides Hinckley, the towns of Pokegama (Brook Park), Mission Creek, Sandstone, and Partridge (Askov) were leveled to ash. The recorded death count was 418, and numerous families were uprooted and homeless. Governor Knute Nelson appointed Charles Pillsbury to lead a commission to oversee and coordinate relief efforts. All aid dispersed by the commission, including money, donated materials, and transportation totaled $184,744, which in today's dollar is $6.8 million.

As overwhelming as those statistics are, what sticks with me are the human stories of bravery, survival, tragedy, and unwavering resilience. There's the image of a mother, fiercely corralling her young children, guiding them to safety, and clutching them tightly to prevent their flight into the flames. Then there's the father who, after securing his entire family on a train to escape, turns back toward the inferno to aid others. A train car porter emerged as a hero, helping numerous frightened and injured strangers flee from the blazing train. And, in the aftermath, a tireless doctor worked relentlessly in the fire zone for seventy-two hours straight, sleeplessly striving to save lives —while his own daughter, who was in Hinckley during the fire, remained missing.

These are just a few examples. I read of countless others in memoirs and firsthand accounts of fire survivors. In this novel, the main characters, Anna and Karl, and their families are fictitious. They are products of my imagination, but many of the experiences they had before, during, and after the fire are based on real events. Some of the characters they encounter were real people including Anna's friends at the dance party (Belle, Archie, Charlie, and Clara), Jake and Kate

Barden, Angus Hay, John Craig, John Blair, the Kelsey family, John Roper, Dr. Codding, Dr. Barnum, Antone Anderson, Bishop Gilbert, J.D. Markham, and Robert Saunders. I am responsible for any errors of fact or interpretation.

One final note before you dive in: as a reflection of the place and time in which Anna and Karl live, there are instances of underage drinking and marriage that do not fit with what is acceptable in our day and age. Please remember that in Minnesota in 1894, there was not a legal drinking age, and the legal age for marriage was 18 for men and 15 for women.

Kristina Shuey
September 2024

When we again hear the songs of the birds in the summer, and the golden grain is being gathered in autumn from the fertile soil around Hinckley, the tale of the great Hinckley fire will be still being told.

-Angus Hay

Swedish and Norwegian Words

Swedish Accent in English:
Ch becomes Sh; Th becomes T or F; Interchanging V and W:
Sweden becomes Sveden; Hard Jay becomes Yee

Swedish words (in order of appearance):

min älskling - my darling

tack så mycket - thank you very much

nej tack - no thank you

Äpple - apple

kom hit - come here

Goddog - Good day

God eftermiddag - Good afternoon

kom kompis - Come on, buddy/friend

ja - yes

God natt - Good night

skål - cheers

God morgon - Good morning

Lyssna, Pappa - Listen, Father

Lova, mig - Promise me

Jag lovar - I promise

Stanna! Vända om! - Stop! Turn around!

Kors i taket - interjection of surprise

Aj - interjection of pain

Pappa! Du är här! - Father! You are here!

Själviskt barn! - Selfish child!

Norwegian words (in order of appearance):

Bedre sent enn aldri - Better late than never

Nei! Ikke omvendt! - No! Not reverse!

Lefse - A soft flatbread made with riced potatoes, butter, and milk or cream. It's cooked on a large, flat griddle and has a texture similar to a thin pancake.

Slang and Colloquial Phrases

In order of appearance:

Skalley - An express train route, officially called Limited No. 4, between St. Paul and Duluth with limited stops. Hinckley was its mid-point station, and the total time between St. Paul and Duluth was five hours. This express train was available twice a day in both directions.

Cowcatcher - The strong metal frame attached to the front of a train that pushes objects off the track as the train moves forward.

Dickens - Euphemism for "devil" and is used to express surprise, irritation, or as an intensifier to describe a high degree of pain.

Shanty boy - An earlier term for a lumberjack, particularly in the late nineteenth century in the area around Lake Superior. "Shanty" refers to the temporary shelter the men used during the winter logging season.

Gal sneaker - A man who tries to seduce every woman he sees.

Jammiest bits of jam - A phrase used to describe beautiful young women.

Cat lap - A derogatory phrase used to describe a weak drinker. It refers to when a cat delicately laps up a bowl of milk.

Asking for a quiet word - Someone is requesting a private conversation.

Knock me stiff - Surprises me.

Poked up - Embarrassed.

Scarlet woman - A derogatory term for a promiscuous woman.

Dandy - A man who is excessively concerned with his dress and appearance. The term originated in the late 18th century and is possibly a shortened term for "Jack-a-dandy" which described a conceited man.

Sauce box - Mouth.

Chemise - A loose straight-hanging dress worn as an undergarment.

Bloomers - Underwear that looks like loose fitting trousers, gathered just above the knee.

Hogshead - A large cask used to store liquids. A hogshead equals sixty-three gallons.

Prologue

Saturday, September 1, 1894
Hinckley, Minnesota

He doesn't know it yet, but Engineer Jim Root is driving his train straight into an eight-mile-wide inferno.

Two hours ago he started his journey at Union Station in Duluth. His employer, the St. Paul and Duluth Company, runs a popular and speedy passenger service between Duluth and the Twin Cities every day. Root's locomotive, Engine Number 69, has made this run all summer. He's learned that the locals along the line affectionately call this train the *Skalley*. He assumes the nickname originally came from immigrants when they purchased their tickets, asking in Swedish, "*Jag skulle vilja gå till . . .* " which in English is "I would like to go to . . ." But that's just his theory. He has yet to confirm it with anyone else.

They had started on time with no surprising incidents except for the unusually dark skies to the south, the direction in which they are headed. Root was hopeful that a storm was ahead of them because maybe then the temperature would drop, and the state would gain some much needed rain.

The summer had been exceptionally hot and dry, and the first day of September is no different. The heat inside the cab where Root and his brakeman, Jack McGowan, now stand is unbearable. Root pulls a handkerchief out of his jacket pocket and dabs at the sweat accumulating above his large, droopy mustache. The heat radiating from the cab's lantern does not help their situation, but it is necessary.

All the lanterns inside the train and the locomotive headlamp were lit forty miles back when visibility dropped to a few dozen feet. Root decelerated the train then too, much to his chagrin, since he values being on time more than anything else.

The darkness is due to smoke. There is a forest fire in the woods near the tracks, but Root and McGowan are not alarmed. Fires frequently occur in Minnesota's dense pine forests; however, this summer's drought has exacerbated them, causing unexpected delays. Root returns his handkerchief to his breast pocket and retrieves his pocket watch. The time is 4:03 p.m. He frowns, and his eyebrows bunch together in concern. He would be a few minutes late pulling into Hinckley which means he will also arrive late to St. Paul. He sighs and returns his pocket watch to his vest. Not much he can do now.

The train clears the top of Hinckley Big Hill which begins the mile and a half descent into the town of Hinckley. Root leans his head out of the cab's window for a moment of relief from the heat. The wind hits his face, but there is something else. He wipes at his cheek and looks down at his palm. Black streaks run across his hand. He sticks his hand out again and watches as little, black snowflakes appear on his skin.

But they aren't snowflakes. They are cinders. The forest fire must be closer than he thought. Root turns to McGowan, about to remark on the falling cinders, when something in front of the train catches his eye. Running out of the smoke is a large crowd of people. Alarmed, he immediately eases off the throttle and hits the bar for the air brakes. His quick action causes an eruption of sound. The air brakes thump under the train carriages, the blast pipe blows out smoke and steam, and metal squeals against metal as the train stops abruptly. Root and McGowan both grab onto something and brace themselves for the sudden stop. They can hear screams behind them, coming from the startled riders in the train's passenger carriages.

Root grabs the window ledge again and thrusts his head out. It is smoky, but he can see the crowd descending on the train. More people appear from the woods on either side of the tracks. Some are half naked, their clothes shredded and torn. All are running and screaming.

"Jack!" Root yells, "There must be something wrong!" He doesn't wait for a response as he swings down from the cab and runs up the tracks ahead of the train. The smoke clears for a moment, and Root sees the men and women running towards him. They are black from head to foot, covered in ashes and soot. The whites of their eyes glow bright with fear. He stops in his tracks and gapes at them.

The first to reach him is an elderly woman being pulled by two younger women. They don't stop to greet him; they just keep moving towards the train. Root stammers, still in shock, "What . . . what's happened?" But he can barely hear himself over the screams coming from the woods and an overwhelming roar in the distance. It almost sounds like another train is coming down the tracks.

The two younger women completely ignore him as they push past. Their eyes are set on the train, and they will stop at nothing. He yells this time, "What is going on in Hinckley?"

The elderly woman, barely able to keep up anymore, pants a response, "For God's sake, will you save us?"

Soot-streaked individuals rush by Root without a glance his way. A blast of searing wind sweeps across the tracks, nearly toppling him over. A billowing smoke cloud ensues, triggering a bout of coughing. Taking a step back towards his train, Root pulls out his handkerchief and covers his mouth. Men, women, and children are climbing onto every carriage down the length of the train. Even if he wanted to, there is nothing he could do to stop this invasion.

A man runs past Root, knocking into his shoulder. Through the soot, Root recognizes his face. "Benjamin! Wait!" he shouts and runs up to Benjamin Bartlett, the owner of the Hinckley Eating House, and yanks on his elbow.

"Benjamin! What is happening?"

At first the man just stares at Root before recognition flickers in his eyes. "Jim. Everything is burned up. The depot is gone." That's the only explanation Root receives. Mr. Bartlett turns away, runs down the tracks, and jumps onto a passenger carriage.

This is madness Root thinks. More men and women scramble up the embankment from the woods and throw themselves onto the train. Children are picked up and tossed onto the train, screaming and sobbing. Through the mayhem, a familiar figure emerges from the opposite direction of the crowd. It's Root's conductor, Thomas Sullivan. He runs up to Root and shouts, "Jim! We can't stay here long! There are flames on the underside of the coaches. We have to go back to a place of safety."

Root thinks for a moment. Five miles behind them is a marshy bog next to the railroad tracks. He calmly answers, "I'm going back to Skunk Lake."

"We will never get there alive," replies Sullivan.

Root walks around him and heads back to the front of the train. He climbs up the locomotive and shouts back to Sullivan, "Then we will die together!" Standing higher above from the ground now, Root can see farther down the tracks. Behind the crowd, a wall of flames rises twenty stories high. The sheets of fire reach and stretch into the sky like fingers grasping for souls. Root is terrified, shocked into stillness for a moment as he gazes at the sheer size of the fire.

Behind him a ringing sound echoes from inside the cab. It rings two more times before Root snaps out of his trance. The bell is a signal from Sullivan that the train is ready to back up. There are still people running to the train, but Root has no choice. He swings into the cab and throws the Johnson bar into reverse, opening the throttle. Slowly, the train comes alive and begins to back up. Men and women running towards it scream as they throw themselves on.

At this very moment, unknown to Root, something else is happening less than a mile down the tracks. Just outside of the now burning town of Hinckley is the Brennan Lumberyard and Sawmill. Because it is September, the yard is covered with stacks of freshly cut lumber. All summer long mill employees have been stacking boards, posts, shingles, and beams in huge piles to cure in the sun. Now as the flames reach the yard, all twenty-eight million feet of lumber ignite causing the temperature of the air to soar to almost 700 degrees Fahrenheit. The sudden release of energy results in an enormous explosion. A blast of superheated air surges across the land straight towards Root's train. It hits the side of the train with such force that all the glass windows shatter, including the front windshield of the cab that Root and McGowan stand in. The carriages shake, but the wheels stay on the tracks, and the train continues to back up.

Glass rains over the men in the cab, slicing Root's face and neck. A sharp stinging pain grows from the wound, and Root's hand instinctively shoots up to his neck and touches it. Wet, red blood appears on his fingertips. He fumbles for his handkerchief with his other shaking hand. Screams erupt from the passenger carriages again, but they are drowned out by the increasing crescendo of the fire's roar as it approaches them.

Above the passengers' cries, the fire's roar, and the pounding in Root's head, he hears shouting coming from outside. He looks out of the now broken front window and sees three men running toward the train. At first he does not trust his eyes. The smoke is so dense, maybe he is imagining them. He squints and confirms that, indeed, there are three, soot-covered men running on the tracks, screaming at the train to stop.

Root's first instinct is to save them, so he begins to apply the air brakes, but Sullivan's warning repeats in the back of his mind, "There are flames on the underside of the coaches." If Root stops now, those flames could burn through the air hose and stop the train for good. He can't let that happen.

He whispers to himself and to God, "Please, forgive me," as he releases the brakes and shoves the throttle back into the open position before the train has a chance to slow.

McGowan yells at him, "Jim! You're bleeding!"

Root tries to answer, but he is caught in a coughing fit from the smoke that is infiltrating their cab. The coughing intensifies the pain in his head. He walks to the front window, glass crunching underneath his shoes, and peers out the front. Two of the men have managed to throw themselves onto the locomotive's cowcatcher. He does not see the third man. Helplessly, he watches them hold on for their lives. The only way to save them and everyone else on board, is to make it to a place of safety. He turns to McGowan and yells, "We must make it back to Skunk Lake."

He wants to say more, but the pain in his head is so strong now, it feels like his skull is crushing into his brain. Root's shirt is sticking to his chest, drenched in sweat and now blood from his neck wound. He walks back to the throttle and grips it. Suddenly, he can't focus, and the edges of his vision blur into blackness. With his hand still on the throttle, he slowly crumples to the floor.

"Root!" McGowan screams, running to his colleague. He lays Root on his back and quickly adjusts the Johnson bar. This valve switch controls the amount of steam entering the cylinders which in turn controls the speed of the train. McGowan pulls it as far back as it goes, reversing the train at full speed towards Skunk Lake.

Root's last thoughts before he passes out are of the two men outside holding onto the train's cowcatcher, holding on for their lives. He wonders who these men are, and if they will survive. But their story doesn't start here on the cowcatcher of the Skalley. It begins days before the fire, days before their world turns to ash.

PART ONE

BEFORE

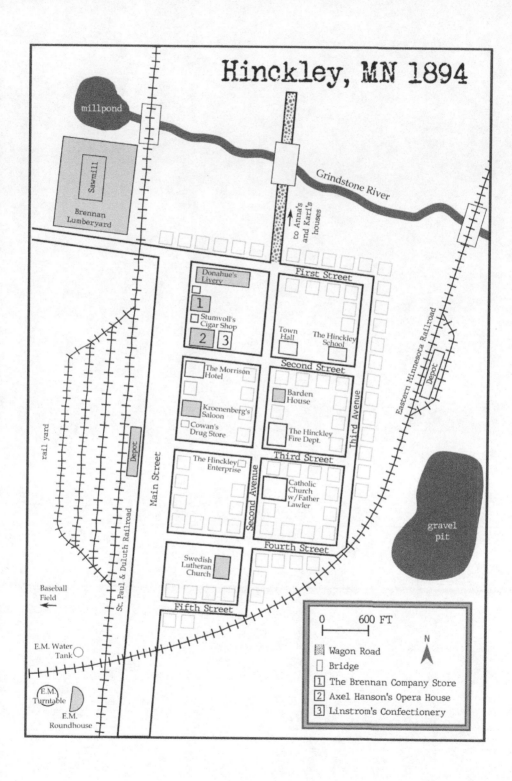

Hinckley, MN 1894

millpond

Sawmill

Brennan
Lumberyard

Grindstone River

to Anna's
and Karl's
houses

Donahue's
Livery

[1] The Brennan Company Store

Stumvoll's
Cigar Shop

[2] [3]

First Street

Town
Hall

The Hinckley
School

The Morrison
Hotel

Second Street

Barden
House

Kroenenberg's
Saloon

Cowan's
Drug Store

The Hinckley
Fire Dept.

Third Avenue

The Hinckley
Enterprise

Third Street

Second Avenue

Catholic
Church
w/Father
Lawler

Eastern Minnesota Railroad

Depot

gravel
pit

Fourth Street

rail yard

Swedish
Lutheran
Church

Main Street

St. Paul & Duluth Railroad

Depot

Fifth Street

Baseball
Field

E.M. Water
Tank

E.M.
Turntable

E.M.
Roundhouse

0   600 FT

▨ Wagon Road
▯ Bridge
[1] The Brennan Company Store
[2] Axel Hanson's Opera House
[3] Linstrom's Confectionery

N

1

Anna

Saturday, August 25, 1894
Hinckley, Minnesota
7 days before

Leaning against the corner of the Brennan Company Store, I wait for Mother to finish our weekly shopping. Just moments before, I was with her as the store manager, Mr. Walter Scott, collected sugar, flour, coffee and bacon for us. But the heat was too stifling, so I left before he was finished. Although the heat is inescapable, at least there is a comforting breeze outside.

People walk slowly past me on the wooden plank sidewalk, and wagons and buggies roll by on Main Street, kicking up a cloud of dust. I turn my head around the corner to look down the alley between the mercantile building and the cigar shop. That's when I see it, the bicycle. My body is drawn to it while my mind is still in disbelief, and like a shiny beacon of light, it calls to me from across the dust and heat. Polished black paint reflects the glaring August sun, and the steel frame clashes with the withered, wooden building it leans against.

Like two magnets drawn together, I take a step off the platform. My feet carry me a few more steps before I stop, just an arm's length away. I can see now that it is not just any bicycle. This is the Featherstone Model F, also called The Road Queen. I look up and down

11

the alley, but there is no one else. It's just me and The Road Queen. I don't dare touch it, but I close my eyes and allow myself to daydream.

I imagine riding on the dirt road into town, men and women staring at me when I fly by. I'd wave to my friends as I pass them on our way to school. Then I dare to dream further. I'm riding on the busy roads in Duluth or St. Paul. Sturdy brick buildings and lampposts on either side rush by as I race down the street. There are so many other cyclists that I have to weave in between them. Some are young women wearing the latest cycling attire including shortened skirts, mutton-sleeve riding jackets, elaborate hats and matching neck bows.

Mother would not approve of my ankles appearing in public. In fact, I can hear her chastising me with that voice—"Anna!" My eyes snap open at the sound of my mother's call. "Anna! Anna!" She yells behind me. I turn my head, expecting to see her, but she has not rounded the corner yet.

I turn my attention back to the bicycle. Just one touch; that's all I need for now. I reach out my hand toward the curved metal handlebars—"Good morning," a confident female voice appears out of nowhere, and I retract my outstretched hand. A woman walks up to the bicycle from the back of the mercantile building. As if plucked from my daydream, she is clad in a fashionable riding outfit including a mauve mutton-sleeve jacket and matching . . . pants! "Are you a cyclist too? It's a beautiful day for a ride although there is quite a bit of dust," she says while brushing some of it from her pants.

I can't move my lips to respond because I'm surprised. I've seen riding pants before in newspaper advertisements, but never in Hinckley.

"Anna, there you are," my mother says behind me. "I was wondering where you went."

She stands at my side before taking notice of the female cyclist standing next to the bicycle. These two women could not be more opposite. My mother is short and hearty, while this woman is tall and lean. My mother's face is round and soft compared to this woman's high-boned cheeks and pointed chin. Even their hair is different. Mother's is light brown and plaited in a no-nonsense knot at the nape of her neck while this woman's is swept up in a soft pompadour underneath a straw boater hat. The silk ribbon on the hat matches her neck tie. If she wasn't conjured from my daydream, then surely, she stepped right out of a newspaper ad.

Mother's eyes inspect the woman's outfit, not at all concerned that her stare is impolite. Her gaze stops at the riding pants, and I notice the smallest lift of her eyebrows.

"Hello," the woman beams at my mother and offers her hand. "Valerie Johnson. I'm here with my husband for the day. He has a few meetings soliciting property insurance."

"Britta Andersson," Mother gingerly takes the woman's hand and shakes it softly, "I'm not interested—"

"Oh, no," Valerie laughs. "I'm not selling you anything. When my husband told me this morning that he was coming to Hinckley, I thought it would be a wonderful opportunity for a ride in the country. Don't get me wrong, I love riding my bicycle in St. Paul, but I must say the air here is more pleasant." She inhales through her nose and closes her eyes, "Fresh and crisp. Not nearly as stuffy as the heat in the city."

This woman, Valerie Johnson, smiles when she talks as if nothing would make her happier than conversing with two complete strangers like my mother and me. I turn to see if Mother is going to introduce us, but her face is still stunned; I imagine she is still trying to process the riding pants. I seldom see Mother with nothing to say, but right now, it is one of those rare moments.

Mrs. Johnson continues conversing as if Mother is participating, "I fear that I must be going, but it was lovely to meet you ladies. Your daughter, I assume she is your daughter, seems intrigued by my bicycle. It's a lovely machine. I highly recommend you consider one for her in the future. They have become so much lighter and more portable due to the substitution of iron and wood with steel frames." She grips the handlebars and effortlessly pulls the bicycle away from the building before swinging her leg over the seat. Mother gasps softly at the display. "Goodbye," Mrs. Johnson calls out and pedals away into the street, leaving us to stare at her as she rides off. The fabric of her pants moves casually up and down with each pedal rotation.

As Mrs. Johnson turns the corner of the mercantile building and disappears into the street, Mother gives her head a slight shake. Then she turns to look at me and says sternly, "Anna. I had to set down my bags in the store in order to come find you. Please follow me back inside to fetch them. I have one more stop to make."

"Yes, ma'am."

After picking up our groceries, and saying a quick farewell to Mr. Scott, we leave and walk south on Main Street. Hinckley is busier than usual as Saturday is a day for shopping for most families. We pass Stumvoll's Cigar Shop, Hanson's Saloon and Opera Hall, the Morrison Hotel, and Kronenberg's Saloon before reaching Cowan's Drug Store. Mother goes inside alone and quickly makes her purchase. I know what it is even if she doesn't tell me: Dr. Worden's Female Pills to help with monthly symptoms of female weakness.

We return to Main Street and start walking north, turning the corner onto Second Street just as a train arrives at the St. Paul and Duluth depot behind us. I wish I could go to the depot and watch the hustle and bustle of the passengers on the platform, but it would be cumbersome holding all of these bags.

The St. Paul and Duluth railroad tracks run north and south parallel to Main Street. On any given day, I can hear German, Swedish, Norwegian, and a dozen other languages from all of the train passengers and families that move through the depot. The most popular ticket on these tracks is for the Skalley, a fast passenger train with limited stops between St. Paul and Duluth. There is one more rail line that cuts diagonally through Hinckley from southwest to northeast. Those trains bring people and goods from St. Cloud and Superior, Wisconsin.

Turning the corner of Second Street and Second Avenue, Mother and I smile at each other as we pass the clapboard house. That was our first home, so we always acknowledge it when we pass by. We lived there while Father built our log house north of town. When I was five years old and my older sister Mary was seven years old, our family moved into the log house, and we have been there ever since.

Mother says that Hinckley has changed in the years since she and Father moved here. They both immigrated from Sweden when they were children and relocated once more to Hinckley after their wedding in '75. She tells my sister and me that the population of our town has exploded since then. I believe her too since the community had to build a two-story, brick school building last year to accommodate over 150 students.

The houses, chicken coops, and outhouses thin out as we leave town and continue on the wagon road. The Brennan Lumberyard now dominates our view to the west. Father is there now finishing his last shift of the week. The yards are thirty-six acres of flat, treeless earth, now covered by dozens of stacks of freshly cut lumber. The whine of the circular saw cuts through the air, and the smokestack on the far end of the sawmill pumps out smoke which drifts lazily off to the northeast. It gives the north side of Hinckley a permanent scent of husky, woodsmoke.

I'm sweating underneath my dress, stockings, and petticoat. This summer has been so unbearably hot and dry. We are in desperate need of some rain. "Dickens," I think to myself. This bag I'm carrying for my mother is heavy, and I keep having to adjust it on my shoulder as we walk home. She must have bought extra flour for this week. As we cross the wagon bridge over the Grindstone River, I stop to look down at the water, what's left of it anyway. This summer drought has all but dried up the Grindstone. To be honest, it doesn't even look like a river. It looks like a slight ravine with scattered, shallow pools of warm, stagnant water.

"Anna," my mother says. "Come along."

I hurry to catch up to her, jostling the heavy bag on my shoulder.

"Anna, I know you were delighted to see that bicycle machine, but I have to mention the woman. Mrs. Johnson or whatever her name is was very polite, but. . . a respectable woman does not wear all the fashion trends just because they are fashionable for the moment. Trends change faster than you can save up enough money to buy them."

I knew she would mention the riding pants to me.

"Yes, ma'am."

"A respectable young woman does not show her ankles in public. That is private, only for your husband's eyes."

I giggle at the thought of a husband.

Mother smiles at me. "Anna, what fascinates you so much about the bicycle, anyway?"

I switch the heavy bag to my other shoulder and say, "The speed, for one. Did you see how fast she moved down the street?"

"You can ride that fast on a horse, Anna. Even faster."

I thought about her comment for a moment. "Yes, I suppose," I respond, "but a horse needs water, food, brushing, and a place to sleep. A bicycle is convenient, efficient, and . . . autonomy." I put emphasis on the last word and wait for her reaction.

The wagon road cuts through a wide marshland north of the bridge. Tall willows grow on either side of the road, and usually the soggy marsh grasses are a nuisance to cross. Early this spring someone laid sapling logs side by side to create a firmer roadbed. The saplings are still here, but they are no longer necessary as the summer months have brought no rain. The marsh grasses are pale and bone dry.

Mother stops walking on the logs and looks at me. Her eyebrows are furrowed, "Anna," she scolds, "you sound like those silly women from the city with their funny talk about independence and equality. What do they call themselves? The New Ladies?"

I answer, "The New Women."

"Yes, The New Women. Coming to our town and telling us how we need to live our lives. They tell us to complain and disregard all our blessings." Mother turns her heel on the log and continues north with more vigor. "I have all the independence and equality I need. Did I need to ask your father to come into town today? No, I did not. Does your father, or any other man in our community for that matter, act disrespectfully towards me or your sister?" She answers for me, "No, they do not. Those young city women need more tasks at home to occupy their minds." She shakes her head and adds, "You don't pay any mind to that kind of talk. Soon you will have so many suitors knocking on our door that you will not have any time for New Women nonsense."

"Mama," I blush thinking about suitors coming to see me.

She smiles at my embarrassment but doesn't push the topic further. I think about telling her that my sixteenth birthday is near and a bicycle would be a wonderful present. I would even concede to accept it as both a birthday and Christmas present, but I bite my bottom lip instead, and keep my thoughts to myself.

We walk up Hinckley Big Hill in silence. The slight incline is not enough to describe it as a hill, but everyone still calls the land north of town Hinckley Big Hill. The sun beats down on us, and my blouse sticks to me from my sweat. There isn't much to look at now on either side of the wagon road. The land is marked by stumps as far as I can see. There are also abandoned piles of tree limbs and cut brush left years ago by the lumber companies. Young Jack pines and tamaracks have started to grow through the brush as the forest starts to make its slow comeback.

And here among the stumps, brush, and new growth is home. Surrounded by a split rail fence, we live in the log house Father built. Dozens of chickens and one proud rooster wander lazily in the yard. A clapboard shed behind the house is home to our milking cow. I step onto the porch after Mother, following her through the screen door into the front room. We pass the staircase and brick fireplace on our way to the kitchen before finally setting our bags down on the small, work table.

"Anna," she says, "fetch some water for your father and meet him on the road. I will start lunch. Hurry, he should be home soon."

I grab the tin pitcher and cup off the counter and run outside to the well. Father walks home from the lumberyard for his lunch break on Saturdays. I pull up the bucket, pour the water into the pitcher, carry it to the road, and lean against the fence. While I wait, I pour myself a small amount of water and drink it. Those bags from the store were heavy, and we walked in the midday sun, so I'm parched. I tip my head back to catch the last drops from my cup. That's when I see them out of the corner of my eye. Father, our neighbor, Mr. Sundvquist, and his son, Karl Sundvquist are walking down the road together.

Father is of medium height and build, but he looks short walking next to Svard and Karl, both of whom are over six feet. Svard and Karl have the same blue eyes, but Svard's always look weary and tired. His hair is clipped short, but he keeps his beard long. The sandy blond hair has started to fade to gray, and the gray is even more apparent in his facial hair. Karl, on the other hand, has a shock of blond hair, but he always keeps it hidden under his floppy hat. I have noticed this summer that he is starting to get uneven patches of blond facial hair, but he shaves it back pretty regularly. I have poked fun at him once or twice for this.

"Anna, *min älskling*," Father's face brightens when he calls me, "my darling", in Swedish, his native language. I grin from ear to ear because he is always happy to see me. I offer the pitcher and cup to him. "*Tack så mycket*. Thank you," he says and takes them from my hands and pours a cup. "Svard, Karl, would you like some water before you head home?"

Svard lifts his hands up, "*Nej tack*. No, thank you." He speaks with a thick Swedish accent, so the *th* sound in "thank" becomes "tank." He adds, "We will be fine. It is a short walk from here." The letter *w* sounds more like a *v* and "short" sounds more like "chort." He turns his attention from Father to me, saying, "Anna, I thought you were your mother from down the road. You must have grown since the last time I saw you."

"Well, I fit in Mary's old dresses now, so I must have grown this summer," I reply, smiling at him. I have always liked Mr. Sundvquist.

"Of course she's grown, she eats like an ox," Karl grins as he takes the pitcher from my hands and drinks straight from it. I playfully punch him in the side of his ribs which makes some of the water spill over the sides onto his sweaty shirt.

"Hey, now," he says as he wipes his face, "I have to go see my favorite lady after this. She won't approve of this messy appearance."

"You might as well change your shirt then for your girl," I say, plugging my nose and keeping the joke going, "because she won't approve of your smelliness."

He feigns shock and places his hands over his heart, "*Äpple* loves me no matter what I smell like." Ducking his head down to sniff under his arms, his face blanches. "Well, maybe I'll stand farther away today. I do smell."

Father, Mr. Sundvquist, and I laugh at Karl's silliness. *Äpple* is the name of his milking cow. Karl, Mary, and I have always gotten along easily ever since we were children. We shared chores between our two homesteads and walked to the schoolhouse together. We spent summers swimming in the Grindstone, running around town with our friends, and finding new ways to annoy Mother. Unfortunately, this summer has been a bit different. Since Karl started working at the mill, I don't see him every day, and with Mary gone, I feel like they both grew up and left me behind.

"We must go," Svard says to Karl, before speaking to Father, "Say hello to Britta for us."

"I will. See you soon."

Karl hands the pitcher back to me, "Do you want to go to the baseball game tomorrow afternoon?"

"I wish," I say sadly, "but, Mary and John are coming to visit and

Mother has a whole lunch planned for them."

"That will be nice to see Mary. I wonder what Pokegama is like."

I shrug my shoulders. I have never been to Pokegama where Mary now lives with her new husband.

He starts walking backwards towards his father who has already started walking down the road and says, "Maybe you and Mary can sneak out early and catch the last few innings?"

"We'll see," I call after him as he catches up to his father. They only have a short walk to their log house which is just north of ours. Mr. Sundvquist built it around the same time that my father built ours. Once his house was complete, he sent tickets to Sweden for his wife and Karl to come join him. When he went to the train station to pick them up, seven months later, only Karl was on the platform. His mother died somewhere along the journey from Sweden. He was only six years old when it happened, and he has never brought it up to me as long as I've known him.

My father's hand touches my shoulder, "Lunch, *min älskling?*"

"Yes, please."

In the dining room, we eat thick slices of bread slathered in fresh butter with strawberry preserves. Mother tells Father about our trip to town, but she leaves out the woman in the pantsuit and her bicycle. My Father smiles at my mother while he eats. Even after he finishes, he sits silently at the table and continues to listen.

"Mother, did you buy extra flour for this week?" I ask, chewing my last bites of bread. "The bag felt heavier today."

"Oh, no, I bought our usual amount of flour," she holds my gaze for a moment and smiles mischievously, "and something special for Mary."

"For Mary? It's not her birthday coming up. What did you buy?"

She stands up from the table and walks into the front room as I turn to Father and ask, "Why does Mary get a present? Her birthday is in January, and mine is in sixteen days."

"Anna, your mother and I didn't have a chance to buy John and Mary a proper wedding present back in June. Mr. Scott has been advertising an exclusive line of home goods for weeks. I told Ma to find something nice for the newlyweds."

Mary and John. Of course the new present was for them.

Nevermind that they hadn't come home to visit us once this whole summer. No one seems to care that Mary decided to forget I even existed.

Mother comes back into the kitchen with something in her hands. It is loosely wrapped in brown paper. As she sets it on the table, it makes a sturdy clunk sound. She folds the paper back to reveal a large cast iron skillet.

"All the way from Pennsylvania," she informs us, "The Griswold Manufacturing Company. Here is their brand," she says as she flips the skillet over to show us the circle brand. "They put an enamel coating on it, so Mary doesn't have to season it, and it will never rust."

I trace my finger along the indented circle glaring at the skillet's brand. Mother must have seen me pouting because she folds the brown paper back over the skillet quickly and returns it to the front room. My father stands up from the table as he gets ready to return to work and says, "They will love it." He leans down and kisses the top of my head. "Please help your mother clean up a little. This house needs some attention before your sister visits tomorrow," He says and winks at me.

"Paulus!" Mother reappears in the doorway, holding onto the frame and pretending to glare at my Father. He kisses her on the cheek and pinches her side before walking out of the kitchen. Mother mumbles in Swedish under her breath, but I don't catch what she says. Her eyes linger on Father as he leaves the house, and she smiles. Then, she looks at me with a determined look in her eyes and says, "Anna, take off that nice dress and put on something else. We can sweep, mop, then wash the windows before supper."

"Why?" I ask since we scrub the pine-plank floors once a week with vinegar and water. "Floors are on Fridays. I'm not going to do it after just one day of wear."

"Anna, you should be happy your sister is coming to see us. Stop complaining and go change."

I walk upstairs to my room and shut the door. It used to be Mary's and my room before she left. I kneel at the foot of the bed and reach underneath it to grasp the cigar box I keep there. I drag it across the floor until it bumps into my knees and then I spread my fingers out over the top of the box. All my treasures in one place. My two favorite people in the world may have grown up without me this summer, but my treasures are still here.

I open the cigar box to see my loon feather, two stone arrowheads, and a broken bone hair clip that Mary gave me when we were little. There are also several newspaper clippings and advertisements from Sears and Roebuck catalogs. I pull out one of the newspaper clippings. It's a sketch of the Central High School in St. Paul, a three story, brick building with over forty classrooms inside and an annex for laboratories. I had cut it from a newspaper article in the *Pioneer Press* last year. The article reported that the high school had its own newspaper, and the two female students in charge of the newspaper read the articles aloud to the entire student body.

When I was younger my school teacher came to our house and talked to my mother about my potential to be a teacher. I stood on the other side of the kitchen door and listened to her explain that I'd have to attend high school in a bigger city. Then, I would attend normal school where teachers are trained. She offered to help my mother find a high school and help with all the application papers. My mother was polite but calmly refused telling her that my schooling would end here at the Hinckley common school. Despite my mother's refusal, I saved that clipping, even if it held a future that I could no longer grasp.

I put the clipping back into the cigar box and unfold one of the advertisements. It's for the John Pritzlaff Hardware Company. In the center is a woman riding the Road Queen bicycle. Sitting tall on the bicycle, she wears riding pants and a mutton-sleeve blouse. "Agents .. . Milwaukee, Wisconsin" is printed on the top in all capitals. "A Featherstone & Co." is printed on the banner behind the woman rider. I wonder if Valerie Johnson bought her Road Queen from this hardware store in Milwaukee. I trace my finger on the worn out clipping, around the bicycle tires, then along the curved handle bar and end with a swirl around the puffed sleeve of the woman's blouse.

My sister enters my thoughts again. The Mary from my memories would prefer a bicycle over a cast iron skillet. This new Mary, the one I haven't seen since her wedding, the one who hasn't come to visit, the one who hasn't invited me to her new house yet, this Mary, I guess, prefers a skillet.

2

Karl

Saturday, August 25, 1894
Hinckley, Minnesota
7 days before

A dry heat, hazy skies, and the pungent odor of charred wood is an apt description for this summer. The combination makes me feel tired and lazy, but there's so much to do before winter, and we are heading into autumn. Since starting at the lumber mill, I've barely kept up with chores at home, nevermind having spare time for anything else. I can't even remember the last time I went to the depot and drank Coca-Colas with Anna. Was it all the way back in May? It was well before her sister's wedding. That's for certain.

I pull up a full bucket of water from our well, one handful of rope at a time, before pouring it into a wooden pail sitting next to the curved stone wall. I drop the empty bucket back down the twenty-five foot hole and head to the barn. Our horse and cow need fresh water. Inside the barn is slightly cooler than outside, but it is still dense and thick with humidity. I call out, "*Äpple, kom hit, min älskling.*" *Äpple* swishes her tail side to side as she walks towards me. Father bought her before I came to live in America with him. I don't remember the first time he introduced me to her, but he likes to tell of how shortly after I arrived in Hinckley, he lost track of me one afternoon. He looked all over the house and the yard, even running down the wagon road. He finally found me in the barn with a bucket of apples trying to feed the cow. I offered her one and said *"äpple"* in Swedish over and over, trying to get her to eat it. That's how she got her name. Father says it was the first word I spoke after arriving in America. I don't know if it's true, but it makes Father happy to tell the story.

Äpple dips her head down to the water and starts to drink, so I let her be. I give some water to our horse Jack and go back outside. I gaze at our home and feel pride swell in my chest. My father built the log house himself with help from Anna's father. They dug the well together too. When I was ten, I helped Father construct the barn.

The grass is so dry, it crunches under my boots as I walk towards the house. With such little rain, everything is dry this summer. Our vegetable garden on the south side of the house has struggled this season. Most of the leaves are yellowing and starting to curl upward, but that is also a sign that the potatoes are ready for harvesting. They'll have to wait, though, because Father and I need to return to the mill. I open the back door to the kitchen, hang my hat on a nail, and sit down. Father has laid out smoked ham and bread for our lunch. I glance at him as we eat in a comfortable silence. I know that he is the same age as Mr. Andersson, but he seems older. His face has more wrinkles and his beard more gray. He has droopy eyelids making him seem tired all the time too.

After I finish, I pick up the plates and knife. Father is picking at some food in his teeth with his jackknife that he always carries. He smiles at me when I take his empty plate, and his whole face lights up and his eyes crinkle at the corners. I take the dishes to the dry sink and give them a quick wash and rinse, set them on the drying board, and fetch my hat. Father returns the smoked ham to the pantry before he follows me outside where I am overwhelmed yet again by the sun, heat, and far off smell of smoke. Cicadas hum to us while we start back south on the wagon road to finish our Saturday shift. As we walk down Hinckley Big Hill, I catch the acrid scent of burned wood lingering in the air above us.

"I smell something burning," I say.

Father nods and replies, "Small fires near Sandstone reported yesterday. Maybe they started up again today."

It's a common occurrence where we live. Our pine forests, full of giant, white pine trees, fell logs, old stumps, and piles of slash left from the timber drives, provide plenty of fuel for a fire. This summer has been especially prone to the fires on account of how little rainfall we've had. It is easy to imagine one small spark from a passing train flying into the dry brush and finding something to catch on. The *Hinckley Enterprise*, our town's newspaper, has reported on the uptick in fires throughout the county. Last month two sawmills burned to the ground, one in Kerrick and one just a half mile south of us.

Even with the dry conditions and the repeated news stories, I'm not worried. The Hinckley Fire Department is one of the best in the country. Two years ago, we came in second place in a competition among all the fire departments west of Chicago, and now we have a brand new steamer from the Waterous Engine Works Company of St. Paul.

Father and I start to cross the wagon bridge, but I stop halfway and stare at the Brennan Lumberyard. The sawmill is quiet since everyone is at lunch. Empty carriages sit on the track between the millpond and the long ramp up to the sawmill. Millwork is not for the faint of heart. A man has to be strong, determined, and careful. One mistake rolling a massive, white pine log, and it could crush you, but it isn't the certainty of another afternoon of hard labor that leaves a heavy weight in my stomach. Returning to the sawmill today increases my chances of running into Ivar Gunnolfsson, another millworker just a few years older than me.

Father notices that I've stopped. He turns around and walks back to me putting a hand on my shoulder, "Everyone has a hard time their first summer. At least you speak American and can understand the orders." He turns my shoulder back towards the road and we start walking again, "I never understood what the foreman was shouting at me for almost a year," he chuckles.

He started working at the mill in the summer of '82, a couple of years before he sent for me. He's told me before how difficult it was being here alone, but he found friends quickly, other immigrants from Sweden and Norway. They helped each other as much as they could, and eventually everyone picked up on the new language and life became easier.

My favorite stories of Father's are the ones he tells of the two winters that he worked as a skidder on a logging team in the woods. He helped roll felled logs onto sleds pulled by oxen which carried them on a logging road to the Grindstone River. He stacked the logs on the frozen waterway, and then in the spring after the ice melted, the logs floated and he drove them down river to the millpond in Hinckley.

My bedtime stories included frozen toes, overcrowded bunkhouses, stacks of pancakes as tall as me, and tree trunks longer than a ship's mast. I was captivated by my Father's tales of these bold men, the shanty boys as everyone calls them, whose strength and grit motivated them to survive Minnesota's harsh winters. Soon I hope to be a shanty boy. I'm planning to join a team when the Brennan Lumber Company hires new men this fall. When I was eight years old, Father taught me how to swing an ax, and by the time I was twelve, we were felling trees together with a crosscut saw in preparation for winter. I'm ready now to test myself. I just have to wait two more months.

Father and I cross the St. Paul and Duluth train tracks and enter the lumberyard. A man guiding a horse-drawn cart full of fresh-cut pine boards crosses our path, and the smell of hot, sticky sap oozes from them as he passes us. We turn north toward the sawmill, a large wooden building with a giant smokestack coming up from the boiler. Ten hogsheads full of water line the roof's ridge board. If there was ever a fire in the sawmill, someone would climb the stairs to the roof and run down the center, tipping each hogshead of water as he went, dousing the flames with each barrel. A system of tracks and carriages feed the pine logs into the sawmill to be cut into boards. Tracks exiting the sawmill take the boards to either the lumberyard to be stacked or down a long ramp to the railroad tracks for loading onto the train cars.

Father and I greet other millworkers as we enter the sawmill. Father is a sawyer and sometimes lets me come watch the engine start before I work in the lumberyard. I'm curious about the mechanics of steam-powered engines, so I enjoy helping him oil the engine and let out the water from the steam chest.

Father and I make our way back to the boiler that creates the steam which powers the stationary steam engine. I follow him as he starts his routine. First, we check the boiler's water level before firing it up. The water level needs to be above the crown sheet; otherwise, the fire becomes too hot, and there is a chance the boiler could explode. Father nods toward me, giving me the confirmation that the water level is high enough. I pick up some wood scraps and add them to the fire. The boiler was lit earlier this morning, but after the lunch break it needs some extra fuel to pick up again.

While it's heating, Father and I fill the engine's oil cups on the crank case and grease the caps and bearings. Oil is a steam engine's best friend. We walk back to the boiler and read the pressure gauge. It reads almost one hundred pounds of pressure. We're close. Once it hits 110 the boiler whistle will scream, indicating to the millworkers that the saw will start soon and everyone needs to be in his place.

The boiler whistle screams outside, *Weeeee-ouшиишиии. Weeeee-ouшиишиии.* The engine starts turning, and the piston begins pumping in and out, in and out. The rumble of the carriages fills the shed as the metal gears spin in place. The sight of the engine moving captivates me. I wish I could take it apart and put it back together again. Maybe that way I could learn how all the pieces work. For now, I get to watch it start before I go back and finish my shift.

I follow my father away from the engine and towards the sawmill mechanism where the large circular saw stands. Father is an experienced sawyer and uses his sharp eyesight and quick hand movements to direct the logs into the blade. He walks up to the paper clutch, a long metal arm attached to a horizontal pulley system that directs the carriage on the direct drive. Slight hand movements from the paper clutch control the carriage direction, forward or backward, and the speed, slow or fast. He is responsible for transforming a log into a straight piece of lumber and has to know the size and thickness of the pieces of lumber he wants to create, then plan ahead to know which cuts to make.

He stands at his post and grasps the paper clutch as the first carriage of the afternoon shift brings him a long, pine log. A few other sawyers show up and stand at their posts along the carriage track waiting to pull off the first cut of bark. Father shouts to them over the sounds of the sawmill, "Two by fours, *pojkars*." The men nod back to him. The carriage is almost at the teeth of the sawblade and my father is concentrating on the log. He moves the paper clutch and the carriage speeds up feeding the log into the teeth of the blade. As the teeth spin into the bark of the log, the contact makes a high-pitched scream.

The log passes through the blade making the first cut. The other sawyers pull back the bark and discard it. Once the log is through the blade, they loosen the feed dogs, which are heavy metal hooks which hold the log in place, and roll it to its side. Then, they tighten the feed dogs and send it back into the saw for a second cut, making another side square to the flat face. They roll it and repeat this cut two more times. My father guides the carriage through each cut as he counts in his head to create as many two by four boards as possible from the log. I leave them to it and head to the entrance of the sawmill where the logs need to be rolled onto carriages. Before I step outside, I take a deep breath and pray I don't see Ivar this afternoon.

The hot sun shines down on me as I make my way to the carriage track. Three other millworkers are there already, waiting for me to get started. One of them is my friend Kristoff Ericksson. He is chatting with the other two men, and his arms are moving in large circles, animating whatever story he is telling them. Both men throw their heads back and laugh. Kristoff is a cheerful person only a year older than me. We are the same height, but his frame is lean. His reddish-blond hair is always a mess on top of his head, even when he doesn't wear his signature straw hat.

Kristoff notices me approaching and waves me over, "Karl! I pick Karl!" He lifts his hat and fans his face. "Glad I got the first pick. Now I don't have to work as hard in this heat."

I grin and joke with him, "Oh, I'll lay off a bit, so you don't get bored up there."

All four of us pick up our cant dogs and climb onto the horse-drawn wagon next to the carriage tracks. It is stacked high with logs ready to be sent into the sawmill. We climb to the top of the pile and line up. The work is done in pairs so every other man in the line must move as one to double our strength. Kristoff picked me, which means he places himself between the other two men in the line. It's dangerous work due to the weight of the logs and the risk of logs shifting underneath us. Kristoff and I will have to mirror our movements to roll it, and trust the other two men to do the same. If we make a mistake, the log could roll over one of us and crush our bones.

We will use the cant dogs to shift the logs off the wagon and onto the carriage. Cant dogs are handy to have because of the movable, metal hook on the end of the long, wooden handle. The hook, or dog as we call it, adjusts to the width of the log. The first one is always the hardest. I squeeze the handle at the same time as Kristoff does, and we transfer our combined body strength to the cant dog and rotate the log forward. The other two men follow suit and finish the rotation as the log rolls off the pile and slams onto the carriage. Horses and men slowly pull the carriage along the tracks into the sawmill. Another carriage lines up below us, and we do the exact same thing. We continue this way for hours, emptying one wagon just as another one arrives full of more logs to roll. The afternoon sun beats down on us, and the heat is stifling.

Kristoff keeps the mood light and starts to whistle his favorite song, "The Shanty Boy and the Farmer's Son," before belting out the lyrics:

> *Oh, how you praise your shanty-boy, who off to the woods must go.*
> *He's ordered out before daylight to work through storms and snow.*

He hums the rest of the verse as we roll another log onto the carriage. As it's secured in place, we stand next to the last log. This one is wider than any we've moved yet today.

Kristoff puts one leg up on the log and flexes his arms, belting his favorite lines:

> *That's the reason I praise my shanty boy. He goes up early in the fall.*
> *He is both stout and hearty, and he's fit to stand the squall.*
> *It's with pleasure I'll receive him in the spring when he comes down,*
> *And his money quite free he'll share with me when your farmer's sons have*
> *none.*

We all cheer and whistle at Kristoff's performance as he steps off the log, but a slow clap continues below us even after we've stopped. I look down and see Ivar Gunnolfsson. Immediately, my smile disappears and my shoulders tense as I prepare for the pestering and criticism that I know will come. Unfortunately, it's something that I've grown accustomed to these past weeks. No matter the situation, he finds a way to badger me.

Ivar pulls himself onto the wagon, and stands next to Kristoff. He is a head shorter than him and paler. How has he not bronzed yet like Kristoff and me? He catches me staring and smiles, "Sundvquist, hot out here today, isn't it? You probably need a break. Why don't you go stand over there in the shade and let me roll this one. You look tired."

"No thank you, Ivar. I'm not tired," I say and turn my attention to the carriage track. Two men are pushing the next empty carriage toward us.

"No? Your face is red, and it appears you've sweat right through your shirt," Ivar is still talking to me.

I ignore him. "C'mon Kristoff," I say as I fit the cant dog around the massive log on the wagon. Kristoff fits his cant dog on the log, and we both roll it ninety degrees, struggling just a little due to its immense weight. The other two men position their cant dogs, and the log is rolled another ninety degrees. It balances at the edge of the wagon. All four of us hold the log in place and wait for the carriage.

"You're doing it wrong, Sundvquist," Ivar complains, "Here give me your dog, I'll show you."

His shoulder presses into my side, and his hand grasps the handle of my cant dog. I lose my composure at his closeness and yell at him, "Get back!" But he doesn't listen; instead, he bumps his hip into me, shoving me out of place. The shift in weight unbalances the log, and it starts to roll on its own.

"Hold it!" Kristoff yells.

The other two men grunt as they use all their strength to hold down their cant dogs and stop the log from rolling off the wagon onto the ground. It is so heavy that it would be impossible for us to lift the dead weight onto the carriage. We need to hold it until we can roll it onto the carriage, but Ivar won't let go of my cant dog.

"Karl, it's slipping out!" Kristoff shouts.

Using one hand to push Ivar in the chest I shove him out of my place. My other hand grips the cant dog, and I immediately feel the extra weight. Ivar falls back behind me, and I quickly put my hand back on the handle, laying all my weight onto the cant dog, hoping it is enough to hold the log in place for another moment. I hear the metal wheels of the carriage below us, so I cry out, "Now, let go!" Everyone lets go at once. The giant log crashes onto the carriage, and the cant dogs are ripped from our hands. They spin over the edge of the log, flipping over and spinning out of sight.

The two men pushing the carriage yell angrily to us, "What's going on?!"

The four of us stand atop the wagon out of breath. Kristoff takes off his hat and wipes his brow with his shirt sleeve, "That was a close one."

"No!" I shout angrily between heavy breaths, "That was him!" Ivar slowly stands up and I jab my finger at him, "You need to leave me alone."

Ivar puts his hands in the air and shrugs, "Whoa, whoa, whoa. You don't need to get so upset. Calm down, Sundvquist. I was only trying to help."

"I didn't need your help. Stay away from me, Ivar."

Ivar laughs, "My, my, what a temper you have. Heavy logs roll off the wagon all the time. It's nothing to lose your head about, Sundvquist."

The man standing beside me says, "Reminds me of that log roll last winter, eh Ivar. It started a chain reaction on the wagon, and the whole load rolled off into the snow. Crushed that poor mule standing in the way."

Ivar turns his attention to the man, "I do remember that, Sven." He smiles wide, "It took so long to clean that mess up that by the time we got the log off the mule, it was frozen solid."

Sven shakes his head remembering the gruesome scene no doubt.

Kristoff frowns, "Poor mule."

Ivar folds his arms and locks eyes with me, "Log rolls do happen."

Anger and embarrassment surge through me, but Ivar looks calm and collected. He has a nasty smirk on his face like he's satisfied that he was able to finally get under my skin.

Sven clears his throat, "I do believe congratulations are in order, Ivar. I heard about your promotion to logging crew foreman."

Ivar breaks eye contact with me and responds to Sven, "Why thank you, Sven."

"With summer almost at an end, I bet you'll be putting together your team soon, eh?"

"Yes, I have some experienced loggers already interested, but there will be spots for new recruits."

I can't believe my bad luck. Ivar is in charge of hiring men for the logging team. He leisurely jumps off the wagon and walks off into the lumberyard, whistling. My dream slips further and further away with each step he takes. There's no way he'll let me be on his logging team, especially after I just yelled at him. Kristoff appears at my side, putting an arm around my sweaty shoulders and lowering his voice he says, "Don't let Ivar fool you, Karl. It is a setback when a log rolls off a wagon, and we have to waste time getting it back up." Sven and the other man jump off the wagon and fetch our scattered cant dogs. I don't answer Kristoff right away. I still feel shaken by the confrontation and disappointed by the horrible timing. Kristoff squeezes my arm, then lets go, "I need to buy Ma some laundry soap and bluing after our shift is over. Come into town with me. We can use the rest of my $5 to buy ice cream at Lindstrom's."

"All right," I finally answer, exhaling for the first time since Ivar showed up. "I'd like that."

He grins at me and nods as another wagon pulled by a horse arrives filled with more logs for us to roll. "Back to it," Kristoff cheers, jumping off our empty wagon.

I allow the corner of my mouth to turn up in a half smile, "Back to it."

3

Anna

Sunday, August 26, 1894
Hinckley, Minnesota
6 days before

The room is stale and full of hot air from everyone exhaling. Ladies fan themselves and men wipe their brows with handkerchiefs. They've opened the windows in the church, but there is a scant breeze outside, so we continue to sweat. I think I'm one hymn away from passing out. I was in a sour mood the entire walk here, complaining about my sister and her absence this summer. Mother had chided me and Father had reminded me that Mary is a grown woman with her own life.

While we waited in the churchyard before the service began, I had hoped that when John and Mary arrived, she would run up to me and apologize immediately, explaining why she had ignored me for months. Unfortunately, my hope was extinguished upon her arrival. Greetings, salutations, and hugs were exchanged, but it had felt stiff and forced. Mary said no apologies to me. In fact, she said very little, and her initial embrace did not feel genuine. Now I'm stuck in between Mother and Mary, sitting in our church pew, sweating through the service. It feels as though I'm seated next to a stranger, not my sister. The games that once filled our services with concealed laughter now fall flat; she disregards my attempts to engage. Even our playful foot tag is met with distance, her foot retreating further away as she resettles in her seat. I stop trying and refocus on the sermon, but it's difficult in this unbearable heat. Just when I really think I can't take it anymore, everyone stands for the preacher's final farewell and prayer. The congregation swiftly exits the building. I think everyone is sick of sitting in that hot room. The sun is shining outside, warming the late morning air. We stand in the churchyard and greet families as they walk by. Everyone wants to speak with Mary and John. It seems I wasn't the only person she neglected this summer.

I watch them as they make conversation. John is tall and lean with dark brown hair which he always styles with pomade. His mustache is full and trimmed, coming to a stylish point at each end. He always wears a black or gray coat, matching vest, and floppy bow tie. Today he chose a black coat and crimson tie. He looks out of place standing among our congregation in his fancy suit even with everyone wearing their Sunday church clothes.

Our group changes size and composition as families come and go. John speaks the most, answering questions, making jokes, and proudly speaking of Pokegama's progress. Before he moved to the small settlement, John was a real estate broker in St. Paul, but last fall he started selling land and houses here in Hinckley, taking the train and staying in a boardinghouse during his business trips. On one of these trips he met Mary. Their engagement was short, and they both moved to Pokegama in June after their wedding. Mother says he works for the Kelsey-Markham Land Company now. That must make him an important man because Father says the company owns 15,000 acres of woodland.

Mary seems quiet and looks down at the ground during the conversation. She is much shorter than John. Her long, light brown hair is swept up in loose curls on the top of her head in a high pompadour in the front and a large bun at the center crown, the new Gibson girl fashion. My hand reaches up to fluff my small, tightly curled bangs. Before she moved away, Mary curled both of our bangs before church every Sunday. She must have grown hers out this summer and decided to start pinning them back.

Mary's satin dress is new and looks store-bought. The fabric is white with small, pink flowers printed all over it. The tight bodice accentuates her tiny waist, but the skirt falls naturally over her shapely hips. Her leg-of-mutton sleeves puff at the shoulder then become tight around her arms and wrist. Two thin, black cuffs embroidered on the wrist and lapels give the dress definition and distinction. She looks terrific, older, and out of place among our home-sown wool and cotton dresses.

I try to smooth the wrinkles out of my pale, pink dress and white pinafore. The dress is a hand-me-down from Mary, so it doesn't fit quite right even though I hemmed the skirt to fit my height. Mary is a much better seamstress than me. Her stitches are tighter and smaller than my large, sloppy ones. Sewing comes easily to her, and she is so much faster than me. Many things come easily to Mary, and she is beautiful too. She has such large, brown eyes and womanly curves. I suppose I'm a bit jealous. My body is still thin and boyish as my curves have not yet grown in. I never need much fabric to cover my bosom—not like Mary's dresses. I think, though, her lips are her most feminine feature. They are full and shaped in a perfect bow. Mine, on the other hand, are small and thin. I touch my cheeks and nose, checking for any small blemishes that may have appeared overnight. They always seem to pop up nowadays, but not on Mary. Her soft skin is flawless and smooth, like a porcelain doll.

Karl and Mr. Sundvquist walk up to us and greet Mary and John. Our two families have made a large circle with Karl, Mary, and me on the far end. John leads the conversation into politics, something about reducing tariffs and President Cleveland. Svard and my father seem interested and move closer to him making the circle tighter on their end.

I'm bored, so I decide to poke at Mary again and try to get her to talk. I spin on my heel and turn my back to the adults, forming a triangle between Mary, Karl, and me. "Mary, did you know that Karl started working at the mill with Father and Mr. Sundvquist?" I ask. She finally looks up from the ground, not at me, but at Karl.

She speaks to him, her voice sounding like a dainty bell, "How wonderful, Karl. Do you enjoy it?"

Karl puts his hands in his trouser pockets and answers, "Sure. The days are long, though. And, I don't have as much free time as I used to."

"And what does a typical day look like?"

"Well, we move a lot of pine logs through the sawmill, and then we stack the boards in the lumberyard. We run the circular saw all day and night, so I can still hear it in my dreams after I've fallen asleep."

Mary's soft features seem to brighten even more as she smiles at Karl, "Oh, dear. I suppose that comes with the occupation. Our lives sure have changed in the past year, have they not?"

Karl nods, "Yes, and hopefully, mine will change even more this fall if I get hired on as a skidder or a swamper."

"You're joining a logging team?"

"I hope so," he says, rubbing the back of his neck nervously. I know how much he wants this, but I don't think he has to be so concerned. Karl's clearly qualified to be a shanty boy; it's only a matter of time before they start recruiting him. Personally, I don't care for those men. When they come to town in the spring and summer, they are loud and rowdy, and sometimes rude. I hope spending a winter with them doesn't change Karl.

Mary asks, "Anna, what will you do? If Karl and I are gone, no one will be here to play with you."

My eyes widen in surprise and my hackles raise. "I am not a child, Mary," I answer, glaring at her, "I do not need playmates."

"You know what I mean, Anna," she quickly averts her eyes and says quietly, "How have you spent this summer without us?"

"I've kept very busy running the house with Mother. Karl and I attend the baseball games when we can. Besides, I have a close group of friends from school, and we take turns hosting the most exciting dance parties." No one in Hinckley has more fun than we do.

"I'm glad you have friends, Anna. I will have to come to one of your dance parties the next time you host one at home." Her eyes dart to John then back to the ground. "When I find the time of course. There is a lot to do running your own homestead, and John is a leader in the community, so we have responsibilities and obligations."

Responsibilities and obligations? I'm her sister. Her first responsibility should be to me, her family.

Mary continues, "In fact, John just finished helping build the new schoolhouse. It's two stories. We anticipate many families moving to the settlement, so the large school building is necessary. The town promoters are hosting a school dedication ceremony next weekend." She and John talk of Pokegama like it is a booming metropolis when it is barely a smattering of shacks in the woods. I don't think there are more than two dozen families in the settlement.

Crossing my arms, I let out a heavy sigh through my nose and begin to say, "Well, Mary, I think that—"

"*Goddog*, Mary!" A young man runs up to our circle and claps his hands. Mary jumps and grabs her chest.

It's Kristoff, Karl's best friend. He is a little older than Mary, but she knows him from dance parties and church events. I wasn't old enough to attend them yet, but I remember Mary telling me that Kristoff was very kind and funny. He lives in town with his mother who runs a laundry business in her home.

Kristoff is grinning from ear to ear, "Mary, I have not seen you for months. How are you?"

Mary regains her composure and smiles at him saying, "Kristoff, it's so great to see you, but you surprised me."

"I'm sorry Mary, I was just so excited to finally see you. Your father told me that you and John moved to Pokegama. He talks about you all the time."

She chuckles, "All the time?" then inquires, "How often do you cross paths?"

"I see him every day. I work at the sawmill now."

A delighted gasp escapes her, "Oh. Of course."

John strides into our circle at Mary's side, and holds onto her shoulders.

She gestures to Kristoff, "John, this is Kristoff Ericksson, an old friend of mine from school."

"Good morning, sir," Kristoff says as he shakes John's hand.

"Nice to meet you, Kristoff," John replies before offering his hand to Karl. "And you?"

Karl shakes his hand, "Karl Sundvquist. We already met at your wedding."

"Oh, yes of course." He turns his attention back to Kristoff and says, "I heard you mention that you work at the sawmill. Pokegama has one too, and I know the foreman there. If you are interested in land ownership, I can show you some parcels later today. Forty acres at a decent price."

Mary seems to shrink next to John as he speaks. She must be

embarrassed that he is attempting a sales pitch to her friend.

Kristoff chuckles, "No thank you, sir. Maybe someday, but not today. Today, I'm going to dance with a bear."

Mary and I giggle at Kristoff's peculiar statement.

"Dance with a bear, my friend? And where do you intend to do that?" John asks.

Kristoff grins, seeming very pleased with himself. "Rumor is that a group of forty gypsies camped outside of town last night. They are passing through on their way to Duluth, but they intend to sell trinkets, read palms, and play instruments before they move on. They have a trained bear that dances on command. I heard it stands over seven feet tall on its hind legs, and I intend to dance with her. If I can tame a beast, I can tame any young lass in the county."

Everyone laughs at his joke.

"*Kom kompis,*" Kristoff holds Karl by the shoulders. "Come, my friend, You are even braver than me. I believe you could teach a bear to waltz."

Karl and Kristoff take off together, Karl waving at Svard while he leaves the churchyard. Svard acknowledges him but keeps on talking with my parents.

John touches Mary's back and steers her toward the larger circle of adults, saying, "Mary, you had interesting schoolmates growing up, I must say." He winks at me and offers me his free hand. "Nothing I wouldn't expect in a logging town, though. Anna, are your schoolmates as colorful as Kristoff?"

I smile back and take his hand. He spins me around into the middle of the circle. Father takes my hand next and twirls me again. I squeal, "No more. I'm getting dizzy." Just then a flash of color breaks through the circle and hugs me.

"Anna!"

"Belle!"

It's my closest schoolmate, Belle Barden. Her parents follow her to our group. Her father, Jake Barden, stands next to my father and Sven. All three work at the sawmill. "Are you coming to my party? Please say yes," Belle turns toward my mother. "Mrs. Andersson, please tell Anna that she has to come to my party Friday night."

My heart skips a beat from excitement, "Oh Mother, please! Please, can I go?"

Mother places her hands on her hips, "I haven't heard of your party until this very moment, Belle."

Belle's mother, Kate, walks over and hooks her arm through my mother's and says, "That's my fault, Britta. Jake and I only just decided to host the party last night. It was mostly my idea in fact. I'm so excited for all the plans and events for the new holiday. I want the kids to have an event for themselves to celebrate the end of summer and a new school year."

Belle's mother is referring to Labor Day. Several churches in Hinckley will host parades, dances, and picnics for the new holiday. President Cleveland designated it early this summer in response to a deadly railroad workers' strike.

She continues, "So we decided to host a party for them Friday night. We'll end the month of August with dancing, games, and food. Jake and I will be there to chaperon, of course."

"Well, that sounds like a splendid idea," Mother replies. "Anna, would you like to go?"

This whole time Belle has had her arms wrapped around my waist, and now she is squeezing the air out of my lungs as she answers for me, "Yes. Yes. Yes. Anna has to come."

I giggle and squeeze her back. "Of course I want to come. Now let go, so I can breathe again."

Our mothers start to discuss the food for the party, so Belle lowers her voice for me, "I have a secret for you."

"Oh really. But, if you tell me it won't be a secret anymore, will it?"

"I suppose not, but this one involves a boy coming to the party who asked me specifically if you were also coming. He said that he wouldn't bother if you weren't going to be there."

My eyes widen in surprise. One of our friends asked about me?

"Who?" I whisper.

Mother turns her head to me, but just glances, then she continues talking to Belle's mother.

Belle says in my ear, "Edwin."

"Edwin?"

"Shhh," Belle shushes me.

Edwin is my friend and classmate. I enjoy his company, just like I enjoy spending time with the other boys who come to our dance parties. But I don't consider him, or any of my schoolmates, to be more than just friends; although, the news that he asked specifically for me is exciting. I wouldn't mind receiving extra attention, especially from a boy.

"Oh, I almost forgot," Belle says. "I heard there is a band of gypsies camped south of town, and there is a lady in a painted wagon who will read your palm for a dollar."

"Kristoff was here earlier and mentioned the gypsies, but what does 'read your palm' mean?" I ask.

"She looks at the lines on your hands because everyone's lines are unique. She knows how to interpret them and see your future," Belle holds my hands as she speaks, and the energy inside her must be contagious because I'm feeling lighter and happier since the disappointing encounter with Mary.

Belle pleads again to Mother, "Mrs. Andersson, can Anna please come with me to see the gypsies? A woman there will read our palms if we pay her a dollar."

"Gypsies?" Father asks, entering our conversation.

John adds, "Oh yes, Kristoff, just informed us of the group camped outside of town. Apparently, they have a dancing bear."

"Anna, a dollar is a lot of money," Mother says. "That's a day's work at the mill for your father. Besides, you need to come home with me to prepare the meal for John and Mary. We should start heading that way soon."

"No, Britta, we will go to the Eatery for lunch," John says. "My treat. Mary and I insist."

Father replies quickly, "You don't have to do that. Britta and Anna have a meal planned, so you don't need to spend that kind of money today."

"Please, sir, I want to impress my in-laws. I won't take 'No' for an answer."

Belle interjects, "Say yes, Mr. Andersson, then Anna can come with me."

"What a wonderful son-in-law, Paul," Belle's father adds. "You don't usually see that kind of behavior in Hinckley."

"Isn't that the truth, sir," John agrees. "Come now, Mr. Andersson, I'll buy lunch. You buy us a couple of cigars at Stumvoll's while the ladies see the gypsies. Then, we'll meet at the Eating House at 1:00 o' clock sharp. Here, girls," he hands Belle and me a dollar each. "Go have yourself some fun and take Mary." He hands her a dollar as well.

"Woo-hoo!" Belle hollers.

She is jumping up and down beside me, but out of the corner of my eye I see my mother's face. She seems a little disappointed. I wonder if she is upset that we had cleaned the house yesterday for nothing or that we peeled two dozen potatoes this morning. I should be upset too since I wasted all that time helping her, but now I am too excited to go and see the gypsies.

My father laughs and says, "Well, I can't get in the way of the girls' fun. Britta, what do you think? Do you want to go dance with a bear? He is probably a better dance partner than me."

"Heavens, no," Mother utters. "I am going back home to grab John and Mary's gift. I will meet you all at the Eating House."

She points her finger at me and Belle, "Girls, stay by Mary, and don't be late."

That is all the confirmation Belle needs. She quickly grabs Mary's hand and pulls us both on the road toward the gypsies. We walk arm in arm through town while Mary follows close behind us.

Belle leans in and whispers, "So, what do you think about Edwin? Do you think he's attractive?"

"Belle," I grind her name out through my smiling teeth. "You are too forward, sometimes."

"It's not everyday that a young boy asks about your best friend."

She is right about that. No boy has ever shown me much attention. I whisper back to her, "I'm not sure, yet. This is new for me."

I withhold more of the truth from her, that I wouldn't call Edwin handsome. He is not ugly, by any means, but I am not attracted to him that way. We are the same height and he has dark brown eyes and brown hair that he parts down the middle. He recently started growing it longer, so he can use pomade to style the sides.

"What are you two whispering about?" Mary asks. She tries to walk in stride next to me, but the wooden plank sidewalk is not wide enough.

Belle looks over her shoulder at Mary while we cross the street and answers her, "Just about the boys coming to my party on Friday night."

"Anna, I don't think it's—" Mary begins to say, but she is cut off when a group of young children run in front of us chasing a ball. We stop quickly to avoid crashing into any of them.

"Let's just get to the gypsies in one piece shall we?" Belle says. She lets go of my arm and moves between my sister and me. She grabs both of our hands and starts skipping. Mary and I have to skip as well to keep up with her.

By the time we arrive on the south end of town, the scorching sun is high in the sky. I try to shake some of the dust off of my pinafore and dress, but it is difficult. There were so many wagons and buggies in town today that it was impossible to avoid the clouds of dust from the street.

We are not the first to hear about the gypsies. There is a decent crowd gathered across the train tracks in front of us. As we approach, I can see a few blankets set up near the road with various items laid out. A couple families stand over them looking at the handmade trinkets the gypsies have for sale. It's mostly jewelry, small wooden carvings, and clothing. About fifty yards behind the blankets, I see a small campfire with a couple of wagons parked nearby and a dozen small, white tents in a circle around it.

Belle and I walk by the blankets arm in arm again and stop near a group of men gathered in a large circle. "Do you think the bear is in the middle?" Belle asks me.

"I don't know, let's go see."

Mary doesn't stop us when Belle moves ahead through the edge of the crowd. She lightly touches the men's elbows, and they slowly make a small path for us to wiggle through. Finally, as the bodies open up to the small clearing, I see a large mass of black fur pass before me.

It is a bear! A great big black bear on its hind legs! He walks away from us, slowly, shuffling in a small circle. The mass of the animal is impressive; he is at least three times as wide as Father and two or three heads taller. I can't believe my eyes.

As he turns the perimeter of the circle, I am able to see his front side. His arms are stretched ahead of him like he is using them for balance, but my eyes are drawn to his massive paws and sharp claws.

Shivers run down my spine. A dozen violent scenarios play in my head, and I squeeze Belle's arm.

"Can you believe it, Anna?" Belle squeals.

"No, I really can't."

Then, I notice a man standing in the circle with a long, gray beard. He is dressed in a weathered, black, three-piece suit with a matching silk top hat. The suit is wrinkled and faded, and the hat is frayed.

He is speaking to the bear, and he lifts up his right hand and starts waving it in small circles in the air. The bear stops walking and clumsily begins to turn in a tight circle. His large feet are too big and clunky, so the twirl is not graceful. The crowd doesn't mind though, and everyone applauds. The man in the top hat claps too and then slowly walks up to the bear and holds out both of his arms. The bear stops twirling and approaches the man, paws stretching out to meet his shoulders. The paws land on their target, and the crowd stops clapping. The people hold their breath at the contact, wondering what will happen next. The bear-man couple slowly shuffle to the middle of the circle. The man leads the bear, and they start to make stilted movements, a slow, awkward waltz between man and beast. The crowd exhales and cheers at the performance. After a few moments of dancing, the bear lets go of the man and returns to the ground, now on all fours. The man takes off his top hat and bends down into a deep bow, his head almost touching the ground. Then he walks around the circle with his hat upside down, receiving coins and dollars for the performance.

Some of the men in the crowd leave the circle, and more fill in their places. Belle turns around quickly and drags my sister and me away from the group. She leads the way back to the main road and stops when we are all out of the crowd. "That was amazing, but now it's time for the real entertainment." She points to a covered wagon behind the large group of men. The wood panels have green vines painted on the sides with small, yellow flowers and red birds. The wagon's canvas is layered with several large, embroidered tapestries. One large, black one is draped across the rear entrance like a curtain. A paper sign is pinned to it that states "Palm Reading $1."

A young man standing on the bottom step at the rear entrance of the wagon sees us staring. "Ladies," he says. "Come this way. Madame Catrina can see your future in the palm of your hand."

"I'll go first," Belle says, leading the way. Mary and I follow her to the painted wagon and Belle hands her dollar over without asking any questions.

The man smiles wide, puts her dollar in his pocket, and says, "Right this way, my lady." He holds her hand and guides her up the steps while holding back the flap. Belle disappears into the wagon, and the man returns to his position at the bottom of the steps and stares at Mary and me. Behind us the crowd around the bear is cheering again. I look over at Mary, but her eyes are on the ground, so I look back at the man. He doesn't look away when our eyes meet, so I decide to try a conversation.

"Have you had many customers today?" I ask.

"Yes."

I continue, "Do you travel a lot?"

"Yes."

"Where have you been?"

"Everywhere."

Well, this conversation is a bit one-sided, but it's better than the awkward silence and staring.

To my surprise, Mary snaps her head up and asks the man her own question, "Is it real? Or is she taking young girls' money for sport?"

"Mary," I hiss in embarrassment. "Don't be rude."

The man doesn't answer. He simply stares at her.

She asks again, "Well, is it?"

He slowly opens his mouth into a wide, toothy grin, but his teeth are brown and rotten, and some are missing, "Oh, yes, it is real, ma'am. Madame Catrina has a gift. If you look her in the eyes, she can see into your soul and understand your darkest secrets. She also has visions about what may come." He pauses for a moment, then his smile turns dark and he asks, "What are you hoping to hear, ma'am? Love, fortune, children? What do the young women of Hinckley dream about?"

My sister's face turns red. Before she can answer, the curtain to the wagon whips open and Belle appears. She looks content and extends her hand to the man who helps her down the wagon steps.

"Thank you," she says to him then turns to Mary and me. "Who's next?"

I walk past Mary and hand my dollar to the man before she can try to stop me. He helps me up the steps, and I crouch down into the wagon. Once the curtain falls behind me the wagon is dark. The air is hot and smells strongly of cigar smoke. My eyes take a moment to adjust to the darkness, so I stay still until I can get my bearings. When they adjust, I see a woman on the far end of the wagon. She is sitting on the floor which is layered with soft, velvet blankets and pillows. A board lays across the middle of the wagon as a makeshift table. There is a space on the floor in front of the table directly across from her. I lower myself to the floor and swing my legs to the side, grabbing my ankles.

Suddenly, the wagon is flooded with light. The woman shields her eyes, but now I can see her clearly. She is dressed in a simple, black dress, but she has several strings of small, white pearls hanging around her neck. The curtain closes behind me, and the wagon returns to darkness.

Mary's voice comes from behind me, "I can't let you be taken advantage of, Anna. I'll sit here."

She touches my shoulder and guides herself down to the floor next to me. She settles in at my side, keeping her hand on my shoulder. I feel close to her, and it is more than a physical closeness. Now I can feel the love she has for me and her instinct to protect me. All morning during the church service, she felt like a stranger, yet only a moment near her on the floor of a gypsy's dark wagon and I can feel her again. My sister, Mary.

"Well, it is very unusual to read two for the price of one, but I sense a close bond between you two," says the gypsy. Her accent sounds Irish, but her voice is a smoky alto, rich and deep, with a gravelly tone that hints at too many smoked cigars.

"I paid for my entry, ma'am," Mary responds, "but I can't see anything. Will you please light a candle—"

A flame ignites, cutting Mary off, and the gypsy's face is illuminated. Her skin is weathered, and she has deep wrinkles framing her mouth and eyes. She wears black, kohl liner around her eyes, and her long, gray hair is tied up in a loose bun on top of her head. She is holding a match, and she uses it to light a small candle on the table in front of us. Once lit the candle produces a faint, flickering light.

The gypsy inhales and exhales slowly and then closes her eyes. "My name is Madame Catrina, and I have been gifted with the Sight."

She lays both of her hands on the table, palms up. "Your hands, child," she says to me.

I carefully place my left palm into her outstretched hand. It is cold despite the heat inside the wagon.

"Both hands, little lamb."

I place my right hand into her left, outstretched hand, leaning into Mary to do so because the space is tight.

Madame Catrina grabs my hands and pulls lightly. Then she slides her fingers up to my wrists and twists them palm side up. She traces the pads of my thumbs with her fingertips, then my palms and fingers. Finally she lets go of my right hand and holds just my left.

She opens her eyes and says, "You don't live in town."

I sit up straighter, "I live north of town on the wagon road."

"A homesteader, then? You know what hard work is."

She leans forward and examines my palm closer.

"There are three lines here on your palm which give me hints to your character and to your future." She points to a curved line around my thumb pad, "This is the line of life. This in the middle is the line of head, and finally the line of heart." She makes a humming sound then continues, "Your line of heart is very long, little lamb. Someday, you will be a fine lover, sweet and romantic."

Even in the dark, I blush. Mary shifts beside me.

"See how it starts here at the index finger? This means you will have a happy love experience. And these two, short lines under your smallest finger? These indicate your marriage will produce two children."

I giggle, "A happy marriage and two children."

Madame Catrina squeezes my hand, "Eh, eh, little lamb. That is not what I said. The lines can only tell so much. I see a happy love experience, yes. I see a marriage with two children, yes. Someday, you will learn these two are not always the same."

I tense a little bit at her ominous explanation.

"Don't be alarmed, dear. You may be right. I can only read so much. Let me learn about your character, and then we will have a better judgment." She traces the middle line and continues, "The line of head reflects the intelligence and mentality of a person. Yours tells me that you are clever, creative, and determined. I don't think you have anything to worry about in terms of character." She pats my hand and smiles. "And finally, the line of life," she says concentrating on my hand, and the smile slowly disappears. "Your line of life is broken, which means your life as it is now is moving in this direction." She traces the short line in the middle of my palm, "but then it breaks here." She lifts her finger at the end of the line and points to a new line which curves us around my thumb. "Hmm," she ponders, "two lines of life? The second is a different path. That is interesting."

I don't know what to say. Madame Catrina holds my hand a moment longer before letting it go and turning to Mary. She offers her withered hand to my sister.

"Me? No, I don't think so. I am here to make sure you don't rob my sister, that's all," she places her hands on the table, palm side down, and leans her weight down on it to push up. "Thank you for the palm reading. It was very insightful, but we really must be—"

Mary gasps as Madame Catrina grabs her hands quickly and flips them, palm up on the table.

"Ahh, sweaty palms means you have a secret. What are you trying to hide, older sister?" Madame Catrina taunts.

"Let me go," Mary raises her voice and yanks her hands back, but Madame Catrina doesn't let go. She tugs back and laughs darkly.

Her laugh is a nasty cackle that suddenly turns into a coughing fit. She coughs so hard that she starts gasping for breath, still holding onto Mary's hands. She drops her head between her arms and the coughing stops. Mary and I sit still as Madame Catrina slouches forward so far that her head almost hits the table between us.

"Mary," I whisper, unsure what to do. Is this woman ill? Is she still breathing?

Madame Catrina's head snaps up abruptly, her face tilts toward Mary, and her eyes open wide. The candle's light dances across her face. Her eyeballs are rapidly vibrating side to side.

"I see him," she whispers. "He's a dark shadow on your soul. Pain. Sorrow. Loss. The flower of youth blossomed, yet wilted and shriveled all too quickly." She pulls Mary's hands up to her wrinkled cheeks. "Anger. Your body is burning with a hot, red, hatred, but you hide it.

Be cautious. Holding onto your anger is like holding onto hot coals. You will burn."

"Enough!" Mary shouts.

She yanks her hands away from Madame Catrina's face and shoots up from the floor. Her knee jostles the table as she bolts up, and the candle tips onto it. My hands move quickly by instinct, and I grab the candle snuffing out the flame before it can start a fire inside the wagon. Mary leaves, and the curtain moves too quickly for any light to help me see, and I am alone in the dark with Madame Catrina.

I hear her soft breathing only inches from my face. Slowly, her gnarled, cold hands enclose mine and the candle. My heart starts to race, but I can't move. I'm frozen with fear. Madame Catrina's voice is gravelly and low, cutting into the silence, "Beware the Red Demon."

Terror energizes my body, and I heave myself up and out of the wagon. I hear men shouting and whistling outside. At first the sunlight blinds me as I pull back the curtain and stumble down the steps. As my eyes adjust, the fear from Madame Catrina's warning is replaced by a new feeling. My mouth drops open in shock by what I see in front of me, but the shock is quickly replaced by anger.

4

Karl

Sunday, August 26, 1894
Hinckley, Minnesota
6 days before

Kristoff and I leave the churchyard and walk through the busy streets
of Hinckley. Dust kicks up from the horses as they trot through the
streets, and the smell of manure hangs heavy in the dry, summer heat.

I feel more comfortable the farther we walk away from the
churchyard. I don't mind going to services with Father, but I prefer
not to stick around afterwards. I never feel like I have anything
interesting to say, so I always end up feeling out of place and fidgety in
the crowd. Most people prefer to speak with Father anyway because
he is friendly and polite. I usually find a reason to leave early and skip
the conversations in the churchyard, but today I stuck around to say
hello to Mary.

Kristoff and I arrive at Main Street and turn south. We keep
walking on the wooden plank sidewalk, passing shops, houses, and
chicken coops. At the edge of town, the sidewalk ends and the two
railroad tracks cross. The St. Paul and Duluth railway and the Eastern
Minnesota railway intersect at a diagonal junction next to the Eastern
Minnesota roundhouse. The shiny, sheet metal of the circular building
reflects the midday sun.

The Eastern Minnesota rail yard is buzzing with activity. Men are walking over the maze of tracks to the roundhouse to service engines inside or operate the turntable, and a freight train is stopped underneath the water tank. The train's fireman standing atop the tender carriage wrenches down the water spout into the train's tank. Kristoff and I cross the tracks and continue south until the sounds of the rail yard are behind us. Finally, a smattering of small, white tents appear near the road. In the middle of the encampment, there is a small fire, a few wagons, and some blankets on the ground. We walk past the blankets toward a small crowd made of mostly young men from the mill along with a few families.

I'm excited the gypsies decided to stop in Hinckley. It's always fun when the caravans pass through, but my happiness disappears when I see Ivar's familiar figure standing at the edge of the crowd. He is talking to two young men I also recognize from the mill, Jan Hrbek and Nathaniel Henderson.

I stop in my tracks. "Um, I think I might head over to the baseball diamond a little early today."

"What?" Kristoff asks, looking surprised. "Why?"

He follows my gaze and sees Ivar. He puts his hands on his hips and exhales, "Pfff, oh, I see."

I turn around back towards town, and say, "I don't care to see him today, not after what happened yesterday. I'm heading home."

"No, Karl," he says, standing in front of me and putting his hands on my shoulders. "Listen, I've been meaning to say this for a few weeks now, but after yesterday I realized I should have said it sooner."

"Oh, boy," I say, crossing my arms, half smiling, and ask, "What wise words of advice do you have for me?"

He scratches his chin, thinking before he says to me, "I've seen how Ivar has been treating you, and I don't blame you for being irritated. But you can't avoid him, and you can't let him know that his behavior bothers you."

"So, you want me to just stand there and take it?"

"Hear me out. I think since you confronted him yesterday, he's going to come at you harder. You can't let him get to you again."

"I'm not playing games with him."

"Karl," he sighs, "do you want to be on a logging team this winter?"

I shove my hands in my pants pockets, not sure where he is going with this conversation. "Yes."

"Yes. Of course you do. You've wanted that for years. Then you have to play the game to some extent. At the very least, show him that the game doesn't bother you."

I shake my head, "What does that even mean?"

"Do you want me to spell it out for you? That's fine. I was never much of a speller in school, but I'll give it a try." He cracks his knuckles, like he's preparing for an epic solo at the piano. "Ivar is in charge of recruiting men for the logging teams, right? Well, he needs to know that the men he recruits are tough enough to work through frostbite, strong enough to run sixteen hour days, and man enough to share a one room shanty with twenty other Ivars all winter. Karl, we see the shanty boys in town, so we know who they are." He ticks off fingers on his left hand for each trait saying, "They are going to smoke, drink, and gamble. And most importantly, they are going to badger you all winter. They're going to try to get under your skin to see how you react. You're going to need a sense of humor to spend that much time in close quarters. You can't let everything offend you."

"You're not wrong," I groan, hating that my physical strength isn't going to be enough. "Fine, I'll stay. Teach me how to do it, then."

"How to do what?"

"How do I not react to him," I answer. Everything about Ivar offends me, so I hope Kristoff has some tips.

"Just ignore him. And remember, he's probably miserable underneath all his jeering. I suspect that anyone that mean is trying to compensate for something." We turn back towards the crowd and walk towards it. "Besides," he adds, "we have more pressing matters at hand. Forget him and just enjoy the show."

Kristoff looks around and wonders out loud, "Now where is that man and the bear?"

I examine the area and see a flash of black fur directly behind the small crowd. "There," I point out.

Kristoff's gaze follows my finger and he slaps my back when he sees it. "Dickens! It's huge."

The black bear is walking on all fours into the crowd. The men near the animal jump back, and I see Ivar throw his cigar down on the ground and run out of the way. The crowd disperses somewhat, some men jostling our shoulders as they run past us. But the bear stops and sets its weight back on its hind legs. It doesn't run or chase. It just sits on its haunches and looks around, not disturbed by the group of people or the frightened shrieks. The sense of immediate danger has passed, so the men who had run the farthest away slowly make their way back. Kristoff and I walk towards it, and we all form a circle around the animal who is silently watching us.

A thin man breaks through the outer ranks of the circle and walks up to the bear. He has a long, gray beard, and he is wearing a black top hat. He sets his hand on the bear's arm and speaks to it. It's not American or Swedish, so I can't tell what he is saying. The bear growls and snarls at the man with the top hat. The crowd collectively jumps, and a man behind us bolts out of the crowd, running down the road. The man with the top hat only laughs at the bear's reaction. Then he spits on the ground in front of the bear and yells at the crowd, "Now that we trimmed the weak from the crowd, we can begin the show." He gestures to the bear, "This is my brother Bartholomew. We're twins if you can believe it."

I laugh nervously with everyone else in the crowd, not really sure what we are about to see.

"Bartholomew, how old are we?" the man asks the bear. Bartholomew holds up both of his paws, spreading his claws apart for the crowd to see. I hear a woman gasp at the sight of the extended claws. "Ten years old! That's right. We are aging gracefully, aren't we?"

The bear nods his head up and down.

"Are you enjoying your time in Hinckley?"

The bear shakes his head side to side. Everyone in the crowd laughs again, this time with a little more vigor.

"And why is that, brother?"

The bear waves his paw in front of his face, back and forth like it is fanning the air from an unpleasant smell.

The tension in the air fades away. Everyone laughs easily at the man and the bear's humor. I notice the crowd has gotten larger, more people eager to watch the act, now that we know the bear is trained and won't charge at us. The bear is standing on its hind legs, and he is at least two feet taller than the man even with his top hat on. He speaks again to Bartholomew, and the bear responds by moving its legs in a slow shuffle around the circle.

It is impressive to see a black bear so tame. I'd seen them before in the woods while hunting or fishing, but they were always skittish and ran away quickly. I watch Bartholomew walk in front of us. He's so close that I could stretch out my hand and touch him if I wanted to. I can't help but smile as he passes me and continues around the circle.

That's when I notice another familiar face, on the other side of the small clearing made for the show. It's Anna. Her attention is on the bear, and she looks fascinated. Mary stands on one side of Anna, but she looks scared. Belle is on her other side, and she is clapping and cheering. The bear is back sitting in the middle of the circle, and the man in the top hat is walking around the crowd asking for tips.

He approaches us with his top hat turned upside down. It jingles when he shakes it as the coins inside hit each other. Kristoff and I throw in a few coins, and then the man continues through the crowd. I gaze back across the clearing to find Anna, but she is gone. She, Mary, and Belle must have moved on.

A new man walks into the circle holding a large coin purse. The man with the top hat empties his earnings into the coin purse and then returns to the bear. He waves to the crowd, "Did you know that Bartholomew is a great dancer? For only one dollar, you can dance with him!"

Well, there was truth to the rumor Kristoff had heard earlier. This bear can dance too. The crowd murmurs quietly, but no one steps forward. The man in the top hat wiggles his eyebrows and scans the crowd. Kristoff takes a deep breath next to me, then shoots his hand up into the air. He's holding a dollar and waving it to catch the man's attention as he calls out, "Sir, I'd be honored to dance with Bartholomew."

The man in the top hat grins widely and answers, "Step up, young man, and join your partner."

Kristoff walks into the clearing as the crowd cheers for him. When he reaches the bear, he bows dramatically, almost touching the ground with his head. He doesn't hesitate as he offers Bartholomew his hand.

The bear looks at his hand for a moment, not moving from his sitting position. The man in the top hat says something to Bartholomew, and the bear lumbers up onto his hind legs, towering over Kristoff. I hold my breath. The bear lifts his paws and leans toward Kristoff. They make contact and the crowd gasps. Slowly, the bear starts to sway back and forth, leading Kristoff. Some men in the crowd laugh while some holler Kristoff's name for encouragement.

The same man who had the coin purse a few moments ago now walks into the circle holding a fiddle. He places the instrument under his chin and starts playing a lively tune as Kristoff and Bartholomew shuffle back and forth. It's quite a show. The crowd is applauding and stomping their feet in time with the fiddle. The man ends the song with a swish of the bow, and Kristoff swings his leg up high and gradually tilts his body back, imitating a woman dipping down at the end of a waltz before strutting over to me, smiling from ear to ear. He grabs my arm as men in the crowd part for him, patting him on the back he passes. He pulls me out of the mass of bodies until we are in the open space between the bear show and the gypsy encampment.

"I can't believe you did that," I hold onto his shoulders and squeeze.

He grabs my arms and admits, "I was so scared, but it was amazing. I've never been that close to a bear before."

Out of nowhere, Ivar's voice speaks up behind me. "That was hilarious." He stands beside Kristoff, delivering a hearty slap on his back. Jan and Nathaniel are just steps away.

"Oh, hello, Ivar," Kristoff greets him and nods to the other two men we recognize from the mill. "Nathaniel. Jan."

Remembering Kristoff's words, I clear my throat and pretend like I don't detest the man standing next to him, and ask, "Did you see Kristoff's dance?"

Ivar answers, "We did, Sundvquist. Why else would we come over here?"

I steel myself and keep my face calm. Don't react. Just let it slide.

Behind me the fiddle starts playing again, and the crowd cheers for Bartholomew's new dance partner. The five of us naturally create a small circle, separate from the larger group. Nathaniel and Ivar light up cigars, so I guess they are staying with Kristoff and me. They start talking about baseball and today's game. All three of the young men play for our local team, the Hinckley Crescents. The baseball diamond is on this side of town, not too far from where we are standing. Hopefully, they have to arrive early for their game and will leave Kristoff and me alone.

As Nathaniel talks about Ivar's batting swing, I notice a painted wagon behind him covered with colorful blankets on top of the stretched canvas. It catches my eye because Anna and Mary are standing next to it. There is a sign pinned to the entrance of the wagon, and I squint my eyes trying to read it.

"Sundvquist, what are you looking at?" Ivar shouts, snapping me back to the group. He follows my gaze behind his shoulder and spots the wagon. "Oh, I see. You want to go see the gypsy? The one that can see your future? Well, go right ahead." He gestures towards Anna and Mary who thankfully haven't noticed us looking at them. "Go line up with the women and wait your turn for a palm reading."

My cheeks burn from embarrassment as Nathaniel and Jan laugh. Kristoff doesn't; instead, he looks at me and shrugs his shoulders. He wants me to ignore it. I push my anger down and stay silent.

Nathaniel shakes his head and points his cigar towards the painted wagon, "Now, there's a scam if I ever saw one. Ladies pay a whole dollar to hear made up stories about romance and finding their true love."

Ivar turns around and throws up his arms, shouting, "Look no further, ladies, your true love is standing right here!"

Nathaniel and Jan laugh, and Kristoff smiles. I glance back towards the gypsy wagon and see Anna walk up the steps, pull back the curtain, and disappear inside the wagon. Jan takes a small flask out of his coat pocket. He unscrews the top and takes a swig, then passes the flask to Ivar. Ivar drinks some and passes it to Kristoff. He takes a swig and chokes a little before passing it to me.

I've had ale with Father before, but I've never had hard liquor, and I don't care to share that experience in front of Ivar. I shake my head no, so Kristoff passes it on to Nathaniel.

Ivar whines, "Ah, don't be a cat lap, Sundvquist! Take a big swig!"

This ignoring thing might be harder than Kristoff made it sound, but I really want to be on a logging team, so this is good practice for this winter. "The baseball game doesn't start for another hour," I say. "What do you all do as a warm-up?"

Jan lifts the flask up in the air and jiggles it.

"Oh," I half laugh, "Ha, right."

"Let's walk by the Catholic Church. They should be getting out now," Nathaniel proposes as Ivar takes another swig of the liquor.

"Why should we do that?" Ivar passes the flask to Kristoff, but this time he declines.

"Christine McElroy, that's why," Nathaniel answers. "Have you seen her lately?" He whistles and uses his hands to imitate curves in the air.

"You're a gal sneaker," Jan laughs. "You'll try to seduce anything with two legs, I swear. I'm not walking over there just so you can steal a kiss from Christine."

"From what I hear, you don't need to steal anything from her," Ivar adds, wiggling his eyebrows and handing his cigar to Jan. "She is willing to give it away if you know what I mean." He pulls a handkerchief from his pocket and starts promenading around our group, flicking it with one hand and twisting his mustache with the other, saying, "Oh, Miss McElroy! Miss McElroy, won't you please look my way?"

Nathaniel doesn't look impressed with Ivar's show. He is still imitating a lovesick Nathaniel as he walks around us a second time, "Why, Miss McElroy, I think you are the jammiest bits of jam. An absolutely perfect young lady." He walks his fingers along Nathaniel's shoulders and pinches his cheek. "Won't you take a stroll with me behind the church?" Ivar says as Nathaniel bats his hand away.

"They don't actually fall for that, do they?" Kristoff asks as Ivar walks to Jan and takes his cigar back.

"Oh, you bet your backside they do," Ivar answers. "Women hear what they want. You just have to figure out what it is they want to hear, and then give it to them. A perfect example," he gestures over to the gypsy's wagon again. "Women paying money to listen to a stranger lie to them. It doesn't matter if it's true or not. Those women want that gypsy to tell them that they will be happy, that they'll fall in love, and then get married. Filling their heads with nonsense is what she's doing."

Jan says, "Those ladies don't need a gypsy to tell them where the real men are. We're only a short walk away."

"We have what they want right here," Ivar says as he puckers his lips and makes a smacking noise.

Nathaniel huffs, "God's gift to women, huh?"

Ivar snaps back, "Christine McElroy wasn't complaining last weekend."

"Oh, yea?" Nathanial says looking irritated, "If you're so great with the ladies, then kiss the next gal that steps out of that wagon. Let's see how she reacts."

"What will you give me?" Ivar asks.

Nathaniel answers, "Two days' pay because you're all talk. You won't actually do it."

Jan pipes up, "I like these odds. Count me in."

Ivar points at Kristoff and then at me asking, "Did you boys hear it? That's four days' pay."

I frown. Anna is in that wagon.

"I have witnesses, so you both better pay up," Ivar says to Nathaniel and Jan as he turns and takes two steps towards the wagon.

"Wait!" I yell. "I'll take that bet."

Ivar turns around, looking surprised. "I didn't take you as a betting man, Sundvquist. All right, six days' pay for one kiss. That's a whole week."

"No, that's not what I meant. I'll give you a week's pay not to kiss her."

"Where's the fun in that?" Ivar shakes his head, "Not interested." He turns around and keeps walking toward the wagon.

I run to him and grab his arm, "Stop!"

He shoves my arm aside, "Get your hand off me."

I stand in front of him, blocking his path. "You can't kiss Anna."

"Anna?" he looks confused.

"I mean, you can't just go around kissing girls."

"For four day's pay, I'd do more than kissing. This is easy money," he says and tries to walk around me, but again, I block his way.

Kristoff runs in between us, "Hey, fellas. Let's forget about this and head to the game."

Ivar points to his chest, "I'm not a man who backs out of a bet. If either of you get in my way again, you'll regret it." He walks past both of us, shoulder-checking me as he does. I jerk backwards from the force of it.

"He's not kissing Anna," I grind out between my clenched teeth.

Kristoff frowns, "What? Who said anything about Anna?"

I run towards the wagon and catch up to Ivar just as he arrives at the bottom of the wagon steps. I stand between him and the entrance, throwing my hands up in front of my chest. "Enough, Ivar. Who do you think you are?"

Belle takes a few steps back away from the wagon.

Ivar glares at me, "I think I'm the guy who's going to knock your teeth out. Get out of my way!"

"You're not kissing her," I say, widening my stance and bracing myself.

There is a shuffling sound coming from inside the wagon and the sound of the curtain being drawn back. Ivar's eyes dart from me to the wagon entrance, and he puts one foot on the steps. I turn around to face the wagon entrance at the exact moment that Anna flies out, so I grab her by the waist and slam my mouth on hers.

She places both hands on my chest and shoves me back—hard. I stumble backwards into Ivar's chest and look up, expecting to see Anna, but the angry eyes staring back at me are Mary's. She looks like she wants to punch *me* in the teeth. The noises around me soften to a murmur while I try to process how Mary is standing in front of me and not Anna. Mary's face changes from anger to fear. Her bottom lip trembles like she is about to cry, but instead she bolts and runs away.

"Karl!" Belle shouts. "What are you doing?"

Ivar grabs my shirt collar and pulls me towards him.

He yells at me, and his breath is hot against my face, "What the hell was that, Sundvquist! You owe me four dollars!"

"What's going on?" Anna asks from behind me. Ivar releases me, and I stare up at Anna who is stepping down from the wagon. She loses her balance and falls to her knees. I quickly crouch down and try to help her up.

"Anna, I thought that—"

"Don't touch me," she says, pushing me away. She and Belle run after Mary.

Nathaniel and Jan slap my back, laughing hysterically.

"That a boy, Karl," Nathaniel cheers.

"I didn't see that coming," Jan shouts.

"Pay up, Ivar," Nathaniel says between laughs. "You didn't kiss her. Karl beat you to it."

I start after Anna, but Ivar grabs my arm and pulls me back, scowling. "Sundvquist cheated. He should pay up, not me."

"What?" I shrug off his hand. "I didn't cheat. I told you not to kiss her."

"And, I didn't. Now, pay Nathaniel and Jan."

"No, I didn't make a bet with them. That was you." I'm through with this nonsense. I stomp away from all three of them. Kristoff meets me, and we continue towards the baseball diamond.

He takes his straw hat off and scratches his head, "Karl, what just happened?"

"I don't know," I cringe. "I couldn't let him kiss Anna."

"Not that, I get that. I mean, why did you just kiss Mary?"

"I thought it was Anna," I shove my hands in my pockets, wondering how things got out of hand so quickly.

"Hmm, well Mary has a husband, so . . . ."

"I know she does. I'll figure out how to fix it."

"And, this is probably a bad time to bring it up, but you might want to start making new winter plans. Ivar looked really angry." He turns towards the baseball diamond, but I don't follow him. "Hey, aren't you coming?"

I shake my head and change direction. "No, I'm going home. I'll see you tomorrow."

My insides twist with regret. I'll have to apologize to Mary and hope she believes that I had no idea she was in the gypsy wagon. Even if she does, her husband will probably take a justified swing at me. But what makes my chest muscles tighten is the furious look that was on Anna's face. That and the reminder that Ivar is never going to hire me to be on a logging team.

5

Anna

Sunday, August 26, 1894
Hinckley, Minnesota
6 days before

"Anna! Wait!" Belle yells at me.

But I won't stop. I run past those laughing men at the fortune teller's wagon and continue along the road all the way to the Eastern Minnesota tracks. That's when I finally stop because a train is parked at the Eastern Minnesota roundhouse. Mary must have beat it because she isn't standing here trapped on the south side of the tracks like me. I bend down and scoop up a handful of dust and pebbles from the road. I throw it at the massive train in front of me, furious that it is blocking the path to my sister. A woman standing nearby frowns at my outburst. I slump my shoulders and look away from her disapproving face. I shouldn't throw rocks at the train. I know that.

Belle finally reaches me and grabs my shoulder to hold her up. Breathlessly, she says, "Wow, Anna, you're fast."

I ignore her compliment, "What just happened, Belle?"

For once my friend's face is not cheerful when she answers, "I honestly don't know."

My hands are shaking, so I try to steady them by crossing my arms in front of my chest and ask, "What did you see, right before

Karl kissed my sister?"

"Well, it happened very quickly. I was standing by the wagon waiting for you and Mary. All of a sudden that man showed up, and Karl stood in his way. I thought that man was going to punch him."

I look down the train and see the boiler man standing on top of the carriage. He swings out the spigot arm from the water tower and places it over the train's water tender. Then he jerks the chain which starts the pump.

Belle continues talking, "Karl told that man that he couldn't kiss Mary."

"He did?"

Belle nods.

I shake my head and close my eyes. Karl, Mary, and I have been friends for so long, and he's never been interested in my sister in that way. The image of Karl's lips on Mary's flashes in front of my eyes, and anger surges through my chest, heating my already warm body. Of course, he must have feelings for Mary. She's beautiful, and every boy she meets eventually falls in love with her.

Belle's hand tugs at my elbow, forcing me to open my eyes, "Mary looked really embarrassed. She probably feels awful."

"Yes, well, it must be terribly difficult when everyone wants to kiss you even when you're married."

"Anna, she didn't ask Karl to kiss her. You're her sister. You should comfort her before she goes to her husband. This might all be a misunderstanding."

"I will go to her once this train gets out of my way."

She smiles at me, "Well, even trains need to refill their tanks from time to time. Honestly, I don't really understand why a train needs water."

I answer her easily with the response I know from memory, "The engineer boils the water from the tender in order to create steam. The pressure from the steam moves the parts inside the engine which makes the train go."

The cheerful glint in her eye is back, "Well aren't you clever," She pokes me in the ribs.

I smile at my friend's comment, but underneath the smile, I feel strange reciting the words that Karl has told me over and over again.

He loves to talk about trains, fire engines, steamboats, really anything with an engine. Last summer when we would get sodas and watch the trains at the depot, he explained the mechanics to me, and I listened.

"That's also why each train has a coal tender as well," I explain to Belle. "The engineer burns the coal which heats up the water."

She shakes her head slightly, "Well, that's one place I'd rather not be, standing next to hot coals and sweating through every train ride."

Hot coals. My breath catches in my throat as Belle's words remind me of something Madame Catrina said to Mary before she ran out of the wagon. *"Holding onto your anger is like holding onto hot coals. You will burn."* Even in this stifling heat, my body trembles at the memory of Madame Catrina's strange behavior and her peculiar warning to Mary.

Just then the train's smokestack releases a plume of steam, and the engineer blows its whistle, warning people to stay clear of the tracks. The wheels slowly begin to rotate. As each train carriage slowly passes us, my mind wanders back to what happened in the gypsy wagon. Madame Catrina's behavior towards Mary had been so bizarre. She told Mary something else that I can't fully remember. I focus on the memory, trying to recall the exact words.

Belle starts to cross the tracks, gently tugging on my hand to follow. Horse-drawn buggies and carts move along the road, so we make our way to the wooden plank sidewalk. Belle hooks arms with me and whispers quietly in my ear, "Madame Catrina told me that I've already met my future husband." I look at each person's face as we cross paths on the sidewalk, certain they are trying to hear our conversation.

I whisper back to her, "Who?"

She giggles, "I don't know. That's the fun part, though, isn't it?"

"Yes, I suppose. It is fun to imagine and speculate. Did Madame Catrina act . . . strange . . . while you were in the wagon?" I feel uneasy asking Belle, but I have to know.

"Strange? How so? She is a gypsy who reads palms, so that's pretty strange in itself, Anna."

"That's true. She did read my palm. I enjoyed that part, but after that she grabbed Mary's hand, and she changed."

"Changed?" she asks.

"Yes, it was so odd. It's hard to describe, but it felt like . . . well . . ." I pause while a woman and her three children walk past us. I lower my voice again, "It felt like she left and something else was in her body, speaking through her."

"You mean like a possession? Like a spirit or a demon was in her body?"

A demon. The memory comes back to me in full force. The darkness of the wagon and the overwhelming smell of cigar smoke invade my senses once more. The icy coldness of her hands on top of mine and the gravelly tone of her voice as she warned me, "*Beware the Red Demon.*"

"Anna?"

I snap back to reality. Belle is standing in front of me, waving her hand in front of my face.

"Anna? Hello?" she giggles, "Where did you go?"

I blink away the memory of Madame Catrina. I have to lie to Belle because I'm not ready to tell her what the gypsy woman said to me. I feel too afraid to repeat it.

"It must be this heat," I say, faking a smile and a shaky laugh. "I should get some water and food in my belly."

Belle looks down at her wristwatch, "It's almost one o'clock. We should run." She hooks her arm in mine and away we go.

We run together for the next two blocks and stop at the corner of Third Street. We can see the Eating House from here. I unhook my arm from Belle's and straighten my pinafore and the skirt of my dress. I pat out the dust that accumulated from the street. Belle turns towards me and pulls some stray hairs back into their pins and uses her fingers to fluff my bangs. The curls from this morning have completely flattened, but I appreciate her trying to help me look presentable.

"Don't fret too much about what happened with Karl and Mary. You three have been best friends forever. I have a feeling that this will all work out. Nothing to lose your appetite over."

I hug her tightly and tell her, "You are such a good friend, Belle. I don't know if I believe you yet, but you make me feel better."

She squeezes me back, "Either way, meet me at the Beanery on Wednesday afternoon. You can tell me how your lunch goes, and how angry Mary's husband is about Karl kissing his wife." The Beanery is a small café in the St. Paul and Duluth depot that sells coffee, soda, and small snacks to train travelers.

"I'd be more afraid of Mother than John," I respond, releasing Belle and turning toward the Eating House.

My mother spots me immediately as I enter the restaurant. She waves her arm in the air to flag me down. It isn't necessary since their table is second nearest to the door. Since I'm the last to arrive, I head to the only empty chair between Mary and Mother. Everyone except Mary greets me as I sit down. She keeps her gaze down at the white linen tablecloth in front of her.

"Anna," Mother says, "You are late, *älskling*. How did your sister make it on time, and you did not?"

"I apologize. There was a train refilling its water tank, so Belle and I had to wait for it to pass."

My father, sitting across from me at the table, asks, "How are the gypsies, Anna? Did one of them read your palm?"

I smile at him, "Oh yes, it was unusual. First, Madame Catrina told me that I would fall in love, get married, and have two children."

Mother, Father, and John clap their hands energetically for me.

Father asks, "And, how can she tell that from your palm?"

"Well, everyone's palms have distinct lines on them. See?" I hold up my hand. "These three lines are the head line, the heart line, and the life line. I can't remember which one is which, but the shape and length of the lines tell something about the individual's character, relationships, and the paths her life will take."

"My goodness," Mother exclaims. "All this from looking at someone's hands."

"Well, my palms are covered in rough blisters," Father jokes. "I can't even see the lines underneath. What does that say about me?"

Mother places her hand on top of Father's, "It means you work hard for your family."

Father smiles at her and squeezes her hand. Then he turns his attention back to me. "And what happened next, Anna? You said it was unusual, but that seems like a pleasant future for you."

"You're right, that was nice to hear, but then Madame Catrina acted strangely. She grabbed Mary's hands as she tried to leave and she told Mary—"

Mary interrupts me, "She said that I would become rich beyond my wildest imagination."

Father laughs, "Oh that's wonderful news, Mary."

Mother and Father clap for Mary this time.

"Anna, why is that unusual?" John asks after my parents are finished applauding.

I'm about to explain what really happened in the wagon, but Mary speaks over me, again. "John, you know how those gypsy games work. The men and women see small details about your clothes or the way you talk, and they make vague assumptions about your lifestyle. The woman must have seen my beautiful, new dress and assumed that I come from an affluent family."

"It is such a beautiful dress, Mary," Mother says. "Where did you find time to sew such a wonderful garment?"

"I bought it for her, ma'am," John replies. "Only the best for my wife."

"Thank you, Mother," Mary says. "Now, no more talk about the gypsies. It was a silly children's game and it's over. The wagons will be gone by tomorrow morning, onto another town to make money off children and young women."

I stare at Mary in disbelief. That's not what happened at all. She just lied to our parents and to her husband. It really scared me how Madame Catrina acted in that wagon, and I want to tell our parents about it, not keep it a secret from them.

"Anna, would you like something to drink?" Father's voice breaks my concentration, and I notice everyone at the table staring at me. A waiter dressed in a crisp, white dress shirt stands next to Father. He has a long, white apron tied around his waist, and he is holding a small notepad and pencil.

"She'll have tea as well," Mother orders for me. She leans over to me and whispers, "Anna, stop daydreaming. We only come here once or twice a year, so please have some manners and don't embarrass us."

Each of us at the table give the waiter our orders. When John orders the fried liver and boiled potatoes, I shift my eyes to Mother. Her face is still and her mouth is smiling, but I see a quick flash of something else when John ordered potatoes. Disappointment, perhaps? She hides it well and continues to smile and make conversation, but she doesn't bring up the fact that we have two dozen peeled potatoes at home ready to be eaten.

The rest of the meal carries on quite smoothly. I keep waiting for an opportunity to have a side conversation with Mary, but she refuses to look at me. She is engaged in the table's conversation and turns her body away from me. Father, John, and Mary are discussing the financial panic and high unemployment that is gripping our country. They carry on until the waiter brings us our food. I am just finishing my pork chop when Mother lifts a large heavy package onto the table and says, "Mary, this is for you and John. It's from your father and me. I apologize that it's late, but this is your wedding present from us."

Mary wipes her mouth delicately with her napkin, "You both didn't need to do this."

"Of course, we did," Father says. "You are our daughter, and we're proud of you."

"Oh, Father, thank you," Mary says. "Really, this means a lot."

John sets his fork and knife down and tells Mary, "Mary, are you going to open it?"

"Oh yes, of course," she gingerly unwraps the layers of brown paper.

"A cast iron skillet," Mary exclaims. "Oh, thank you so much." She stands up and walks around the table, kissing my father and then my mother on the cheek. She makes a wide arc around my chair, careful not to make eye contact with me.

"It's from the Griswold Manufacturing Company, all the way from Pennsylvania. And look, here," Mother slides her hand across the inside of the pan and says, "there is an enamel coating on it, so it will never rust."

John picks up the skillet and inspects it, "It won't rust, but will it prevent burning? Mary will have to practice a little more before she uses this new skillet. I think I've lost a few pounds since our marriage on account of all the burned dinners."

Mary looks down at the table and whispers, "Oh, yes of course."

A group of four men enter the restaurant and walk by our table. One tall man, just a few years younger than Father stops and places his hand on Father's shoulder.

"*Goddag*, Paul" he greets him.

"*God eftermiddag*," Father stands up and shakes his hand. "Sven, this is my son-in-law, John Larson." John stands up and shakes Sven's hand. Father continues introducing each of us, "And you know my daughters, Mary and Anna. My wife, Britta." The men continue to stand as Sven greets everyone at the table.

"Hello Britta, Anna, and Mary," he says smiling then his eyes look mischievous, "I mean Mrs. Larson," I expect him to say a joke or something along those lines, but he just continues to stare at Mary.

Mary continues to smile, but her eyes dart between John and Mother. A few moments pass, and then Sven chuckles and puts his hand on Father's shoulder, and says, "Paul, I just heard the strangest story from Ivar Gunnolfsson over at the baseball game."

"Oh yea? And what was the story he told?" Father asks.

"Well, Ivar told me that he and his friends were hanging out south of town, checking out the gypsy wagons passing through, and he mentioned one of the new millworkers was kissing your daughter."

Mary's smile disappears, and her face turns white.

Mother gasps, "Who?"

Sven answers, "Your neighbor."

"You mean Karl?" Father says.

Sven continues, "Yes, but, Ivar seemed pretty angry—"

Mother interrupts him, "No, I meant which daughter. Who did Karl kiss?"

Sven looks at Mary and says, "Her."

"Excuse me!" John roars. "My wife has not been kissing anyone." He takes two, long strides towards Sven who holds his hands up defensively.

"I'm only telling the story that I heard."

"How dare you spread such lies!" John yells, and a few other restaurant patrons turn their heads to the commotion.

Father raises his hands putting one on John's chest and one on Sven's, but Mother pulls Sven towards her out of John's reach. "There must be a mistake, Sven. Are you sure that Ivar said it was Mary?"

"He said it was Paul's daughter getting her palm read in the gypsy wagon."

"Paul has two daughters," John says as he walks back to his chair and sits down, smoothing his hair back into place. The legs scrape against the floor as he scoots the chair closer to Mary whose face is set like a piece of stone, not a muscle twitches or an eye blinks. She is staring at Sven. John reaches under the table and takes one of Mary's hands and places it on the table. He covers it with one of his hands and cups Mary's chin with the other.

A hand grabs mine from underneath the table, and I jolt in surprise. It's Mary's other hand, and she is gripping my own tightly.

John slowly guides Mary's face away from Sven and towards his own, speaking slowly, "Tell me what happened, Mary."

Mary blinks at him a few times before speaking, "Belle, Anna, and I went down to the gypsy wagons to have our palms read."

"Yes, dear. I know that part," he says, still holding her face, which makes me uncomfortable. "Did you kiss that boy Karl while you were there?"

"No," she calmly answers. Her hand, the one holding mine squeezes so hard, I think my fingers might break.

Father clears his throat, "John, why don't we—"

Mary blurts out, "Anna did. Anna kissed Karl."

"Anna?" John asks, turning his gaze to me. "You kissed the boy?"

My face turns crimson, and my cheeks heat from his piercing gaze and the judgment radiating from my parents. The truth bubbles within me threatening to come out so I can defend myself, but Mary's grip is excruciating, a clear signal to obey. I'll say anything for her at this moment if she will just let go of my hand. I meet John's gaze and the words rush out, "Yes, Karl kissed me."

John's eyebrows go up a little at the same time that Mary releases my hand. Instantly, the pain is gone, but at the same time the reaction across the table is immediate. "Anna!" Mother gasps dramatically. "Why didn't you tell us?"

Sven scratches his chin, "Anna? Oh, it must have been Anna."

"Is kissing all that you've done?" Mother asks.

"Britta," Father says sternly. "We'll discuss this at home."

Father turns toward Sven, "Thank you for saying hello, friend. I will see you tomorrow at the mill."

Sven nods, looking like he regrets coming to our table in the first place. He walks away quickly. Father returns to his seat as John gets up and leaves the table. Father calls to him, but he keeps walking.

"Paul," Mother grabs his arm, pulling his attention back to our table. "Fifteen is too young."

"Britta, not here," Father repeats himself.

They start to argue quietly, so I turn to face my sister. She needs to explain to me what just happened. My hand is still throbbing from her warning grip to go along with her lie, and I want to know why.

"Mary? What's going on?"

She ignores me. Instead of answering, she pulls the cast iron skillet towards her and puts it back in the brown paper wrapping.

I place my hand on top of hers to get her attention. "Mary," I quietly plead, "please talk to me."

She pauses but does not look up from the half-wrapped skillet.

"Mary, where did John go?" Mother asks.

Mary slowly pulls her hand out from under mine and answers flatly, "He probably went to pay the bill."

"I think it's time everybody went home," Father says.

"I agree," Mother says and then adds, "Anna, I have never been so embarrassed."

My stomach twists, and I feel tears forming. Her words hurt. I feel a pressure in my chest, begging me to tell her the truth, but Mary speaks first, "Mother, have you talked to Anna about kissing?" She is holding the wrapped skillet tightly against her body. "If you haven't told her your expectations, then how is she supposed to know how to act?"

Mother looks shocked from Mary's forwardness but says, "She's still a child."

Mary calmly replies, "She's almost sixteen and can hardly be called a child anymore. You need to explain to her sooner rather than later."

John appears at the table, holding his hand out to Mary and announces, "I just paid the bill for everyone. I believe Mary and I will return to Pokegama early today. If you don't mind, we'll be on our way." His words are stiff and lack his usual friendliness.

Mary takes his hand and stands up. Mother rushes to her side and gives her a hug. "John, I apologize for Anna's behavior. You don't have to leave so soon," Mother pleads.

John places his hand on Mary's back and guides her away from the table towards the door, calling out, "Goodbye, Paul. Goodbye,

Mary." They leave without saying anything to me.

Mother looks down at me, "Anna, you are excused from the table. We are going straight home to discuss your behavior."

I want to scream that it wasn't me, but then I would expose Mary's lie, and I'm not sure if I should do that yet. Instead, I reply, "Yes, Mother," and silently leave the Eating House. I need to talk to Karl as soon as possible and let him know that my parents think it was me he kissed and not Mary.

6

Karl

Tuesday, August 28, 1894
Hinckley, Minnesota
4 days before

I plunge my hands into the soft dirt of our potato patch. Father and I are harvesting the last of our potato plants before the sun sets. The soil is so dry, the dirt falls off the potato's skin easily as we brush them off and place them into baskets.

Anna wants to meet me tonight in the old sod house where we used to play as kids. I don't know why I didn't think of it first, but Anna's always been smart. And impatient. She probably can't stand that I haven't tried to talk to her yet.

There is a one-room, sod house between our two homesteads that was abandoned years ago. The roof is gone, and one wall has crumbled from weather and time. As children we would play "Family," and Anna and Mary would take turns being the mother. Anna loved to act out historical events too. Another game we played was the story of Paul Revere. In school, we read the poem "Paul Revere's Ride," by Henry Wadsworth Longfellow. Anna directed us in the sod house to re-enact the night of his famous ride. Either Mary or I would be Paul Revere, riding around the tree stumps on our horse looking for the signal. We didn't have lanterns like the poem described, so the house's abandoned and broken kitchenware acted as lanterns. One tin pitcher with a hole in the side meant the British were coming by land. The broken tin pitcher and a rusty spoon meant they were coming by sea. Anna would place them on the rotted window sill. After seeing the signal, whoever was acting the part of the British would chase our Paul Revere character either from a boat or on a horse, depending on what signal Anna put in the window.

This morning as Father and I walked on the wagon road to the mill, I saw the broken tin pitcher standing on the window sill. It caught me off guard at first. We haven't played the game of Paul Revere or even been in the sod house for at least five years. But the pitcher sitting on the ledge felt so normal, as if we played the game yesterday. I half expected Mary to come running up behind me acting as a British soldier. I knew that Anna must have placed the pitcher there as a signal to me, just like in the game. She is asking for a quiet word, and this is the only place we can be alone.

I need to square things with Anna and Mary, but I already feel embarrassed just thinking about what I did. I close my eyes and take a deep breath. Down here, the air smells like soil, but it lacks the dampness of summers past. I exhale it all out, but I still feel uneasy.

"Something on your mind, Karl?" Father asks me, holding up a potato plant by the stem. The dried shriveled up leaves look as if the plant is dead, but just below his hand are the roots and about five medium-sized potatoes caked with dirt.

"No, nothing," I say, holding up a potato and rubbing the dirt off it.

"Are you thinking about Anna? I heard that you kissed her on Sunday."

His words knock me stiff and my hands freeze in the dirt. I frown, shocked but also confused by his statement. *Anna?* He said I kissed Anna on Sunday, not Mary.

"Who says that I kissed Anna?" I ask him.

"Men at the mill and Paul," he answers.

I throw the potato in my basket, thinking about what Father just said. If Mr. Andersson thinks that I kissed Anna, she must have told him that.

"Are you angry with me? Is Mr. Andersson angry with me?"

"No, I'm not angry with you and neither is Paul, but I think it's time that we have a conversation about courting."

My stomach twists inside my belly. I do not want to talk about courting and tell him, "Father, I'm not courting Anna."

"I understand that, Karl," he replies, standing up and holding his basket of potatoes. "That's why Paul talked to me."

Father starts walking towards our barn, so I stand up and lift my basket following him as he explains to me. "If you have feelings for Anna, you must ask Paul and Britta if you can court her when she is a little older. There will be consequences if you two keep acting this way."

"Consequences? What kind of consequences?"

He opens the barn door without answering me and walks inside to the far corner where potatoes are already spread out on the floor. We harvested these ten days ago and set them in here to cure. Potatoes need time to heal nicks and blemishes and completely dry out before we store them for winter in the root cellar. We both kneel on the floor in an empty spot beside the curing potatoes and unload the basket of freshly-dug ones.

Father doesn't answer my question but says, "I assume that you kissed Anna because you have feelings for her. That's why young men steal kisses from girls. It's easier than actually saying it out loud. You just turned eighteen this month and are most likely taking an interest in girls. In fact, that's the age that I started courting your mother."

My arms stop moving for a second. He rarely speaks of my mother, so I'm surprised that he mentions her now.

"Our parents matched us," he continues, "We had no say in the matter. It's different here, though, you and Anna can decide if the match is right. She is too young now, but if you talk to Paul and Britta and tell them how you feel, then when Anna is older, you should be able to court her. And by that time you will have enough money from the mill and logging to offer her a good life."

We finish setting out the fresh potatoes and stand up to look at them. I don't think he's going to tell me anything else Mr. Andersson said, so I want this conversation to be over. I tell him what he wants to hear, "All right. I'll talk to Mr. and Mrs. Andersson." The truth is I'm planning to talk to Anna first. I need to know why she made her parents believe that I kissed her, not Mary. It makes me a little uncomfortable keeping the whole truth from my father, but there must be a reason that Anna lied.

"Yes, I think that is a good plan," he scratches his beard and groans, "but I also have to forbid you from seeing Anna unless her parents or I am around."

I glance at him, hoping my face isn't giving away the secret meeting that we have planned, "I used to be with Anna all the time without anyone watching me. Even this spring, we went into town whenever we pleased," I say, crossing my arms against my chest. He's treating me like a child.

"That was all well and good, but now you changed things."

"Father, it was one kiss."

"Karl, she's not a child anymore. Her good name means something. If you ruin that for her, she'll be climbing a steep hill for years to come. If you care about Anna, you need to protect her."

Oh, if he only knew that I was protecting her, from Ivar.

"Karl," he continues, "there are two groups in Hinckley. There are families that work slow and hard for everything they have. Millworkers, carpenters, and shopkeepers. And then, there are others like the shanty boys. They work hard too, but they get paid fast and all at once. Then they spend all that money just as fast in the saloons and sporting houses over on the east side of town. As long as you live with me, you belong to the first group, and we have rules about how you behave around the women. Do you understand me?"

I nod, "*Ja.*"

He nods back, "Good, good."

Then, he bends down and grabs two large potatoes from the ground and hands them to me and says, "Now, wash these for supper, *ja?*"

I hold the potatoes but remain next to him asking, "What about the second group? What if I want to be a shanty boy? You did it for two winters."

"I did, and I saw their behavior," he says, shaking his head. "It's great money, but I raised you differently. Anna deserves better." Now he crosses his arms across his chest, "Karl, I know you want to work in the winter camps. You can cut down the trees, drive the logs, and then get the big pay envelope, but you don't have to act like them."

I agree with him just to end this strange conversation. "*Ja,*" I mumble.

We both pick a spot in the barn to stare at instead of looking at each other. We rarely have conversations like this, so neither of us know how to move on. I push my boot into the dirt floor and make small circles. I feel Father's eyes move to my face, but I don't look up at him until he suddenly pulls me into a hug, and says, "*Jag älskar dig.*"

I'm not sure how to react, so I mirror his words, "I love you too."

He squeezes me harder and says, "I want you to know that I'm proud of you."

It's odd he picked this moment to tell me. I know he loves me, and I know he's proud of me. But I thought we had a silent understanding between us that we don't talk about feelings. I love him too, that was not a lie, so I feel guilty leaving his embrace and walking away, knowing that in a few hours I'm going to do the exact thing he just forbade me from doing. I'm going to meet with Anna.

Father finally retires for the night around ten thirty, and I am able to leave the house. The wagon road is dark and empty, so my walk is uninterrupted. I turn east where I think the sod house is, but it is so dark that I am not completely sure where I am. There is a crescent moon tonight, so it is not much help for sneaking around. I wonder if Anna is waiting for me and if she brought a lantern.

Either way my presence won't surprise her. She will hear me before she sees me. With every step my boots make a loud crunch on dry grass, pine needles, and twigs. The snapping sounds blend with the chirping crickets.

Finally, the outline of the sod house appears. I weave through the overgrown brush and tree stumps, mindful not to trip over one as I approach the south side of the house and walk around to the east side which is the side with the wall missing. I touch the scratchy, mud corner of the house and heave one leg over the crumbling mound of dirt and debris.

"Karl," hisses a voice.

I look into the darkness of the house. A small movement near the front window catches my eye. I can barely distinguish her from the darkness, but it's Anna. She walks slowly away from the wall into the light. Faint moonbeams shine through the roofless house onto the top of her head. My eyes adjust, and I can make out her small silhouette. She has a long sweater over what must be a nightgown, and boots on her feet. Her long hair is braided to one side and tied with a ribbon. She's empty-handed, no lantern to provide a light, so we'll have this conversation in the dark.

"You made it," she whispers. "I wasn't sure if you would notice the sign or remember the game we used to play."

"Of course, I remember," I whisper.

"I hoped that you would understand its meaning, and that I needed to talk to you without our parents."

"I understood. That's why I'm here."

"Yes, I suppose you are," she clears her throat and speaks a little louder. "No need to whisper. I don't think anyone will hear us from the road."

I speak louder as well, but my deep voice carries, so I still keep it just above a whisper, "No, I don't think anyone else is out tonight."

She smiles, "This is the first time that I've sneaked out of the house. It's a little exciting."

I smile back at her and wait for her to explain why the secrecy was needed, but instead of talking she looks away from me quickly, like she is embarrassed. Maybe she wants me to talk first, but I assumed that she would lead this secret meeting. A few more awkward seconds drag on, before she finally speaks. "Karl," she says, "I understand why you like Mary. She's beautiful and kind. She never disagrees with anyone, but . . . "

Hold on. What did she just say?

"Nothing will come of this infatuation. She's married, Karl. You were at her wedding."

"Wait a second—"

"What if people find out the truth? Think of how it would make her look. This could hurt her marriage, her reputation, her husband's reputation, even his business dealings."

"Anna," I raise my voice, "I don't have feelings for your sister."

"What?"

I repeat, quieter, but with the same conviction, "I don't have feelings for Mary. That's not why I kissed her on Sunday. Let me explain. You already know about my troubles at the mill."

She crosses her arms against her chest before asking, "You mean Ivar?"

"Yes, him. Well, I finally confronted him on Saturday."

"Well, I suspect he deserved it. From what you've told me he sounds like an awful person."

"He is," I agree. "That's why I wouldn't allow him to kiss you."

"Me? What are you talking about?"

"When Kristoff and I went to the gypsy camp, Ivar was there too. He spotted us in the crowd and came over after Kristoff danced with the bear."

"We saw that too," she says. "I can't believe Kristoff danced with it."

"Me either," I say, clearing my throat and continuing, "well, Ivar and his two friends from the mill were pretty impressed by Kristoff, so they came over to us and talked for a bit. While we were standing there, I saw you go into the gypsy wagon, the one with the woman who reads palms, but, I swear, I didn't see Mary go in. Someone dared Ivar to kiss the next girl that came out of that wagon. He agreed, and he started walking over there. I tried to stop him, but he is so stubborn. He wouldn't listen to me."

Her face is still, so I must not be getting my point across. "I kissed Mary because I thought it was you. I couldn't stand the thought of Ivar kissing you."

She blinks a few times before responding, "You didn't want to kiss Mary. You wanted to kiss me?"

"Well," I stumble over my words, not sure how to answer. "I . . . Um . . . he had his foot on the step, Anna. He was going for it. I needed to protect you."

"From Ivar?"

"Yes. I wasn't going to let him touch you."

She looks down at the ground, so it's hard to see her face in the dark, but I think she's smiling when she says, "Thank you, Karl. But kissing a girl is an odd way to protect her from being kissed by someone else."

My cheeks heat from embarrassment and I say, "I hope you aren't going to laugh at me. I'm already poked up about it."

She tilts her head up and looks me in the face, softly saying, "I thought you liked my sister."

"Not like that," I shake my head, "but is that why you lied to your parents? Did you tell them that I kissed you because you wanted to protect Mary from me?"

She places her hands on her hips and huffs, "No, not exactly. I wasn't the one who first told my parents. After I yelled at you and ran away from the gypsy wagon, I met my parents, Mary, and John at the Eating House. Mary didn't mention the kiss to them and neither did I. After our meal, a man walked into the restaurant and came up to our table to say hello to Father. He was at the baseball diamond earlier and heard from Ivar that you kissed Mary." She twists her hands nervously in front of her before saying, "She was sitting next to me at the table, and when John asked her if what this man said was true, she said that I kissed you. She lied to everybody."

"Really?" I question it. "Mary never lies."

"Yes," she looks away from me and stares into the darkness, "and I can't be certain why, but I imagine she understood what could be said about her and wanted to take action before the rumors could start."

That doesn't sit well with me, so I ask, "What about you? Doesn't she care about the rumors that will start around you because of this?"

She turns her head back to face me and says, "I had an earful Sunday night from my mother about how this affects my reputation."

"Exactly," I say, shaking my head. "Mary knows that too. It would have been easier to tell the truth right away. Your father or John could have taken care of the matter with a right jab to my jawline."

Anna snorts, "Father would never hit you."

"What I mean to say is that it's out of character for Mary to sacrifice you."

She shrugs her shoulders, "I guess she's changed."

"But why did you lie too?" I ask.

She thinks for a moment and then grins mischievously and says, "I had to be kissed in order to protect Mary from being kissed by you."

A laugh escapes me as I echo her words from earlier, "Kissing is an odd way to protect her." She laughs with me, and I notice a familiar discomfort in my belly. It's a mix of nerves and thrill I usually get when the young women in town flirt with me, but this is the first time that I've felt it while talking to Anna.

She slowly stops laughing and explains, "I lied because Mary basically asked me to, and I think we should keep lying to our parents."

"More lying?" I ask. I hate lying to my father, and I really don't want to have to lie to the Anderssons. "Don't you think the truth would be easier?"

"I'm afraid if we explain everything now, the situation might be worse. I'll be labeled a liar, and Mary will be known as a scarlet woman."

Regret washes over me as the meaning of my father's words finally sink in. I created this problem for Anna, and he's right. She does deserve better. I can't let her, or Mary, ruin their reputation because of my stupid mistake, but how do I take it back? "I'm so sorry Anna. Please, tell me how to fix this."

"I think the best path is to make this look legitimate," she throws her hands up in the air. "We kissed, and we intend to court each other."

"Anna, you're fifteen."

"Almost sixteen," she says with her hands on her hips. "Mary was seventeen when boys started coming to our house to court her; I'm not that far off."

I shake my head, "Father already had a talk with me. You are too young."

"Oh really," she rolls her eyes. "Well, I recently found out that someone in town may be interested in me, so I must not be too young in his eyes."

I furrow my brow, "Who?"

"Edwin Meyer. He'll be at Belle's dancing party on Friday night."

"Meyer?" I rack my brain trying to remember all the names of Anna's friends.

"Is it so hard to believe?" She's fidgeting with her hands again.

"No, not at all. But if you want people to keep thinking that I kissed you, and we want to court each other, why would you go to this dancing party?"

"Oh, I didn't think of that," her eyes widen, "but I already told Belle that I'd come. It's the last one of the summer."

I really hope she doesn't ask me to come. I am not a good dancer, so I try to avoid dances as much as possible. Girls usually get an escort home after these events. If Edwin Meyer really is interested in Anna, he'll partner up with her at the end of the night. "Let me walk you home," I say.

Her hands stop fidgeting. "You want to walk me home?"

"Well, it would help convince people that I want to court you."

"That's actually a really good idea, Karl, but my parents already told me that I'm not supposed to be alone with you."

I wave my hand to the dark, empty sod house we stand in, "Too late for that now."

"They are waiting for you to stop by and ask about courting, but I suppose, you could wait to talk to them until after the party."

"I can do that," I say, eager to hold off that conversation for as long as possible. Mr. Andersson may not be as forgiving as his daughter.

"What about Kristoff?"

"I can explain the situation to him."

"I'm meeting Belle tomorrow afternoon at the Beanery."

I had forgotten that she was also there at the gypsy wagon. "When you talk to Belle, can you please leave out the part about Ivar? I don't really care to have anyone else know how mad he makes me."

"She'll want a reason for why you kissed Mary."

"Well . . . " I rub the back of my neck. There are too many lies to keep track of, so why not the truth. "Tell her that I thought it was just you in the wagon."

"The truth? But you just said not to mention Ivar. I assume that includes the dare as well."

"I won't be able to remember anything else we make up, so keep the dare, but say it was me."

She frowns, "Um, all right."

"Say it happened like this, my friends from the mill dared me to kiss the next girl that came out of that wagon, and I already knew it was you, so I did it."

"That's pretty audacious behavior, even for you. I don't know if she will believe it."

"I don't know what that word means, but I think this version is believable," and I tick off my fingers for each reason. "First, I really wouldn't back down from a dare."

She snorts, but I keep going, "Second, I get to steal a kiss from my girl."

"Your girl, eh?"

I shrug, "My father already thinks that I have feelings for you. If he didn't take any convincing, then Belle probably won't either."

"My parents think that too."

"See? If we are going to keep lying about my supposed feelings for you, let's make me bolder than I actually am and keep the dare." I laugh at myself, but this time Anna doesn't join me. She takes a deep breath and tilts her head up to the night sky. A long time ago, Anna told me that there are animals, hunters, and kings in the stars. I've forgotten their names and their stories, but I bet Anna remembers.

She's quiet for a moment before saying, "All of this for Mary." I can't tell if she is talking to me or her heroes in the sky, but she sounds sad.

I wait a moment for her to look at me, but she doesn't so I ask, "Do you know when you will see her again?" She shakes her head no. "Well, when you do, will you apologize to her for me? You can tell her everything. I mean, I will too, eventually. I just don't know when I'll see her. She might not want to speak to me again, and I'd understand that."

"Mary doesn't really get angry," Anna lowers her head back down and looks at me before adding, "It's getting late. I should head back before my parents notice I'm gone. I can't imagine how much trouble I'd be in if they found my empty bed at this hour."

I nod. She's right. That would be terrible.

She walks by me but stops at the crumbling wall of the sod house. "Are you coming?" she asks.

"No, I think I'll stay for a little bit longer."

"*God natt*, Karl," she says and quietly climbs over the broken wall of the sod house before disappearing around the corner. I hear the familiar crunch of dry earth as she walks away.

I sit down and lean my back against the dirt wall. I pick up a few broken pieces of glass next to my legs and throw them aside. Tilting my head up towards the sky, I stare at the stars. I don't see the same characters that Anna sees, and there's no point in remembering their names since their world is so far from our own. Besides, they don't have any answers for us.

7

Anna

Wednesday, August 29, 1894
Hinckley, Minnesota
3 days before

"I can't believe it," Belle hisses. Her eyes grow to the size of saucers.

She leans in to whisper, "Mary told the whole table that Karl kissed you, and you agreed."

I nod just having finished telling her all about Sunday's lunch at the Eating House. She stares at me in disbelief. We are sitting against the wall of the St. Paul and Duluth depot building, drinking Coca-Colas that we purchased from the Beanery inside. The time is almost four o'clock, so the platform is humming with activity as passengers wait for the Skalley.

Some of the men wear dark suit jackets and vests. They keep their hands busy, puffing on cigars or pulling out their pocket watches to check the time. In the same crowded space, other men wear coveralls, frayed shirts, and work boots. Those men, the farmers and laborers, are more comfortable waiting in silence. Huddled together, a large group of women wearing purple, blue, and black dresses with large leg-o-mutton sleeves chat endlessly. Their wide-brimmed hats bob up and down with each nod making the ribbons, feathers, and flowers shake. A few of the women hold parasols to hide their faces from the blistering sun. Two older women sit on a bench in the little shade available on the platform. They wave paper fans in front of their sweaty faces.

Belle asks cautiously, "So how did your parents react?"

"As you can probably imagine," I reply. "My mother was in hysterics. She gave me a proper scolding at home Sunday night. My father came in and out of the room during her rage, but he was mostly quiet."

A mother rushes by us, trying to collect her four, small children, but her attempts are in vain. She can only grab two of the smallest, slowest ones. The two oldest run out of her reach, and she lets them scamper up and down the platform, zigzagging between the groups of people.

Belle clucks her tongue, "It's unearned, Anna. You did nothing wrong. Why did you agree?"

I watch the mother hold onto the two smaller children, hugging each one in an arm. She plants kisses on their cheeks, and they giggle yet still try to squirm out of their mother's embrace. They are little girls—sisters, I assume.

I turn my attention back to my friend, "She's my sister, Belle. What was I supposed to do? Should I have called her a liar in front of her husband?"

Belle exhales, "No, I suppose not. You are a good sister. She's lucky to have you."

"If anyone asks you about it, will you please say that it was me Karl kissed, not Mary?"

She pinches her lips together. I know she wants to say no because she does not want to lie to anyone, but I believe that she will say yes because she is my friend. Finally, she agrees. "Yes, if that's what you want."

I smile, "Thank you, Belle."

"Of course, but what about Karl? If he's lovesick over Mary then someone should talk to him, make him understand how inappropriate that is."

I chuckle, "He's not in love with Mary."

"What? How do you know that?"

"I met him last night at the sod house after our parents fell asleep, and he told me so." I take another swig from my Coke bottle and watch her eyes grow wide again.

"Anna Andersson," She playfully punches me in the arm. "Did you sneak out?"

"I had to warn him about Mary's lie, that my parents think that he kissed me. What if he came to the house to apologize for kissing Mary? My parents expect him over any day now to ask for their permission to court me."

She chokes on her soda, "Courting! Anna, are they making you court Karl because of this?"

I laugh, "No, of course not. Let me explain. Last night, Karl made it very clear that he does not have romantic feelings for Mary. It turns out that he and a group of millworkers were standing not too far away from Madame Catrina's wagon. Karl saw me go into the wagon, but he didn't see Mary go in."

I pause. Now, I have to lie to my friend.

Belle lifts her eyebrows in anticipation, so I swallow down my reservations and keep going. "While I was having my palm read, he was dared by one of the men to kiss the next girl who came out of the wagon. And, you know Karl, he wouldn't back down from a dare, but he would also never kiss a married woman. He honestly didn't know that Mary was there with me."

She frowns, "But he saw you go in?"

"Yes, he did. He thought he was going to kiss me, not Mary."

Belle gasps and places her hand over her heart, "Anna, he wanted to kiss you. He just used the dare as a way to steal it. He must like you." Belle is easily convinced by my story. My parents, Mr. Sundvquist, and now Belle all think I'm worthy of Karl's attention. "This is the most exciting thing that's happened all summer!" she squeals, "Gypsies and stolen kisses. A mistaken identity and secret meetings."

I shush her, "Belle, keep your voice down."

She giggles, "So who do you like more?"

"What do you mean?"

"Karl or Edwin?"

A shrill whistle cuts through the air causing everyone on the platform to stand taller and turn their heads to the north. The Skalley is here. Belle slides back her shirt sleeve and looks at her wristwatch, "Right on time, it's 4:05, on the dot."

A cloud of black smoke precedes the train as it slowly comes to the station. We hear the screech of the brakes first before the locomotive appears through the smoke. The front reminds me of a man's face, despite its true nature as a steel workhorse. The round headlamp is a lidless eye able to see everything down the tracks, and the cowcatcher underneath the smokebox, is a bristly, metal mustache covered in soot and grime from the journey.

The locomotive sputters and chugs past us like an old man coughing and hacking. Immediately followed by the coal tender, its side displays the engine number, "69" in bold white letters. Two more carriages slowly pass us, their large metal wheels and brackets losing momentum until they finally come to a stop. This train brings mail and passengers all the way from Duluth. They'll pick up more mail and passengers here before heading on toward St. Paul.

Belle and I watch a steady stream of men, women, and children disembark the train's passenger cars onto the platform. The movement of bodies coming and going creates a buzz of energy. Disembarking passengers hurry on their way; embarking passengers clamber onto the train. Station employees move packages and deliveries to and from the freight room. A man in an ironed, blue uniform hauls a large mailbag from the station to the mail car.

Belle is content to watch the commotion for now, so I don't have to answer her question yet. After a few moments I feel a presence near us. Turning away from the passenger cars, I glance towards the front of the train. A modest man of medium height is slowly walking along the platform towards us. He seems calm and unhurried. His dark, blue uniform is clean and pressed, and the shiny, gold buttons reflect the searing, August sun.

It's the engineer, Jim Root, a familiar face on the Skalley. He comes to a stop only a few feet away from Belle and me, but he doesn't look at us. His bushy mustache is the same shape as the train's cowcatcher, and the corners of his eyes turn down towards his cheeks.

Another man, also in a crisp, blue uniform, walks up to Mr. Root and speaks to him. It's Thomas Sullivan, the conductor. Belle and I have seen him on the Skalley when he checks our tickets. After the men share a brief conversation, which I can't catch over the noise of the passengers, Mr. Root checks his pocket watch and nods to Sullivan before he heads back to the locomotive. Mr. Sullivan cups his hands around his mouth and shouts down the platform, "All aboard!"

Belle's hand grabs my wrist and tugs, "Anna, look who just got off the train," she says as she points down the platform. "It's Edwin."

Edwin catches Belle pointing at him and smiles. He changes direction and walks over to us. Bells gets up quickly, pulling me up off the ground. The train whistle screeches again, and the steam engine slowly begins to depart. The air on the platform is thick with smoke and heavy from the afternoon heat. My face grows hotter and hotter with each step Edwin takes toward us. My mouth dries up, so I lift my bottle up to my lips, but, unfortunately, my Coca-Cola is empty.

"Edwin," Belle shouts over the noise of the train leaving the depot, "where are you coming from?"

Edwin smiles at her, "Hi, Belle. I spent the day in Duluth with my mother."

He turns his attention from Belle to me, "Hi Anna, how are you?"

"Me? I'm . . . terrific."

He laughs at me, "Well, that's great to hear. Is anyone else here?" He looks around the platform for the rest of our friend group.

"No, just Anna and me today."

Edwin looks at my empty Coke bottle, "Would you like another one, Anna?"

"Oh, no. I have to save the rest of my money for a newspaper."

He laughs at me, again. "I mean, can I buy you another one?"

"Oh," I stammer on my words. "Um . . . yes, I suppose. Belle?" I turn to Belle, hoping she can save the conversation.

"We both would love another one, but only if you can join us."

He grins, "Of course. Let me check with my mother first. She's in the freight room checking on a few items she bought today in Duluth."

He turns and runs into the depot.

"Anna," Belle whispers to me. "Why are you acting strange?"

I set my empty Coke bottle on the ground and whisper back, "Because, you told me on Sunday that Edwin specifically asked if I was coming to your party. That he wouldn't bother coming if I wasn't there."

"Yes, so?"

"Well, doesn't that mean he likes me?"

"Yes, I think it does."

"Belle, I don't know if I like Edwin in that way."

Edwin is walking briskly back over to us, so I stop whispering to Belle and turn towards him.

"I apologize," he says, "but I can't stay. I have to help Mother carry a set of chairs home, and then we are expecting our neighbors over for supper. How long will you two be here? I can come back."

Belle's shoulders drop in disappointment and she says, "I'm supposed to fetch my brothers from their friend's house and bring them home before five o'clock."

I quickly add, "Yes, I have to be home soon too."

Edwin snaps his fingers, "Darn, it. Well, next time then."

"Yes, next time, absolutely," I am relieved that I don't have to fumble through a conversation with Edwin.

He bends his head down and touches his hat to us as he leaves.

"Wait, Edwin," Belle grabs his arm. "Are you still planning on coming to my party on Friday?"

"I'll be there," he answers. His eyes lock on mine, "Anna, will you be there too?"

My cheeks burn. Am I embarrassed? Excited? I'm not entirely sure. I don't know how to talk to boys that fancy me because it has never happened before. Edwin's still my friend. I should be able to answer him without turning into a hot, sweaty tomato. "Yes, I'll be there," I answer.

"Fantastic. See you ladies there." He walks into the freight room, and my muscles relax.

"Anna," Belle whispers, "are you all right? Your face is beet red."

"Yes, I'm fine," I answer even though I'm not. It's not affection that sets my nerves on edge around Edwin. Instead, I feel a need to please him or maybe an urge to protect his feelings from my disinterest.

"You never answered my question earlier. Is that why you look embarrassed? Do you like both of them?"

"Belle," I scold her, but in a playful tone. "Honestly, I don't."

She smiles mischievously, "Then, which one?"

"Karl is my neighbor and my oldest friend. I've known him since we were little. Edwin is also my friend, and he's so kind, but I don't really know him that well. Not as well as I know Karl."

"Well, either way, I am a tad jealous. I wish one young man would pick me, and you have two!"

She's right. Karl and Edwin both chose me. Edwin addressed me directly here on the platform. He specifically asked if I was going to Belle's party. A boy has never cared before if I was present or not. And even though Karl denied having feelings for me, he said that he had intended to kiss me. After years of living in my sister's shadow, it feels nice to be seen even if it was just to protect me from Ivar.

For the first time in my life people are noticing me, listening to me, and seeking me out. Maybe this is what it feels like to be a woman, to be keenly aware of how your presence affects others.

❧ ❧ ❧

Before I left the train station, I purchased the newest edition of the *Hinckley Enterprise* for Father. He enjoys reading it every Wednesday night when he comes home from the mill. The Skalley brings daily editions of the *Minneapolis Tribune*, the *St. Paul Pioneer Press*, and the *Duluth News Tribune*, but Father prefers to read the local newspaper. He is a fan of the editor, Angus Hay, and his political views. I think Father likes reading Mr. Hay's articles because he pokes fun at President Cleveland's weight.

I set the newspaper on the table next to Mother. She is slicing an onion at the kitchen table. "*Tack*," she says without looking at me.

"You're welcome," I say sitting down across from her.

She nods toward the paper, "What does it say?"

She is referring to a drawing of a ladder on the front page. I slide the newspaper to the middle of the table and point to the small text on the left side of the ladder. I trace my finger under each word for her as I read it out loud, "Hinckley is a city that is rich in good schools and churches. Its people are bold in enterprise, firm in purpose, liberal in supporting public measures, moral in their lives, warm in their hospitality, and ever glad to," my finger follows the rest of the sentence as each word is a step on the ladder in bold capital letters, "help you climb the ladder of success."

Her eyes follow my finger across the page. She is a smart woman, one of the most capable women I know, and she reads from her family Bible each night in our parlor, but that is written in Swedish. She has never learned to read or write American English.

"Quite true," she returns to her slicing. "Who was at the depot this afternoon?"

"Just Belle and me," I answer. "Well, Edwin was there with his mother. They were on their way home from a day trip in Duluth. He said hello to us."

She stops slicing her onion for a moment but doesn't look at me. I think she is going to say something, but instead she starts cutting again without any comment.

"Belle and I talked about her party on Friday night. It should be a good time. Can I wear a piece of your jewelry, please?"

"Yes, that's fine. I washed your woolen cashmere blouse for the party. It's hanging outside. It should be dry now; you should bring it in."

"Thank you, Mother."

"Please be mindful of it Friday night. When you get home, hang it up immediately. I want you to wear it Saturday morning with your brown woolen surge shirt."

"What's happening on Saturday?"

"The Pokegama School dedication ceremony. You will go with Mary. I'll give you money for a ticket, but I want you to catch an early morning train, so you can spend some time with your sister before the afternoon ceremony. Just remember Pokegama is a stop on the Eastern Minnesota tracks, so you'll have to buy a ticket at the depot on the east side of town."

I lift my eyebrows, "I've never been to her house before."

"It's a small settlement. Everyone knows where everyone lives. All you have to do is ask someone."

I play with the edges of the newspaper, nervous to question this decision. My mother is giving me quite a bit of freedom for this trip even though I know she is still upset about the Karl incident. So I wonder why she is allowing me to go.

"You're letting me go alone?"

She stops slicing the onion, looks at me and says, "Yes, this ceremony is the most important event held thus far in Pokegama. The town promoters, including your brother-in-law, believe the town has the potential to be another economic center, like Hinckley. Mary deserves our support. Your father will be working at the mill, and I am meeting with a friend in town to plan the Labor Day picnic at church. You can go and represent our family. Mary will appreciate it."

"Does she even know that I'm coming?"

"Well, no. I didn't have a chance to talk to her about it after lunch on Sunday." Her eyes narrow, "That day didn't really go according to plan, did it?"

I sink a little in my chair and avoid her eyes.

"This will also give you a chance to apologize to her and John."

That's the real reason she is sending me to Pokegama. She wants me to apologize to Mary for embarrassing her and John on Sunday. Oh, if she only knew the truth.

"Can I wear my new oxfords?"

"Your new school shoes?"she asks.

I nod.

"Yes, I suppose, but don't scuff them up. We can't afford two new pairs of school shoes."

I sit up a little straighter in my chair, "Yes, ma'am."

Her stern face disappears and she smiles at me. She reaches her hand across the table and cups my cheek.

"*Min älskling*," she studies my face intently. "When did you grow up?"

I lean into her hand, "Just recently, I believe."

"*Ja*," she exhales and lets go of my face. "Now, go fetch the laundry on the line outside." I stand up from the table and walk toward the door, but Mother clears her throat, so I turn my head back. "Anna," she points toward my outfit. "It's time to take off that pinafore. They are for children."

8

Karl

I can't find Father anywhere. He isn't in the kitchen or the front room. He's not in the barn, the root cellar, or the garden. I even came around to the front of the house and looked up and down the road but still no luck.

I'm meeting Kristoff at Kronenberg's to play billiards before I walk Anna home from her party, so I won't get back until late. I need to tell Father, so he doesn't wonder where I am. I run up the stairs two at a time and check his bedroom. The door is open, and the room is empty.

I yell out to the seemingly empty house, "Father! I'm going out!"

I wait a moment at the top of the stairs. When no response comes, I make my way back downstairs and enter the kitchen, stopping in the doorway because our table, which is normally pushed up against the corner of the room, is now in the middle. We keep the table in the corner, so we don't have to walk around it when we move through the kitchen to the back door of the house. When the table is pushed up against the corner, it blocks the doorway to the spare room adjacent to the pantry.

Right now the door isn't blocked, and it's cracked open. Father and

I never use that room. It's where he keeps the sewing machine he bought for my mother that she never got to use. I gently pull open the door and hot, stale air hits my face. Empty, narrow shelves line the walls and cobwebs clutter each corner of the room. A window inside is crusted over with dust, but enough sunlight comes in for me to see Father facing away from me, looking down at the machine.

"Found you," I say, taking two steps inside to stand next to him. He is examining the sewing machine that sits on a wrought iron and wooden stand in the middle of the room. Both are covered in a fine layer of dust. Cobwebs twist between the iron embellishments of the stand. The room is small, not much larger than our pantry, and the hot, stale air clings to my face and clothes. The tight space suffocates me with feelings I wish to walk away from, but I stay next to Father. With each inhale, a strong musty smell invades my nostrils. He is quiet for a long time, but then he sighs and says, "This is your mother's sewing room," he says as if I didn't already know. "In Sweden, we didn't have much, but I did my best with what we had. I knew you and your mother deserved more. I had heard stories of men finding a better life in America, higher wages, owning their own land. The men sent back money to their families and letters describing how Minnesota was so much like Sweden. I came first to build us a home. I wanted to create something your mother would be proud of. Once I finished, I went to Duluth to buy two steam ship tickets and send them back to Sweden for you two. While I was walking downtown, I passed a shop and this," he gestures to the sewing machine, "was sitting in the window. I walked inside that shop, found the shopkeeper, and I told him, 'Sir, I'm buying that sewing machine for my wife.'"

I wipe the dust off the black body of the machine and see 'SINGER' printed in gold letters. Father doesn't often speak of Mother, but when he does an unsettling sensation builds in my stomach. I can't think of a mature response, so I resort to humor. "Since you spent all your money on this, I suppose you had to steal the steamship tickets, eh?"

"No, no, I still had enough for the tickets too," he laughs. "But I had to wait in line holding this stand and the machine. The cashier must have thought I was mad." The atmosphere in the room lightens, but the conversation stops. We both stare at the sewing machine for a few moments, then he continues, "It was my idea to move to America, but this house, this was all for her. I wanted her to have the best life here. I built this two-story house, bigger than anything she had ever lived in before. She was so important to me, Karl. I'm not sure why I came in here tonight. I suppose the thought of you courting Anna made me think of your mother. I guess I wanted to be near her."

I look around the abandoned room, "Do you feel her in here?"

He sighs again and answers, "I do and I don't. You know this sewing machine is the only thing that is hers in this entire house, but she never even saw it."

I shove my hands in my pockets and push down the emotions thickening in my throat. It's my fault that he has none of Mother's belongings. I was too weak to pull my trunk and hers on the steamship after she died.

"It's time we use this room for another purpose. There's no reason to keep it this way. I should sell this too," he sets his hand on top of the sewing machine, wiping away more dust. "Or, maybe, I should keep it for a little while longer. Maybe one day, you can give it to Anna."

The ball of nerves in my stomach drops to the dusty floor. My face flushes, and I keep my eyes downcast. My shoulders slump with the weight of my recent behavior and from the guilt of lying to Father.

He places a hand on my shoulder and asks, "I heard you say that you are going out?"

"Yes," I respond, clearing my throat. "I'm meeting Kristoff in town. I'll probably be late, so you don't need to wait up for me."

"All right, I'm pretty tired today, anyway. Say hello to Kristoff for me."

"I will," I answer. This is my chance to leave, so I slowly back out of the room. "Good night, Father."

"*God natt*, Karl."

Once past the door frame, I turn around fast and bump into the corner of the table. It begins to tip, so I grab the sides of it to keep it from falling over. I set it right and walk to the door as fast as I can. I want to be as far away from that room as possible. Like my father, I've kept my mother's memory hidden away in an abandoned room. Only the room I keep for her is in my head, and it's just easier to keep that door closed.

❧ ❧ ❧

The sun is setting now, so the sky on the horizon is a fiery red that melts to bright orange and pink. Even with evening approaching, the temperature is still unbearable. I pray that this summer heat and drought will end soon, and the changing of the seasons will bring rain and cooler weather.

Hinckley is still busy as I walk down Main Street's wooden plank sidewalk. Men and women come and go through the large white doors at the Brennan Company Store. The sun's reflection paints the large, glass windows, so they look orange and pink. I smell Stumvoll's Cigar Shop before I walk past it. The sweet, heavy scent of cigar smoke drifts over the sidewalk and hangs in the air. A few men are standing on the front porch, puffing hand-rolled cigars and making conversation around the wooden Indian statue which is always on display. I take a deep inhale as I pass and savor the scent.

The next large, two-story building is Hanson's Saloon and Opera Hall. All of Hinckley's public meetings take place here, but I've heard men at the mill talk about burlesque shows that also share the stage from time to time. I wonder how much of what they say is true. I cross Second Street and pass two horse-drawn carts filled with hay. The horses kick up dirt and dust, and I use the glass windows of the Morrison Hotel as a mirror to wipe off my pants and shirt.

Kronenberg's Saloon is next. Welcoming piano music and muffled conversation spill out of the open doors into the street. After stepping over the threshold, I'm met with an explosion of smells, sounds, and sights. Just like the front porch at Stumvoll's, the saloon is surrounded in a cloud of sweet, heavy cigar smoke. Kerosene lamps line the walls which are covered in velvet wallpaper. The tables are full of men and women from all walks of life. There are finely dressed gentlemen with vests and jackets, shopkeepers from town, farmers in torn overalls, and millworkers with sawdust on their jeans. Friends and families relax, socialize, and enjoy something cold after a long, hot day.

I walk by a table near the door occupied by two small girls. Tiny porcelain tea cups sit in front of them, and they are pretending to serve tea to their dolls which sit on the table. The piano music is interrupted for a moment by the loud crack of someone splitting the colorful, ivory pool balls at one of the felt billiard tables along the wall. Two barkeeps stand behind the elaborately carved wooden bar, wearing long, white aprons over their pressed white shirts, with matching black bow ties. I spot Kristoff trying to flag one down at the far end.

I pass more tables and walk through one group of men standing in a circle smoking clove cigars and clay tobacco pipes. They discuss the price of wheat threatening to drop under a dollar per bushel. I tip my hat to them as I pass by, finally making my way to Kristoff.

"Karl, I thought for a minute you weren't coming," he grins at me, not upset that I'm late.

"I was held up for a moment," I answer as I settle in between Kristoff and another man at the bar who is spitting tobacco into one of the ceramic spittoons that sit on the floor.

"What are you drinking tonight?" he asks.

I look up at the shelves behind the bar. There are green glass bottles full of red wine, mineral water in orange-and-tan colored stoneware jugs, clear glass decanters, and dozens of empty glass beer mugs waiting to be used. "Soda water," I answer.

He nods and tries to catch a bartender's attention. "So, have you apologized to the Andersson's yet?" he asks.

"No."

He laughs, "Well, what are you waiting for? An invitation?"

Finally, a barkeep appears in front of us, and Kristoff orders me a soda water and an ale for himself. The man turns around and dispenses beer from a wooden keg with a white porcelain spigot into one of the clean, glass mugs from the shelf. He sets it in front of Kristoff and then walks away.

"Not exactly," I rub the back of my neck. I've been avoiding this conversation all week and am lucky Kristoff didn't run into Father or Mr. Andersson at the mill. Tomorrow that luck will probably run out because we usually all see each other when we pick up our pay envelopes. I need to tell Kristoff the truth, now, so he doesn't accidentally say something tomorrow.

The barkeep returns and sets a glass bottle down in front of me. He uncorks it, takes money from Kristoff, and walks away.

"Thanks. I'll get the next one," I offer as I pick up my soda water.

"Skål," He says, tipping his mug to my bottle, and we clink them before we take our first sip. Mine is cool and bubbly, a perfect refresher after the sweaty walk into town.

"Kristoff, I have to tell you something."

He wipes the foam from his upper lip, "Yeah? What is it?"

"Mr. Andersson believes I kissed Anna on Sunday afternoon, not Mary. My father believes the same thing."

"What?" Kristoff looks confused. "Why would they believe that?"

"Because that's what Anna told her father, and he told mine."

"You didn't set either of them straight?"

"No, when my father mentioned it to me on Tuesday, I was surprised, but I assumed there must be a reason that Anna would lie. Later that night I met her in that old, abandoned sod house on the east side of the wagon road."

"You met Anna alone?" he wiggles his eyebrows.

"It's not what you think."

"I don't believe you, but please continue, and don't spare me any details."

I frown at him but carry on, "She explained to me that it was Mary who first told her parents and her husband that I kissed Anna at the gypsy wagon. Anna assumes that Mary lied about it to protect her and her husband's reputation."

"Interesting," he says. "Not how I thought it was going to turn out. I figured that fancy-dressed man was going to punch you in the jaw for stealing a kiss from his wife," he chuckles to himself and takes another drink.

I shake my head, "I doubt he would have hit me. He's a dandy, so he wouldn't want to wrinkle his shirt."

Kristoff laughs, "That's probably true."

"Well, now our parents believe that I have feelings for Anna and that I intend to court her in a year or so. She asked me to continue this until she can talk to her sister, so I only have to pretend that I'm going to court her until then."

"Hmm, that's pretty brave of Anna to take the blame for her sister."

"I agree."

"You'll have a brave wife that's loyal to her family."

I choke on my soda water, and the carbonation burns going down my throat, "Wait a minute! My wife? Not you too," I wipe the water dribbling down my chin, "Father just mentioned marrying Anna before I left the house. I'm not marrying her. We're just doing this to protect her sister."

Kristoff pokes me in the chest, "You only court someone if you intend to marry them, and right now you intend to court Anna."

"I'm just going along with it, and need you to go along with it too. If anyone asks you about it, you have to tell them that I kissed Anna."

"So, let me see if I have everything in order. Mary lied to everyone and said you kissed Anna. Anna went along with it. Her father told your father. Then your father told you that you need to court her before you two do any more kissing, and both you and Anna feel comfortable lying about liking each other?"

"Correct."

He folds his arms across his chest and says, "This is a strange scheme you two are entwined in. What about . . . no, never mind."

"What?"

"Well, what are you going to do if this plan is successful? If both of your families and everyone in town believes that you kissed Anna, what's your next step if not to court her?"

"Nothing. Hopefully, I'll be leaving with a logging team soon, and by the time spring comes around, no one will remember this happened."

Kristoff scratches his chin, "Do you like Anna?"

"Do I like her?" I repeat. "Well, yeah. She's my neighbor, we've known each other forever. She's kind and easy to talk to, but I don't have feelings for her. Not like that."

"Then why was it so important for you to keep Ivar from kissing her?"

"Because he's vile. I won't let him anywhere near her."

"Mmm-hmm," he murmurs as he drinks. He sets his mug down. "You know, he's still pretty mad at you."

I shake my head, "He better not hold us back from the winter logging camps just because I made him lose four dollars."

"Us?"

"Yes, us."

Kristoff shakes his head while I finish my soda water and set the empty bottle on the bar, "I'm not going to be on a logging team. I'm only working at the mill until I can save enough money for college. My mother has a purse at home with cash too. We think in a couple years I'll have enough."

I stare at Kristoff in disbelief. I can't believe he doesn't want to be on the logging team, and that this is the first I'm hearing about college.

"I had no idea. What do you want to go to college for?" I ask.

"Veterinary sciences."

Of course, Kristoff loves animals. "I think that's a great idea. Why have you never told me?"

"Haven't I? I thought I had."

"No, I definitely would have remembered that."

He shrugs, "Well, it's a lot of money, and it's a long way off. It's still just a dream at this point."

Over his shoulder, I see two men leave a billiard table. I point over to it, "Do you want to play now? A table just opened up."

Setting his mug on the bar, he says, "Yes, but I want one more ale."

"Run over there and save our spot. I'll get you another one. It's my round anyway."

"Sounds good to me," he says and walks away as I flag down a barkeep and pay for another ale. On the way to the billiard table, I have to turn my body to the side to squeeze between two chairs when suddenly a man stands up from one of them, bumping his chair into me and spilling Kristoff's full mug of ale down the front of my shirt.

"Pardon me," the man says as he turns around and pulls the chair out of the way. "Come with me. I'll ask for a towel." He leads me by my arm back toward the bar and raises his hand to the same barkeep who served me, "Edward, I need a towel for this young man. My clumsiness has gotten the best of me."

I set the empty mug down on the bar and peel my wet shirt away from my chest, attempting to air it out while I wait. The man who bumped into me leans against the bar but turns his body towards me. He is older than me, but still young, probably the same age as Ivar. His face is clean-shaven, and he wears a large, black silk tie. His dark eyes are piercing, and I feel a little intimidated by his determined look.

He extends his hand out to me and says, "Angus Hay. Editor of the *Hinckley Enterprise*."

"Karl Sundvquist. I work at the sawmill, " I say as I shake his hand.

His serious expression softens, "Ah, a Swede. Common, especially in this area. Your accent is almost gone, so I assume you have lived in America for some time?"

"Yes. I immigrated here in '84. My father and I live north of town on the wagon road."

"A homesteader, too. That's hard work. And what are you and your father's political inclinations?"

"Um, I don't know."

"I only ask because I'm also the secretary of the county Republican Committee, and we are always looking for new members." The barkeep hands Mr. Hay a white cotton towel, as Hay continues, "Edward, another one for Mr. Sundvquist, please." He sets money down on the bar. Edward takes the money and the mug before walking away.

I wipe the beer off my shirt, "Thank you, sir, but you don't need to do that."

"Of course I do. I spilled your entire drink, and I'm thankful you didn't take a swing at my head. I've been challenged for less around here."

I smile and set the damp towel on top of the bar and say, "I suppose you need to ask folks personal questions from time to time to get a good story. That might offend some people."

"Exactly. You understand," he grins, and it makes his face look younger. "Do you have a good story? I have a few days to finish next week's edition of the *Enterprise*, so I can interview you anytime before next Tuesday night."

"No, no story from me. Not much to report lately except this terrific heat and drought."

"Yes, you should be glad you are not a farmer. I read that a weather station in St. Paul reported only two inches of rainfall since June. All this drought doesn't help the fires burning in the woods outside of town. They are destroying a great deal of timber and tons of hay. Unless a heavy rain comes soon there will be a great loss sustained. Everything is as dry as tinder." He shakes his head and knocks the bar with his knuckles.

I nod as Edward returns with my full mug. Mr. Hay picks it up off the bar and hands it to me. "I must get back to my table now, but it was a pleasure to meet you, Mr. Sundvquist. I hope we talk again soon."

🐦 🐦 🐦

While playing pool, Kristoff and I overheard that a lively poker tournament was going on at Hanson's Opera House. Neither of us had been inside before, so we decided to check it out. It is easily the fanciest room I've ever been in. The room is well-lit by an intricate gaslight system. Decorative brass fixtures and valves dot the walls giving the room a warm, yellow glow. The stage has unlit candles ready for the next show lining the edge, and a thick, velvet curtain hangs in the background.

While we watch the poker game, a man walks around and offers the players slices of cold beef and mutton on a large serving tray. They all drink dark liquid in short, thick glass tumblers. I still have to walk Anna home tonight, so I keep checking the wall clock near the door. When it hits midnight, I lean in to whisper to Kristoff. "I have to head out."

He nods, and we stand up and walk through the crowd of onlookers. As we open the heavy doors and walk outside, another group of men make their way in. They smell like stale whiskey, and I hear Ivar's voice among them. I keep my head down and hurry out. Once in the empty street, I look back and see the doors have already swung shut. He must not have noticed me.

Kristoff clears his throat. "He didn't see you."

"What?" I ask, turning to face him. The glow from the gaslights inside shines on his face.

"Ivar. He didn't see you. If he did, he'd be out here right now."

I shake my head, "I'm not scared of him."

"I know." Kristoff nods, "Midnight lunch at the mill is starting. Should we bring the overnight shift a pint?"

"No, I'm all out of money," I laugh. Then it slips out, "Besides, I have to be somewhere soon."

"Now?" he looks confused.

"I ah . . . " I feel silly telling Kristoff, but I don't know what else to say. "I told Anna I'd walk her home from her friend's dance party tonight."

He grins from ear to ear and says, "But you don't have feelings for her, right?"

"Oh, not this again," I playfully whine, rolling my eyes.

Kristoff throws up his hands defensively. "I'll head home then. I don't want to interrupt anything, be it real or pretend."

"Very funny." I say pushing his shoulder.

He turns the other direction and calls out, "See you tomorrow, Romeo!"

9

Anna

Friday, August 31, 1894
Hinckley, Minnesota
1 day before

It took an hour to replicate the Gibson girl hairstyle that my sister wore on Sunday, but somehow my mother and I did it. I'm holding her hand mirror in front of my face, inspecting the high pompadour which was the most difficult part of the look.

Mother stands next to me, holding an iron tong over the candle flame. I set the hand mirror down and stick my fingers in a glass of water before dampening my bangs. Mother picks up a strip of brown paper off the kitchen table and sets a piece of my bangs on it. Then she uses the hot tong to curl the hair which sizzles on contact. She is careful not to burn my forehead or scorch my bangs.

When she is finished, she blows out the candle and picks up one of her shell side-combs. The teeth scrape against my scalp when she places it underneath the bun at the crown of my head. I pick up the mirror again and stare at the final look. It's perfect. The young woman staring back at me looks soft and gentle, beautiful and mature.

Mother has helped me get ready for each dancing party that I've attended this summer. In the past, as she curled my bangs, I hoped and prayed that the fancy hairstyle or Mary's hand-me-down dress would help me get noticed, but tonight I expect to receive attention. This party feels different, or maybe I'm different. The events of the past week still confuse me, but they've also lit a sense of excitement.

Before we leave, I pull out my new oxford shoes from under my bed and try to sneak them down the stairs, but Mother catches me and tells me to put them back. She explains that they would get scuffed from all the dancing, so I'll have to wait to wear them until tomorrow morning when I to the Pokegama School dedication ceremony.

My parents walk with me to Belle's house and, like every other day this month, it is hot. I take my time and lag behind them because I do not want to break a sweat and soil my woolen cashmere shirt. Along the wagon road, I walk with my elbows up by my ears in order to create an airflow near my underarms, but once we reach town, there are too many people, so I put my elbows down. We eventually make it to the Barden house, mostly sweat free, and I say goodbye to my parents. The boys are running around the yard, throwing a ball. I wave to them, but they are too busy with their game. I'm not worried. I'll talk to them eventually, so I head inside to find the girls.

As I walk into the dining room, Belle is telling Clara and Helen about the gypsies that were camped out last Sunday. I stand next to Clara and quietly say hello. Belle continues describing her time with Madame Catrina, but then she locks eyes with me and raises her eyebrows. It's a silent question for my permission to share what happened, and I nod my approval. She grins and continues her story, explaining that I also went into the gypsy wagon, and that Karl stole a kiss from me as I exited.

The girls gasp as I expected they would.

"He kissed you!" Clara exclaims before grabbing my hand and pulling me in to whisper, "Was he a good kisser?"

I blush, not sure how to answer, "Um, yes."

Clara squeals. I look at Belle who is smiling too. She must not be concerned that I'm lying, so I decide not to dwell on it.

"So, is he going to ask your parents to court you?" Clara asks.

I open my mouth to respond, but Helen answers for me. "No, of course not. She's only fifteen. That would be inappropriate. He'll have to wait until she's older."

"I think he's the most handsome boy in Hinckley," Clara adds.

"You mean the most handsome man," Belle corrects her. "He's eighteen and has a job at the mill."

"In a couple years, we might all be bridesmaids at Anna's wedding!"

"Clara," I gasp, as she and Belle squeal.

Belle playfully pushes my shoulder, "Well, your sister married right after she turned eighteen. That's only two years away."

My plan to make people believe that Karl had kissed me is working all too well. My cheeks redden at the thought of marrying him. Or maybe I'm blushing because deep down I feel guilty for lying to my friends. Just then the boys come in from outside, panting and sweating. Edwin and Daniel sit down at the dining room table, but Charlie and Archie walk over to us girls. Archie is Belle's brother, and Charlie is Clara's. We visit for a few minutes until two men come into the house, one carrying a fiddle and the other a harmonica. Belle recognizes them and walks over to say hello.

She quickly turns back to us and shouts, "Everyone, grab an edge of the carpet. We need to make a dance floor." We all follow her instructions and help roll up the carpet rug. The boys carry it outside and set it in the lawn. Belle's parents push the dining room table into the sitting room, and the musicians pull two chairs against the wall. They sit down and immediately start playing.

We all recognize the tune and form two squares, one for boys and one for girls. It's a fast-paced song, and I'm already bobbing my head to the melody. We all stomp our feet on the wooden floor and clap our hands, and the party begins in earnest. The harmonica player shouts, "Partner up!"

Belle grabs my hand and throws me at Charlie before she partners up with Daniel. We hurl ourselves around the room with the other couples. Song after song, we dance, changing partners randomly. At first I dance with Charlie, next Archie, and then Edwin grabs my hand, and we start dancing together.

He is smiling and sweating. He gently places his hand on the small of my back before he swings me around and reels me back in. I am having so much fun. Edwin is a great dancer, and he is easy to follow. He twirls me around, and we promenade. All the while he keeps his attention on my face and grins from ear to ear. We dance for another three songs before Daniel taps on Edwin's shoulder indicating he wants to dance with me. Edwin nods, but he squeezes my hand before he lets go of it.

I watch him as he walks away, trying to figure out if that squeeze meant something more, but Edwin doesn't look back before he partners up with Helen. I don't have much time to interpret it because Daniel and I start moving around the dance floor, and I have to pay attention before I lose my balance. We continue dancing into the night. I have the chance to dance with each boy at least twice. Even Belle's parents hop in and take turns dancing with everyone. My second time partnering with Edwin is uneventful. He is still cheerful but doesn't give me another hand squeeze.

After some time, the musicians stop playing and everyone claps wildly for them, hooting and hollering. They stand up and bow, and some of the boys shake their hands. Belle's father asks Archie and Charlie to fetch the carpet rug from outside before he leads the musicians to the porch. I notice that it's dark outside, so the sun must have set while we were dancing. Mrs. Barden walks around the house turning up the oil lamps, so we have more light.

Archie and Charlie carry the carpet roll back inside, and Edwin and Daniel help them unroll it back on the wooden floor. Belle and I collapse onto it and sprawl out. I lay my head on Belle's stomach and take a moment to catch my breath. Everyone else joins us on the floor.

"Let's play a game," Clara suggests.

"Yes, let's play Post Office," Archie says.

"No, not Post Office," Helen disagrees. "That one takes forever."

Belle chimes in, "We'll only play a few rounds, so it doesn't get dull. Then we'll play a different game after that."

We both sit up, and Belle looks at Helen, "You can be the first postman if you like."

Helen agrees, so we start the game. She goes outside to the porch and closes the front door. Belle stands next to the door and waits. After a minute, Helen knocks on the door.

"Who is it?" Belle sings.

Helen answers from the other side, "It's the postman. I have a letter for Charlie."

"Oh," Belle smiles. "How much is the letter?"

"Two pennies."

Belle turns toward Charlie who is sitting on the floor and asks, "Charlie, do you accept or decline?"

Charlie stands up and says, "I accept."

He walks toward the door as Belle swings it open for him. Helen stands on the other side with her hands behind her back. When she sees Charlie coming toward her, she smiles and makes room for him in the door frame. Charlie gives her two quick kisses on the cheek.

"All right, Charlie, it's your turn to be a postman. Helen, you be the doorman now," Belle instructs them before she sits back down on the carpet.

"Anna," Mrs. Barden calls from behind us. "Please come and help me in the kitchen."

"Yes, ma'am," I answer, standing up and joining her. She places a hand on my shoulder and leads me out of the dining room and into the kitchen. Heat hits my face as we enter the room.

"Sit with me for a spell," she says. I do as she asks and sit down next to her at the table, slowly baking along with whatever she has in the oven.

"I saw your sister briefly on Sunday in the churchyard. How is she doing?"

"Mary?" Everyone cares about Mary. "She's well. We had lunch at the Eating House together."

"Oh, wonderful. I'm glad that she is feeling well enough to go out." I'm not sure how to respond since Mary is not ill, but there is no need to answer because she continues, "Sunday was also the day that you kissed Karl Sundvquist."

I stiffen. Her tone is not judgmental, but for some reason, I feel like I am about to be scolded for that kiss, again. I steel myself, ready to bear it, since it is my plan to make everyone, even Belle's mother, believe that Karl has feelings for me.

"Yes, Karl kissed me at the gypsy encampment."

"Your mother told me. She is very fond of Karl. She always has been, and I know she thinks you two would be a good match."

My jaw drops open in astonishment. Mrs. Barden must be mistaken. My mother was angry with me about kissing Karl. Why would she tell Mrs. Barden that she thinks we are a good match?

She chuckles, "You look a bit confused, Anna."

"I . . . well . . . yes, I suppose I am," I stumble on my words. "I thought my mother was upset with me."

She sighs and leans back in her chair, saying, "Your mother loves you very much, Anna, and she's happy that Karl has taken a romantic interest in you. She's just being cautious since your sister got married so quickly. You are still very young and impressionable. Once you are older, she will be just as excited as you are."

"She will be?"

"Oh yes, she already thinks of Karl as a son. But I'm not surprised that she's being protective, especially, after your sister's short engagement. Until the day comes when your mother is ready to accept you and Karl, you may want to be a bit more conservative. I wouldn't recommend kissing Karl—or any other boys for that matter." She stares at me, knowingly.

I think I know what she is hinting at. "So no more kissing games?"

"No more kissing games."

I nod, "Yes, ma'am."

"Young women should guard their purity and innocence while they still have it. You don't want to create a soiled reputation for yourself before you are fully introduced to society."

I shake my head, "No, ma'am."

"We live in a very interesting time, Anna. There is so much opportunity for women, but we still need to act properly. Women are the backbone of the family, and we set an example for the community."

"Yes ma'am."

She nods, satisfied with our conversation. Then, she stands up and uses a woven pot holder to take out a pie from the oven. She sets it on the open window sill and says, "Help me set the table while the raisin pie cools." As Mrs. Barden and I set plates, forks, and cups on the dining room table, I peek at the party to see what I'm missing. They have moved onto another game: Kiss Your Shadow. Each player takes a turn trying to kiss their own shadow even if it lands on a chair, the floor, or a person.

When we leave the room for the ice box, laughter erupts behind us. I know that I'm missing out, but I agree with Belle's mother. Together we set out cold fried chicken and a pitcher of milk. Immediately, the game is forgotten. The boys practically run over each other to fill a plate. The girls follow, then Belle's father. Halfway through the meal, Belle's mother takes the pie off the window sill and cuts it. I help her serve each person a piece. Only then, do she and I fill our plates.

The heat from the oven has warmed the entire house, so after our meal everyone decides to go outside and cool off. The boys, having been fed, have found a new source of energy and run across the lawn, throwing the ball back and forth again with Belle's father. We girls sit on the edge of the porch and discuss the first day of school. Mostly, we talk excitedly about our new clothes and shoes.

After some time, Belle's mother walks up to us and says, "Girls, it is well past midnight. Time to head back home." We all stand up, and she hugs each of us and gives us all a kiss on the top of our heads. "Thank you so much for coming. I hope you all have a wonderful school year."

"Yes," Belle adds. "Thank you for coming, it was such a wonderful party. The perfect way to end the summer."

"Boys!" her mother shouts, "We need each of you to pair up with a girl and walk them home. Helen and Daniel, you two live on the south side of town, so you can leave together. Clara and Charlie, you two head on home." She turns to Belle's brother, "Archie, dear, you can take Anna home."

Archie groans, "Mother, that's so far away, and I have to come all the way back. It will be past one in the morning."

Edwin runs over to Archie but keeps his eyes on Belle's mother, "I don't mind taking Anna home, ma'am. I don't live on the wagon road, but my house is near the north side of town. It's not far out of the way for me."

Belle's father jogs over from the boys game and claps Edwin on the back, "Thank you for volunteering, Edwin."

"Thanks, Ed. I owe you one," Archie shakes Edwin's hand and then rushes up the porch steps and inside.

My heart skips a beat because Karl is supposed to walk me home.

Clara and Helen start walking towards their escort as Belle embraces me. "Goodnight, Anna."

"Belle," I whisper in her ear. "Karl is walking me home."

"What?" She pulls back and frowns at me. "Is he coming here?"

"No," I answer her, keeping my voice low. "He's meeting me along the way, so your parents don't see us together."

"Oh," she bites her lip. "Well, then, you better tell Edwin."

"How should I do that?" I ask.

She just shrugs.

"What are you girls whispering about?" Belle's mother asks. "It's late, Belle, you better let Anna head home." Belle hugs me again and squeezes my shoulders before she walks up her porch steps and into the house.

The chicken and raisin pie churn in my stomach as I walk over to Edwin. We leave the Barden yard together just like the other two groups moving in different directions into the dark streets of Hinckley. I wave my goodbyes to Charlie and Clara, then to Helen and Daniel. I turn back around and wave to Belle's parents who are standing on their porch.

Edwin is not a loud, boisterous boy, like others my age, so I bet it took a lot of courage for him to request to be my escort. I don't care to hurt his feelings with rejection, but there's no way around it. He's going to see Karl in a few minutes. I twist my hands together, trying to find the best way to bring it up.

Even at this late hour, the boys are still energized and in high spirits. One of them, I think Charlie, starts to sing from around the corner of the street. It's the beginning verse of The Shanty Boy and the Farmer's Son. Daniel and Edwin, join him:

> *As I walk'd out one evening just as the sun went down,*
> *I carelessly did ramble till I came to Hinckley town.*
> *I heard two maids conversing as slowly I passed by.*
> *One said she loved a farmer's son, the other a shanty boy.*

Charlie and Daniel's voices fade as the distance between us increases, but Edwin still keeps singing. I can't think while he sings, and I need to find the right words before we run into Karl.

"Shhh, Edwin. Please, stop singing," I plead.

He is walking backwards behind me and cupping his hands over his mouth to project his voice back to the other boys who all have all turned down other streets and are out of sight.

Edwin belts out the line about the farmer:

He'll stay at home all winter, to the shanties he will not go,
And when the spring it doth come in, his land he'll plow and sow.

I stop walking and raise my voice, so he'll hear me over his singing. "Edwin! Please."

He stops abruptly and turns his head towards me. "I'm sorry, Anna. I'll stop. I didn't mean to aggravate you. Don't you like this song?"

I shake my head and keep walking, "Just not right now."

He catches up to me and holds my elbow, "I'm your escort, remember?"

I can barely make out his features, but I can tell that he is smiling as he peers into the darkness. Guilt twists in my stomach because what I say next will probably make his smile disappear. I thought having attention from boys would be entertaining, like I was finally growing up, but I don't know how to tell Edwin I just want to be friends. If I'm frank about it, he will probably be upset or angry, and he might want to avoid me.

How did Mary handle all of this? I wish I could discuss my feelings with her and ask her for advice, but our relationship is so different now. I doubt she would care to hear my concerns. Gone are the nights when we would stay up late giggling under the bed covers and sharing our secrets.

"Anna?" Edwin interrupts my thoughts about Mary. "What are you thinking about? You look sad."

"Oh, nothing. I just miss my sister sometimes."

"I bet. You should go visit her. Pokegama isn't that far away."

"I am. In fact, I'm going to visit her tomorrow. There's a dedication ceremony for the new schoolhouse."

"Pokegama has a school now?" Edwin asks.

"Yes, but I don't want to talk about their school right now, Edwin. There's something I have to tell you."

"What's that?"

"Do you know Karl Sundvquist?"

"Yes. He's your neighbor."

"Yes, he is." I swallow down my indecisiveness and go with directness, "Well, he wants to walk me home tonight."

Edwin stops walking. "He does?"

"Yes, he kissed me the other day, and our parents are expecting him over soon to ask to court me."

"I heard that rumor," he says and lets go of my elbow.

"You did?"

"Yes, but I didn't think it was true. Or maybe, I didn't want it to be true." He shrugs his shoulders.

"I'm sorry Edwin. I don't want to hurt you—" he puts up his hand to stop me.

"Don't apologize, Anna. There's nothing to be sorry about."

I frown, "You're not mad at me?"

He laughs, "Why would I be mad? I understand why you like Karl." He starts walking ahead of me, "If anything, I'm disappointed in myself."

I match his pace, "In yourself? Why?"

"Well, I should have made my feelings known earlier this summer, but I didn't have the courage, and I thought I still had time. I should have known that others would start to pursue you."

"Me?"

He laughs again. "Of course. You must know that you are quite a catch."

I blush and playfully scold him for his boldness, "Edwin."

"It's true. I should have been honest with you from the start. Now, I will have to suffer the consequences of seeing another man sweep you off your feet before I come of age."

I snort, "Karl is not sweeping me off my feet."

"No? Well then, maybe in the future I will still have a chance."

Suddenly I smell the sweet, smoky scent of a cigar, so I turn around to find the source, but the streets are too dark to see anything.

"Where is Karl meeting us?" Edwin asks.

I turn my attention back to him, "Oh, well, I'm not sure. Probably at the end of this street." Wait. Did Edwin say, 'meeting us'? "Edwin, I can walk from here. You can head home if you want."

He shakes his head, "No, I told Mr. Barden that I'd walk you home."

Now the smell of hay, manure, and horses invades my nostrils. We are at the intersection of Second Avenue and First Street, directly behind Donahue's Livery. A kerosene lamp is lit inside the stables, and insects swirl around it. The glow from the lamp casts shadows across the street onto a dark figure sitting on a stump used for chopping wood. Rising to his feet, Karl makes his way over to us; his face obscured, yet his distinctive gait and movements unmistakable.

He sticks out his hand to Edwin and says, "Karl Sundvquist."

Edwin shakes his hand and answers, "Edwin Meyer."

"I thought . . . " Karl chuckles, "I mean. . . you're Anna's age."

"Yes." Edwin lets go of Karl's hand and asks, "Did you expect someone else?"

Karl smiles, "No, no of course not. How was the dancing party?"

"We had a swell time, didn't we Anna?" Edwin doesn't let me answer. "I told Mr. Barden that I'd walk Anna home tonight."

"I figured as much," Karl nods his head and looks at me for the first time. "Are you ready, Anna?"

"Yes, I am." I say and touch Edwin's arm to get his attention, "Edwin, Karl lives right next to me, you really don't need to—"

"Good evening!" a rough, male voice rudely interrupts me, "My, my, my aren't you out past your bedtimes?"

We all turn our heads towards the voice and see a dark shadow approaching us from the direction that Edwin and I have just come. A tiny, red light glows in the dark, the ember at the end of a cigar. Karl grumbles under his breath, "Ivar."

"You," the man stumbles into our circle and jabs his cigar at Karl, "you owe me four dollars, Sundvquist." Instinctively my muscles tense at the man's aggressive tone. He smells like a saloon.

Karl takes a step in front of me, blocking my view, "Go home, Ivar. You're drunk."

"Not until you give me my money."

Edwin clears his throat, then speaks in a shaky voice, "Good evening, sir. What seems to be the problem here?"

I peer around Karl's arm and see Ivar turn his attention away from Karl. "My problem?" He inhales from his cigar before taking an unbalanced step towards Edwin. "Karl owes me money, and I'm going to get it." He blows smoke into Edwin's face.

Edwin blanches and fans the smoke away, "I'm sure there is a way to work this out like gentlemen." I know Edwin, so I understand that he is trying to act older and calmer than he really is, but from what Karl has told me about Ivar, he won't appreciate someone my age telling him what to do.

Ivar barks out a laugh and then leans into Edwin until he's only inches from his face, "I'm no gentleman. And I sure as hell am not going to listen to you, so shut your sauce box."

The tension is palpable; something violent is about to happen. I can sense Edwin's and Ivar's fists clenching. Ivar is much older than Edwin and has probably been in fights before, so the odds are not in my friend's favor. I step in front of Karl and grab Edwin's arm trying to tug him back, away from Ivar, "Please Edwin, just leave him be."

"Hey!" Ivar shouts, making me flinch. "You must be the girl that was in the gypsy wagon. That was supposed to be my kiss and my money."

"What are you talking about?" Edwin asks.

Ivar takes one step towards me and leans in, "I owe you a kiss, darling." This time Karl grabs my waist and pulls me back behind him just as Edwin grabs Ivar's shirt and pulls him back away from me.

Ivar screams, "Get your hands off me!" I hear a scuffle and then a loud thud followed by Edwin grunting in pain. Karl lets me go and bear hugs Ivar. I stand frozen in shock, trying to comprehend the scene in front of me. On one side, Edwin is moaning in pain, doubled over with both hands covering his right eye. On my other side, Karl is holding Ivar's arms tight against his sides while he struggles against Karl's chest, trying to free himself.

Suddenly Ivar elbows Karl in the gut which releases his grip. Ivar falls out of his arms onto the ground. My heart is beating so fast, but I don't know what to do. I can't run away and leave my friends, but I don't know how to help them. Ivar gets up and pants, "Where was I?" He smiles and advances towards Edwin, ripping his hands away from his face and pulling him up into a standing position. Edwin's eyes are wide with fear which seems to energize Ivar. He lifts him off the ground and sneers, "Still want to work this out like gentlemen?"

Out of nowhere, Karl's arm wraps around Ivar's neck and yanks him backward. I cover my mouth in shock, stifling a scream. Ivar drops Edwin who crumbles to the ground. I recover my ability to move and run over to him. "Edwin!" I crouch down and hold onto his shoulders, trying to lift him up. "Get up, we have to get out of here."

A crunching noise distracts me, and someone yelps out in pain. I jerk my head up, just in time to see Ivar's head snap back from the impact of Karl's fist. He falls to one knee and clutches his nose. Karl is standing over him, grinding his teeth and shaking his right hand. Ivar folds over to all fours and blood gushes from his nose, pooling in the dirt.

"Karl!" I shout. He looks away from Ivar and sees me struggling to lift Edwin. He runs over and puts Edwin's arm over his shoulder. I put Edwin's other arm over mine, and we both lift him up off the ground. The horses start to snort and wake up in the stables behind us.

"Ah!" Edwin moans. "My ankle. I think I fell on it wrong."

Out of breath, Karl pants, "Where do you live? We'll take you there."

"No," Edwin shakes his head. "I have to take Anna home."

On the street Ivar spits out more blood and growls something at us. The horses start to shuffle and whinny.

"Let's go, then," Karl says and leads us north, pulling Edwin with him. I step quickly to keep up, and we leave Ivar in the street, moaning and cussing. Eventually the sounds of the sawmill, the rumbling of the carriages and the whining of the circular saw, drown out Ivar's voice as we make our way on the wagon road.

PART TWO

SEPTEMBER 1, 1894

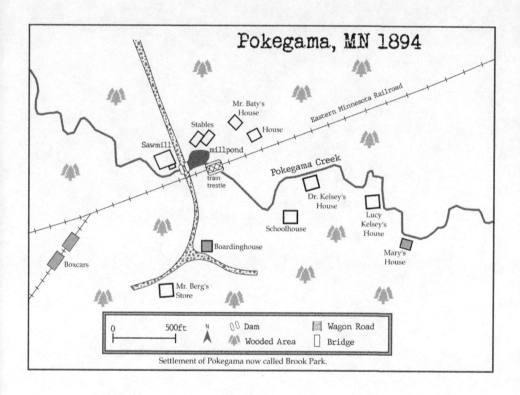

Pokegama, MN 1894

Eastern Minnesota Railroad

Mr. Baty's House

Stables

House

Sawmill

millpond

Pokegama Creek

train trestle

Dr. Kelsey's House

Lucy Kelsey's House

Schoolhouse

Mary's House

Boxcars

Boardinghouse

Mr. Berg's Store

0	500ft	N	⌒⌒ Dam	▨ Wagon Road
		▲	🌲 Wooded Area	☐ Bridge

Settlement of Pokegama now called Brook Park.

10

Karl

Saturday, September 1, 1894
Hinckley, Minnesota
12:45 a.m. - 10:00 a.m.

The three of us make our way to Anna's house in silence. She doesn't need to help me hold Edwin up, he's light as a feather, but I think she wants to help in some way. He's putting most of his weight on me anyway, so I don't say anything.

My hand stings from punching Ivar. Father taught me how to throw a punch, and how to take one for that matter, but he never mentioned the sting. I'll have to tell him about it someday. That day might be sooner than I wish, though. If Ivar tells anyone from the mill that I slugged him in the face, Father will surely find out.

I exhale out a long strained breath, "Strange night."

"I'll say," Edwin agrees.

I smile. If Edwin didn't have feelings for Anna, I think I'd like him. That was a brave thing he did, standing up to Ivar. It was stupid since he's so much weaker, but brave nonetheless. There's no moon out tonight, so we only have the stars to guide our way. That and the fact that Anna and I could make this walk with our eyes closed, we've done it so many times. I'm secretly pleased when Edwin keeps asking

119

if each of the houses we pass is Anna's. He must not have walked her home yet this summer. Finally, when we do reach the Andersson homestead, one flickering candle is still lit in the house. I hope her parents aren't waiting up for her. What a sight they would see, the three of us staggering down the road.

"Here," Anna says, pulling Edwin toward her split rail fence, "this is home."

I take his arm off my shoulders and shift him towards the fence. He leans onto the railing and sighs, "That was an interesting way to end the summer."

Anna agrees, "Yes, I suppose. Well, thank you Edwin for walking me home tonight. I hope your ankle is all right."

"Don't worry about me. I'll set it up on some pillows when I get home, and then rest it tomorrow."

"You might have a black eye, too," I add.

"Really?" he asks, excitement in his voice.

Anna shakes her head and says, "Well, I'm going inside. Um, good night."

"I'll walk you to the door," I tell Anna as I climb over the fence and offer my hand to her. She takes it and climbs over next to me.

"Karl," Edwin clears his throat and Anna drops my hand. "Do you mind . . . would you be able to . . ."

"Yes, I'll help you home. Just give me a minute."

"Yes, of course. I'll wait here," he says and gets comfortable on the fence, facing the road. After Anna says goodbye to Edwin, we walk to the house. When we get to her front steps, I turn to her and whisper, "Are you all right?"

She whispers back, "Yes, I'm fine, but what about you?" She motions to my hand. "I saw you shaking it after you hit Ivar. Does it hurt?"

"This?" I hold up my hand, "No, I'm fine, but I think I ruined any chance I had to be hired for the winter logging camps," I say it jokingly, but deep down it hurts because it's the truth.

"What?" She asks, "Why is that?"

"I just punched the recruiter in the face."

"Oh, no," she says, covering her mouth with her hands. Then she whispers, "You've wanted that for so long. If I hadn't asked you to lie .

.. this is all my fault. I'm so sorry, Karl."

I shrug my shoulders, look down at my boots, and tell her, "You're worth it, Anna."

She doesn't respond, so I lift my gaze to see her face. Our eyes meet, and I know this is the moment I should tell her that I'm beginning to feel different about her. That maybe, we should try courting when she is a little older, but instead, I nod and tell her, "*God natt.*"

🐦 🐦 🐦

Abruptly, I sit up in bed, panting. I'm drenched in sweat. Disorientated, I look around at my room, and the familiar objects give me a sense of comfort and safety. I swing my legs over the side of the bed and put my head in my hands. My face and hair are slick with sweat, and my nightshirt clings to my skin, so I take it off, slip into my work pants, and find a clean shirt in my dresser. I stuff it in the back of my pants for later. I'm too hot to wear it now.

I take my time walking down the stairs, still waking up. A plate of bacon and eggs wait for me on the kitchen table, but Father is not in the room. I glance at the dry sink and see his plate and fork already washed and drying. I'm hungry, but breakfast will have to wait. I need water first, so I go out the back door and head toward the well. Even this early the air is already warm, but the sky is calm and clear. The usual pall of smoke is missing, so I take a deep breath, relishing the fresh air. Our rooster crows in the yard, and in the distance, a dog barks in response. A few birds fly above my head, singing a morning song to each other. Besides that, it's a quiet morning. I pull up a bucket of water and splash my face and hair a few times. I take a handful of water and rinse my neck and shoulders, squeezing the tension from my sore muscles. I bend down and pick up a tin cup on the ground next to the well and use it to drink the cold water from the bucket. My dry mouth and throat feel instant relief.

After putting the cup and bucket back, I set my hands on the stone rim and look out on our land. The sun is rising over the horizon casting a bright light on the tree stumps and brush. A cicada buzzes in the distance, interrupting the silence. It's a tranquil morning. Even the aspen trees behind the barn are still. Their leaves, so easily stirred by even the faintest breeze, are motionless. Everything around me is at peace. Except me.

I can't shake the nightmare I had. I close my eyes, trying to remember every detail. First, I was walking on the sidewalk with Anna. I was holding her hand, and it felt soft and warm. I felt at ease walking through town with her, like it was a normal thing we did every day. Then a large, angry crowd of men came running down the street. They yelled at me, but I couldn't understand what they were saying. A few of them grabbed Anna's other hand and started pulling her into the crowd. I lost my grip on her, and she disappeared behind the angry men. I started swinging my fists at them, hitting them as hard as I could, trying to reach Anna, but each punch landed softly against the men. No matter how hard I hit them, it was useless. My strength vanished before the punch landed. The men began to laugh at me and my weakness. I felt embarrassed and tried to hit harder and harder. I swung my arms so fast, but the men just kept laughing at me.

The sound of a door closing interrupts me. I open my eyes quickly and glance at the barn where the sound came from. It's Father, finishing up feeding and watering the animals. He notices me by the well and walks over.

"*God morgon,*" he greets me.

"Good morning," I answer.

"Another hot one today."

"At least that blessed stink is gone," I grumble.

Father frowns at me, "It's too beautiful of a day for words like those, Karl. What is wrong?"

I pull out the clean shirt from my waistband and set it on the edge of the well and say, "Nothing is wrong. I just had a strange dream."

"What did you dream about?" he asks.

"A large crowd of men were attacking me and Anna. I was trying to hit them, but no matter how hard I swung, my fists landed softly. The men laughed like it tickled them."

"I see," Father says. He sets down the buckets in his hands and folds his arms across his chest.

"Well," I prompt. "What does it mean?"

He chuckles, "The meaning is clear to me."

He walks toward the house, leaving me at the well. I pick up my shirt and follow him inside.

"What meaning?"

He picks up two pails off the counter, "You'll have to eat your breakfast on the way. The seven o'clock whistle is near," he says, lifting up one of the pails for our lunch, indicating that it is mine. "You can set your breakfast plate in here when you finish."

Then he walks out of the kitchen without explaining the meaning of my dream.

I retrieve my plate off the table but leave my fork. I put my hat on with my free hand and walk to the front room picking up my boots along the way. Father is holding both pails and waiting in the front yard while I sit on the steps and lace up my boots.

I put a piece of bacon in my mouth, and we set off for the sawmill. Scooping the eggs with my hand, I finish my breakfast as quickly as possible while walking down the wagon road. Then I take my lunch pail from Father and set my plate inside the pail next to the smoked meats and cheese.

Father whistles and shakes his head, "Already the sun is unbearable. Glad, I'll be working in the shade of the sawmill." Most of the two hundred men on the day shift today will be outside, like me, stacking lumber in the yard, but it's Saturday which means everyone receives their pay envelopes at the end of the day. We'll all be in a good mood despite the heat.

Father and I pass Anna's house. Maybe I could use some of my pay envelope to buy her dinner at the Eating House. I've always wanted to take a girl there. I glance at Father, wondering if I should run my idea by him. Since he already warned me not to meet with her alone anymore, I doubt he would approve of me taking her out for dinner. Maybe I can buy her some candy at Lindstrom's and bring it to her house. I've been putting off my conversation with her parents about courting, so I should do that today or tomorrow.

As we continue south on the wagon road, more men like us walk from their homes toward their ten-hour shift at the sawmill. The anticipation for our pay envelopes, in addition to the clear morning sky, makes for a hopeful start to the day, almost making me forget about my nightmare.

"Father, what meaning is clear to you from my dream?"

"You care about Anna," he responds quickly, "and you want to protect her. It makes sense. You two have always been close. Now you are beginning to see it too."

I smile. I won't have to lie to Mr. Andersson later when I talk to him about courting Anna.

🐦 🐦 🐦

The winds have picked up, and a low cloud cover has blown over Hinckley. The bright, early morning sunlight which made me feel so hopeful this morning has faded into a dull, stale light muddied by a gray-white smoke. It descends into the lumberyard bringing back the awful smell.

I'm stacking boards outside, sweating through my shirt, but my mind keeps replaying the scene in the street last night. I'm trying to find another way to make Ivar back down without breaking his nose, but I only end up shaking my head in frustration. I can't change the past. I hit him, and now I'll have to live with it even if it means I won't be a shanty boy. Maybe I should tell Mr. Andersson about what happened. He probably wouldn't like that Ivar threatened to kiss his daughter. We could team up and pressure Ivar, run him out of town or something before he has time to hire a winter logging crew. Almost as quickly as the idea forms in my mind, I decide against it because then Anna's father would learn that we were together last night.

"Karl!" a voice shouts behind me. I turn around and see Kristoff walking toward me from the sawmill. I set the board in my hand down onto the pile I've been working on and wait for him, wiping the sweat from my brow.

"*God morgon*," he smiles at me as he closes the distance between us.

"*God morgon*," I answer.

"You're brooding. I could see it all the way over there. What happened last night with Anna?"

I groan, tilting my head up to the sky, "You're not going to believe me." The sun is hiding behind the cloud cover and smoke, which is so thick that I can stare at it without hurting my eyes. It reminds me more of a pale, blue-gray moon than the sun.

I turn back to face him, telling him everything that happened, including the part where I walked Anna up to her front door. At the end of my story, he whistles loudly and claps his hands together saying, "I knew that you liked Anna."

124

I laugh at him and ask, "Is that all you heard? What about Ivar? There's no way he's going to ask me to be on his logging team. Ever."

He shrugs his shoulders and says, "There are other ways to make good money."

"It wasn't just that."

"I know, I know." A strong gust of wind blows in between the lumber stacks, rippling our shirts. I grab onto the brim of my hat to keep it from blowing away. We wait a moment for it to pass. After the wind dies down, Kristoff continues, "Now, I didn't come over here just to talk about Anna, Ivar, and your midnight shenanigans. The managers sent me to get a dozen men, a team of horses, and a wagon. We're going to haul barrels of water to Snake River Road, the one just beyond the west side of the yard."

"Why?" I ask, curious.

"There's a marsh fire over there. It's been burning for a few weeks now, but with this wind picking up, the managers are worried it might come too close to the lumberyard."

"I'll go with you. Beats working in this scorching heat and stink."

"It's so hot, I might just have to ride in one of the water barrels," he jokes.

"Well, you should. It's about time you took a bath."

He elbows me in the ribs, and we walk through the maze of stacked lumber to find more men.

11

Anna

Saturday, September 1, 1894
Pokegama, Minnesota
10:00 a.m. - 11:00 a.m.

I step off the train in Pokegama, expecting to see and hear the usual commotion and sounds I am familiar with at the Hinckley train stations, but to my surprise, it's completely silent. There is no train ticket office, no freight room, not even a building. My oxford shoes echo on the five by five foot square wooden platform next to the tracks.

"Excuse me, sir," I say quickly, spinning on my heel to face the train again, questioning the conductor, "Is this Pokegama?"

"No, this is just a flag stop. We usually don't stop here unless there are passengers flagging us down, or as in your case, someone being dropped off," he answers me.

"Oh, I see," I respond. The gentleman who sold me a ticket at the Eastern Minnesota depot forgot to tell me this. "Well, my sister lives in Pokegama. I'm joining her this morning for a school dedication ceremony."

"You'll want to head to the city center then," he answers, pointing back behind the train, "Follow the tracks east, back the way we just came. Before the bridge and trestle is Pokegama."

126

The train starts up and slowly starts heading west to St. Cloud. "Thank you, sir," I raise my voice over the clanking of the train gears and wheels. He nods to me before disappearing back inside the train car. I stand on the platform and watch the train leave. Once it is out of sight, I turn back and face east. I peer into the woods on either side of the tracks. On one side, I spot a small wooden building. It's likely a line house for the railway company. Behind that is a rough wagon road cut into the trees that leads to two, old wooden shacks on either side of the road. Both are dark. With a deep breath, I step onto the railroad tracks and begin walking to Pokegama.

The trees are thick here, and their branches hang over the railroad embankment. The mosquitoes swarm even thicker, like a living, buzzing fog. I snap off an overhanging tree branch and use it to fan them away as I walk. The pests irritate me, souring my mood and sending my thoughts to Mary. It was such a short train ride; I can't understand why she didn't take it once all summer to come back and visit. I'll ask her when I arrive at her house, but first and foremost, she needs to tell me why she lied to our parents and to John. My life would have been a lot easier this past week if she had just told the truth at the Eating House. I wonder, though, if she had told the truth and they had sorted it all out with Karl, would he still have walked me home from the party last night. At first, he insisted that he only wanted to walk me home to strengthen the lie, but now, after what he told me last night, I think he had another reason. I smile, remembering the sweet words he said on my front steps.

Finally, a trace of civilization appears among the forest. A shallow creek runs parallel to the tracks, and there is a small sawmill and millpond next to it. This must be the Pokegama Sawmill. I don't see a lumberyard, though, not like the massive one in Hinckley with dozens and dozens of stacks of boards curing in the sun. My feet reach a small, dirt road that crosses the tracks, and I smell the distinct odor of hay and horse manure, so a stable must be nearby. Looking ahead on the tracks, I can see a wooden trestle. The conductor said Pokegama was before the trestle, so this road must take me to the city center. Instead of turning toward the mill, which is quiet, I turn the other way and make my way down the dirt road.

Very soon, the thick trees clear somewhat, and I can see a few shacks with stacks of firewood leaning against them. Hammocks are tied between several trees near the shacks. Beyond that, among a variety of evergreen trees, stand two, large, handsome log buildings. The closer of the two looks like a boardinghouse because it has a wide, wraparound porch, and several glass windows, all spotlessly kept. The other building, a bit further down the road, only has two windows by the front door. A sign hanging above the door reads, "Teas & Coffees." This must be their general store.

I'm surprised. The settlement is so much smaller than I had imagined. Surely there must be more houses. They must be hidden among the forest. I'm surrounded by so many mature trees, I can't see where anything is beyond the dirt road that I'm walking on. As I near the boardinghouse, I see a woman sitting in a chair on the porch. She notices me approaching and waves me over.

"Good morning, young lady," she smiles down at me. "Welcome to Brook Park. What brings you down the tracks today?"

"Good morning," I greet her and walk up the steps. "Brook Park? I thought this was Pokegama?"

"Well, yes, the post office is marked as Brook Park," she points to the log building with the "Teas & Coffees" sign, "but the train stop has always been Pokegama. We use both names."

"Is that so?"

"Yes, dear."

"Hmm, well I'm here to visit family and to attend the school dedication ceremony."

Her face lights up when I say that. She's smiling from ear to ear, clearly proud and excited for the community celebration. "Oh, I'm so glad to hear that. We are proud of our new school. Mr. Kelsey and a few other men in town spent three weeks building it."

"Mr. Kelsey, of the Kelsey Markham Land Company?" I ask.

"Why, yes, dear, he is. Caleb Kelsey and his brother, Dr. Chauncey Kelsey, are the leaders of our town promoters. How are you acquainted with the Kelsey family?"

"I'm not, but my brother-in-law is part of their firm."

"Oh, are you related to the Markham family in Rush City?"

"No, ma'am. I'm Anna Andersson of Hinckley. My sister married John Larson, and he works with Mr. Kelsey."

She frowns at me for a moment before she answers, "I thought their firm only consisted of the three Kelsey brothers and J. D. Markham of Rush City."

I'm not sure how to respond, but thankfully, she smiles again and answers for me, "Well, what do I know of their firm's business, anyway," she laughs to herself. "I keep myself too busy as it is, cleaning and cooking for the weary plodders who pass through my boardinghouse."

I was right. It is a boardinghouse. I look down at the painted, white floors of the porch, "Yes, ma'am. Your floors are spotless."

"Oh, thank you. Now, what was the name of your kin, again? I know all the families in Pokegama, so I can help you find your way."

"Mr. and Mrs. John Larson."

"Oh, yes, Mary Larson," recognition flashes across her face, "She is a lovely woman, a good cook and housekeeper, and so kind and even in her manner. I wish I saw more of her, but she mostly keeps to herself. She and her husband live about twenty minutes east if you follow that evergreen path." She points towards the woods. I follow her finger and find the trail she is referring to. It is almost entirely swallowed up by tree branches, so I would have never found it myself.

"Caleb Kelsey and his wife Lucy live down that road too. Their house is before your sister's. Lucy and her five children moved here in July about a month after your sister. The Kelseys are a wonderful family. We have so many respectable families here in Pokegama. Usually there are one or two of them here in town, but it is quiet today as most of the men are busy haying. Are you Jewish, by chance?"

"No, Lutheran."

"That's a shame. You look about the same age as Jakey Braman. Now there's an industrious, young man with a bright future. There are a few other German Jewish families too." She scratches her chin and thinks, "Or are they Russian? I can't remember."

Two girls walk up onto the porch beside me and set down two buckets full of cranberries. The older girl looks to be around Mary's age while the younger girl is just a year or two younger than me.

"Good morning," I greet them.

"Good morning," the older girl answers.

"Good morning, Mrs. Carver!" the younger girl exclaims. "We

brought you cranberries."

"Oh, thank you, Mabel. It looks like you picked them all." the woman in the chair responds, amazed at the girls' overflowing buckets. "The Indians will be disappointed. They usually show up in the fall and pick them."

The older girl asks, "Have any passed through town recently?"

"No, not recently. But I know that a group of twenty or so are camped out near Shadridge Creek," the woman says before turning her attention to me. "Anna," she says, "this is Alice and Mabel Nelson. They live in the Eastern Minnesota Section House."

"Nice to meet you," I say to the girls, "I'm Anna Andersson."

"Where are my own manners?" Mrs. Carver says. "I just get so carried away when newcomers come down the tracks. As sweet Mabel just said, I'm Mrs. Carver, and my husband and I run this boardinghouse." She stands up from her chair and picks up a bucket of cranberries saying, "Are you girls coming to the dedication ceremony this afternoon? Rumor is the doctor will have a short speech, then we'll have food and music."

"That's my school," Mabel says happily. "I can't wait to start going there."

Alice smiles at her younger sister, "I hope we can make it. Mabel and I are picking more cranberries while Pa works on the tracks. We came in a handcar with him from south of town."

"I told Alice that we had to bring you some cranberries."

"Oh, you are so sweet, little Mabel. Thank you again."

Alice touches her sister's shoulder, "We should head back now if we want to have lunch with Pa."

"All right, girls, I hope to see you this afternoon," Mrs. Carver says as Alice and Mabel walk down the steps.

I nod to Mrs. Carver, "I best be on my way as well. Thank you for the directions."

"Anytime," Mrs. Carver smiles at me.

I walk down the porch steps and make my way to the evergreen path.

🦢 🦢 🦢

At first, the path is bordered by young maples, raspberry bushes, and various kinds of undergrowth, but soon the woods become thicker, making the path narrower as mature balsam and pine trees appear. Their branches stretch out above my head, interlacing to create a beautiful archway. In some places the branches are so close to each other, they block the sun, creating a magical twilight.

The ground is spongy and soft, not hard and dusty like all of the wagon roads around Hinckley. Ferns, mosses, and other growth spring up around me. It's an enchanting forest, and I imagine the fun that the squirrels must have scurrying from branch to branch. Occasionally I step over fallen logs, taking my time because I don't want to stain my new shoes. A house eventually appears on one side of the path. White pine trees, just feet away from the house, make the structure seem like it grew up from the forest floor. It is a handsome home, two stories tall, and built out of gigantic ash, tamarack, and basswood logs. Tree stumps litter the front yard, likely where the family cut down trees for their home. Two large, glass windows stare down at me from the front of the house. The door is covered by an elaborate gable, giving the house a regal appearance.

This must be the Kelsey house that Mrs. Carver mentioned. I stop and admire it. On the east side is a clearing of blackened and dead trees spread out before the forest, probably from a brush fire. Two, small boys chase each other around the corner of the house. One sees me and stops running. He smiles and waves, and then he continues chasing the other boy around the stumps.

I wave back, then continue on my way to Mary's house, wondering if it looks as beautiful as this one. The path meanders through the forest back and forth. It remains narrow and covered with arched branches from the trees on either side. The forest here seems untouched by the logging companies. I imagine this is what the forest that used to cover Hinckley Big Hill looked like, years ago, before the Brennan Lumber Company logged it. I remember the sawmill on the other side of the train tracks in Pokegama, and the reason that I am here today, to attend a ceremony for a new school building. More families will move here, and soon this area will look similar to Hinckley. The thought makes me sad for the forest because it is so beautiful. The trees are so thick on either side of the evergreen path that I have no doubt I would get lost if I wandered off. I can only see a few yards deep before the leaves block the sunlight from above. I take a deep breath in through my nose. The familiar smell of woodsmoke fills my nostrils, but it's not as strong here. Instead, I smell the damp, earthy scent of the forest, and it is delightfully cool.

My only complaint is my sore feet. I should have worn my new oxfords at home for a few days before taking them out. They are stiff and not yet molded to my feet. I'll have red, swollen heels by the end of this journey, and it is a long journey. I didn't think I would do this much walking. Even in the coolness of the forest, I feel the perspiration seeping through my wool cashmere blouse, so I unbutton my brown, wool surge shirt and pull my arms out of the leg o'mutton sleeves. I hang it over my shoulder and lift my elbows up hoping to air out my blouse.

A carpet of acorns blankets the path as a massive oak tree looms above. It feels early to have dropped so many of its acorns, but maybe that is normal in a drought year. That would also explain why some of the trees have already started changing colors. Just as my feet stop crunching the acorns, the path stops, revealing a small clearing. Chickens slowly walk around tree stumps and stop to peck at the brown, dead grass. A simple log house sits among the stumps. It has two stories, but it is tiny in comparison to the Kelsey home that I passed only minutes ago.

There are no windows on the wall facing me, but the door is wide open. Small stacks of firewood line the path to the house. There is an outhouse on one side of the house in front of the tree line, and on the other side is a potato patch, a well, then more forest. This must be Mary and John's house since the path ends here. I find it odd that the front door is wide open, but maybe Mary is baking and the heat of the oven is unbearable. Not that it's any cooler outside. Once I leave the forest path and enter the clearing, the reprieve of the trees disappears and the scorching sun hits my face. Still, I must look presentable, so I put my surge shirt back on, slowly closing the buttons in the front. I try my best to straighten it and smooth out any creases. I pin back any flyaway hairs that have escaped my pompadour, which I kept intact from last night.

Though my frustration with Mary still lingers beneath the surface, I'm eager to share my excitement about the dancing party and what happened on the way home. If she chooses to be honest with me, she'll give me advice about Karl. I close my eyes and try to compose myself. My mother's voice echoes in my head: Be kind and be polite. You are a guest. Mind your manners. I open my eyes and walk toward the tiny house.

As I approach the threshold, I can immediately tell something is wrong. Chairs are overturned at the table. Plates, dishes, and silverware lay scattered, and shards of glass litter the floor. Across the room, sunlight reflects off the jagged edges of a broken window. Eggs and bacon lay on the floor in a heap next to a cast iron skillet.

I hold onto the door frame and tentatively step inside. The house is only one room, with a ladder leading upstairs. My feet nudge silverware out of the way as I walk toward the skillet. I pick it up, flip it over, and run my fingers across the indented circle. This is the skillet my parents bought for Mary. I set it quietly on the stovetop and turn around. Thoughts swirl around my head as I try to figure out what happened.

What if they had a burglar? It's so remote out here that it would be easy to come and go quickly while John and Mary weren't home. My mind races wondering what I should do next. Should I run back along the path to Mrs. Carver? Should I stop at the Kelsey home and ask those boys if they saw anyone else come down the path today? What if the intruder is still here, lurking somewhere outside. I run to the door frame and stick my head out. I scan the edge of the forest, waiting to see a figure in the trees, but I don't see anyone. All I see are the tree limbs and leaves blowing in the wind. Besides the chickens, I am the only one here.

Then I hear a noise. It's a whimper coming from inside the house, and I spin around and scan the room again. Table, overturned chairs, oven, dry sink, pantry, nightstand, bed, ladder. I look at the dark square in the ceiling where the ladder leads up and shiver. What if the intruder is upstairs? But something shifts in the corner of my eye, so I whip my head back to the first floor. In the corner of the room at the foot of the bed, someone is crouching there in a tight ball.

12

Anna

Saturday, September 1, 1894
Pokegama, Minnesota
11:00 a.m. - 12:00 p.m.

"Mary!" I shout, running over to my sister. I can't believe my eyes. She is crouched down, hugging her elbows, and leaning her head against the wall. I bend down next to her and softly touch her shoulder. She flinches from the contact and squeezes her body into a tighter ball, so I retract my hand quickly, scared that I hurt her.

"What happened," I whisper. "Were you robbed?"

Mary blinks a couple of times and turns her head slightly toward my face.

"Anna?" she whispers softly.

"Yes, it's me," I answer and attempt to touch her again. This time I carefully place my hand over hers. She doesn't flinch, but she still doesn't move.

"Mary, please tell me what happened. Are you hurt?"

She pulls one arm out and wipes both of her eyes, "Anna, what are you doing here?"

"Mother sent me. She wants me to go with you to the school dedication ceremony."

Mary blinks a few times, staring at me, but says nothing.

134

At this very moment, I realize this is the first time that Mary has looked me in the eye since her wedding day. Her large, brown eyes are red and watery, and her hooded eyelids are swollen. She has been crying for some time. My heart aches to see her pain.

"Oh yes," she sniffles and wipes her nose. "The ceremony. I completely forgot. Help me up, I'll have to change and fix my hair. What time is it?"

She starts to unfold herself from the corner, and I help her up. She's only wearing a chemise and bloomers.

"Ahhh," she cries out in pain, grabbing the side of her body.

"What? What is it?"

She blows air out of her mouth, repeatedly. "My ribs, Anna, I think I bruised them."

"Please come to the table," I say, leading her to the kitchen table and picking up a chair that was tipped over on the floor before I gently guide her down.

She takes a few slow, deep breaths, focusing on each inhale and exhale. "There is a bottle of laudanum in the pantry behind the jars of jam. Please fetch it for me and a spoon as well."

I nod, heading toward the pantry. The dry sink and stand had been thrown to the floor in front of the pantry, so I have to tip it upright and nudge the broken sink pieces out of the way.

Just as she said, behind the jam jars is a square, glass bottle. The label on the front says, "laudanum" in large blue letters surrounded by a leaf border. I pick it up and start rummaging through the drawers, looking for a spoon. All the drawers are empty, so I scan the floor until I find one.

I bring the bottle and spoon back to the table, uncork it, and pour out the clear, liquid pain killer. I hand the spoon to Mary and set the glass bottle on the table between us. She swallows it quickly before slowly pouring herself another dose. When she is finished, I return the spoon and bottle back to the pantry.

I pick up another chair off the floor and set it right side up next to Mary.

"Please, Mary," I softly plead. "Tell me what happened."

Again, she doesn't answer me.

"Where's John?" I ask. "He needs to know that you've been

attacked."

Mary stares at me silently. Her hair has completely fallen out of her pompadour, so it looks haphazard and wild. Her face is red and puffy, and snot glistens above her upper lip. Mary never looks like this.

I grab both of her hands and squeeze them under the table, mirroring what she did to me at the Eating House, not even a week ago. "Please, Mary, please speak," I beg.

She licks her lip and then swallows. "I suppose I can't hide it from you anymore, Anna. No one robbed me. I had an argument with my husband. He lost his temper and made a little mess." Her voice cracks a little, so she clears her throat and tries again, "He is under a lot of pressure lately, and sometimes when he is angry, he throws the furniture around. I'm sorry that you have to see the house like this. I can pick it up in a few moments."

My breath catches in my throat, and all I can manage to say is, "But . . . why?"

"Business. Finances. Disappointment. As I understand it, he was never able to establish a business partnership with the Kelsey brothers, so now in a way he competes with their firm for real estate deals. Since the Kelsey firm owns almost all of the land in Pokegama, John is struggling. He hasn't brokered a sale here or in Hinckley since February, I believe, so money is tight."

My mind tries to make sense of the words coming from Mary. John made this mess. He doesn't work with the Kelsey brothers. The information washes over me, but I still feel confused. I scan the room again looking for something. All I see is chaos and destruction. I realize that I'm looking for someone else, a parent, an adult, someone who can take charge.

Mary squeezes my hand, "Really, it was my fault. I was nagging at him this morning, even though I know he is under a great deal of pressure. I will do better next time to hold my tongue."

I want to tell Mary something that will comfort her, but my tongue is numb, and my mouth is dry. I can't think of anything to say. This is all wrong. I was supposed to confront Mary about lying. I wanted to brag about the dancing party and having two boys walk me home. Mary was supposed to give me advice about Karl.

Mary smiles, and her face lightens, despite the wet tracks on her cheeks from crying, "Come on, now. Today will be fun. Help me get dressed, and we'll fix our hair together. It looks like yours needs some attention. I told my neighbor Lucy that I would meet her at her house before heading to the ceremony, so we must hurry." She stands up from the table, pulling me along with her.

Still unable to form words of comfort, I pull her towards me, giving her a tight hug. Instantly, she hisses in pain. I jerk back, "I'm so sorry. I forgot about your ribs."

She squeezes my arm and says, "Not to worry. I'm fine. Wait here, I'll go get clothes from upstairs and be back in a minute." She turns around and slowly climbs up the ladder to the second floor.

I look around the room again, and a chill crawls up my spine making me rub my arms for warmth. Feeling uneasy with the scene, I attempt to restore a sense of order. I pick up silverware off the floor and set it inside a drawer. My hands move on their own without much thought, picking up spoons and forks. My legs feel heavy, and each step is a struggle. The ladder creaks as Mary sets her weight on it, coming back down to the main level. She walks towards me holding a white blouse and black skirt.

"I have a matching jacket, but with this terrific heat, I'm not sure if I can wear it," She sets the blouse and skirt on the table. "Can you help me into this blouse? My ribs are still a little sore, so I can't reach over my head."

"Sure," I agree, taking one step towards Mary, but then I stop suddenly and jerk back.

Her smile turns upside down from my reaction, "Anna? What's wrong?"

Her ribs. My mind has finally caught up, and the discovery hits me like a train.

I swallow the lump of nerves in my throat and speak barely above a whisper, "Your ribs, Mary. Did John hurt you?"

She flinches, and the color instantly drains from her face which is all the confirmation I need. We stand for a moment staring at each other. She's struggling to tell me the truth, and I know why. She knows if she answers my question, she can't take it back. She won't be able to hide that her life is far from perfect. Guilt burns in my gut because I feel ashamed that my sister's first instinct is to hide this from me, to ignore it and continue on with our day.

She surprises me by saying, "Yes." The word escapes her mouth in a rush of air and emotion which opens the floodgates. Her bottom lip trembles, and she begins to cry, "I think John may have broken my ribs."

Her sobs come fast and hard, overpowering her posture. I run to her to keep her standing up, but her body trembles against mine, so I wrap my arms around her, dropping the silverware. They hit the pine wood floor with loud clangs. She sobs on my shoulder, and I let her. I hold her and rub her back and don't stop until she does, but even as she becomes quiet, she doesn't pull away. So we stay in this position, and I slowly start to rock back and forth on my heels. Finally, she lifts her head up and looks down at my face. I put my hand on her cheek and wipe away the last of her tears. "Oh, Anna," she whispers, "I'm so scared. It's worse every time. I think he's going to kill me."

I frown, still so confused, "I don't understand."

She shakes her head and pulls on my hand, lowering us down to sit at the table. She places her hands on top of the table and takes a deep, shaky, breath. "John has been hitting me since Independence Day. We celebrated the holiday separately. I was at the community picnic, but I'm not sure where John was. That night he came home very late and very drunk, so I confronted him. I told him his behavior was inappropriate and how embarrassed I was to be alone at the picnic. He hit me in the face, pretty hard."

I gasp, covering my mouth.

"I lost consciousness, but when I woke up, I was in our bed next to John. At first, I thought it was a dream, but the pain and the bruise were proof enough of what had happened. We both ignored it for a while. Then a few days later, he apologized and said it would never happen again. But it did. Not even a week later. Sometimes it's just a quick slap, but other times . . . " she chokes on the words, "Well, you see." She waves her hand towards the room, indicating the mess.

After a few moments, I somehow manage to find my voice, "Mary, I'm so sorry. I had no idea. I . . . I just never expected this. John is so polite and kind."

"Oh, no, of course not. He's charming in public. That's why I fell so hard for him last winter." She fidgets with the blouse sitting on the table and adds, "I was a fool. I thought I understood men from the few dates I had with some local boys, but I was so naive."

"What do you mean?"

She wipes a new tear falling from her eye, "Anna, didn't you ever wonder why we married so quickly? My God, we were engaged for only a month."

My mind is blank. I don't remember anything strange about their engagement. Tears quietly fall down Mary's face, and she makes no attempt to wipe them away, "I was pregnant."

My eyes widen in shock, and my heartbeat quickens.

"We threw together a quick marriage in order to make the child legitimate. Thankfully, I hadn't started showing yet, so it never became town gossip but—"

"Pregnant," I blurt out. "But . . . Mary, I don't understand . . . how could . . . I mean . . . "

"It doesn't matter anymore. As you can very well see, I am no longer pregnant, and there is no baby in our house."

My eyes dart to her very small waist, then back to her eyes. She turns away from me and gazes out the front door which is still wide open, "I lost the baby. Only two weeks after the wedding as a matter of fact."

Time stops as her words echo in my head. This is too much. The room spins, and I have to close my eyes. Pain erupts on my hands, and I realize that I've been squeezing them together under the table. There are red marks on my skin from where my fingernails have dug into my palm. I can't hold back any longer. Large tears form in my eyes and fall down my cheeks in streams. I try to suppress a whimper, but it comes out. "Oh, Anna," Mary cries. She leans over and holds me as I start sobbing. I shouldn't behave like this in front of her; in fact, I should be comforting Mary, but I can't control it. I just keep sobbing into my sister's chest.

"Mary . . . I'm so sorry . . . I didn't know," I cry in between sobs.

"Shh," she brushes my hair back and says, "I should have told you the truth, right at the beginning. I kept it a secret from you because I was ashamed." My heart aches for my sister. I shake my head side to side against her as she continues, "I'm ashamed of my behavior this year, but I thought we made it right when we got married . . . apparently not."

I lift my head up, "Mary, you can't blame yourself for losing the . . . baby. That wasn't in your control."

"No, I suppose not," she leans back into her chair. "Those things do happen, but . . . " her lip trembles, "I never imagined he would become so violent."

That was never a possibility in my imagination either. Mary and John were supposed to be happily married, financially stable, and leaders in their community. It's difficult to break that image and accept the reality of what Mary is telling me, but the destruction in the room and the pain on Mary's face is proof.

"What should I do?" she whispers.

My heart wants to tell her to leave right now, at this very moment, but a voice in my head disagrees with that advice, warning that it would be a sin. My heart and my head fight against each other inside me, but eventually my heart wins. "Come back home. Mother and Father won't let him hurt you anymore. I won't, either."

Mary wipes the tears away from her swollen eyes, "Leave my husband? No, I can't go back home, Anna. What would people say?"

"Your safety comes first. Father will talk to John and sort this out."

Mary doesn't look convinced, "I don't know, Anna."

"Please, Mary. Our room has been so empty this summer without you," I smile, hopeful that she will come home with me. "Sleep next to me again. I have so much to tell you. This past week has been outrageous, and I need my big sister's advice."

Her lips turn upward, almost to a smile, "Outrageous? What sort of trouble have you gotten into, Anna?"

I take a deep breath and dive in, "Well, Belle hosted a dancing party last night. Mother let me wear one of her shell side combs, and she curled my bangs."

"Did she burn your forehead?" Mary asks.

"No. She was very careful. Anyway, after the party Edwin asked to walk me home. He had also asked Belle, days before, if I was going to attend, and told her that he wouldn't bother coming if I wasn't there. That's strange because our group of friends has been the same all summer, so why would he specifically ask if I was going?"

"Maybe he likes you more than a friend, Anna."

"Oh, he does. He practically said so while we walked through town."

Mary props her elbow on the table and rests her chin on her hand, "Do you like him as well?"

"No, I don't. I mean, I can't. I'm trying to convince everyone that Karl likes me and intends to court me."

"What," Mary sits straight up in her chair, now at full attention. "Why would you try to convince people of that?"

"I had to do something. You told everyone at lunch that he kissed me."

Mary's eyes widen and she grabs my hand saying, "I'm so sorry about that, Anna, but that man put me on the spot. It was the first idea that came to my mind. I couldn't have John know that Karl kissed me. He would have been very angry."

Goosebumps rise on my skin at what Mary is implying. She didn't lie to protect her reputation. She had to lie so John would not retaliate against her. She was scared for her safety and what he would have done to her if he had found out Karl kissed her. That's why she said it was me.

Mary asks, "Does Karl know?"

"Yes, he knows. He agreed to say it was me that he kissed. We are both telling people that he has had his eye on me for some time. It makes it more believable that he kissed me and not you."

She looks stunned, "Why go through all the trouble?"

"For you," I answer. "We are lying to protect you, Mary. I don't want people in town knowing that Karl kissed you, a married woman."

"You're lying for me?" she squeezes my hand.

"Yes, of course. But last night, Karl walked me home, too."

"Karl and Edwin?"

"Yes, and and when he brought me to our front steps—"

"I knew it!" A voice interrupts my story. We both jump in our seats, and Mary lets out a shriek. A large hand is on the front door, fingers splayed out against the wood. I follow the arm up and see it's John standing in the entryway, glaring at us. His face is flushed red with anger, his nostrils are flaring open with each inhale, and a vein in his forehead pulsates as he screams, "I knew you kissed that boy!"

Mary stands up fast, knocking back her chair, "John, please, let me explain," she cries, holding up both her hands defensively in front of her face.

The "gentleman" that I saw last Sunday is nowhere to be seen. This John looks like a monster. "You," he spits at my sister. "You tramp, you whore!"

Terrified, I cover my mouth with both of my hands, stifling a scream. Mary stands in front of me, "Let's go outside and talk."

He lunges at her, arms out in front of him. Mary flings up her elbow defensively, trying to block him, but he shoves her arm away with one hand and grabs her neck with the other. He moves like a train, fast and powerful, pushing Mary through the chaotic mess of the room. Her back hits the far wall with a loud thud. She makes an awful, guttural sound of pain, but it is choked back by her blocked airway.

He lifts her off her feet, and she grabs onto his wrists, kicking her feet wildly. The image of Ivar holding Edwin up in the street last night leaps to the forefront of my mind, except John is holding Mary by her throat, not by her shirt. She is trying to breathe, but only a rough, choking sound escapes her throat. Her eyes bulge and roll backwards.

My body moves before I have time to think. I step up from the chair to the top of the table and leap onto John's back. My arm reaches around his neck, just like Karl did to Ivar, and I pull back with all my strength, but it's not enough. Mary's hands drop from John's wrists, and her body goes limp.

She's going to die. One command screams inside my head: *Stop him. Stop him. STOP HIM!* I wrap my legs around his waist and squeeze hard enough to hold my body upright. A strength I didn't know I possessed surges through my fists, and I swing them wildly. They punch him over and over, wherever I can make contact. I hit him on his chest, in his face, on the side of his head and his neck.

Suddenly, Mary drops to the floor, and John takes a step back, then another. My fingers find his eye sockets, and they dig in. He screams in pain, falling backwards. We crash into a wall, my back hitting it first, and the impact takes my breath away. I panic from the sudden shortage of air, and I let go of John's face and untangle my legs from his waist. My body crumples to the floor, and I roll over to my side, trying to breathe.

A hand grabs my hair and pulls me up. The intense pain on my scalp burns as I take my first gulp of air after hitting the wall. John is pulling me up by my hair, and my hands instinctively grasp onto his hand. He pushes my head against the wall and grabs my chin with his other hand. He is panting, and his breath smells like bitter coffee. He is holding my head so close to his face, I can see up his nose. There are so many black, bristly hairs.

I've never been restrained like this, and I've never been this close to a grown man. It's so disturbing, I feel my stomach roil like I'm about to throw up. As if reading my thoughts, John leans in closer, pushing his nose into my cheek. His mustache scratches my lips as he whispers, "You're just like her, aren't you?"

I sob, a terrified, gurgling, panicked sob. I'm trapped, and I know it. I wiggle, trying to break free, but his grip on my chin tightens as his other hand yanks hard on my hair. The pain silences my sobs, but the tears keep falling down my face. Mary's voice suddenly cries out, sharp and desperate, followed by the dull thud of her fists as she punches him in the back. She's screaming at him to stop, her voice raw and filled with anguish.

He finally lets go of me to turn around and shove Mary back hard. She falls to the ground, knocking over a chair. I start to run away, but he yanks me back by my hair. The shooting pain on my scalp has me seeing stars, and I scream.

"Enough! Both of you!" He shouts, grabbing me by the neck. His large hand covers my throat easily. I feel pressure from the large pad of his thumb and fingers before his whole hand squeezes down on my airway. My throat muscles tighten and push back which makes the pain intensify. More pressure than I could have ever imagined weighs down on my throat, and I twitch, trying to find air. I think my eyes are still open, but I see nothing. Panic rushes through my body like hooves beating on the ground in a hard gallop. The pressure on my throat overpowers it, though, and the hooves stop suddenly. A calm slowly falls over my muscles, and they relax. The lack of air is so overwhelming, I give up fighting. I give up thinking. I give up breathing. All there is now is pressure, pain, and darkness.

13

Anna

Saturday, September 1, 1894
Pokegama, Minnesota
12:00 p.m. - 1:30 p.m.

Father had told us there was probably a weasel attacking our chickens. He was right. Mary and I just didn't expect to find it in the hen house that morning. "Weasels can be vicious creatures," he told us. "They can eat a chicken whole, or simply suck all the blood from its body, leaving behind the empty carcass."

When Mary and I came here to collect eggs, she could tell immediately that something was wrong. Blood and feathers covered the floor, mixed with dirt and chicken poop. A few stray feathers floated in the air, mimicking a light snowfall. Once I stepped inside, she shot out her arm to shield me and pushed me back behind her. I was angry because her elbow bumped into my hand which was inside my mouth, as I was sucking my thumb. My thumbnail hit the roof of my mouth, and I was just about to yell at her, when something growled.

I swung my head around my sister and caught a glimpse of the weasel against the far wall of the hen house, half of a chicken's body hanging from its mouth. The weasel's eyes grew wide, and it dropped the corpse. It curled its lips back and snarled, showing us its needle-sharp teeth. It understood that the only way out was through the door Mary and I had just come through. It was ready to fight to survive.

Fear overtook me, and I opened my mouth to let out a scream for my mother,

144

but the sound of the shovel hitting the weasel's skull stopped me. Mary had moved so fast that I didn't realize what had happened until the weasel was lying on the floor. Its skull was crushed and unrecognizable, a mangled mess of blood, bone and fur. A chicken feather floated down, sashaying back and forth through the air until it landed on the wet, bloody mass of what was once the weasel's head.

Crack! Iron hits bone and crushes it. The impact is so intense, it vibrates through my teeth. I can feel his skull fracture and splinter before I fall. The impact with the floor jolts me awake, and my eyes snap open. I'm not outside, and I'm not at home. There is no weasel and no dead chickens. I cough a few times and rub my throat. I'm lying on the floor against a wall inside a house that is unfamiliar. I turn my head to the side and see large shoes. They are a man's shoes. They are John's shoes, and he's wearing them, lying on the floor, but not moving.

I bolt up quickly, panic setting in as the memory of John attacking Mary and me floods back. The sudden movement is too fast, and my head is overwhelmed with pressure and pain. I hold the back of my head, and my throat. Both are throbbing. I cough again, trying to clear my throat, but the air seems to burn as I inhale and exhale. After a few more breaths, I scan the room. John is lying face down on the floor in front of me. I stare at his motionless body. Mary must have stopped him from choking me. I look up and see her standing over him. Her face is as white as a bedsheet, and she's staring at John. Her hair has completely fallen out of its pins and cascades down her back and bare shoulders. Her chest rises and falls with each breath, and she's holding a large, black cast iron skillet.

I clear my throat, which is painful, but I manage to croak, "Mary, what happened?"

Mary blinks a few times, still staring at John.

"Mary?" I repeat.

She snaps out of her trance and quickly walks over, kneeling down next to me and holding my face gently with one hand. She gingerly touches my throat with her fingertips.

"I stopped him," she says.

"My throat," I whisper.

"It might bruise a bit, but that will fade," she tells me and touches her own throat. It's red and blotchy. I wonder if mine looks the same.

"How did you stop him?" I ask.

Mary doesn't say anything, but I hear the clank of the skillet as she sets it on the floor. I stare down at it, realizing it's the same skillet I set on the stovetop when I first walked into Mary's home. When was that? It feels like it was so long ago.

"Mary? Did you—"

She interrupts me, "I stopped him, Anna."

I look into her eyes, but she stands up and walks away, leaving the skillet on the floor between me and John's feet. She folds her arms across her chest and stares out the front door. My eyes travel down to the skillet absorbing its black surface, the curved lines, and the grease from the last cooked meal. I reach out and trace the rim with my finger until I touch something wet. I turn my fingertip towards my face and see the blood. A few hairs are stuck in the blood, John's hair.

I look at John's head and finally see. The back of his head is dented. It's not crushed like the weasel's was so many years ago. There's not a mangled mess of brains and skull, but it's definitely not the correct shape for a head. Mary hit John with this skillet, and his blood and hair are on my finger. Bile rises in my throat. Shooting up from the floor I fly through the room, tripping over a chair and falling to my knees. I get up again and run out of the house; I never want to enter it again. The air outside is a wall of heat. It hits me hard as I escape that house of horrors, but I run through it to the well and yank open the pine board cover with my clean hand. I try to pull up the bucket with one hand, but it keeps falling back down the well. I let out a scream of frustration, and hold my blood-stained finger as far away from my body as possible.

Suddenly, my stomach twists in warning, and I buckle grasping the edge of the stone wall. It twists again, stronger this time, and I fold over into the grass, bracing my hands on my knees as my stomach empties itself. Breakfast burns coming back up my throat, and my eyes squeeze shut. Sweat rolls down my face, along my nose and drips off the tip, mixing with the contents of my stomach that has spilled onto the dry grass.

Saliva drips from my mouth, but I can't wipe it away. After a few moments of breathing, Mary is standing next to me at the well. She quietly pulls up a bucket of water and sets it on the ground next to me. I plunge my face into the bucket and drink. *That's not ladylike.* My mother's voice echoes in my head. I whip my face out of the bucket and use my hands to pull back my wet hair.

"Let me see your finger," Mary requests.

I forgot about John's blood on my finger and look at my hand. It's mostly gone. I must have smeared it on my skirt when I threw up. Mary gently holds my hand, then bends down to cup some water into her other hand and rinses my finger. She rubs the last of the blood off. She doesn't let go of my hand; instead, she leads me around the well to the side facing the forest. She gently pulls me down, and we sit, still holding hands. Minutes pass, but neither of us says a word. I'm too exhausted to speak or even think, so I lean my head against the well and close my eyes. The wind hits my face, and I hear the chickens cluck and peck at the ground behind us. Images of John choking my sister come uninvited to my mind, so I open my eyes, looking upward. For the first time I notice that the sky is alarming. There is a blanket of crimson and black clouds hanging low to the tree line. They look menacing and evil, like a painting from biblical times. The sun hides behind the dark clouds, casting an eerie darkness on us. The hair on my arms stands up, and a chill races down my neck.

"He's not dead," Mary says.

"What?"

"He's still breathing," she answers. "I checked after you ran out of the house. He's alive."

"Oh, I thought you killed him."

"I did too," she lets go of my hand and rubs her eyes. "This complicates things."

"What do you mean?" I frown, not following. "Isn't this a good thing?"

She bends her knees up and rests her chin on them, "I didn't kill him but, I severely injured him. I imagine his brain is bleeding." She says the words without any emotion.

"How do we save him?" I turn my head and look around the tree stumps in their yard, trying to find a wagon or a sleigh that we could carry him in. "Is there a doctor in Pokegama?"

"Dr. Kelsey."

"That's right, Dr. Kelsey."

"Anna. Stop and think for a moment. What will happen after we bring John to Dr. Kelsey?" She pauses, waiting for me to answer, but I can only frown in confusion. She stares intently at me and continues, "I will be arrested. If not for murder, then for sure manslaughter."

"Arrested?" I gape at her.

"Yes, I believe so."

I stand up and point towards the house and say, "That was self-defense, Mary. He tried to kill us!"

She doesn't get up. She just shakes her head and looks down at the ground, "I suppose, they'll take me to the jail in Hinckley since we don't have one yet."

"I won't let you go to jail for saving my life."

"If we bring John to Dr. Kelsey, that decision won't be up to you." She's right. The minute someone else gets involved, Mary will be at the mercy of the law.

"But . . . John, he . . . " I stammer.

Mary hangs her head between her knees and whispers, "But, if we leave him . . . "

My skin prickles. She's considering that we still go to the school dedication ceremony. "Mary, if we leave him, he'll die."

She keeps her head down but still answers, "It would be easier to hide a dead body than explain an injured one."

I gasp and cover my mouth, taking a step backward. She finally looks up at me, "Anna, I'm just considering all our options right now. There is not a clear answer for this. If we try to save his life, I will be arrested, and I don't know what will happen next. If we leave him, he'll die, but we might have more control over the situation."

My head spins and I think I'm going to get sick again, but Mary's voice interrupts me, "Either way, we need to move him out of the house." She slowly stands up and brushes the dried grass off her bloomers.

A strong gust of wind blows up my skirt, and I push it down with my hands. Mary's hair whips wildly around her head, obscuring her face. "Follow me!" she shouts over the wind. I trail behind her to the back of the house where a small cart is parked next to an ax and a chopping block. The cart is full of chopped wood. She picks up a log in the cart and throws it on the ground. I copy her, and we slowly empty the cart, log by log. All the while, the wind is howling at us, blowing my skirt and Mary's hair. At one point she leaves me, going around the corner of the house without a word. She arrives a few minutes later holding the blouse and skirt that were on the table. Her hair is swept to one side and woven into a long braid that cascades over her shoulder.

She calls out against the wind, "Can you help me?" Carefully I slip her arms into the sleeves, but it is difficult buttoning it since the wind takes the fabric faster than my fingers can work. It doesn't help that my hands are shaking too.

After she puts on her skirt, we finish emptying the cart and then each hold onto the shaft and pull it around to the front of the house. Panting, we set it down between the two piles of wood in front of the door which is still wide open. Another fierce gust of wind blows by us, bringing dust, leaves, and chicken feathers into the house.

Mary walks inside without pause, but I make it to the door frame and then hesitate when I see John on the floor. I can't help but stare at the dent in the back of his head. Mary did that. "Anna," my sister calls from inside. I hear the table legs being dragged across the floor as she clears a path for us, but I can't look away. I touch my throat and remember what it felt like to be choked. A trickle of doubt breaks my earlier conviction that we should save him. I don't know if he deserves a second chance. Even though I told Mary that we should try to save his life, I'm terrified to go near him, near the monster.

Mary walks over and stands in front of me, blocking my view of John's head, "Grab his feet, and I'll hold his shoulders." Her instructions are firm and confident and snap me out of my deliberations. I cross over the threshold and stand by my sister's side.

14

Karl

Saturday, September 1, 1894
Hinckley, Minnesota
1:30 p.m. - 2:15 p.m.

Kristoff and I spend an hour hauling barrels full of water to the Snake River Road. It is a nice break from stacking lumber in the yard, but the second task of fire prevention is grueling. On the last load of barrels, we also bring shovels to expand the firebreak in the ditch on the west side of the road. The old logging road will act as a natural firebreak, but this extra effort will ensure the bog fire can't advance towards the mill. We stick our shovels into the dried grass, a perfect source of fuel for the fire, and turn it over to reveal the dirt underneath. We turn over the entire ditch, shoveling dirt on top of anything that could catch fire. If the flames even reach this far, there will be nothing to burn once it reaches the firebreak.

The air on this side of the mill is noticeably smokier, and breathing is hard while we dig. The pungent smell of smoke and ash fill my nostrils with each inhale. Tiny cinders fall from the sky onto our heads and backs, remnants of the bog burning nearby. That must be where the wall of heat is coming from. Kristoff and I have sweated through our shirts, and look as if we just climbed out of one of the water barrels lining the road.

When we finish, we ride in the back of the wagon to the lumberyard just in time for the noon lunch break. We choose a spot to sit along the sawmill. The other men who helped us at Snake River Road join Kristoff and me as we lean against the building in the only sliver of shade to be found. Facing the south side of the yard, we can clearly see a column of smoke billowing up to the sky. There must be another fire south of Hinckley, perhaps near Mission Creek. I feel sorry for the farmers in that area since it is time to cut the last hay crop. If their hay burns this time of year, animal bedding will be stretched thin.

As I eat my lunch, I scan the yard to catch sight of Ivar, but I don't see him anywhere. When the mill whistle sounds off, we end our lunch break and walk back to the yard. As we walk, a foreman comes running up to us. He seems alarmed and speaks to one of the men and points behind him towards the southern horizon. The man he is talking to nods and turns to us as the foreman runs up to the sawmill.

"Looks like we are not going back to stacking lumber or sawing logs today," the man informs us. "The rest of our shift will prepare and protect the sawmill in case the fire south of Hinckley reaches us." He points over his shoulder to the looming, black column of smoke.

Our lumberyard and sawmill have the most thorough system of waterworks in the county. There are water mains and hydrants throughout the yard, and the hose has recently been pressure-tested. The sawmill has several hogsheads of water along the roof that can be tipped over to put out fires inside the building. I'm not concerned that anything here will burn, but I wonder how well the rest of the town is protected.

Kristoff whispers to me, "We have an entire year's supply of cut lumber sitting in the yard."

"I wouldn't worry too much," I reassure him. "The foreman is being overly cautious."

The man who spoke with the foreman assigns our group of men to various tasks. Some will stay in the yard and use shovels or buckets of water to snuff out any falling cinders that blow here from the fire. Others will continue filling water barrels from the millpond and use wagons to place them around the yard and sawmill. He points to Kristoff and me and directs us to follow him to the stables. Our task is to plow the ground around the yard, extending the firebreaks which will form a perimeter of dirt.

I see Father and Mr. Andersson hooking up a team of two horses to a sulky plow, a horse-drawn, single-bottom riding plow. Kristoff and I walk over to them. Father acknowledges me with a smile, but then pulls Kristoff aside, leading him to a different team of horses. He's left me to work with Anna's father. A ball of nerves forms in my stomach since I assume he will bring up the kiss, but after he greets me, we only discuss the task at hand. We hitch the horses to the sulky plow, and then lead them to the south side of the mill yard.

We lead the horses in silence. He's on one side of the team, and I am on the other. Once we reach the southern border of the yard, Mr. Andersson sits in the plowman's seat to add more weight, and I lead the team of horses. Then we plow, working in the heat and the haze.

The smoke columns start to bend and drift over Hinckley, sending ashes down that cover the land with a light, gray dusting. The sky is slowly but surely changing too. The overcast clouds of midday have darkened from the black smoke now surrounding the town. The sun hides behind the smoke, so the day takes on a strange, ominous atmosphere. It feels like dusk. That time of day when the fading light tricks your eyes and muddles your vision.

It's unsettling. The horses are skittish and difficult to lead. I assume they are confused by the lack of sunlight too. They whinny and whimper as sweat runs down their large legs. I turn back to look at Mr. Andersson in the plowman's seat. I open my mouth to shout back to him, to tell him that the horses need a break when a hot gust of wind hits us hard, kicking up a wall of dust and smoke. I shield my eyes from the sting and place one hand on the horse nearest to me, attempting to calm him down. I grip the reins tighter, hoping it is enough to keep the team from bolting while Mr. Andersson is still on the plow.

He scrambles off the plowman's seat and runs to the other horse. Once the wind dies down he shouts to me, "Unhook them, Karl. We need to get them some water." We set the sulky plow in the dirt and lead the horses to the nearest water barrel. "There's no doubt in my mind that a fire is coming," Mr. Andersson says to me.

"Do you think it will get close to the mill? To town?" I ask, splashing a handful of water on my face.

"I'm not sure. It might. I'll stay as long as I can to save the mill, but if the fire line gets too close to town, I have to leave. Britta is in Hinckley today."

I nod, understanding that she is more important than the mill and a year's supply of cut lumber.

"Thankfully, Anna's not here," he adds. "She's in Pokegama with Mary."

I meet his eyes when he says Anna's name. I can't ignore the mention of Anna, so I'll have to talk to him here, next to a water barrel of all places. I clear my throat and say, "I've been meaning to speak to you about Anna. I had hoped to stop by this evening and talk with you and Mrs. Andersson . . . about courting Anna." I finish quickly in a rush of air. He doesn't respond right away and doesn't move. He just stares at me which makes me more nervous. "I apologize for kissing her the other day. That was inappropriate. I won't do that again."

He still doesn't move. Not even the muscles in his face. I try to mirror his expression, but it's hard when the thoughts racing through my head are anything but calm. Finally, he says, "Britta and I never had a son. We have two beautiful daughters that we love dearly. Our eldest married a stranger. I had my reservations about John, but Britta and Mary insisted it was a good match." He scratches his chin, scraping at the stubble. "Britta was upset when she found out you kissed Anna—how you did. I agree with her, that you and Anna shouldn't be stealing kisses behind our backs."

I want to defend myself, but instead I bite my tongue to hold back the truth. I look down at my shoes and the dirt as he continues, "But I wasn't upset. I know you have feelings for Anna. I've always known that. She has feelings for you too, but I think she's too young to understand them. I'd be honored if you courted Anna."

My head snaps up, and I look at him. He's smiling at me. "Karl, I've been your neighbor since you were this tall," he motions with his hand to just below his waist. "And I've watched you grow up into a man. I think you're a great match for my Anna. You are strong, loyal, determined. Everyone makes mistakes now and then. Just learn from it." He puts a hand on my shoulder and chuckles, "I was young once, too. As long as you learn something from this, all is forgiven."

"I have, sir. I won't do that again."

"It's not that we don't trust you. It's just how things work."

Mr. Andersson is a man of few words. This may be the most he's ever said to me in one conversation. Certainly, it is the first time he has shared his opinion of me so openly. I don't want to lie to him anymore, but I can't tell them the whole truth, not until I can confirm with Anna.

He turns away from me and back to the horses, signaling that we don't have to talk anymore, but I can't hold back, so it just comes out. "Ivar tried to kiss Anna."

"What?" he asks, turning back to face me. "I thought you kissed Anna."

"Yes, I did. I mean, last night, on the way home from the dancing party Ivar tried to kiss Anna."

He lifts his eyebrows, "Were you at the party?"

"No, but I wanted to walk Anna home. I'm sorry, I know I shouldn't have been with her alone, but I didn't want anyone else walking her home. Ivar was drunk. He stopped me in the street and started messing with Anna. He was going to kiss her, so I hit him."

His face shows clear concern. "Is Anna all right?"

"Yes, she's fine."

The muscles in his face relax, "Are you talking about Ivar Gunnolfsson?"

"Yes, sir. But don't worry, he didn't touch her."

"You hit him?"

"I did," I hang my head a little. "I doubt he'll let me be on his logging team this winter."

"Well, it sounds like he deserved it. Wait," Mr. Andersson shakes his head, "Did you say his logging team? Karl, Ivar doesn't choose who is hired or not. He was promoted to foreman, but the Company hires anyone who wants to be a shanty boy."

I stare at him in shock, but he only chuckles, "Did Ivar tell you that you can't be in the camps?"

"He . . . I thought . . ." I stammer in disbelief. "I can still be on a logging team this winter?"

"Only if you want to," he replies, still smiling.

"I do!" Joy radiates to my fingertips.

"It's hard work."

"I know, but I can take it," I'm grinning from ear to ear. "I'm going to save the money I make and buy my own land, build my own house.

Just like my father did for my mother. I don't want to court Anna, now," I add. "Someday when I have something to offer her, that's when I want to do it. I want to build her things and take her places she hasn't been before."

It's not a lie. I almost laugh out loud at the realization. I do want to court Anna. I want to take her fishing with me and show her how the sunrise reflects on the stillness of the lake. I want to ride the train with her to Duluth and see Lake Superior. I want to build her a house with a sewing room.

As if he's reading my thoughts, Mr. Andersson answers, "I think she'd like that."

My heart races with excitement, "Maybe today after we receive our pay envelopes, I can—"

Phweeeeeeeeeeeeeeeeee!!

The mill whistle blasts through the air, interrupting me. It's long and hard, not short like at the end of the lunch break.

Mr. Andersson's happy face changes to concern. "That's not normal. A firebreak must have fallen." We both scan the area around the southern border, but see no flames. He says, "It must be on the west side near the bog fire. I'll take the horses back to the stable. Run back and see how you can help." I nod and turn back toward the sawmill.

I have emotional whiplash from all the feelings I just experienced in one conversation. Pride from Mr. Andersson's praise, shock that I can still be a shanty boy, and excitement at the realization of my true feelings for Anna. But there is no time to think about them if a fire is really coming towards Hinckley. I sprint all the way back, pumping my arms to go faster. A few other men from other places in the yard run too. A general sense of alarm is noticeable. Another gust of hot wind hits me, pushing more ash and dust into my face. I wipe it off and keep running. A small crowd of men stand around a stack of lumber nearest to the entrance of the sawmill. A foreman is standing on top, speaking to a man on a horse next to the stack. I find Kristoff and my father standing together, so I part the group of men and stand next to them.

Now that I'm closer, I can see the man on the horse is Hinckley's Fire Chief John Craig. I've seen John around town, but I don't know him that well. He's twenty-three and lives on the east side in one of the new, painted frame houses. He nods to the foreman before galloping quickly out of the yard.

Our foreman yells out to the crowd, "Chief Craig says a fire is headed towards Hinckley and with this wind, firebrands are being thrown out ahead of it, creating spot fires. Already, two houses and a barn are on fire south of town, near the end of Main Street. Craig is headed there now with his crew of nineteen volunteer firefighters. He asked us to blow the whistle as a warning of general alarm."

"The south side of town, not the west?" I wonder out loud.

The foreman continues to address the crowd, "The mill managers told me to release you for the rest of your shift. Go help the firefighters stop the spread. We don't want the fire to reach the mill." He claps his hands together and yells enthusiastically, "Everyone grab a bucket and follow me."

He jumps off the stack of lumber onto a cart full of buckets and starts handing them out to the men. Jan and Nathaniel are among the first, hands outstretched for a bucket, when the foreman notices them. "You two! Where is Ivar?"

Jan answers, "We don't know. We've been putting out yard fires for the past two hours. We thought he was with you and the other foremen."

"Maybe he went home to nurse his nose," Nathaniel jokes.

The foreman shakes his head, handing Jan and Nathaniel their buckets and says "He better not be. This isn't a day off."

Kristoff and I smile at each other and grab our buckets. We fall in line with the other men, but I realize Father is not with us, so I search the lumberyard and see him talking to another foreman. I pull on Kristoff's arm to follow me, and we run over to him. By the time we reach Father, he is done speaking with the foreman who walks in the other direction.

"Father, are you coming with us?" I ask.

He shakes his head, "No, they want me to stay here with a few other men and watch the mill. We'll keep putting out the small fires caused by these falling embers. You and Kristoff go, hold the fire line, so we don't lose any more homes."

I don't like the thought of being separated from him. The concern must show on my face, because he grabs my shoulder and says, "It's all right, Karl. You'll be fine without me. Tonight at supper you can tell me how that brand new fire engine works. John Craig says it will generate enough pressure to spray a stream of water right onto a burning house."

"I'm not worried about myself, Father. I don't like the thought of you here, almost all alone."

"We'll be fine. Besides, there's a boy here that's assigned to blow the mill whistle if the sawmill is threatened. So as long as you don't hear that whistle, you will know I'm safe."

"All right," I concede. "What about home? Jack? And *Äpple*?"

He nods, "After we get settled here, I'll go home and pack a wagon. I can hitch Jack to the wagon and tie *Äpple* behind it. I'll bring them back here, and they can wait in the stable. If I have to, I'll ride them out of town."

I feel a little better knowing that Father will collect the things we need to survive, but I hope it doesn't come to that. "If the fire line breaks, I'll come back here to collect you. We'll ride northeast away from the fire."

Father shakes his head, "Karl, you have nothing to worry about."

I square my body to him, putting my hand on his shoulder and look him in the eyes, "*Lyssna, Pappa,*" I plead, "If the fire reaches here before me, get on Jack and run. Don't save the mill. The lumber is not worth your life. Promise me. *Lova mig.*"

He nods and smiles, "*Jag lovar.* I promise. Don't worry about me. Now go, both of you, they need you."

He embraces me and squeezes, this time; I hug him back. I want to tell him about my conversation with Mr. Andersson, but there's no time. Kristoff pulls on my sleeve, "Let's go. We don't want to be last."

I pick up my bucket and follow Kristoff to the crowd of men where each holds an ax, shovel, or bucket. It's an exodus of over two hundred millworkers spilling out of the lumberyard gates. On Main Street, we stop the usual Saturday traffic of carts, buggies, and people. Shopkeepers even come outside to stand on the sidewalk and watch. It is still early afternoon but their lanterns are lit as dark clouds and smoky haze have created an eerie blanket of darkness over Hinckley.

15

Anna

Saturday, September 1, 1894
Pokegama, Minnesota
2:15 p.m. - 2:30 p.m.

We both get into position. I kneel down and hold John's ankles firmly.
Mary hooks her arms under his armpits. His upper body moves with
her support like a puppet. Mary and I lock eyes before she says, "On
the count of three, Anna. One. Two. Three."

We both lift up, but I'm faster because Mary is lifting the majority
of his weight. She may move slower, but she doesn't hesitate. She
pushes me forward, so I back up toward the door. She trips over
something on the floor, then falls to one knee. John's shoulder slides
out of her grip and hits the floor with a thud.

"Mary," I scold, struggling to hold onto John's legs at waist level.

"You're not carrying any of his weight, Anna," she says. "Hold his
thighs, not his ankles."

"Absolutely not."

"Do you prefer to carry this end then?"

Her face is serious, so I set John's feet on the ground and shuffle
forward between his legs. I can't believe I'm doing this, but I kneel
down anyway and take a deep breath. I circle my hands around his
thighs as Mary gets into position again and looks at me.

158

"One. Two. Three."

We rise again. This time more balanced. John's legs bend at the knee and dangle freely. We move through the house and out the door. The sky seems darker, and the air is significantly hotter than when we entered the house. The chickens are huddled together near the cart, squawking madly. I have to kick one out of my way, so I don't trample it. Walking backward, my backside hits the edge of the cart, so I straighten John's legs, one at a time and set them down. I step out of Mary's way and away from John as fast as I can. Mary, still holding his shoulders, huffs, "The cart is too short. Bend his legs, so he fits."

I frown at her, frustrated that I have to touch her husband again, but I do as I'm told and fold John's legs, bending them at the knees. This is by far the strangest thing I've ever done. It feels almost like I'm watching myself from far away. If it weren't for Mary, I might still be sitting next to the well, crying hysterically.

Mary grunts as she slides John into the cart. His face is turned toward the side, and the back of his head is cradled by his shoulder. Thankfully, the head wound is hidden from my view. My stomach twists just thinking about it, and I grab myself wondering if I'll puke again. His eyes are closed, and his face is calm. He looks like he is sleeping. I wonder if he'll even remember that he attacked us. Mary puts her finger under his nose and is still. I assume she is checking his breathing, but the wind is so strong, she has to kneel down next to his face. Her cheek is right next to his, and I hold my breath, covering my mouth. I'm shocked that she is brave enough to be that close to him after what he did to us.

She shouts over the roar of the wind, "He's still breathing."

I nod and walk to the front of the cart, kneeling down and grabbing the shaft. Mary crouches down on the other side of the shaft but pauses. She holds my gaze, like she's going to say something to me, but the wind is so strong, it whips my hair into my face. I let go of the shaft and pull the pieces of hair back, re-pinning them. When I'm done, I grab the shaft once more and look at Mary. Small black spots dot her forehead and cheeks like small, black freckles.

"Mary!" I shout, "What's on your face?" Then I feel it too. The wind is blowing something onto my head. It feels like snowflakes. I wipe my own cheek and stare into my palm. It's smeared black. I look up at Mary and see alarm flash across her face. Her eyes are wide, and her hair and face are now covered with more black snowflakes. We both look up at the sky. The clouds are pitch black and hanging low over us like a heavy curtain. Mary bolts up quickly, turning on her heel, to look at the forest. She is scanning the trees looking for something.

Frightened by her sudden change in behavior, I stand next to her and grab her arm asking, "Mary, what is it?"

She doesn't answer me but points to the forest and down the evergreen path. The wind is whipping the leaves and scattering them frantically. Tree limbs sway wildly back and forth. It's so dark in the forest that I have to squint to see farther down the path. Finally, I notice what my sister is pointing at. There are dozens of rabbits, chipmunks, and squirrels running down the evergreen path towards us. When they reach the clearing, they dart every which way, running frantically.

I clutch my chest in astonishment. Some of the animals run toward us, and I fear they will run over my feet, but they hurry past us, not even frightened by the flock of chickens under the cart. Others run in wild patterns across the clearing, switching directions randomly on a whim, turning around and then, running back the way they came. It's unnerving to see them so disoriented.

Mary rips my hand off her arm and practically drags me back into the house. I tug at her and pry her fingers off, stopping in front of the doorway and refusing to go inside.

"Mary! What are you doing?" I shout.

"Fire!" She whips her head back to look at me, "Anna, it's a fire!"

I quickly turn around and look to the horizon, but it's impossible with so many trees. I peer up into the sky but see no flames, only the dark black clouds. Then I realize they are not clouds at all. They are massive columns of smoke. The wind blows more black snowflakes onto my face, and I wipe at them again and look down at my palm. It's not snow; it's cinders blown from the fire up into the sky to rain down on us. It is a warning that, indeed, the forest is burning.

My heartbeat races, and I panic. "It's a fire . . . a fire," I stammer to myself. "Oh, Jesus, a fire is coming! What . . . what do we do? Where should we go?" I pull on my hair trying to sort through my dread. "This can't be happening. Not now."

I run into the house looking for somewhere to hide. I pace around the room, talking to myself, not quite sure what Mary is doing. Sobs escape my body, tears streaming down my face. "I want Mother and Father. I'll never see them again. I'll never see Belle or Karl, or anyone else again."

"Anna!" Mary appears in front of me, shouting my name. My face and scalp are burning with pain, and I realize I've been scratching at my cheeks and pulling my hair as I've been pacing. She holds my wrists and pulls them down from the top of my head.

"Anna!" she has to shout over the roaring wind outside. "Strip the bed! Now!" Her eyes are piercing, and her voice is firm. Her rational behavior calms me, and I follow her directions without hesitation. My mind is numb as my hands work to take off the quilt first and then the sheets on Mary and John's bed. I throw them into a ball on the floor and wait. Mary is rushing through the house, throwing things into a carpetbag set on the table. I stand next to the bed and cry silently, doing everything in my power not to look out the front door. The roaring wind crashes against the walls of the house, and it shakes. I cry harder, unable to hold back my fear.

Mary quietly picks up the quilt and thrusts it into my arms before she bends down again and picks up the ball of sheets. She nudges me towards the door. When I hesitate, she pushes. I choke back a sob and walk through the house and out the front door. The instant I'm outside, I stop in my tracks because I've stepped into an oven. The air is unbearably hot against my face. My eyes sting, and I close them immediately, shoving my face into the quilt to escape the heat.

"Mary!" I yell, but no one answers. I try again, but I can barely hear my own voice over the roar. I lift my head off the quilt and squint. Everything has disappeared behind a black wall of smoke. As I breathe it in my lungs, I choke and gag. The heat and taste is overpowering. I stumble around, fighting to keep my eyes open because the air is so hot that it stings my eyeballs. I hold the quilt over my mouth and cheeks to help me breathe, and as a shield against the heat. I take small steps in the darkness until my hip bumps into something hard, and I look down to see the side of the cart. John is still lying in the same position as when we left him. I drop the quilt and hook my arms under his head and shoulders. As I brace myself to bear his weight, a hand suddenly grabs my arm, its force startling me.

"Stop!" Mary shouts into my ear. She pulls back hard on my

shoulders, and I release John from my grip, falling back into my sister. Still clinging to my arm, she bends down to snatch up the quilt before yanking me away from the cart. I think she's going to pull my arm out of my socket.

I struggle against her and shout, "We can't leave John!"

She pulls on my arm even harder, and we crash into a tree stump. I fall onto my back and choke on the smoky air filling my lungs. As I lay on the ground, the black curtain opens for a moment, and I see a sliver of the forest again. Except now, the trees are all on fire as long, fiery tongues lick, bite, and burn.

Madame Catrina's voice echoes in my head: "*Beware the Red Demon.*"

I don't struggle when Mary begins pulling on my arm again. She helps me up, and I run with her as fast as I possibly can. We run through the smoke as the roar of the Red Demon behind us grows louder. Abruptly Mary stops in front of the well. The pine cover is leaning against the side wall, and the top of a ladder is set against the inside wall. She must have taken the one from inside the house.

I clutch the ladder with both hands, and hoist myself up and over the side of the wall placing my feet on the nearest rung. Fear propels me down, but my feet stumble on the carpetbag which Mary must have shoved in between two rungs. I lose my balance and crash into the water below. It's so cold that it shocks my skin which was burning from heat only seconds before. I stand up in four feet of water, gasping for air. The bedsheets are floating on top of the water next to me. I look up in time to see the quilt falling down the well and reach my hands up to catch it. I shove it aside in the water and wait for my sister.

From the depths of the well, the world above is a circle of black. Small, bright sparks shoot and swirl around like red-orange fireflies. Then a flickering glow at the edge of the opening casts shadows on the stone walls. They dance wildly, growing more frantic as the flames draw nearer. The air becomes thick with the acrid scent of smoke, and suddenly the light intensifies, casting an eerie orange-red hue on the stones, making the confined space seem even more claustrophobic.

"Mary!" I scream but hear nothing. My voice is useless against the roar. I force another scream from my body, pushing it through my throat, feeling the vibrations. Still the scream is soundless. My ears hear only the all-consuming roar of the fire.

Then a different kind of darkness occurs as Mary appears on the ladder, pulling the pine cover across the top of the well. Since the ladder is taller than the well, she can't completely close the opening. She is careful coming down the ladder and does not trip over the carpetbag. Once she's in the water, I grab her and pull her towards me. We both look up towards the opening which is now a small crescent. The roar of the fire peaks, ringing in my ears and overwhelming any other senses. Without warning the crescent above us shines brilliantly, and we both shield our eyes from the heat and the light. The fire is here. I hear the monster above, the Red Demon.

16

Karl

Saturday, September 1, 1894
Hinckley, Minnesota
2:30 p.m. - 3:50 p.m.

Under different circumstances, the sight in front of me would have ignited my curiosity and wonderment for steam-powered engines, but the backdrop of flames, black smoke, and men shouting, limits my excitement. The new fire engine's brass-plated boiler and stack reflects the bright flames as large clouds of steam shoot up into the black sky. Two men hold onto the reins and struggle to keep the horses from jostling the chassis. Another man in the back of the fire engine is using a shovel to push coals under the boiler and feed kindling to keep it going. Four nozzlemen hold the hose which is pumping water from the fire engine onto the burning house. I recognize three of them, Axel Rosdahl, Horace Gorton, and William Merrigan.

From atop his horse, Chief Craig is shouting orders at groups of men from the mill. He points to a group of men including Kristoff and me, "Use those buckets to get water from a nearby well and put out that hen house!" he shouts. The urgency in his voice breaks the spell I am under from watching the fire engine. I swivel my head left and right looking for a well. We are standing on the crossroads of Main Street and Fifth Street, so there are plenty of houses and wells to choose from. I grab Kristoff's arm, and we run to the nearest one. We work fast to pull up the rope, fill our buckets, and race back to the flames. I stop abruptly when my face hits a wall of super-heated air. The hen house is only a couple of yards away from me, so I toss the water onto the flames, then turn around and shield my face from the heat.

I stumble back, blinking away the heat from my eyes. It stings something awful. As my eyes recover and adjust, I notice groups of men spread throughout the street and buildings. Some are using shovels to create fire breaks, but most are using their buckets to put out the flames on several houses. A man wearing a black cassock and white stole runs past me with a bucket of water. He's the Catholic priest, but my mind goes blank as I try to remember his name. Kristoff grabs my arm and tugs me back toward the well. We fill our buckets again and again. Before I know it, an hour has passed like this. An hour of filling and tossing buckets of water, first on the hen house, then on a home right next to it. The strong winds keep throwing burning embers from one building to another, creating more fires.

The nozzlemen have already pulled the entire two thousand feet of hose from the fire engine cart. It is stretched to capacity, snaking through the street and buildings. Chief Craig appears next to me on his horse, shouting at the man who is keeping the fire lit under the boiler. "We need more hose. I'm sending a telegram to Rush City." I watch him ride off, disappearing into a cloud of smoke before following Kristoff back to the well. We fill our buckets, race back to the house, and throw more water onto the flames.

Most of the water is swept up in the wind and splashes back on my face. This time when we run back to the well, the air doesn't cool off even though we are far from the fire. I have to cover my mouth and nostrils because the air hurts to breathe. This sets off an alarm in my head. My body immediately feels the need to run, to get away from the dangerous heat. I throw my bucket down on the ground and yell at Kristoff, "We need to leave!" He doesn't hear me above the roar of the fire and the chugging of the steam engine parts. He's standing still, looking behind me.

"Kristoff!" I yell again.

He grabs my shoulder and turns me around yelling, "Karl! Look!" He shoves a finger out towards the horizon.

A massive, black column of smoke shoots up into the sky. The black mass reaches hundreds of feet above the treetops, and it is moving, pumping out smoke and embers in circles and waves. Above that bright, red flames lick and dance across the sky. A thunderous roar erupts from behind the black curtain, and the flames leap and jump onto the tree line south of town. Hell has opened its gates and released its fury. It will reach us in minutes.

"We have to leave, Kristoff," I shout to my friend. "Now!" Heated air rushes down my airway, causing me to choke and gag on it.

"Others have already left," he yells back. "I've been watching them in between hauls. One look at that," he points to the gates of hell, "and they dropped their buckets and shovels and ran back into town." He coughs on the words, covering his mouth to protect it from the heat.

I had been too busy and focused on the house fires to notice the other men from the mill leaving. I turn my head now to look, but it is too smoky. I can't see that far away from the well.

Kristoff yells out, "There's probably only a couple dozen left of us from the mill, and the firefighters working the engine. I'd hate to leave them."

"But we can't stay here. We have to find our parents."

He nods, leaning close to me, so we don't have to shout. "I have to find my mother."

"I have to convince my father to leave the mill."

"I don't think he'll argue with that," he says and tips his head toward the black smoke column.

I've seen fires before, and I've seen the smoke they produce, but I've never seen something of this magnitude. The sheer size of it is astonishing. Fear starts to grow inside my belly as I calculate how large the fire must be behind the black curtain. It has to be miles wide in order to produce a black column of smoke as large as that. I push the fear down deep, willing it to hide or disappear. I can't waste energy on fear right now. I need to focus on the task at hand. First, we warn the firefighters, and then we run. "Let's go!" I shout.

Kristoff drops his bucket and we are off, running back to the fire engine. The heat and driving smoke intensifies as we approach, but we push through it. Only one man remains at the fire engine. He is standing next to the horses, struggling to hold onto the reins. The animals whip their heads back and forth, as they try to escape.

Kristoff runs to them and uses a knife from his pocket to cut them loose. The firefighter sees what he's doing and begins to shout at him, but I grab his shoulders and turn him towards the horizon, "We have to leave! Look!"

The man's face quickly changes from anger to horror. The horses, now free, gallop past us towards town. I watch them disappear into the smoke and let go of the man's shoulders. Kristoff runs up to us, putting his knife back into his pocket as the engine makes a strange, gurgling noise. It shakes slightly, and I put my arm in front of my friend, pushing him back away from the engine. Just as quickly as it started, it stops. The shaking and gurgling is gone, and the engine is still.

Shouting catches our attention, and we look in the direction of the noise. It's the four nozzlemen, standing near a house on fire. They are screaming at each other, dropping the hose, and throwing their arms over their faces. My eyes follow the hose backwards and see that it has caught fire. The flames are growing by the second, inching toward the nozzlemen and back towards the fire engine. Towards us!

Everyone runs. The nozzlemen, the man standing next to us, all of the volunteer firefighters, and any men remaining from the mill. The sense of urgency is immediate. If our strongest weapon, the fire engine and hose, has fallen to the fire this early in the fight, then we have no defense against such a strong opponent. Our only option is to flee and pray we are faster than the fire.

My legs carry my body north on Main Street. Kristoff is right at my side, pushing me forward with his arm. A deep, rumbling sound like thunder erupts behind us. The fire is closer than I thought. I wonder how much time we actually have before it is here.

A man on a horse races past us yelling, "We can't save the town! Don't lose a moment, but fly!"

As his horse gallops ahead, the man turns his body, so that I can see the side of his face as he cries out, spit flying from his mouth. It's John Craig. For a moment, I tense thinking he will turn around and scold us for leaving the fire line. Then the meaning of his words hits me, and a wave of despair rolls over me. If the fire chief has no hope to save the town, then this is really happening.

Hinckley is burning.

I pump my legs harder, running faster than I've ever run before. Main Street is full of smoke, making it hard to see beyond a few yards ahead of us. The wind pushes us forward, rattling buildings, and slamming against shop windows. The street is pure chaos. Men, women, and children run in different directions. Horse-drawn buggies and carts race past us. The horses pound their hooves on the dirt road, kicking up dust that mixes with the smoke, swirling in the heated air.

Suddenly, a large crowd appears in the street, men and women yelling and shrieking in fear. They're running toward the St. Paul and Duluth depot on the left side of the street. Some are dragging trunks and holding onto suitcases. I recognize one woman in the crowd as I run past. She is a teacher, holding up two beautiful dresses—one in each hand. I also see children sobbing, being dragged by their frantic mothers. The crowd must be running to the depot to catch the afternoon Skalley. I wonder if the conductor knows what lies ahead on the tracks just south of town. I scramble through the crowd, slowing down a bit to avoid knocking into anyone, but I keep heading north. A pack of dogs runs past me, barking wildly, abandoning their owners and saving themselves. I point this out to Kristoff, but when I turn my face to look at him, he isn't by my side. I stop abruptly, my shoes sliding on the dusty street. My head swivels back and forth, but Kristoff isn't here. I must have lost him in the crowd near the depot. A horse-drawn buggy appears out of nowhere, almost knocking me down. I step out of the way just in time as it flies by. I race back the way I came, back toward the depot.

Just as my legs are picking up speed, a searing wind blows up the street, lifting me off the ground for a second. It is blistering hot, and I have to shield my face and shut my eyes or else risk them being seared off. The next breath I take burns down my throat. I choke and sputter, dropping down to the dirt, covering my head with both arms. I think of the buggy that almost hit me moments before, and I know I need to get off the street. I hurry to the sidewalk, but the air is still too hot, so I drop to my hands and knees, crawling on the wooden planks. The sidewalk burns, and I gasp in pain which makes me choke again on the superheated air. The wood is so hot that it burns my skin. I desperately try to breathe, but the smoke and heated air just make me cough more. Pain assaults me from the inside of my throat and on the skin of my palms and knees.

I can't die here on the sidewalk, alone. I have to keep moving.

I force myself up, covering my mouth and nose with my hands. I hold my breath and keep my eyes shut. It's disorientating. Then my shoulder slams against the wall of the building, and I use it as a guide to get off the sidewalk and farther away from the street. After I round the corner of the building, the heated wind immediately stops.

I rub my eyes to adjust my vision to the smoke and the darkness. I'm standing in between the drug store and another building which must be blocking the wind. The air is still hot, but bearable. My lungs burn from holding my breath for so long, and relief instantly rushes through my body with each new breath I take. After what just happened, my instinct is to run and survive, but I have to find my friend. I push myself off the building and run into the backyard of a house. The wind picks up, so I shield my face and keep going. I race through two more backyards, hopping over each fence. I run past a clothesline, the wind whipping the clothes so violently a shirt rips off the line in front of my face. It flies up into the black, smoky sky, until the sleeves start to glow red and ignite.

I'm running out of time.

I sprint through another yard, Mayor Lee Webster's backyard, in fact. I hop over his white picket fence and into the busy street. There are men and women running and screaming out names of loved ones. They are searching for spouses and children in the chaos just like I'm searching for Kristoff.

A cloud of dense, black smoke blows into the street, and I have to stop and cover my face. The screaming stops for a moment, and I hear a bell ringing in the distance. When the cloud of smoke passes, the screaming continues. I yell Kristoff's name over and over, running around the corner and down the street, not fully understanding which way I am going. I join a group of men, women and children all running together. Fist-sized coals start to rain down on us. The woman next to me screams as one hits her shoulder. She begins to fall to the ground, but the man next to her grabs her by the waist and pulls her up, dragging her as we keep running.

We've made it to the end of the street, and our group starts running north toward the Eastern Minnesota depot, but I stop. Should I follow them? Or should I keep searching for Kristoff? I have no idea where to look, and I will surely die trying. I almost sob in frustration because it is so loud. I can't think with all the noise, so I shove the heels of my palms into my ears, trying to block out the screams and the roaring wind.

I turn south, attempting to estimate the distance between me and the fire. But the land disappears into the deepest night, broken only by brief flashes of flames when the black curtain of smoke lifts. Something appears in the sky during one of these short flashes of light. It's a giant bubble of gas, floating silently above the rooftops. It is full of light and color, but it's translucent, almost like a soap bubble. I lose it for a second in the darkness, but as another flame illuminates the sky, the bubble reappears. Silently, it drifts over the rooftops, like a ghost. It's hypnotizing me and I can't look away. Then, a thunderous roar breaks the silence. The sound is so loud, I think the earth has cracked. The floating ghost changes. The light and airy nature of the bubble darkens, and it sinks onto a house, erupting in white hot flames.

The brightness mimics daylight for a moment, so I can see much clearer. A block away from me, a woman and a boy are running on the train tracks coming my way. She stops mid stride and crumples into a heap onto the tracks. The boy runs to her, but he also stops as if he hit an invisible wall and falls down. I know in my gut that I just saw them both die. They won't get back up ever again. Tears well up in my eyes, and the fear I had attempted to bury now surges within me. I've only seen one other person die. Life left her quietly, one last breath before an eternity of sleep. My mother's face appears in my mind even though my gaze is on the two bodies on the train tracks. Her image is blurry, like I'm looking at her through water, but I know it's her face. She's there for only a second, but it helps me focus.

I will die in minutes if I don't move. There is nothing more than that, so I spin on my heels and run. I run past the screaming children, I run past the crying mothers, and I run past the men trying to help others escape. Nothing stops me this time. Horses, cows, and chickens race with me. I swing my arms and pump my legs, leaving behind everyone and everything. When the smoke burns my throat, I keep running. When the cinders and firebrands fall on me, I keep running. The back of my shirt catches fire, but I keep running.

I'm running toward the lumberyard, toward Father.

Anna

Pokegama, Minnesota
3:30 p.m. - 3:50 p.m.

The Red Demon snarls and sticks out its fiery tongue, licking the top of the well. My muscles tense in anticipation, waiting for the fire to shoot down the well and burn us alive. I have never been this afraid in all my life. Only twenty-odd feet and a simple piece of pine board separate me from death. I may not reach my sixteenth birthday after all. Tears swell in my eyes at the thought. Will this be how my life ends? As if hearing my thoughts, Mary pulls me closer and rubs my arms against the chill of the water. The simple contact makes me want to fight back the sadness. I don't want the last thoughts I have to be ones of despair.

Twenty, maybe twenty-five feet between us and the fire. That is something. It's more protection than we had only moments ago. I peer up at the top of the well. The sliver of sky between the stone wall and the pine board cover is small, but I can see so much color and light. Bright reds, oranges, and yellows spin around and around, and then the sliver grows into a pool of bright, white light. I have to cover my eyes. Then the heat comes, and the air fills with sparks. A gust of wind swirls down the well towards us, shooting hot air and debris onto our heads. When I breathe, it feels like the inside of my throat is on fire. My skin is burning, tingling pain crawls all over my head and neck. Next, the embers fall on us. Chunks of hot burning wood make splashes around Mary and me, painting us with well water. The embers sizzle on impact. I cover my head with my arms, trying to protect myself from the falling firebrands.

Squinting through the gap between my arms, I see the pine board cover is on fire. Mary acts quickly and grabs the floating bedsheet and quilt. She drapes them over my head, drenching me in cold well water. I scream out in surprise and pain when the wet cloth hits my burning skin. She struggles to cover herself, but eventually appears at my side under our wet shelter.

"The cover!" she yells in my face. "It's burned up!"

I try to be brave, but I can't help it. A sob escapes me. With the cover gone, there is nothing between us and the Red Demon.

17

Karl

Saturday, September 1, 1894
Hinckley, Minnesota
3:50 p.m. - 4:10 p.m.

With each breath my throat burns as I run north, past the town hall and the schoolhouse. My eyes sting something awful, and I have to squint through the pain to see. The muscles in my legs burn from running, but I keep going. My instinct for survival is the fuel my body needs to continue.

The wind is horrible, and the smoke is so black and dense that it is impossible to see more than three feet in front of me. I pass shadows and figures in the smoke. Everyone is in a state of panic, humans and animals alike. Horses, cows, and people zig-zag through the blackness, stumbling over abandoned trunks and suitcases which were left in the street as their owners fled.

A large, dark form appears in my path, but the smoke has hidden it from my view. I try to stop in time, but my feet skid across the dirt as I run into it. It's a buggy. I grasp the back wheel and make my way around the side, where I see a woman and two children within. The children are crying and clinging to their mother. She is holding them tightly, trying to console them. A man, their father I assume, is trying to fix the shaft between the buggy and their horse. Something must

172

have broken as they tried to escape. Before my mind can argue against it, I climb up the side of the buggy and yell at the mother, "One! I can take one!"

The fire roars in the distance, and the horse bucks wildly. The buggy jerks, and I almost fall off the side. The father quickly grabs the reins and tries to calm the horse before it bolts away with his family.

The mother has yet to acknowledge me, so I yell again, "We must flee! Give me a child!"

The mother's face whips toward me, her floppy hat shaking in the wind. She looks surprised to see me at first, but then I lock eyes with hers and point to her child. I repeat my offer to her, yelling over the wind.

Her eyes widen in understanding, so I lean forward toward the nearest child who has his face buried in the mother's bosom. Just as I'm about to grasp the child, the mother pulls both her children closer and shakes her head aggressively.

At that moment, sparks rain down onto our heads, and the heat on my neck intensifies. I jump off the buggy and use my hands to shake off the embers burning through my shirt. Pain, like a thousand tiny bee stings, ignites on the skin of my neck and back.

Still brushing off the embers caught in my hair, I start to run again away from the danger. I leave the buggy and the family. Guilt twists in my gut, but I snuff it out quickly. Turning my focus back towards Father, I shake the image of the buggy out of my head and pump my legs harder against the street. I need something faster.

As if God himself hears me, a horse neighing catches my attention. The wall of smoke parts for a moment, and I see the outline of a small wagon parked next to a hen house. It's already hitched to the horse, and a man is behind the cart, setting a trunk onto it, next to a barrel. I race to the cart, praying I reach him before he leaves.

The man jumps into the driver's side at the same moment that I throw my body up into the seat next to him. He looks startled for a moment but doesn't push me off. Instead he grabs the reins and snaps them, shouting, "Y'ah! Y'ah!

He turns towards me and yells, *"Bedre sent enn aldri!"*

The words are Norwegian, but it's similar to Swedish, so I understand what he said, and I agree with him: Better late than never.

We race through the street, and the Norwegian shouts and hollers above the wind and the roar of the fire behind us. He's older than me, but younger than Father. He wears laborer's clothes yet, I don't recognize him from the mill. I notice holes in the back of his shirt, singed from falling embers and firebrands. My hand absentmindedly touches my own shoulder, and I feel the tattered material of what was once my shirt. The edges of the fabric are stiff and brittle. My fingertips brush the raw skin underneath and I hiss. Pain radiates across my skin. My shoulder and neck feel incredibly hot and dry as if the skin is being stretched over too large of a space.

The Norwegian pulls the reins back sharply, forcing my hand away from my skin to grab onto the sides of the cart. Not a second too soon, the horse jerks to the right, and we narrowly miss another cart that materializes out of the smoke, quickly disappearing as we fly past it. We pass more people and animals running on foot. The smoke thins considerably, and I realize that we've made it out of town. We are on the wagon road, almost to the bridge that crosses over the Grindstone River.

I panic and scream, "Stop! Turn around!" We have already passed the street that runs to the mill. The Norwegian doesn't change course, so I repeat myself in Swedish, grabbing the reins, and pulling back as hard as I can, "*Stanna! Vända om!*" The horse's neck rears back sharply, slowing her down, but she doesn't stop. The Norwegian leaps into action, shoving me aside with his shoulder and regaining control of the reins. He snaps them again and yells something to his horse. She listens to her owner and races, north on the wagon road, farther away from the mill. I reach for the reins again, desperate to turn around before we pass the bridge.

The man swings his fist through the air, and it lands square on my nose. My head snaps backwards, and the force pushes me back in the seat, my body almost sliding out of the cart all together. Instantly, my eyes water, and liquid gushes out of my nostrils. I'm paralyzed from shock and intense pain. I squeeze my eyes shut and see bright explosions of color. Cradling my nose between my palms, I taste blood pooling in my mouth. It's warm and coppery.

I open my eyes, but everything is dark. The impact has blinded me or maybe its damage from the smoke. I can't tell. The pain won't subside, and I can't keep myself upright anymore, so I bend forward, one hand grasping the wagon edge, the other still on my face. I can't focus on anything else except the throbbing pain. Each breath burns from the heat and the smoke, and my eyes won't stop watering. After a few more painful breaths, the shock of being hit in the face subsides, and I regain control of my senses. I'm still sitting in the Norwegian's cart; he hasn't pushed me out. We are still racing away from the fire, north on the wagon road. I should feel relieved that I've escaped, but I don't. Fear, despair, and guilt wash over me. I lost Kristoff, and I failed Father. My chest tightens like a hand has reached in and is squeezing my heart.

I sit up straight and look behind me. The world has turned upside down, and Hell has replaced Hinckley. The sky is black, and all of the buildings are on fire. Some walls melt, revealing the rooms inside while others are ripped apart as the wind bites into them. Boards, branches, dust and other debris whirl through the air, whipping around like a tornado. The roar of the wind is deafening as the sky bursts into a living sheet of flame. The sight is magnificent and terrifying.

I wipe the tears from my eyes and blink a few times, wondering if I passed out from the blow to the head, and this is just another nightmare. But the scene doesn't disappear or change. Mrs. Andersson's voice suddenly appears in my mind, repeating a Bible verse she read to us as children, "*Och änglarna skall kasta dem i den brinnande ugnen, där det skall vara gråt och tandagnisslan.*" She always made me translate it from Swedish to English for Anna and Mary, "And the angels will throw them into the fiery furnace, where there will be weeping and gnashing of teeth."

I turn back around to face the wagon road, our only chance to escape Hell. Others, like us, race on the road in carts and buggies full of people and belongings. The tightness around my heart intensifies when I start to see the houses along the wagon road. We're approaching home. Everything my father and I own is there. Soon it will be gone, and there's absolutely nothing that I can do to stop it.

We fly by the Andersson homestead, and I know mine is only seconds away, on the other side of the road. First, the split rail fence appears, but our cart is parked next to it. It's empty, but it's there, not in its usual place in the barn. My eyes dart up to the house, and there is a figure struggling through the front door. Father! I scream at the Norwegian man, "*Stanna! Min pappa!*" I jab my finger towards Father.

"Min pappa! Stanna! Stanna!"

He grumbles something to himself, but with the roar of the fire behind us and the thunder of horse hooves on the road, I can't hear what it is. But he does pull back on the reins. The horse slows to a stop, and I jump out of the cart, running to Father. He is dragging my mother's sewing machine and stand down our front steps, heading towards our cart. The stand's wooden legs drag behind him through the grass, leaving two tracks behind him.

"Father!" I shout, throwing my arms around him in a tight embrace.

He jumps from the surprise, *"Kors i taket!* Karl!"

"You're here!" I yell into his shoulder. I squeeze him harder, and the tightness in my chest disappears. I lean back to look at him.

He is smiling, but the smile quickly disappears, "What happened?"

I pull back and touch my nose and mouth, realizing that he's referring to the blood still dripping from my nose onto my lips and chin. I use my shirt sleeve to wipe it away, shaking my head, "There's no time, Father, we need to go. The fire is coming," I say and point to the sky south of us.

His eyes widen as he follows my finger, "Go, fetch Jack. I'll load this while you get him."

"Leave it. We have a horse and cart ready to go." I point to the Norwegian who is standing in the horse cart and yelling at us from the road. His voice is carried away by the wind, but I assume he is threatening to leave us.

"I can't leave it, Karl," Father says. "That's all I have of her."

Mother. A memory of her surfaces, robbing my focus of the task at hand. Instead of pulling Father toward the road, I lean into the memory, trying to piece together the image of her.

She is sitting at a table next to me, laughing. It's a loud belly laugh. She throws her head back and shuts her eyes, and I smile, looking up at her. I think I'm the one that made her laugh. Her dress is blue, but she wears a white apron around her waist. Something is sitting in her lap. Green beans? I can't remember, but the memory makes me feel happy, peaceful, even love.

I shake my head vigorously, physically trying to push the image away. We don't have time for this! The fire is coming now! I grab

Father by the shoulders and pull, but he doesn't budge. I look back to the Norwegian in the cart. He's still there, struggling to keep his horse from bolting. He's angry and will leave us if I can't convince Father to come. We don't have time to hitch up Jack to our cart. This stranger is our only chance to live.

I turn back to Father and see that his brow is wrinkled in a frown, and his eyes look hard and determined. Still holding onto his shoulders, I soften my grip and bend my head down so I am eye level with him and admit, "Please come with us. I can't be alone again."

I am not sure if he heard me or not because he doesn't move. I don't know what to say next to make him change his mind. Then the hard lines in his face smooth, and his eyes soften. He sets the sewing machine down softly on the ground, tenderly placing it on the grass. He slowly stands back up but still looks down at the sewing machine. Wind ripples his shirt and pants, and his hair whips violently around his head. Then he looks at me, tears in his eyes and nods. He grabs my elbow, jogging back to the wagon, leading me.

The Norwegian sits down hard on the seat, and Father sits down next to him. He doesn't greet my Father, and Father doesn't greet him. I jump into the back of the cart between the barrel and the trunk. The Norwegian cracks the reins as Father braces his hands on the edge of the cart. I turn back and face south, but I can't see far due to the smoke. The road behind us, the Andersson homestead, and the ruins of Hinckley are hidden behind the black curtain. I know what comes next, and I pray that our horse can outrun it.

As we ride away, I watch as our house is slowly swallowed up by the darkness. The last thing I see is Mother's sewing machine on the grass in the front yard. The shiny, gold letters reflect the flashes of flames that illuminate the sky.

Anna

Pokegama, Minnesota
3:50 p.m. - 4:10 p.m.

Time spent underneath the quilt is worse, far worse than before. It's wet and heavy, and it's hard to breathe. Mary lifts the edge of the quilt up every so often and splashes water onto the ladder. I think I hear her yelp in pain each time, besides that, nothing breaks up the time. My entire body is numb from the chill of the water. My ears are ringing, and my muscles ache from holding up the water-logged quilt. But the worst part is the darkness. It's so dark that I can't see the quilt even though I know it's right in front of my face. I can smell the damp cloth, and I can feel it on top of my head, seeping water onto my hair; but I can't see it. Fear makes the time move slower too. A steady stream of tears run down my face. I weep from the uncertainty of our fate. I weep for the destruction and loss happening around us. And I weep from guilt and shame.

John is dead. There is no scenario where he could have survived. His body burns in the wagon we left him in, his coffin, engulfed in flames and fire. I pray that he never woke up from the head injury that he suffered at the hands of my sister. I pray he burned quickly in his sleep. If Mary hears my whispered prayers, she does not let on. Instead she holds up her side of the quilt in silence.

The minutes drag on, and my mind wanders. Images of the past emerge from my memory. They are simple tasks that I took for granted like washing the floors on Fridays with Mother or sitting on the split rail fence waiting for Father to come home from the mill. Thinking about Mother and Father makes me cry harder. I will probably never see them again. I miss them so much. My chest tightens, and I yearn to hold them both one last time.

I think about my friends too. Belle, Karl, Edwin and my schoolmates. All of us are in that strange place between being children and becoming adults. I wish I could have spent more time with each of them if only to see how all of their lives ended up.

I wonder what kind of woman I would have become. Would I have been a wife and mother like Madame Catrina predicted? Who would have been my husband? Someone I have already met? Or would I have married a stranger like my sister did? Oh, what a stranger he was. A chill runs down my spine, thinking about what he did to my sister. A black eye, a bruised rib, face-punched. What kind of monster does that to his wife? And for what purpose? Because his life did not go as he had planned? How could he hate her so much? The rage in his eyes when he charged at Mary, scares me still, even though he lays above us burned to a crisp. A tingling sensation crawls along my throat where his hand tried to stop me from breathing.

Is it ironic that Mary and I are still breathing while he is not? I shouldn't have such wicked thoughts. Mary and I may soon see him in Hell. I don't know how long our quilt will last against the flames, or if we have enough air in the well to last through the fire. Or if the ladder burns and we are stuck down here, how long will it take for someone to find us—if there is anyone left.

A body-wracking sob shakes me, and my arms fall down into the water. I'm not ready to die, to meet God. I will be judged and found wanting. I lied to my parents about kissing Karl; I spread a rumor to my friends and Belle's mother, but worst of all, Mary and I left a man to die. We killed him. The quilt hangs heavy on my head, and the wet cloth clings to my face. With the next sob, the material sucks into my mouth, and chokes me. I gag on it, pushing it away from my face. My whole body is shaking, and my legs surrender to the weight. I sink down into the cold water, giving up and letting go. All of the terrors of the day are washed away. Turned over furniture, a broken window, my sister's devastated face, and the image of John choking her just melt away. The black smoke that covered the sky lifts to reveal a bright, blue one dotted with puffy, white clouds and sunshine.

Two strong hands squeeze my shoulders and lift me up out of the water. Against my will, my body gasps for breath. I choke on water, not smoke, and my hair hangs wet over my face. The world is still dark and wet, but Mary is holding me up, embracing me again. The wet quilt is pushed to the side of us, and the air seems easier to breathe without it. I hang onto my sister, letting her hold me above the water. I don't move the hair out of my face or look up into the world. Exhaustion overtakes me.

"I have you, Anna," my sister whispers into my ear, "I have you."

18

Karl

Our horse is fast.

We fly by other larger carts and buggies. Only single riders are light enough to speed ahead of us. Unfortunately, there are more men and women running on foot through the tree stumps and brush. I doubt they will have the pace to outrun the fire.

One cart we pass has four barrels full of water in the back, and in each barrel stands a small child. The parents, riding in front, must have instructed each one to hop into a barrel as they fled. Clever. With all the embers, sparks, and firebrands falling from the sky, the moisture from the water will help prevent their clothes from catching fire.

I'm too big to fit into the barrel of water next to me, so I cup my hands together and throw water over my head and shoulders. My shirt already has several holes burned through it, but I still drench it in water. I splash some water on Father's shoulders, then drench his head and neck. He flinches at the shock of it, but doesn't tell me to stop.

I scoop another handful of water for our driver and stand up to reach him when the cart suddenly veers to the right, and I lose my balance. The trunk slides across the cart and crashes into the back of my legs. I tip over the side of the cart, twisting in the air as I fall, my back crashing into the earth. The impact is strong enough to knock the wind out of me, and I struggle to breathe.

Nothing happens when I inhale, so I arch my neck, silently screaming for air. I panic and bang on my chest, trying to force my lungs to work. The next inhale is successful. Air rushes down my throat, but it's polluted with smoke, and I choke on my first breath. I roll onto my side, pushing my face into the brittle grass, coughing and hacking.

When I stop struggling and finally breathe normally, I open my eyes and am horrified at the scene before me. The front of the cart, the reins, and the horse's backside are on fire. The poor creature is twisting in pain, causing the wagon to rock side to side. The sounds coming from her mouth are unnatural shrieks. In an attempt to save her, the Norwegian cuts her loose from the cart. She bucks at the flames with her hind legs, but it's no use. The flames only crawl up her body faster. She kicks and bucks away from us, running north, still on fire. It's an awful sight, and the image is branded into my memory.

"Karl!" Father shouts as he reaches me. He helps me to my feet as the Norwegian joins us. We stare at the cart, the flames licking the sides and wheels. "We can go back! Jack might still be in the barn!" Father shouts over the wind. He points back south on the wagon road. The Norwegian's eyes follow Father's finger, and he realizes that Father is suggesting we go back. He shakes his head violently and starts speaking rapidly in Norwegian. Father answers him in Swedish, and I can't keep up with what either of them are saying.

I look around us, searching for a better option than going back. Stepping onto the road, I peer north. I think I see a flickering light about a half mile away. I cup my hands around my stinging eyes, trying to stop the smoke from impeding my view. There it is, again. It's not a flickering light; it's a flame. Several large flames, in fact. The woods on both sides of the wagon road are burning. The dry marsh grasses must have caught fire. We are trapped between two fires, one ahead of us, and the inferno behind us!

My mind races between options, making split-second, life or death decisions. The Grindstone River? No, too far and probably too low. Running back to our root cellar? No, too risky. Finding a puddle of swamp water to lay in? No, too unpredictable. The wind grows louder, prompting Father and the Norwegian to raise their voices. I cover my ears to block it all out. Think, Karl! Think of something! Something to save us . . . something reliable . . . trains are reliable, and they are fast . . . faster than a horse . . . the St. Paul and Duluth train tracks are close to us.

I run back to my Father and yank down on his arm which is waving in the air, helping him make a point to the Norwegian. I pull down his shirt sleeve and look at his wristwatch. It is a few minutes past four o'clock. We have a chance, a small one, but it is our only option to survive. I drag him with me, running off the road and into the woods west of the wagon road, screaming, "The Skalley! Run to the Skalley!" The Norwegian follows us, so I scream to him, "Skalley!"

Running through the brush is slow, and I immediately worry that we will miss the train. Prickly raspberry vines and short Tamarack trees snap and scratch our arms and legs, but even in the dense undergrowth of the woods, the smoke still finds us. We choke on it as we breathe it in, and it claws at our eyes, stinging them.

The train tracks run alongside the wagon road, so if we continue straight, we should find them. We don't have time to run around in circles, because if we don't find the tracks within the next few minutes, we will certainly die. I push more vines and branches out of my way, scratching my palms. The small cuts from the vines are nagging at me, laughing at my attempt to lead us to safety. This has to work because if it doesn't, I've led us to our deaths.

Finally, the trees thin, and I stumble into a small clearing, but I can't see beyond a few feet ahead of me. I try to lead, but I'm exhausted, disoriented, and almost blind. My eyelids are inflamed and throbbing with pain. Father grabs my arm and pulls me across the clearing in three strides reaching the embankment of dirt and rocks that go up to the tracks. As we scramble up, the Norwegian grabs my other arm and helps pull me. He has a long scratch on his face that is bleeding, but he doesn't seem to notice. We run on the tracks together. Father leads, dragging me along by the hand, and the Norwegian brings up the rear.

Without warning, a blast of superheated air knocks into our bodies with such force that my legs fly up over my head. Father's hand is ripped away from mine, and we are both thrown off the tracks. At the same time, my teeth rattle and my ears pop. We land on the embankment and roll into a heap. I'm lying on my side, my legs sprawled out atop Father's chest. My skull is bursting with pressure and crushing pain. I move my jaw back and forth, desperate to relieve the pressure. "*Aj!*" I sputter and grab both sides of my head.

Father moves from beneath me and yells, "Karl, get up!"

He lifts me from under my armpits, and we both stumble to our feet. I'm seeing double, but I find stability holding onto Father's arm. Again, we scramble back up the embankment and begin to run. I turn back to make sure the Norwegian is still with us. He is already on the tracks, his form blurring into focus. He is holding his right arm close to his chest. The blood from the scratch on his face is mixed with dirt. In front of me, Father shouts, "I see it. The headlamp. We are saved!"

I whip my head back towards him, squinting, trying to see the train through the pain in my eyes, but the pressure in my head intensifies. My eyesight blurs again, so I tighten my grip on Father's arm to steady myself. I close my eyes and pump my legs, matching his stride and trying to keep up. My footsteps pound on the rail ties, running to the train. Behind me, the Norwegian screams. I stumble from the outburst, and he screams again, "*Nei! Ikke omvendt!*"

"No," Father answers, shouting as well. "No, no, no."

I snap my eyes open, but my vision is blurry. "What?" I scream. "Tell me! I can't see anything!" I squint as we run, trying desperately to see ahead of us.

"The train is in reverse," Father says, dropping my hand to wave both of his arms wildly in the air, screaming, "Stop! No! Stop!"

The Norwegian joins Father and screams at the top of his lungs. I've never heard men scream this way, and it frightens me. Panic surges through my body, releasing the animal instinct to survive. I run, blindly, taking short, frantic breaths. My heart races, pounding against my ribcage. The sole purpose of my existence now is to catch that train. My legs spring off every third railway tie, propelling me towards my last chance to live.

Without thinking, only acting, I launch myself off the last tie. One knee hits something solid, then the other. My pelvis and chest follow, slamming against the train's cowcatcher. Instinctively, my hands grasp onto the hot metal edge on top and my feet find the bottom edge. My legs tremble from exertion, yet they can rest now against the sturdy cowcatcher.

A body slams next to me. I turn my head towards the sound and see Father's face. His skin and beard are almost black, covered in soot and dirt.

"Karl!" he shouts.

I yell back, spit flying from my mouth *"Pappa! Du är här!"*

"We made it!"

He shuffles closer to me and adjusts his grip, his two smallest fingers overlapping on top of mine. We are both gasping for breath, leaning our cheeks against the backs of our hands.

Chug, chug, chug. The train is picking up speed, moving in reverse, away from the fire. The sound drowns out the roar, and it is such a welcome reprieve. I smile at Father, and he smiles back.

A tiredness I have not felt before sinks onto my body, weighing me down. I don't feel the pain in my head anymore, nor the burning skin on my shoulder and neck. I just feel a heavy exhaustion blanketing my body. My eyelids are so heavy, and my eyes sting, so I close them. The train keeps moving, and my breathing normalizes.

I hear my Father move next to me, his hand lifting off of my two fingers. He makes a strange noise, like a grunt or a yelp. The noise and the sudden loss of his hand on top of mine, makes me open my eyes just in time to see the shock on his face as he falls off the cowcatcher. He disappears into a cloud of black smoke.

Anna

Pokegama, Minnesota
4:10 p.m. - 4:35 p.m.

The stone walls of the well shift and slowly move inward.

My cold, dark world is shrinking. The air smells like damp earth, but it's polluted by something sinister. Smoke hangs in the air, it smells like burned timber and flesh. Flames eating away at his clothing, his hair, then his skin. Slowly, consuming him from the outside. The skin peels back easily, and the Red Demon feasts on his insides. Rancid meat that is overcooked and charred. The train arrives, it's so loud this time. The roar and screech makes my ears bleed. A riderless bicycle rolls past me, but it's on fire. The flames are white, blinding me. It's so bright I have to drop my Coke bottle to shield my eyes. I hear the glass hit the platform and shatter.

When I open my eyes again, there is only one small candle, the flame flickering in total darkness. I'm sitting on the floor of Madame Catrina's wagon. I reach for the candle, but my hand knocks it to the floor. Instantly, the rug, pillows, and blankets start on fire. The flames engulf the wagon until it disappears.

I'm standing alone in the fire. The flames dance around me, yet my body shakes from the cold. I will freeze soon unless I find a way to warm my body. The chill sinks into my bones, and it makes me wonder. Would I rather die by flames or by freezing? That question is pointless. I don't get to choose. Mary chose. She didn't choose very well. No, she chose a bad man. He became a dark shadow on her soul.

Madame Catrina's Kohl-rimmed eyes fling open.

I wake up, my head still resting on Mary's shoulder. We are standing in the water at the bottom of her well, leaning against the ladder.

I wonder how long I slept. My lips and tongue are parched, so I use one hand to cup the well water and splash it onto my mouth. It's lukewarm and full of cinders and ashes.

"Can we get out, Mary?" I ask, pulling away from her.

"Just as soon as we can endure breathing outside of the well," she answers.

I stand up on my own and pull the hair off of my face. I blink a few times and wipe the tears away. I'm not sure if they are tears or if it's just water. "I'll check," I offer.

She moves out of the way as I step onto the bottom rung and pull myself up. "Be careful," she warns.

Mary's carpetbag is stuffed between two rungs, so I step around it and move upwards. The sky is black, but somewhere outside flames flicker slowly and cast shadows into the well. I'm only a few feet away from the top when the air changes drastically. A scorching wall of heat hits the top of my head and face. Quickly, I scramble back down and splash into the dirty, ash-covered water.

"Well?" she asks, hopeful.

"Not yet," I tell her, shaking my head.

Her lip quivers and she begins to cry. I pull her close to me and embrace her. She leans against me, clearly exhausted. Now it's my turn to hold her, and it's her turn to rest. I whisper, "Shh, Mary, don't cry." A hymn drifts on the wind, and I sing it. It's a song our mother used to sing to us when we were little:

Jesus loves me; He who died,
Heaven's gate to open wide;
He will wash away my sin,
Let His little child come in.

19

Karl

Saturday, September 1, 1894
Skunk Lake, north of Hinckley
4:35 p.m. - 5:00 p.m.

A child is screaming, a terrible high-pitched shriek. I can't cover my ears to block it out because I'm holding onto the train's cowcatcher, and I can't let go. The air is so hot that it burns my face and neck. Each breath is painful, and the smoke is blinding. Only when the train starts to decelerate, do I realize that it's me who is screaming. I've been screaming since Father fell.

The train makes its final chug and completely stops, but my screams continue. I peel my hands off of the hot metal bar and collapse onto the tracks. The cowcatcher has burned holes through my pants and shirt and onto my skin, but I don't feel it. I crawl several feet away from the train, but my muscles have nothing left, so I fall down onto the tracks, turning onto my back. The railway tie is so hot against my skin, it starts to burn my shoulder, and I scream out in pain. I try to open my eyes, but they are swollen shut.

"Pappa!"

I sob so hard my stomach muscles clench, and I can't breathe.

The skin on my shoulder is burning off, so I flop over and push off the ground. It's difficult to stand up because my legs feel like rubber.

187

My body moves slowly and awkwardly. Each inhale is full of smoke, and I cough through it. I cover my mouth with one hand, desperately trying to breathe. By instinct, I stretch my other arm out in front of me, splaying my fingers wide. I take one step, then another. The air is hot, and I'm walking blindly back into the cauldron. Somehow, I manage to take a few steps without falling. I hear screams behind me and panicked shouting, but the roar of the fire drowns them out.

"*Pappa!*" I sob from behind my hand. "*Pappa!*"

I'm six years old again, sobbing and screaming for my parents who do not answer me. I take another shaky step on the tracks, desperately trying to walk back to Father. My foot hits something hard, and I lose my balance. The world falls on top of me as I tumble down, knocking my head on the railroad track. The impact shakes my skull and radiates down my body through my bones. Crushing pain in the back of my skull consumes me.

There is nothing left but pain. I can't move, and even if I could get up, I wouldn't. Father is gone. My home is gone. There is no point in trying to get back up. This is where I will die. I'll burn quickly, and soon I will see Father again. Wave after wave of pain washes over me, and the roar of the fire is deafening, maddening.

My swollen eyelids crack open, and a sliver of light floods my vision. Slowly, the sky sharpens into focus. It's a dark, swirling mass of smoke, and red-hot sparks and embers pour down like rain. Suddenly, I feel pressure squeezing on my arms. Two hands grasp me under my armpits, lifting me up.

"Sir!" a male voice shouts in my face, "You can't stay here!"

I can't speak, so I only grumble a response.

"We have to move," he shouts as he pulls me up onto his chest. My eyes sting again, so I close them. The man hoists my arm around his neck and starts moving. My skull throbs with pain, and it lolls to the side. My legs move with his, but he is holding most of my weight, dragging me with him. The solidness of his body next to mine helps me find my balance, and I begin to match his steps.

It's hard to hear him, but I think he yells out, "There you go. Don't give up, yet."

I don't know where he's taking me, but he is sure of his direction. The farther we walk, the louder the screams become. He pushes my body down for a moment, and I reach my hand out. My fingers grasp a barbed wire fence, so I turn my head to the side and awkwardly work my way under it. The man never lets go of me, and we continue to walk. The ground under my feet feels soft, like grass, so we must be off the train tracks. The screams are right next to us now. Hundreds of screaming voices. I step in water and feel its coolness against my skin. The cowcatcher must have burned holes in my boots. We keep walking into the water until it reaches my knees. "Here we are, Skunk Lake," the man yells, taking my arm off his shoulder. "Stay here." His body moves away from me, and I'm alone again. I immediately miss his solid presence.

Still feeling unsteady, I spread my legs and push my boots into the muddy bottom. I know Skunk Lake. It's a small, murky pond, covered in green algae. I desperately try to open my eyes. I need to be able to see. The pain in my skull and eyes intensifies, and I scream out in frustration, holding my head in my hands, trying to push back against the pain. Someone touches my chest and neck, pulling me down. The hands are small, and they pull gently.

Water splashes onto my eyelids, and two small hands scrape at them. I thought they were swollen shut, but someone is scraping ash from them. Again, water splashes in my face, but this time, I blink. My vision clears as the water drips down my face. An old woman stands in front of me. Her hair is singed off near her forehead. I blink a few times, making sure that my eyelids still work. Before I can thank the old woman, she walks away, wading through the water to help someone else. I get my bearings and look around the pond. The air is smoky, but I can see men, women, and children in the water. More are jumping from the train and running down the embankment. Everyone near me is screaming or sobbing.

I make a wide circle, looking around the edge of the pond for the fire, but I can only see trees and smoke. Shuffling between sobbing and screaming people, I face the train tracks. The passenger cars are on fire. Flames erupt from the bottom of the cars, licking the sides and finding their way through the windows. My gaze follows the tracks southward, but dread grips me. There it is—Hell's inferno. There is no escape now. A colossal wall of flames, towering two hundred feet and stretching for miles, claws at the black sky. Its relentless advance hurtles straight toward us, consuming everything in its path.

Everyone in the pond must see it at the same time as I do, because a collective scream drowns out the wind's roar. The scream is cut off suddenly when a gust of hot air rolls over the water. It's so strong that it knocks me down, and I splash into the mud. Sitting on my knees, I face the fire which is now moments away from the pond's edge. The air is so hot that my face is melting, but I have to see. I have to see what will most likely kill me. The trees lining the edge of the pond are hit first. The tall evergreens are swallowed up in a bright, white light. The smell of burned timber is overwhelming, and the crackling sound of the forest competes with the rushing wind.

A sheet of flames bends over the lake, rushing towards us, like a hand reaching out to strangle and choke. It is burning the air above our heads, hoping to suck the life from us completely. I take one last breath and dunk under the water just as the flames begin to singe the hair on top of my head.

20

Anna

Saturday, September 1, 1894
Pokegama, Minnesota
5:00 p.m. - 6:00 p.m.

The air is thick with smoke, and I have been coughing on it for the better part of an hour. Mary and I use the wet quilt and sheet to breathe through, creating a filter to catch some of the smoke before we inhale it. We have also been taking turns going up the ladder to check the temperature of the air.

Finally, this time when Mary comes back down the ladder, she tells me the air has cooled, and we can get out. I roll up the quilt and tuck it under my arm, using the other hand to pull myself up behind Mary. She holds the wet sheet and carpetbag. We take our time going up the ladder, each of us exhausted from the ordeal and stiff from standing for hours in water.

After Mary pulls herself over the top of the well, I reach the top of the ladder and almost fall backwards into the well at the sight before me. It's complete and utter desolation. All the beautiful trees that circled this clearing are gone, only the blackened trunks are left, some still on fire. The enchanted forest is gone, leaving only a barren, dismal wasteland.

The air is thick with smoke and ash, and the sky is still dark. I'm not sure if it is night or day. Before the land was obstructed by trees, but now if not for the smoke, I could see for miles. Mary holds my hand as I pull myself up and out of the well. Our dresses are soaked through with water, and I am shivering. Mary sets down her carpetbag and rips strips off the wet bedsheet. She hands me two strips, but I just stare at her blankly. She doesn't say anything. She just wraps a strip of wet fabric around her head, covering her mouth and most of her eyes. I copy her and immediately notice how it eases the stinging in my eyes and throat. It will be easier to see and breathe with this head covering.

Mary starts to walk away from the well, but she stops every few steps and shakes her legs. I'm just about to ask her why when I understand. The ground is still hot from ashes and burning coals. Some of the coals stick to our shoes. I have to shake them off or scrape them on a rock before they burn a hole into my oxfords.

We go over to where the house once stood and look down at the destruction. It is a hot pile of still glowing embers. Looking down into the cellar, we see all that is left of her home are the remnants of a stove which must have fallen through the burning floor and a few spoons, forks, and broken dishes. That's it. The beginning of her adult life and her belongings are all gone. I set my hand on her shoulder, attempting to provide comfort, but she slowly walks away, kicking in the rubble, looking for something. I stay where I am and look out on our grim surroundings. It is bleak. Everything is burned up. I rub my hands up and down my arms in disbelief.

Mary stops her searching and stands still. I walk over to where she stands, shaking hot coals from my shoes. When I reach her and look down, I stop moving as well. I stop breathing. A charred, black mass lays on the ground; its limbs and spine twisted and contorted in odd angles. The clothing has disappeared, but the shoes are still there, each pointing in opposite directions at an unnatural angle. The smell hits me, and I instantly gag as the awful, acrid odor seeps through my head covering. The coppery, metallic smell of hot blood and flesh is too much. My stomach lurches, and I quickly pull my head covering down, and retch onto the ground. Since I already emptied my stomach before the fire, there isn't much to come up. The liquids from my stomach burn as they come up my throat which is already as dry as sandpaper.

Once I'm done, I pull my head covering back over my mouth and nose. Blinking back salty tears, I look back at the body. This mass of burned flesh and organs is John. "We killed him," I whisper to myself. I clear my throat, which is painful to do, but repeat it louder so Mary will hear me, "We killed him." She doesn't even flinch. She just continues to stare at the corpse of her husband. Her indifference enrages me. "You!" I point to her, "You left him to die! We should have saved him!" Still, nothing. "Mary!" I cry out.

She turns toward me, eyes hooded under her head covering. "We had minutes, Anna. Minutes before the fire consumed us. Do you really think we would have been able to carry him to the well, then lift him over the edge, and somehow manage to get him to the bottom? Then, what? Take turns holding a full grown man for hours?"

I wipe my tears away, so I can see her more clearly. Her head covering hides most of her face, but I can see there are no tears in her eyes. She is eerily calm for a woman who just lost everything.

"No," she answers herself. "By trying to save him, we would have killed ourselves."

"I know he hurt you, but you were his wife, Mary," I plead. "You should have at least tried."

Her eyes widen at my response, but her voice remains calm as she answers me, "His wife? Yes, I was his wife. I married him, and I followed him here without question. I was ready to have his child. I was loyal and obedient; good and kind to him. Maybe if he had never hit me or choked me I would have tried harder to save his life." She shakes her head and continues, "The last mistake he made was putting his hands on you."

I swallow down a sob, remembering how it felt to have his hands pushing into my neck, almost choking the life from me. How many times did he do that to my sister? She turns back to look at John. I look at him too, trying to find his face in the mangled mass of charred flesh and peeled-back skin. Mary walks to me and puts her right hand on my left shoulder. It's not a gesture of comfort. She places her other hand on me and swivels my body, turning me away from the corpse. "We didn't kill John. We ran to the well to save ourselves. John did not make it to the well."

I look past her face at the destruction around us.

"Anna," she bends her head down, blocking my view and forcing

193

me to look at her, "John did not make it to the well." Her eyes are piercing when she says, "Repeat it."

I repeat her words, "John did not make it to the well."

"When we leave this place, we will never speak of him again, do you understand?"

I nod.

"We will only say that he did not make it to the well. Nothing more."

I nod again.

"Now, we have to leave. Follow me."

She walks back to the well and picks up her carpetbag and quilt. Besides the wet clothes on her back, these are her only possessions. I pick up the torn bedsheet and ask, "Can't we stay and dry ourselves?"

"No," she answers, "it will be night soon. We have to find shelter, and I have to look for my friend Lucy and her children."

I walk behind her in silence. She sets the pace as we walk out of the clearing into what used to be the evergreen path. It is still a path because there are no tree stumps but it is no longer green. We have to move off the path when we pass what used to be the large, oak tree. Its blackened trunk is on fire, and it gives off waves of intense heat. We circle around it, giving it as much space as we can, worried it might fall on us. The rest of the walk is quiet and somber. The beautiful tree canopy that blocked the sun on my walk to Mary's house is gone. There are only small, black stumps and piles of smoldering ash which cling to our clothes and skin as we walk by.

"There,"Mary stops and points ahead as she says, "that's where Lucy's house should be. See the well?"

I squint to see through the smoke, and find the top of a stone well, standing alone in the barren yard. The big, beautiful house with the large windows and gable over the door is gone. We walk up to the well and see a ladder inside it, but no occupants.

"A ladder," Mary comments. "They must have survived in the well like us. If they already left, I would assume they headed towards town, by way of Dr. Kelsey's house. We'll go that way as well and hope to catch up to them."

Mary starts walking toward a clearing of blackened grass. It's dry, brittle, and crunches as we walk over it. This ground is not as hot as what we've already walked over, so I try to wipe off the clumps of coals that have melted onto the soles of my new shoes. I get most of them, but some are still sticking to my poor oxfords. Then, I follow Mary to a creek bed, and we slide down the banks together. The creek is almost dried up, but we use what water we can from the small puddles to rinse the ash off our clothes and skin. It still clings to our head coverings and stains them black, so we soak the bedsheet in a puddle and rip off new strips to wrap around our heads.

Then we continue down the creek. I'm thankful Mary knows where she is going because I would be lost if I was on my own. The larger trees on the sides of the bank are still burning, and a couple of them fall behind us, crashing onto the creek bed. The noise makes me jump, and Mary leads us around the burning trunks as we continue to follow the creek. Everything is dead, black, smoking, or slowly crumbling into ashes. There are no birds singing, no squirrels jumping from tree to tree, no signs of life. Only the hot wind blowing every now and then followed sometimes by a sudden crash as a burned tree trunk hits the ground.

After some time, I don't know how Mary knows to do this, we leave the creek and walk up over the side into a potato patch. The unharvested plants don't seem to be that burned. The leaves are curled up onto themselves in this heat, but none of them are charred. I pull one up out of the ground, barely tugging as the plant slides easily out of the dirt. The potatoes underneath are untouched by the fire.

"Hmm," Mary ponders, looking ahead, not noticing the plant in my hand, "Dr. Kelsey's house should be just over there, on the other side of this potato patch. It must have burned to the ground as well. This fire must have been exceptionally large and powerful. Nothing seems to have survived."

"Almost nothing," I pull an oblong potato from its roots, dropping the rest of the plant to the ground. "Where do we go now?"

"I suppose, we go to the city center and pray that there are some survivors there," she says as she walks away from the potato patch. She doesn't wait for my response. I obediently follow her through more smoldering tree stumps and piles of ash. Soon another larger creek bed appears. This one has a little more water, but the surface is covered with a thick layer of ash. As we cross it, the lukewarm water reaches just above my knees, leaving a line of wet, gray ash along my skirt.

More blackened, tree stumps, some still on fire, meet us on the other side of the creek. I continue to follow Mary, holding my head covering close to my face. We scramble up the side of an embankment and step onto train tracks. The railroad ties are smoking, and the metal tracks are fiercely hot. I don't dare to walk on them for fear that they would melt the bottoms of my shoes. Even so, it is reassuring to see a sign of civilization.

Mary turns one way and walks alongside the train tracks. I follow her, and we carefully step over the hot railroad ties and tangled remains of fallen telegraph wires. My feet ache from so much walking, and the water from the well and the creek squishes my socks with each step. A cowbell rings in the distance, and Mary and I both stop in our tracks, for other than the crash of the tree trunks falling into the creek bed, this is the first sound that we've heard, the first sound of life. We move a little faster down the tracks, hoping there are people near the cow, but stop in our tracks when flames shoot up into the sky ahead of us, pushing out large billows of black smoke. My breath catches in my throat, and I think it may be the fire coming back for us. But then I see it's the trestle and bridge I saw only hours ago from the other side of the tracks. It's still burning from when the fire passed through. At last, we've made it to Pokegama.

Mary stops in front of me, and I walk to her side. We stand together peering through the smoke and look down at the millpond on the other side of the tracks. At first it looks like more tree stumps on the banks of the pond, but slowly my eyes see movement through the smoke. People are sitting and lying down next to the millpond, and hope surges in my chest at the sight of other human beings. We are not alone.

Karl

Skunk Lake, north of Hinckley
5:00 p.m. - 6:00 p.m.

I try to stay underwater for as long as I can, pushing my body down into the mud of Skunk Lake, attempting to keep my head below the surface. It is the only place to hide from the fire. When my lungs burn from the lack of air and my body twitches, I shoot out of the water to take a breath. We are surrounded by the seething flames of Hell; wave after wave rolls over us. The fire blocks out the sky, creating a bright red and orange canopy. The air is so hot that it burns my throat each time I inhale, but somehow I choke it down. It's a strange existence. My lungs burn both in the water and above it.

At first, the waves of fire come fast and hard. My arms are exhausted from pushing my body down under the surface, but after what seems to be an eternity, the waves of the fire come less frequently. I stay under water less and spend more time above breathing in the heated air. During one of these breaks, I notice the men and women around me. They are all drenched and gasping for breath. Parents hold their children and plug their noses as they go under.

Not too far away from me is a group of children, all different ages, and one solitary man standing in front of them. Standing there with his back to the wind and the flames, he is a willing sacrifice. He is devoting his energy to the protection of the children, splashing them with water, and telling them when to dunk under the surface. I don't think he's their father because his skin is a different color than theirs. I wonder if the children can't find their parents and if this man decided to help them—like the old woman helped me.

I can't dwell on the thought for too long because another wave of heated air rolls over us. Flames will follow, so I take another deep breath and dunk under the water. As I push myself deeper under the pond's surface I wonder if there will be anything left of the world when I come up for air.

21

Anna

Saturday, September 1, 1894
Pokegama, Minnesota
6:00 p.m.- 6:30 p.m.

A man walks over to us from the group near the millpond. He climbs up the embankment and reaches a hand out towards Mary.

"Mr. Baty," Mary says, "it's so good to see you." The man wears a head covering similar to ours, so I'm not sure how Mary recognizes him, but he knows her as well.

"Mary! Thank God, you survived!" Mr. Baty says as Mary hooks her arm around mine, and we slowly make it down the embankment with his assistance. His shirt and pants are tattered and covered in black soot.

He escorts us to the banks of the millpond to two women who are sitting down and leaning against a trunk. Their bodies are completely covered by a quilt. It is pulled up to their necks. Mary sets down her carpetbag in front of them, folds our quilt into a square, and lays it on the ground like a picnic blanket.

"Mrs. Baty, Mrs. Carver," she greets both women as she sits down on our quilt, "I'm happy to see you both."

"Mary?" one of the women under the quilt murmurs. "Is that you?"

"Yes, Mrs. Baty, it's Mary Larson," Mary answers. I sit down next to her and start to untie my shoelaces. My feet are smarting something awful. "This is my sister, Anna," Mary gestures to me. "We survived in our well, but the house is gone. Everything is burned up."

I look at Mrs. Carver, remembering how talkative and kind she was to me when I passed through the city center on my way to Mary's house. But this woman sitting in front of me is quiet and deeply disturbed. She mumbles to herself and stares blankly at nothing. Feeling a little embarrassed for her, I turn my gaze away and take into account the other survivors. Men, women, and children rest in various states of suffering, misery, and despair. A man is stretched out full length on the ground completely covered with blankets. A woman nearby is rocking herself back and forth, curled in a ball on the ground. Another is crouched down on her knees, holding her head between her hands, her face contorted in pain, but the young children's behavior is what disturbs me the most.

They are all so still and quiet. Not one of them is crying, not even the toddlers. Usually full of energy and unrest, these children stare blankly ahead with no emotion showing on their faces. One small boy, sitting next to his mother, I assume, quietly vomits on himself. Neither he nor his mother wipes it off his chin or shirt.

Not sure where else to look, I bow my head and focus on my shoes. I have to tug on them, but they do finally come off my swollen feet. My water logged socks peel off my wrinkled skin to reveal red blisters on my heels and toes.

Next to me, Mary rummages in her carpetbag and pulls out a square, glass bottle and a spoon. It's the laudanum from her pantry. She uncorks it and dispenses some of the liquid on her spoon. She swallows it, pours another, and offers it to Mrs. Baty and Mrs. Carver.

"No, thank you," Mrs. Baty shakes her head. "But, poor Mr. Gonyea may need it. His entire body is covered in awful burns. He can't move, so he's lying over there on the ground."

Mary stands up slowly and walks over to the man stretched out on the ground. She kneels down next to him and speaks. I'm too far away to hear, but he nods to her, and then she helps hold his head up to take a spoonful.

"Mrs. Larson! Oh, Mrs. Larson!" a girl shouts from the other side of the millpond. As she runs past, I notice that she is close to my age, yet younger. A woman, holding two young boys—one by each hand—follows behind the girl who hugs Mary tightly. Mary winces and gently pulls the girl off her shoulders. As the woman takes a step closer, she gently encircles her arm around Mary's waist. Barefoot, I walk lightly over to their reunion. As I reach the group, the young girl is speaking rapidly recounting her family's survival in their well. The woman and the girl resemble each other so closely that they must be mother and daughter.

"Oh, it was so awful!" the daughter wails. "We held onto the ladder forever. And the entire time my racking headache never let up."

"Maidie, dear," the woman gently says to her daughter, "everyone here has a racking headache. The cure is to vomit, so please get on with it, so we don't have to hear you complain about it one more time."

The little boys add nothing to the conversation. Like all the other children, they simply stare blankly into space.

"Lucy, this is my sister, Anna," Mary introduces me. "Anna, this is Mrs. Lucy Kelsey, and this is Maidie, Earl, and Lyle." She gestures to each of the children, in turn. "They are my neighbors."

"Well, we were your neighbors," Lucy states plainly. "Now we are homeless."

Maidie whimpers.

"Ah, nice to meet you, Mrs. Kelsey," I answer awkwardly, shaking her hand. "I'm so sorry about your house. I saw it only hours ago on my walk to Mary's. It was a lovely home."

"Yes, it was, wasn't it," Lucy replies, smiling, "Please, call me Lucy. We are just thankful that we all made it. My husband, Caleb, and my eldest son, Allen, are on the other side of the millpond."

I smile back at her, but it feels forced. I don't know what else to say to someone who just lost her home. Her smile looks genuine, though, despite the circumstances. It brightens her soot-covered face. She stands tall and proud, carrying herself with a quiet confidence that I wish I possessed.

Mary asks, "And what of Caleb's brother, Dr. Kelsey? Are he and his family here?"

"His wife Isabella is over there," Lucy points to a woman sitting down on the ground, wrapped up in a wet blanket. "She survived with her sons, Carleton and Willie. Thankfully, her daughters were not in town."

Lucy lowers her voice, "But, Chauncey is unaccounted for."

Maidie covers her face with her hands openly sobbing now.

"Maidie, please, collect yourself," Lucy scolds her daughter. "We will find your uncle."

I'm trying to follow their conversation, but it's hard to keep up with the new names. Chauncey must be Dr. Kelsey's first name. I'm still attempting to connect the Kelsey family dots when Lucy looks at Mary and asks, "Where is John?"

I freeze, unable to move or breathe. The question was not addressed to me, but I start to sweat.

Mary pauses only for a moment, then calmly says, "John did not make it to the well."

"Oh, no," Lucy gasps and covers her mouth. She whispers. "Mary, I'm so sorry.

Mary nods but doesn't say anything else.

Lucy pulls her sons close to her and says, "Come, let's sit down." She leads the way back to our quilt and instructs her daughter to fetch one of their own. The girl runs into the smoke and returns quickly with it. Lucy shakes out the quilt before setting it on the ground next to ours. She and Mary help the boys lie down and remove their wet shoes, while Maidie and I settle comfortably next to each other.

"Maidie, dear," Lucy says, "please, take off your pinafore and tear it up into strips."

I help Maidie untie her pinafore and she rips it in half and hands one piece to me. We slowly rip off long strips and make a pile on the blanket. Mary and Lucy don't sit next to us; instead, Lucy takes Mary aside and tenderly rubs her hands up and down Mary's arms. She cups my sister's face in her hands and leans in close to whisper. Since Mary's face is hidden behind the head covering, I can't tell if she whispers anything back.

When Maidie and I are finished, Lucy walks back to the quilt and gathers the strips of fabric, saying, "Girls, please keep an eye on the boys. Mary and I will hand these out to those who need bandages for their eyes."

"Yes, Mother," Maidie replies as I nod.

Mary kneels down next to me and asks, "Are you all right?"

"I'm tired," I admit.

She rubs my back and says, "Lie down. I'll only be gone a few minutes, then I'll be right back."

I nod and lean back onto the quilt. My head is starting to ache as well and I feel nauseous, probably from breathing in so much smoke in the last few hours. I don't care to vomit in front of these strangers, so I lie still and hope it will pass. Closing my eyes, I pray for sleep. I need the rest, but even more so, I need to shut out the hopeless world around me.

Karl

Skunk Lake, north of Hinckley
6:00 p.m. - 6:30 p.m.

I do come back up for air and dunk down again, over and over. I lose count how many times I do this when my body starts to move on its own without any coherent thoughts. Life becomes a series of actions on repeat: inhale, dunk, hold, surface, exhale. Eventually, the air changes. This inhale doesn't burn my throat, so I try breathing again. My heart hammers in my chest, and my ears ring, but I keep breathing. Peering through the smoke, I wait for the next wall of flames to jump out, but it never comes. I don't know what to do next besides breathe. Like the others in the pond, I just stand, not speaking, not crying, just breathing.

I don't think anyone in this pond expected to survive. Looking around me, I see faces etched with shock, weariness, and fear. Everyone here fled for our lives, and we may have outrun the fire, but now we have to survive the aftermath. Our feet move together, bound by the horrors of the inferno, but united in our own resilience. Slowly, we drag our weary bodies towards the muddy banks. Each step feels heavy as I trek through the muck and the mud. Once I reach the banks, I drop to my knees and crawl the rest of the way. The train is directly ahead of me, and it's still on fire. Huge sheets of flame swallow it whole, producing a thick column of black smoke that shoots up into the sky.

I find a patch of blackened grass and flop down onto my belly, breathing in the burnt smell. My neck, shoulders, and the back of my head throb in pain. Closing my eyes, which sting something awful, I moan through it. Unfortunately, when I close my eyes, I relive the last moments with Father. He's smiling at me while we hang onto the cowcatcher. Then he falls back into a cloud of black smoke and flames. A raw spot in my heart aches and emotions swirl in my gut. My stomach muscles contract and I start to gag. Painfully, I roll to my side and vomit, but it ends in a violent coughing fit. I spit and hack, gasping for air when someone bangs hard on my back, and thick black mucus flies from my mouth. The person pulls me up to a sitting position. I hold on to his arm for support and take a look at him. It's the black man who was helping those children in the pond. He's crouched in front of me, examining me like a doctor would. He has large brown eyes, a round face, and a thick bristly mustache.

"You have ash caked on your eyelids. Allow me," he says as he scrapes it away. "You'll need a bandage. I'm going to rip off a piece of your shirt and lay it on top of your eyes. That should help cool them off since it's still wet from the pond." I nod and watch as he rips off a strip of my tattered shirt. "Anything else bothering you?" he asks.

I lift my hand up to my head, "My head, sir."

He drops the strip of fabric and gently takes my hand, turning it over to look at my palm. His face changes from calm to worried. "This will need treatment as soon as possible." He holds my palm up near my face, and the flickering light from the train fire illuminates my damaged hand. It is severely burned. The skin is peeling back and underneath is a mass of red and black flesh. My stomach twists again as I realize that I'm looking at a muscle inside my hand that should be covered by skin. Quickly, I lift up my other palm. It is the same.

My heart races, and my lungs tighten, making it hard to breathe. I think I'm going to throw up again. I can't help it, but I start to whimper.

"Look at me," the man instructs, pulling my hands away from my face. I do as he says and look at him through tears that have just formed in my eyes.

"Keep looking at me. That's right," he says standing up and walking backwards. "Keep looking at me. Don't look away from my eyes."

I continue to stare at him, panting. My arms start to shake, but I continue watching the man as he goes back into the pond a few feet, bends down and scoops something up. All the while he is watching me, repeating, "Don't look away from my eyes."

He walks back to me, crouches down, and says, "Don't mind what I'm doing. You just look at my face and breathe."

I follow his instructions and focus on lengthening each inhale and exhale.

"What's your name?" he asks.

I stammer, "Karl."

"Karl, I saw you hit your head on the train tracks pretty hard. I think it's best if you lay back and rest. I'll put this bandage on your eyes to help with the pain, and now your hands should cool off from this mud."

I look down at my hands. He has put wet mud on top of each palm, hiding the burns.

"Don't move your hands too much," he says.

I lick my dry lips and ask, "You saw me fall on the tracks?"

"Yes, I did. You were calling out for someone."

"My father," I say, a lump forming in the back of my throat. "He's . . . he's not here."

"I'm sorry, Karl," he says. "I think everyone here may have lost someone today."

Finally, I recognize his voice. He's the man who saved my life when I had given up.

"Did . . . did you come for me?" I ask, already knowing the answer. "After I fell, it was you, wasn't it? You helped me into the pond?"

He stands up as he says, "Yes, I did."

"Thank . . . thank you, sir." My voice is thick with emotion. "Are . . . are you a doctor?"

"No. My name is John Blair, and I'm a porter for the St. Paul and Duluth Railway Company. I have to go check on the others now, but I'll come back and check on you later. This will soon be over. Now I want you to lie down and rest."

"All right," I nod, feeling so tired I might fall asleep the minute my head hits the ground. I lean back, close my eyes, and set my hands at my sides, palm up. I feel Mr. Blair set the strip of fabric from my shirt gently across my eyes. The relief is instant when the wet material hits my hot, stinging eyelids.

Even though I know the mud is there, I can't feel it on my palms.

Anna

Pokegama, Minnesota
6:30 p.m. - 7:30 p.m.

When I wake, Mary is lying next to me on the quilt. Her arm is around my waist. Blinking the sleep away, I remember our horrible situation. Hearing the groans of the strangers around me confirms it. I adjust my head covering since it slipped a little while I slept. The movement wakes Mary who removes her arm and sits up quickly, gasping.

"Mary," I say, sitting up next to her. "It's all right. We're safe."

"I had a nightmare," she says. "But I don't think I was asleep for more than a few minutes. I must have been exhausted."

"What did you dream about?"

"I dreamed of the fire, and—" She clears her throat. "Just the fire."

My shoulders slump. I'm afraid all of the day's horrors will haunt Mary and my dreams for the rest of our lives. I still don't have any words of comfort for my sister, so I just set my hand on her shoulder. A man walks up to us and stops at the edge of our quilt. He kneels down and offers us roasted potatoes from his bare hands. I don't mind at all. It's been hours since I've eaten. We thank him and hold out our dirty hands. We eat them in a matter of seconds. Mary must have been just as hungry as I. As I swallow the dirt-crusted chunks, I realize that the potatoes probably cooked themselves in the fire, depending on where the man found them.

"If only we had some fresh water to wash it down," Mary says.

I nod, chewing on the last potato. It tastes like burned wood, but I devour it.

After swallowing, I ask, "Can't we drink from the millpond?"

Mary shakes her head, "No, it's completely covered with ash, and there are dozens of dead fish floating on top. The water was spoiled during the fire. Someone will find a bucket and a well eventually, but it's almost dark now. We need to find shelter first."

"Is there anything still standing?" I ask, rubbing my feet, and noticing that the swelling has gone down, but the blisters remain.

"I'm not sure. Mr. Ward left some time ago to look for shelter. We shouldn't spend the night here. The evenings are too cool, and we don't want to be left out in the elements."

I look out beyond the pond at the wooden trestle which is still on fire. The flames are small, but they shine bright through the smoke and waning daylight. Night is coming on fast. The thought of sleeping outside frightens me, and I shiver.

Mary puts her arm around me and rubs her hands up and down my arms.

"So, you and Lucy are close?" I ask through chattering teeth.

"I suppose. She is a kind woman. We both have been learning how to be pioneers."

"Pioneers?"

"'Bound by the bonds of a common belief and a common misfortune,'" Mary recites the line from the poem *Evangeline: A Tale of Acadie*. She adds, unnecessarily, "That's Longfellow."

"Yes, we read that in school last year."

"It's a fitting description of the settlers here in Pokegama. All working towards the common belief that this town would prosper, but now look at it."

"That's a depressing perspective, Mary."

"I suppose it is. I have yet to acquire the spirit it takes to succeed as a pioneer, but Lucy has it. She and Caleb are already planning how to rebuild their home and the city center."

"Already? It's only been hours since it burned to the ground." My mind reels at the immense task of cleaning and rebuilding Pokegama. It would take so much time and energy.

"There's Mr. Ward now," Mary interrupts my thoughts. I follow her finger, pointing into the smoke, and see a man walking along the edge of the millpond. Lucy and another man meet Mr. Ward and speak to him. I assume the man is Lucy's husband Caleb because he is holding her hand. When they finish, the three of them walk over to us.

"Mr. Ward has wonderful news," Lucy smiles down at us. "He has found two boxcars untouched by the fire. We can spend the night there."

"Yes," Mr. Ward adds, "my wife and son are there now, but we should hurry before it gets too dark. It was difficult enough finding them in this gloom. I fear it will be impossible at night."

"How many more will join us?" Caleb asks.

Mr. Ward answers, "I walked around the millpond just now and saw that most of the survivors are not here. They must have left while I was gone. It's only your family and the doctor's left that I can see in this haze."

"They must have left to find another means of shelter," Lucy comments. "I didn't even notice. The smoke has been so thick and suffocating."

"Either way, we best be on our way," her husband adds. "Let's gather the children."

Lucy wakes her children, and Mary and I stand up and shake out our quilt. I roll it up and put it under my arm.

Mr. Ward touches my shoulder, "Miss, you best put your shoes on. The ground is still smoking, and the railway ties are burning."

"Yes, sir," I agree, bending down to pick up my oxfords.

The leather is stiff as a board, and I have to force my blistered feet into them. Each step is painful as I follow the group into the darkness.

22

Anna

Saturday, September 1, 1894
Pokegama, Minnesota
7:30 p.m. - 8:30 p.m.

After walking for nearly a mile, the train tracks split, and we follow the side track to the two boxcars. One contains bundles of wooden lath, the other brick. Lucy's husband informs us that both of the boxcars had arrived earlier in the week to be used as building materials for his brother's house. He is still missing. On that somber note, we climb into the one full of lath.

As Mr. Ward had said, his wife and son are already inside, resting against the side of the boxcar. The stacks of lath are piled high in two tiers on the other side of the car. The highest tier of lath is at the far end of the car next to an opening in the wall to let in air. As our weary group settles in, I wonder how the fire did not burn this. The children lie down, and the adults sit, trying to make ourselves as comfortable as we can.

Mary and I choose a spot near the door since we are the last ones in the boxcar. Mr. Ward sits near his family, and the two Kelsey families take up the rest of the space. I count Lucy's four children, making sure they all made it here safely. Earl, Lyle, Maidie, and Allen. Isabella sits in the far corner with her sons, Carleton and Willie. On

208

the walk here, Mary told me that Carleton is thirteen years old and Willie is eleven. Our group of fourteen fills up the boxcar.

My feet are stuck in my shoes, so Mary has to help me pull them off before we can relax. The stiff leather is cracked and destroyed. Another loss due to the fire. I kick them away with my sore feet, never wanting to wear them again. Just after we get settled, the door to the boxcar slides open. Three men climb up inside and look around. Their faces are covered in soot, and only one has a head covering. They nod to the Wards before turning back to the opening of the boxcar. Slowly, they start helping women and children into the car.

Lucy's husband stands up quickly, "Excuse me, gentlemen. There is another boxcar. You will find much more room there."

One of the men shakes his head, soot falling from his hair, "No, that one is full of bricks, Mr. Kelsey. We'll settle down here for the night."

"No, no, no," Mr. Kelsey says. "There is no more room in here. I must insist." The men at the opening of the boxcar stop helping others and turn to hear the conversation.

The tension in the tiny space is palpable.

"Please, neighbors," Lucy intervenes, walking quickly to her husband's side. "Let's be reasonable."

"I am being reasonable," the soot-covered man calmly states.

"You can clearly see that this boxcar is full," Lucy points out. "You and your families would be much more comfortable in the other. Then all might not be so crowded."

"We've all had an exceptionally long day and need space to rest," Mr. Kelsey adds.

"I agree," the man nods. "We all deserve to rest, and none will be comfortable sleeping on bricks, I can assure you of that."

Mr. Kelsey peers out the door, "There must be at least thirty in your party."

Lucy remarks, "If you all come in here, we will be sleeping on each other."

The man doesn't budge, "My family is not sleeping on bricks tonight. We wish to sleep here."

Mr. Kelsey shakes his head, grumbling, but turns away. He walks back to where Allen sits against the boxcar wall. He crosses his arms and sits next to his son, leaning his head back against the wall, closing his eyes.

Lucy stands in her place next to the soot-covered man for a moment more, then turns her heel and walks back to her children.

The conversation is over.

The men at the door turn back to the opening of the boxcar and continue to help more of their group inside. They make enough noise climbing into the boxcar and shuffling about to find a spot that I feel comfortable that no one else will hear me when I whisper to Mary, "Who are these people?"

Mary is rummaging inside her carpetbag. She finishes what she is doing and closes it back up. Turning to me, she whispers, "They are some of the Jewish families that live in Pokegama."

"Oh," I whisper, "so they are your neighbors?"

"Yes, I suppose. They live on the other side of the settlement. You better get comfortable now. We might not be able to rearrange ourselves once they are all inside."

I do as she says, and lie down on the rough laths, placing my head next to Mary's. We lie there silently as the group settles in. Once everyone is in place, we are, indeed, closely packed together. A Jewish woman holding a young girl lies on the other side of Mary. A man sits next to my feet, leaning his head against the side of the car. In any other situation, I would have been horrified that a man was so close to my bare feet, but today we all escaped death, and I don't have the energy to feel embarrassed. He doesn't remark on my feet either.

Karl

Skunk Lake, north of Hinckley
9:30 p.m. - 10:30 p.m.

My body shivers so hard, it wakes me up. I feel like I'm standing in a raw winter's wind. Then, I realize I'm lying down.

My eyes flutter open, but there is a dirty cloth on top of my face. I move it away with my hand which drips mud across my cheek.

Blinding pain rips through my skull. I have to lay still for a moment until it passes. Once the pain subsides, I remember the fire, the reason that I'm lying on the ground. I wish I had remained sleeping. My eyesight is blurry, but I am able to see. I turn my head each way to see where I am. I'm on the banks of Skunk Lake, but it's much darker now. I wonder how long I slept. There are others lying on the banks next to me, but some people remain in the shallows of the pond, sitting so still that they look like boulders. Others cry out in the darkness, groaning and moaning in misery.

I sit up slowly, careful not to bring back the crushing pain in my skull. The Skalley's coal tender is still on fire behind me, but the flames are small since they are running out of fuel. The tender is disconnected from the locomotive. It's the only light and heat source out here in the wilderness. The air near the tender is warm, but not so hot that I have to run away. In fact, I scoot myself closer to it, trying to gain some warmth from the blaze. The coaches behind the tender are smoldering, almost unrecognizable except for the steel frames that remain. Some of the smoke that surrounded the pond earlier has disappeared, and I can see that the tree stumps lining the edge are glowing red embers, slowly burning down to ashes. A whole forest wiped out in a single day.

Once I am satisfied with my distance to the train, I stop and lay back down. Now I'm away from most of the other survivors, closer to the barbed wire fence and the train tracks. I don't mind being here away from the group. It's quieter. As I stare up into the night sky, I can see the stars. As if nothing had happened, they shine and twinkle, obscured briefly at times by passing wisps of smoke. The stars make me think of Anna. I know she's safe in Pokegama, but I imagine she could see the tall column of black smoke since the fire was so large. She's probably worried sick about her parents. I wonder what happened to them.

The pain in my head comes and goes.

My eyesight blurs.

I drift in and out of sleep.

At times I see Father lying next to me in the grass.

Sometimes he is smiling, but other times, he's just a burned corpse smoldering next to me.

Anna

Pokegama, Minnesota
10:30 p.m. - 11:59 p.m.

I wake up to alarmed voices.

The blackness of the boxcar is overwhelming. I can't see anything, and it reminds me of our time at the bottom of the well. I pull off the damp quilt and sit up, trying desperately to see what's going on. I hear metal scraping against metal as the boxcar door slides open. Two dark figures jump outside into the night.

"What's happening?" Mary mumbles, groggy from sleep.

A voice on the other side of Mary answers in the darkness, "The ties under the boxcar are on fire."

Mary sits up quickly, "Should we get out?"

The voice doesn't answer, and Mary doesn't get up. I hear voices and grunts outside the boxcar. Minutes pass by, and no one moves. I jump when the wall next to me is hit from the outside with a spray of dirt and pebbles.

Mary grabs my hand and says, "They are putting it out. We are safe." She lays back down, but doesn't let go of my hand.

I listen to the men outside throwing dirt under the boxcar to put out the flames. Eventually, they stop and come back inside. After sliding the door shut, they make their way in, but it's impossible for them to move without nudging or stepping on someone. I hear grumbles as they wake others on their way back to their places.

I lie back down and try to relax, but my muscles are tense and my mind is wide awake. My sister's breath becomes slow and constant, so I assume she has fallen asleep. But I don't let go of her hand. I'm too scared to sleep, and I don't have the energy to cry. Instead, I replay the day in my head. Riding the morning train to Pokegama, finding my way to Mary's house, walking into a nightmare, John's hands squeezing the breath from my airway. The awful cracking sound of the frying pan crushing the back of his skull. I flinch at the memory, involuntarily squeezing Mary's hand. She shifts in her sleep, but does not wake up.

I can't wait to go home, see my parents, and sleep in my own bed again. Mary and I will need to figure out how to get there, so I should rest in order to deal with tomorrow's uncertainty. Time in this stuffy boxcar will go by faster if I sleep through the night, so I try to empty my mind and think of anything else besides what happened today. It's difficult, so I focus on each inhale and each exhale. Slowly, my body relaxes and exhaustion forces the tension to ease. The muscles in my shoulders feel heavy and weighed down. My mind is the last to give up, but eventually it does, and I ease into sleep.

Footsteps and a man's voice wake me. My eyes fly open, but I am met with darkness. I hear several other people breathing very close to me, and others groaning and coughing, but I can't remember where I am. A boy's voice cuts through the darkness, "Papa! Papa!"

The scrape of metal makes me sit up quickly, and I remember everything. We survived the fire, and we are taking shelter here for the night. My eyes have adjusted to the darkness, and I can make out a man climbing inside the boxcar.

"Carleton," he whispers.

Mary rouses next to me and lifts her head up.

The man squeezes between bodies until he finds the boy who hugs him tightly.

"It's Dr. Kelsey," Mary sighs with relief, "Thank goodness. All this time, Isabella and the boys were not sure if he was alive. That's Lucy's brother-in-law."

"Chauncey!" A woman's voice cries out, not caring if she wakes up anyone in the boxcar. I bet it's his wife Isabella. "How did you survive?"

"I was with Mr. Gonyea, Big Joe, and Mr. Anderson, trying to help Mr. Collier save his home. When the entire house exploded into flames, we all ran towards the city center to warn everyone."

Lucy's familiar voice speaks, "But Mr. Collier lives north of the settlement. The fire came from the southwest."

"Yes, we found ourselves in quite a predicament. Mr. Collier's house started on fire separately from this larger fire. After we ran from his house, we were stuck between two fires."

Isabella sobs, but the sound is muffled, like she is being held. My mind creates a scene where Dr. Kelsey is holding his wife, and she is clinging to him, as her fears that he was dead gradually disappear.

"Big Joe, Mr. Anderson, and I found a creek bed and lay there splashing water over ourselves. I don't know what happened to Mr. Collier and Mr. Gonyea."

"Both survived," Lucy answers. "Mr. Collier made it all the way to the millpond and held his wife and baby through the fire."

"Thank God," Dr. Kelsey sighs. "I delivered their baby only three weeks ago."

Lucy's voice continues, "Mr. Gonyea eventually made it there too, but he is in a terrible state. He is still lying on the banks of the millpond, unable to move."

"I can't see anything tonight, so hopefully he'll survive, and I can take care of him in the morning."

A cool breeze blows in through the open door which distracts me from their conversation. The doctor must have forgotten to close it in his excitement of finding his family.

I whisper to my sister, "I am going outside to relieve myself."

Mary answers, "I'll come with you."

"No, you don't have to. I'll stay right next to the boxcar, I promise. Go back to sleep, I'll only be a minute."

"Are you sure? How will you get back inside?"

"I will climb up."

"All right, but only a minute, Anna. And don't wander off, or you'll never find the boxcar again."

I stand up, slowly tiptoeing my way to the door. I feel the edge of it, crouch to the floor, and slide down to the ground. The air outside is still warm and smoky, but it is fresher than inside the boxcar. There are small, twinkling lights everywhere. Despite the circumstances, it is a beautiful scene of glowing red embers, smoldering tree trunks, and stars lighting up the night. Red sparks and cinders drift lazily in the air like fireflies. I wonder if this is what St. Paul looks like at night, with so many oil lamps and candles burning. I tilt my head up trying to find the moon, but it's not there. I suppose I should keep my word and get back to Mary. I finish my business quickly, but before I climb back into the boxcar, I say goodnight to the constellations and the twinkling lights.

PART THREE

AFTER

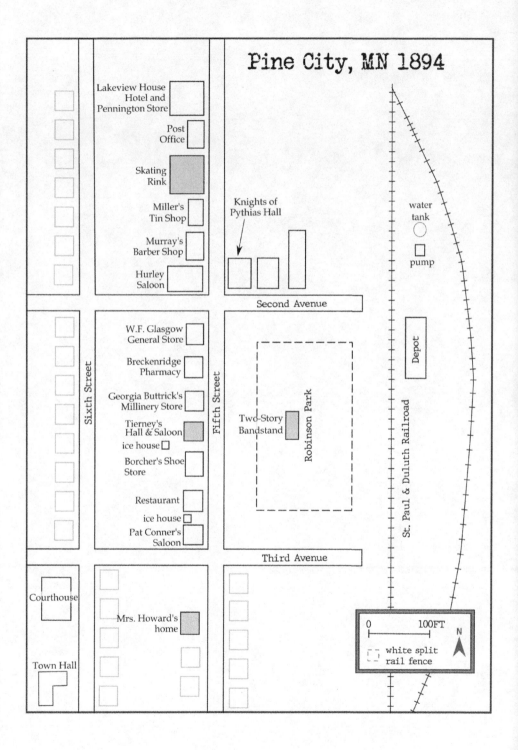

Pine City, MN 1894

Lakeview House Hotel and Pennington Store

Post Office

Skating Rink

Miller's Tin Shop

Knights of Pythias Hall

Murray's Barber Shop

Hurley Saloon

Second Avenue

W.F. Glasgow General Store

Breckenridge Pharmacy

Sixth Street

Georgia Buttrick's Millinery Store

Fifth Street

Tierney's Hall & Saloon

ice house

Borcher's Shoe Store

Restaurant

ice house

Pat Conner's Saloon

Robinson Park

Two-Story Bandstand

St. Paul & Duluth Railroad

water tank

pump

Depot

Third Avenue

Courthouse

Mrs. Howard's home

Town Hall

0   100FT   N

white split rail fence

23

Karl

Sunday, September 2, 1894
Skunk Lake, north of Hinckley
1 day after

I wake up alone, shivering, and whimpering in the darkness. I had a nightmare, but I don't remember the details. Slowly, I sit up and place my hands in my lap, palms up. The mud has dried and cracked in places. I touch the mud to my cheek and feel its coolness against my skin, but I can't feel the mud on my hand, only on my cheek. I'm not sure what that means for me, but it can't be good.

Light coming from the train skips and dances behind me. I turn around to find only the locomotive and the steel frames of the coaches left standing. The coal tender is still on fire, but the flames are small and tame. The light reflects on the surface of Skunk Lake, but the water is still. Nothing moves. Nothing makes a sound except the occasional pop and hiss from the coal tender.

I can't even make out the forms of the survivors anymore. If they lie on the banks, they must have died in the night, for nothing can be that still. Feeling a deep sense of loneliness, I slump forward and let my head hang between my knees. Minutes or hours later, I'm not sure anymore how time is passing, I hear something. Something that is out of place.

It's a squeaking sound, like a metal wheel spinning over a metal plate. It has a rhythm to it: *squeeek-sqoooo, squeeeek-sqoooo, squeeeek-sqoooo*. It gets louder but then stops suddenly. Maybe I'm dreaming again. I hear a thud behind me, followed by more thuds. Boots hitting gravel. Footsteps and then coughs. I lift my head and peer into the water, but still I see no one. Voices behind me cause me to sit up straighter. Certainly that is the sound of men talking.

Two voices begin to sing out behind me, "Hallo! Hallo! Is anyone there?"

I quickly scramble to my knees, stumble onto my feet, and finally stand facing the train tracks. Small, yellow lights are swinging back and forth along the tracks north of the train. Lanterns. Behind me the water shifts, and small, dark forms in the shallows stretch out and uncurl into human shapes. Along the banks, people begin to stir. Not everyone has died. They were just sleeping or sitting still.

Voices emerge from the pond—one, then another, and still another. "Hallo!" someone calls out. "We're here!" a man yells. "Please, save us!" screams a woman.

John Blair appears out of the darkness and flies past me, running to the new voices on the train tracks. I follow him but at a much slower pace, fumbling my way through the marsh that surrounds the pond. He stops running when he reaches a group of six men walking down from the train tracks. They don't look much better off than we do; their faces are covered in soot and sweat. I wonder if they have come to rescue us, or if they are just fellow survivors looking to be rescued.

Two of the men leave the group, carrying small, leather bags, and run towards Skunk Lake. The other four stay where they are, each of them shaking Mr. Blair's hand. When I finally reach the men, I can hear him finishing an explanation of what happened here.

One of the men asks, "And what of Engineer Root?"

"He's alive," Mr. Blair answers, pointing to the Skalley. "He's lying in the locomotive. He refuses to leave it."

The man cusses and walks toward the locomotive; he is followed by another man in their group.

One of the two remaining men reaches his hand out toward me. "Peter Kelly," he says.

I stare at his hand for a moment before I realize he's introducing himself to me. I grab his hand and shake it, "I'mmm Karrr—" My voice gets caught up in a cough, and I cover my mouth.

Mr. Kelly frowns at his hand and shakes off dried pieces of mud.

The other man says, "Let's get you some water and something to eat, Kar. We have a few crates of medicine, water, and food back on the handcar."

Mr. Kelly and the other man run back to the tracks as Mr. Blair helps me back to my patch of blackened grass that I was resting on before.

"These men have come all the way from Duluth, Karl. The world already knows about this tragedy. They are sending more help, but it may take time. Mr. Kelly says there are burned-out trestles and culverts between here and Miller, two miles north of us. Their train can't get past it, which is why they took the handcar. For now, we'll have to make do with the supplies they could carry on the handcar."

I nod at him but end up grabbing my head in pain.

"You stay right here. I'm going to help them pass out food and water."

Mr. Blair helps me lie on my back. I want to help him and the men from Duluth, but I can't even sit up. The pain in my head is too intense. All I can do is lie still and breathe through the pounding in my head.

After several minutes, I sense someone near me. I open my eyes and see a man crouching down at my side. He quietly sets down his lantern and a small leather bag. "Let's see what we have here," he gently lifts up my left arm. "Mr. Blair tells me that you have severe burns on both of your hands." He picks at the mud caked on my palm and hisses between his teeth.

I yank my arm away from him, struggling to ask, "Who arrrre youuu?" I don't know why I'm finding it so hard to speak. Is there dried mud in my mouth?

"Dr. Codding," he answers. Not disturbed by my lack of manners, he lifts up my right arm and gently picks the mud off my palm.

"You need to keep these clean and dry as much as possible."

He puts a hand behind my head and helps me sit up. Then he uses a damp rag to very gently dab at my palms before lightly patting them dry with a different rag. He uses the same wet rag to wipe my eyes. The moisture feels cool against my swollen, stinging eyelids.

"Is there anything else ailing you?" he asks.

"My head," I say. Finally, I'm able to say two words without slurring.

The doctor tilts my head forward and feels through my hair with his fingertips. His fingers find the back of my head and pause.

"Oh yes, you have a large laceration on the crown of your head."

He rummages in his small leather bag and brings out a small tube. He squeezes it onto his fingertip and applies a salve to the back of my head. He pulls out a long, white cloth bandage from his bag and wraps it around my head, tying it together at my temple. He does the same to both of my palms, salve and a cloth bandage for each. As he is wrapping my left hand, a man walks over and sets down a crate next to me.

"The last of the water I'm afraid," he tells Dr. Codding.

"Thank you, Conductor Roper," Dr. Codding replies, not looking up from my hand.

"We're off now. The worst ones are on the handcar. Are you ready?"

"No, I'm staying here with Dr. Magie."

"That's probably best. Williams is itching to get word back to Duluth. More help will come soon, but it probably won't be until morning. We need more light and more tools to rebuild those culverts and the trestle," he says and sets his hand on the doctor's back. "It was an honor to make the journey down here with you. I wish you well."

Dr. Codding stops wrapping, looks up and answers, "And you as well. Please give my regards to your engineer, the yardmaster, and his boss."

The conductor nods and walks towards the train tracks while Dr. Codding finishes tying the last bandage on my palm.

"Why are they... leavvvving?" I ask, slurring again.

"They are taking the severely wounded to Willow River, so they have shelter for the night. That is the first train station north of here that was untouched by the fire. Besides that, Mr. Williams wants to send a telegram to Duluth as soon as possible. The telegraph wires are destroyed everywhere else. The last message we received in Duluth this afternoon was rather grim, so everyone there thinks you are all dead. I expect Williams will also ask for building materials to be sent to Willow River, so they can rebuild the tracks and get a train here as soon as possible to pick up the survivors."

He uncorks a glass bottle of water from the crate and brings it to my mouth. He helps me drink it, and I swear it is the most amazing thing I have ever tasted. My throat feels instant relief, and I suck it down fast.

"Now I'm going to smear mud on your eyelids to help calm the swelling. You won't be able to see for a few hours, but that will help them heal faster. I can't imagine you can see very well as it is."

He walks down to the edge of the water and comes back with two handfuls of mud. I stare at him, wondering if he has lost his mind. He explains, "It's the best we have at the moment."

I bite my lip, but agree, "Ffff . . . fine."

"Lay back, you'll probably want to fall asleep after this."

I lean back on my elbows, slowly slide down to my back, and then close my eyes. Dr. Codding smears the mud across my eyelids and the bridge of my nose. "You have minor burns on your cheeks, so I'm going to cover them as well. This will help keep them from blistering."

He doesn't wait for me to agree. He just smears the mud all over my face and says, "Now, get some rest, son. You'll feel better after you sleep." I hear him wipe his hands on the ground next to me. Then he gathers his lantern and his bag and walks away. The burned grass crunches with each step the doctor takes.

Anna

Pokegama, Minnesota
1 day after

"Is it not nearly morning," a voice calls out, waking me.

My eyes flutter open and are met with darkness again. It seems this night is lasting an eternity. A match strikes somewhere in the boxcar, and the flame casts a light onto the wall next to me. Shadows appear on the wood.

A man's voice answers, "My watch says it's nearly two o'clock. The sun rises in five hours."

I rub the sleep from my eyes, but the movement is difficult. My arms feel strangely heavy and clumsy, and I'm disoriented and dizzy. Even though I'm lying down, I feel like my head is dipping in circles below my body, turning and turning. I push the quilt off my body, sit up slowly, and hold my head in place. That's when the shivering starts. My whole body is overcome by vibrations from my toes to my teeth. My legs underneath me shiver and contort.

"Marrrry," I slur, "Helllp."

Mary wakes and sits upright. My teeth knock wildly against each other. "Doctor!" she shouts.

The doctor gets up and slowly weaves through the crowded boxcar, crouching down beside Mary. He gently touches my face and neck. "She's suffering from an old trouble. Quickly, Mary, take off her shirt."

Mary hesitates. The man repeats himself with urgency, "Now, take it off."

I feel Mary unbutton my wool surge shirt and peel it off. She is slow to do so because I keep shivering and the fabric is damp. Next, she unbuttons my cashmere blouse and peels it off my skin. I squeak a little in protest, but she doesn't hear me. It's becoming difficult for me to breathe.

"Yes, as I expected," Dr. Kelsey says, "The material hasn't yet dried completely. We must warm her up before this chill takes her breath away. Do as I do."

I hear a swishing sound in front of me, speeding up and getting louder. *Swish-swish, swish-swish, swish-swish, swish-swish, swish-swish.* The violent trembling happening all over my body is becoming painful, and my mind is foggy. I think I'm going to faint, but then I feel heat all along my right arm. The doctor's large hands are rubbing up and down my arm. The heat from his palms hugs my skin like a warm blanket. Mary's hands touch my left arm, and she does the same, rubbing up and down my arm until it is warm.

"Now work over her chest and back, and I will work her legs," Dr. Kelsey instructs Mary. As she and the doctor warm me up, the shivering slowly stops. My breaths are coming easier now without all the trembling.

"She may endure more of these spells before daylight. Keep an eye on her until morning, and if she starts to shiver again, rub your hands over her skin to warm up the blood. Don't use that wet quilt anymore."

"Yes, doctor," Mary answers, "thank you." Dr. Kelsey leaves us and returns to his family. Mary and I remain sitting, leaning against each other. She drifts off to sleep, but when my shivers start again, she wakes up quickly. She chafes her hands together before working on me until the trembling stops. She does this for me periodically until the first rays of sunlight leak in through the slits in the boxcar walls.

24

Anna

Sunday, September 2, 1894
Pokegama, Minnesota
1 day after

Mary and I spent the last few hours with our legs curled up under us, leaning against each other, drifting in and out of sleep. She spread my damp clothes out on the floor, hoping to dry them before sunrise. As the first rays of sunlight creep into the cracks of the boxcar walls, Mary picks up my clothes and determines they are dry enough for me to wear. She helps me into my wool blouse and surge shirt before the boxcar is flooded with light.

Slowly everyone wakes up, or rather gets up. I don't believe that many of us slept the past few hours. Besides the sounds of my shivering spells, many have grown hoarse from coughing spells. Needless to say, we are all grateful that the morning has arrived, and we have a chance to stand up and stretch out.

Most of the men leave the boxcar to fetch water and look for something to eat. They leave the door open to air it out, so we have a chance to look out at the world for the first time in clear daylight. The sight makes my heart ache. We can see far off into the distance, miles in fact, because all of the trees are gone. Everything is a shade of black or gray. Lucy's youngest son, Lyle, walks to the opening of the boxcar and says to his mother, "Now, we can see the sunrise. We never saw it here before."

All of the children in the boxcar seem to perk up in the daylight, or maybe, the passing of time has awakened them from their stupor. Hopefully, they will soon be running around and playing games as they did before. In the daylight I can see the state of the survivors as well. We are quite a sorry lot. Many of us wear tattered clothes, and everyone is covered in black soot. Yesterday it was hard to see everyone's faces since most of us wore bandages or head coverings. Today I can see the wounds left from the fire.

Lucy asks Mary if she has a brush or comb in her carpetbag, but she doesn't.

"Well, no matter really," Lucy smiles. "I don't suppose I could get one through this matted mess." Her hair, like mine, resembles a bird's nest. Even Mary's long braid looks messy with strands coming loose. Besides our hair, we are also covered in ash, dust, and cinders.

Noises outside signal that the men have just returned. They set pails of water inside the boxcar and we all applaud. It has been hours since any of us had something to drink. We take turns drinking the water from the pails, and I can hear the pleasure and relief from my fellow survivors. Even so, I'm not prepared for how glorious it feels on my cracked lips and parched throat when it is my turn to drink.

There is barely any water left to wash ourselves, once every woman and child has had some to drink, but a few still try. Mary and I dip our bandages and head coverings in the water that is left and retie them around our heads. Then we step down from the boxcar. Lucy follows us, and we all help the children climb down.

Outside the men have formed a small circle, and each one looks out in the distance with their hands on their hips or folded across their chests. Some hold burned cabbages and raw potatoes. Lucy's oldest son Allen stands next to his father with a pail in his hand. He walks over to us, smiling. "Look, Mother," he says, "I found some eggs near the train tracks. Someone probably dropped them off for Mr. Berg's store yesterday morning. The fire cooked them, so everyone can have a hard-baked egg for breakfast."

Lucy exclaims, "How wonderful." Allen passes around the cooked eggs, and another man passes around the burnt cabbage. It's not a bad breakfast even if it does taste like smoke.

Another man scrapes the dirt off of the potatoes and cuts them into chunks with a pocket knife. He hands one to each person and tells us to use them as poultices to relieve the pain and smart in our eyes. I try it on my own eyes and am pleasantly surprised at the instant relief it brings. Unfortunately, the relief is short-lived. The moment that I take the potato off my eye, the nagging pain returns, so as long as I can blindly walk around holding a potato to my eye, I can feel relief.

I move the potato chunk away from my eye and see that Dr. Kelsey, assisted by Isabella, is slowly coming out of the boxcar. He puts his hand on her shoulder, and she leads him over to the group. In the daylight I see him for the first time. His clothes are tattered and burned. His long, chestnut beard now bears the scars of the fire, its ends singed and charred near his chest. His eyelids are swollen, puffy, and barely open. The whites of his eyes are red and bloodshot. I think he is blind, since he is using his wife as a guide. The hand he has on her shoulder is covered in large red blisters.

"Someone needs to go check on Mr. Gonyea," he tells the group, and at first, no one answers.

"I will," Lucy chimes in. "I am most able, and I can at least walk up and try to encourage him."

"If he is still alive," her husband remarks.

"I do hope so," Dr. Kelsey says.

Next to me, Mary speaks up, "We will come as well. My sister and I need to make our way to Hinckley."

Mr. Kelsey frowns, "I don't think that is a wise choice, Mary. You should stay here with the group until a relief party shows up."

Mary stands a little straighter, "Mr. Kelsey, I need to return my sister to our parents. Besides, I have nothing left here. My family is in Hinckley."

The doctor says, "The fire was moving northeast towards Hinckley. They might have sustained damage and casualties as well."

Mr. Baty adds, "That would explain why a handcar has not come from that direction."

I drop my potato in the dirt. The fire may have reached Hinckley? Our parents, my home, all my friends. My chest tightens, and I place my hand over my heart.

Mary's voice remains firm, "Even more reason then for us to go there and see what has happened, if anything."

Dr. Kelsey warns her, "It's an eight mile walk along the tracks from our city center to Hinckley, and that's if the tracks are unobstructed."

I feel compelled to say, "We have to at least try." My voice sounds exasperated, but I'm proud of myself for speaking up.

Mary nods, calmly explaining, "We will stay on the tracks, and if we must, we will turn around and come back." She takes my hand and leads me back to the boxcar, ending the conversation. She climbs in, retrieves the quilt and the carpetbag, handing them to me before she slides back down.

"Oh, I forgot your shoes," she turns around to climb back in.

"Leave them," I tell her. "I can't wear them. The blisters on my heels are too large for them to fit. Besides, the shoes are ruined. The water from the well soaked the leather."

Mary looks down at my feet, frowning, but she has no alternative to offer me. Lucy walks over to us, hooking one of her arms through mine and the other through Mary's. "Come ladies, we are going to take a morning stroll."

Karl

Skunk Lake, north of Hinckley
1 day after

Waking up to warm sunlight on my skin is a godsend, but when I shift my stiff legs and back, the tension forces me to remember that I'm lying on the hard ground. I attempt to open my eyes, but they are glued shut, and when I try to move my fingers, they are stuck under a bandage. Waking up outside in an unfamiliar, uncomfortable place is disorientating, but not being able to see or have the use of my hands is maddening. I kick my legs about and roll over to my side, pushing off my elbows and standing up far too fast. My head spins, and I stumble around scratching at my eyes with the ends of my bandaged hands.

The pressure in my head grows, and I feel nauseous. I throw my hands out and start to walk clumsily in circles. There are splashes and moaning noises coming from ahead of me, so I walk towards it, but I'm so disorientated I fall in the mud. My boots sink deeply in the squishy ground. I have to yank them up, which makes a sucking sound with each step. On the next step, my boots make a splash. I bend over, and just as I'm about to dip my hand in the water, I hear Dr. Codding's voice in my head, "You need to keep these clean and dry as much as possible." But I have to get the mud off of my eyes. I need to see! I grit my teeth and growl, stomping my foot, which ends up getting my trousers all wet as I splash myself.

"Please, let me help," a female voice requests behind me. "I saw you wake up, and I imagine you must be terribly confused."

I beg to the voice, "Please, my eyes. I can't see."

"Of course," she says. The woman uses her fingernails to chip away at the dried mud on my cheeks first, and then she does my eyelids. She is careful not to scratch too hard. After most of the dried mud is gone, she splashes water onto my face and wipes away the rest of the muck.

I use my tattered shirtsleeve to wipe the rest of the water away and stare down at my helper. Her face is smeared with black mud as well, but her eyes are familiar. She's the schoolteacher I saw yesterday in the street, holding two dresses, running towards the depot. I think her name is Mollie McNeil.

"*Tack så mycket.*" I tell her, "Thank you, Miss McNeil." She nods, then walks away to help a young boy who also has mud on his eyes. As she walks away from me, I cringe at the sight of her dress. It's almost completely burned away, leaving her quite exposed, but she's still holding up the tattered edge of her skirt from the water's surface, trying to keep it dry.

Embarrassed for her, I shift my gaze away and find more groups of people huddled on the banks of Skunk Lake. The daylight shows the true horrors of what happened to our sorry lot. Everyone is in a state of disarray. Some have black mud smeared across their faces, others wear a mask of green slime from the marsh. Clothing is similar to Miss McNeil's, burned away or ripped and tattered, barely hanging on to their owners' shoulders and hips.

The sounds the people make are frightening as well. Shrieks and yelps of pain, sobbing and crying, mumbling and groaning. The children are shivering, their teeth chattering together loudly. I can't stand to hear it, so I make my way out of the water and pass by a woman missing an eyebrow and the skin from one side of her face.

I move as quickly as I can along the edge of the pond, and keep moving until the sounds and the sights are far behind me. I keep close to the edge of the marsh, staring at the land. It's complete devastation. Not a single tree still stands. Blackened stumps, still smoking, stretch out as far as I can see. It must be miles and miles of destruction. The earth is black, covered in a blanket of ash. Not an animal stirs, not even a bird in the sky.

I stop and turn around, looking across the pond to the train tracks. The coal tender which slowly burned all night is now destroyed. The locomotive is several yards ahead of the tender. Someone must have disconnected it from the tender in an attempt to save it. Their idea worked because it is the only part of the Skalley left standing. The white numbers "69" painted on its side are almost completely covered in soot. The metal cowcatcher juts out in front, low to the ground. It's what Father and I grabbed onto yesterday when we fled the fire. Tears form in my eyes, and my lip trembles. I try to hold it in, but I'm too weak. Everything explodes all at once. First, a sob escapes and takes my breath away. A sudden pain erupts in my chest, and it splinters any trace of composure I had left.

I unleash all of my feelings in one long, loud wail. The sound comes from a dark place, deep inside of me. My head tilts back at the end, and I scream up to the overcast sky. My throat burns and my muscles tense. The release empties me, squeezing every ounce of energy I had left. I collapse onto my knees, crashing into the marsh weeds and sinking into a shallow puddle of green water.

"Why?" I cry out. "Why didn't you hold on? We were so close." The tears keep coming, but I don't wipe them away. I let them run down my cheeks and fall. Across the pond, people are staring, but there's nowhere for me to hide. I hang my head between my knees, and I cry. It hurts so much. I think my chest is going to crack open, and my insides will spill out into the mud.

I wipe the snot from under my nose, but the inhale of air up my nostrils causes a sharp pressure between my eyes. "Not again," I groan, holding the sides of my head. A loud ringing in my ears drowns out any other noise or thought. All I can do is stay still and wait until the pain passes. I sit like this, alone in my puddle, until I hear a train approaching from the north. I look up, and since all the trees are burned away, I can see it coming down the tracks from a mile away. The joy I felt when I saw the handcar appearing in the night does not come this time. I don't feel anything, except pain.

I stand up slowly and walk along the edge of the pond back to the tracks and the other survivors. The walk back is more difficult as the ringing in my ears has not stopped, and the pressure in my head makes me dizzy and unbalanced. Everyone is boarding the train, but it is a somber departure. Feet trudge through the weeds quietly, and heads hang low. Pain and despair has numbed us to the gift of rescue. We are all too weary for any more emotions, and we board the train with vacant looks on our faces.

I am just another one of the herd, climbing on board with the help of two men. They pull me up into the coach and smile at me, but I can't smile back. Those muscles don't work anymore. Slowly, I follow the man in front of me and find a seat on a stiff wooden bench. Someone throws a blanket on me, and I struggle to wrap it around my shoulders. Another man sits next to me and assists me. His hands are covered in blisters. Nobody speaks. Everyone coughs and moans. A constant *drip, drip, drip* of water and mud splashes on the floor.

A man walks down the aisle handing out cold doughnuts to everyone. He pauses when he sees my hands, but I hold them both up in the air, so he sets the doughnut in between the bandages. I eat it quickly before it falls on the floor. The grease and sugar mix with mud and pond sludge from my dirty bandages. I don't think I've eaten since lunch break at the lumberyard yesterday before the fire. So this should satisfy me, but it doesn't. In fact, the dough sits heavy in my stomach.

The man sitting next to me with the blistered hands stares ahead and says, "We are heading to Duluth."

"Duluth?" I repeat.

Still, he doesn't turn to face me when he says, "I've never been to Duluth before." He's not excited or scared. He states it as a matter of fact, but my mind begins to race.

"I don't know anyone in Duluth."

"I don't either," he sighs. "Everyone I knew burned up." He says it so plainly, like he is telling me the day of the week.

"No, no, no. I can't go to Duluth," I cry. Faces flash in front of my eyes. People that I left behind: Kristoff, Mr. Andersson, Anna.

The man ignores the panic in my voice and repeats himself, "I've never been to Duluth before."

I stand up quickly, shrugging the blanket off my shoulders and say, "I have to get off, now."

"What?" he asks, finally turning to look at me as I squeeze past him into the aisle. "Where will you go?"

I struggle through the line of people coming into the train. None of them even look up at me, to wonder why I'm going the wrong way. I don't turn back but shout out to the somber man with the blistered hands, "Hinckley. I have to go back and look for my friends."

25

Anna

Lucy, Mary, and I follow the train tracks back to Pokegama's city center. We find Mr. Gonyea lying on the banks of the millpond. He lies still, but answers when Lucy greets him. He asks if we have any food, so Lucy tells Mary and me to look in the ruins of Mr. Baty's house for something that he can eat. I follow my sister to a pile of ash and rubble near the millpond. We find burned bread, crackers, and charred potatoes. Lucy helps Mr. Gonyea eat the bread and crackers while Mary walks to the horse stables on the other side of the millpond to find a bucket and a well. I scrape the ash from the potatoes and use Lucy's pocket knife to cut them into chunks. I carefully place the potato chunks on Mr. Gonyea's hands and feet, using them as a poultice to relieve the pain. His skin, bright red and blistered, emits an overwhelming scent of burned flesh.

When Mary returns with a pail of water, Lucy cups her hands and helps Mr. Gonyea drink from it while Mary holds his head up. We can't help him anymore than that. Mary's bottle of laudanum is empty, and we don't have any other treatment for his pain or the burns. Lucy wants to return to her children, and Mary wants to start

234

our walk to Hinckley. Before we leave Mr. Gonyea alone again, Lucy lays our quilt on him. She is trying to be kind, but the gesture disturbs me. It feels like she is placing a burial shroud over his body.

Lucy hugs me and Mary before we part ways, and then we are off. The eight mile walk without shoes is treacherous. The blisters on my feet burst open, so I have to stop and rip strips of fabric off the hemline of my dress to wrap around my feet. Everything along the tracks is burned up. I walk silently next to Mary, but she stops suddenly and gasps. There is a black charred body on the embankment. It is the corpse of a man or a woman who tried to flee the fire but failed. We stand there a moment staring until Mary takes my hand and guides me past the body.

"We have to keep going," is all she says to me. We continue our walk in silence.

After a couple of hours, the top of a structure emerges in the distance through the lingering smoke. Sunlight reflects off of the metal roof. Mary and I pick up our pace and almost sprint to it, but as we get closer, we can tell something is wrong. As the smoke clears, we both stop in our tracks and gasp at the sight. Hinckley is gone. Dr. Kelsey was right. The fire did come here, and it wiped our town off the face of the earth. The landscape looks like a battlefield. Piles of ash stand where there should be houses and businesses. The shiny metal roof that we thought was a beacon of hope is one of three remaining structures in Hinckley. There's the Eastern Minnesota roundhouse, its water tank, and far off in the distance a crumbling shell of my school. Everything else is annihilated. Buildings, trees, sidewalks, everything is gone.

We both cry, devastated and unsure what to do next. Slowly, we make our way to the roundhouse. The siding has black stains around the sides, but the metal sheets must have blocked the flames and spared the building. We are not the only ones inside. A few other survivors slump between the train tracks, heads hanging between their knees. One of the men stands up and greets us. The side of his head is burned, and he is missing an ear, leaving a mass of red and black flesh. He explains that a train from Pine City has already come this morning. It took refugees back with them and left search parties to look for other survivors. The men on the train promised that they would return this afternoon.

Mary and I stand in front of the man, trying to absorb everything he just said. Mary's trembling voice breaks the silence, "Does anyone know how far the fire spread?" she asks.

The man's reply is a gut punch, "All the way to Sandstone, maybe farther."

My heart stumbles, and the world tilts. Our home—my parents—could be gone. I collapse, tears streaming, and crumble to my knees.

Mary sits down next to me and rubs my back. The man carries over a crate and sets it down beside us. "The men from the train left us milk and bread," he says before he returns to his spot between the tracks. He sits down and looks away, trying to give me a moment of privacy.

Mary rubs my back until I stop crying. Then she opens a bottle of milk and offers me some. I drink it, but I don't taste it. I refuse the bread. I can't eat right now; I'm still in shock. Mary eats and drinks then returns the crate to the man who gave it to us. She talks to him for a while before she comes back and sits next to me. We don't say anything. I can't. I'm afraid if I start to speak I will sob again and never stop.

We sit in silence for almost an hour. The other men in the roundhouse fall asleep. Tears stream down my face, and I don't have the energy to wipe them away. Mary whispers, "Anna, what's wrong?"

Such a strange question to ask when everything is wrong. The world is burned up, Hinckley is gone. Our parents are missing. I don't know if anyone I knew before is still alive. Mary's house is a pile of ash. Everything she owned is gone, and moments before all of this happened, her husband attacked and tried to kill us. Oh, and another small detail, Mary crushed the back of his skull with a skillet, and we left him to die. That's what's wrong!

I sigh and choose the part that worries me the most, "I'm thinking about Mother and Father. Where do you think they are?"

"I'm not sure, Anna," she nods her head toward the man missing an ear and continues, "He said most of the survivors left in Hinckley were already taken to Pine City. The few that have been trickling in this morning are from outside of the city."

"So, Mother and Father might already be in Pine City?"

"They could be. But he also said that some survivors escaped on trains before the fire. They headed north, probably to Superior or Duluth. The Skalley was able to leave Hinckley, but it burned up near Skunk Lake. A few men on handcars left Hinckley hours ago to see if anyone survived there." Her voice is steady and calm, as though she is talking of strangers, when she could be talking about our parents.

My voice trembles when I ask, "How will we know where they are?"

"I don't know," she sighs. "It's impossible to know where to start looking. I honestly don't know what to do, Anna." She is silent for a moment, then whispers, "They might not even be alive."

I hiss through my teeth, "Don't you dare say that. Mother and Father are alive. Why would you even think like that?"

My anger doesn't shake her at all. She doesn't even flinch, "Anna, we have to be prepared for the worst. It's a very real possibility that they didn't make it."

I choke back a sob. She said that without any emotion at all. "It's also possible that they lived," I reply, raising my voice.

"Shh," Mary shushes me and steals a glance at the sleeping men. "This is not an appropriate time to be hysterical."

I shout back, "Hysterical? How should I act? You think Mother and Father are dead."

One of the men twitches and snorts in his sleep. "Shh. Anna, you're acting like a child," Mary hisses.

"No!" I shout in her face. "I will not shush. It is an appropriate time to be upset about dead parents." She turns away from me, and I whisper, "And a dead husband." Mary's hand shoots out quickly and slaps me in the face. Her palm cracks against my cheek, and the sound echoes against the walls and ceiling.

The movement hurts her more than me because she cries out in pain and doubles over, grabbing her ribs. I remain seated, stunned, holding my stinging cheek. Mary struggles next to me, gritting her teeth in pain, but I don't move to help her.

The man with the missing ear blinks away sleep and then stares at us. I look away, ashamed and embarrassed. Then another sound echoes through the building. Heavy footsteps. A figure stumbles through the arched entrance, tripping over the rails and falling to the ground. I think it's a man, but it's hard to tell. He picks himself up and continues towards us. His face and hair are covered in soot, and his clothes are ripped to shreds, so much that I can see his bare chest, which is stained black.

The man struggles to stay upright. He is coughing and hacking so hard it almost knocks him to the ground, again. He turns abruptly and starts to walk away from us towards another entrance. I fear he may be blind from the smoke and cannot see us. I try to stand up, alarmed that he will continue walking out the other entrance into the desolation and be lost forever, but when I put weight on my feet, they give out underneath me. The pain from the blisters is too much to stand on.

Mary notices the man and slowly stands up, still clutching her ribs and breathing irregularly. I pull on her skirt for stability and heave myself up, throwing my weight onto her shoulder. She tries to shake me off, but I grip onto her and shout, "Here! Sir, we have milk and bread."

The man stops at the sound of my voice. He turns back around towards us. He stands there, frozen in place. The whites of his eyes clash with the black soot covering his face. Then he opens his mouth into a wide grin and starts running. He holds his arms out in front of him for balance, and I notice his hands are covered in thick dirty mittens. As he approaches us, I gasp and almost faint from shock.

Karl

Skunk Lake, north of Hinckley
1 day after

I follow the train tracks south towards what is left of Hinckley. At first my pace is quick. I want to get away from Skunk Lake as fast as I can. Even though I survived the fire in the swamp and marsh, I hope to forget the images and sounds of that terrible place.

Anything left in the landscape is black and dead. All of the poplars, birch, and tamarack that used to line the edges of the train tracks are gone. Only some of the larger tree stumps remain, and they are still smoldering and burning. Even the railroad fences and telegraph poles are missing. The last vestiges of civilization are the metal rails and wooden ties of the train tracks. It's my road back to Hinckley but, the fire took a toll on them as well. The ties are unbearably hot, most still smoking, and the rails are twisted in some places. The heat created by the fire must have been so hot that it melted the steel and contorted them into odd shapes.

At one of these places on the tracks, I meet a caravan of five handcars. Men are lifting the handcars, one by one, and carrying them around the twisted rails. I walk over to a woman sitting on the handcar furthest back. Her dress is burned off, and the skin on her back is peeling. She is missing most of the hair on the back of her head.

"Where are you going?" I ask.

The woman turns her head towards me, eyes swollen and red. She has black mud smeared on her cheeks, and she soughs as she says, "Hinckley."

"Where did you come from?"

"Skunk Lake."

"Me too," I'm surprised that we came from the same place. I suppose there were hundreds saved in that marshy pond. This group must have left before the train from Duluth arrived while I was on the other side of the pond.

The woman points to a man in the front of their handcar caravan. "Dr. Barnum is taking us back to Hinckley," she tells me. He says there are relief trains ready to bring us to Pine City. The fire didn't reach—" She has a coughing fit and can't finish her sentence, so I leave her alone.

I walk ahead to the handcar that's being lifted and moved around the melted tracks. I stand and watch. I'm embarrassed that I can't help them. After moving two more handcars, the men set wooden boards across them, creating more seating for the Skunk Lake survivors. Most look similar to the first woman I talked to, charred hair, burned skin, and missing clothes. These must have been the most injured of our group back at Skunk Lake.

I count almost forty survivors sitting or lying across the handcars. A few are moaning and crying, but most of them stare in silence. Seeing an elderly man struggling to lift himself onto the handcar, I hurry over to him. I drape his arm over my shoulder and use my arms to lift him up. The movement pains me, but I can't drop him now. I set him gently on the handcar and hold the back of his head with my bandaged hand, struggling to support him as he leans back and lies down.

"Don't you need a place to sit?" he asks.

"No, I live on the wagon road, north of Hinckley. I'm going there, now."

"You better head that way, off the tracks, then," he points east, into the gray and black wasteland. "We are almost to the bridge." I nod to him and leave the group, walking down the embankment into the sea of burning tree stumps and ash.

The walk is difficult. In some places, the ground is so hot that it starts to burn through my boots. I walk on my tiptoes, trying to make as little contact with the ground as possible. In other places, the tree stumps glow on the inside, still slowly burning. Walls of smoke hang in the air, blocking my vision at times and making me cough and wheeze. My eyes sting, and my head aches, but I keep walking, not knowing what else to do. Part of me wants to turn around and head back toward the railroad tracks. At least, they provide a sense of direction. This landscape has no markers. Everything is gray, black, or burning. I don't even know which way I came from. I'm all turned around, lost in this desolate burned up country.

Finally, my feet step on something other than ash and charred tree stumps. It's firmer than the burned-up ground and not as black. I kick at it with my feet and see dust fly up with only a little bit of gray ash. This must be the wagon road, but now I have to decide which way to turn. I look up and down the road, desperate for a landmark. In one direction, there is a black column of smoke rising up from the horizon. Something big must still be burning, so that way must be Hinckley. My guess is the lumberyard or the mill is still on fire. That's the direction I head. Hopefully, I haven't already passed my home.

Not too far down the road, there is a large, black pile of ash on the right side of the road. A well stands erect among the ash, but nothing else remains. I walk over to the well and peer inside. It's empty, not even a rope and bucket for me to use. I curse under my breath. The water is so close that I can taste the moisture on my tongue. My throat is so parched from breathing the smoke-riddled air, but I don't dare climb down into the well because I'm too weak to lift myself out. I could be stuck down there for days. I shake my head and walk away, dragging my feet through the pile of ash.

I know this isn't my house. This house is on the wrong side of the road, and the well is north of the house; ours is east of the house. I kick through the ash, looking for anything that isn't completely destroyed. My foot hits the hard side of the cellar. The metal hinges remain, but the wooden door must have burned up. I lean back on my haunches and peer down into the darkness. My eyes adjust to the lack of light, and I see a circle of charred lumps. The lumps are unrecognizable except that they have limbs. These were once human beings. Stunned, I cry out and try to run away, only to lose my balance and fall backwards into the rubble. A cloud of ash surrounds me, and I cough and choke on the air—it tastes foul, like burned meat.

I crawl on my hands and knees, choking and gagging and make it back to the wagon road. I stand up quickly and walk away, shaking the hot ash off my tattered shirt. I'm shaking off the ashes of a family who used to live there.

I come upon another pile of ash on the east side of the road, but the well is in the wrong place to be my home, so I keep walking. The next large pile of ash is on the east side of the road, and the well is to the east side of the pile, just like ours. Farther from the well is the crumbling foundation of a building that I assume is the stone foundation of what was once our barn.

I stop walking and stare. Smoke and ash swirl in the air above the pile that used to be my home. There is nothing left. No animals. No buildings. No tree stumps. Nothing. The fire even consumed the top layer of dirt leaving nothing but the clay subsoil and the rocks and stones beneath. Slowly, I step off the road and stumble towards nothing. A flash of light catches my eye, so I look down. Something is reflecting the sunlight. I step towards it and kick it with my boot. Ash shakes off my mother's sewing machine. The gold letters, SINGER shine in my face. They have been damaged, the GER is more black than gold, but they are still there.

Thoughts are wiped away and it's hard to breathe, so I grab my chest. My breath comes in short and shaky, and I choke on each exhale. This was my home, my place of safety and warmth. The log house that Father built for his family now reduced to a pile of ash. Nothing is left except the well and the foundation to the barn. Everything else we owned, everything we worked so hard for is gone. Tears pool in my eyes, hot and salty. I'm tired of crying, so I push them back with my bandaged hands. Then, I trudge through the pieces of my broken home. Each step is heavy, and a cloud of ash follows me as I walk in circles.

I continue this way for hours, it seems, stuck in a loop. I finally stop when the sunlight reflects off something half-buried in the ash. I bend down to see two coins melted together. I claw at it with my bandaged hands, struggling over and over to grab it, growling in frustration until I'm screaming down at it. Anger pulses through my veins, and fury crawls up my dry throat. I punch the ground over and over with my hands, curling them into fists within my bandages. The coin disappears in the black ash, but I keep punching. My fists kick up such a heavy cloud of ash that I lose my balance and stumble backward, tripping on Mother's sewing machine. I fall to my knees next to it, kicking up another cloud of ash which stings my eyes.

I want to pick up the sewing machine and hold it, but it's too large and heavy for me to carry all the way back to Hinckley, especially with my hands as they are. It breaks my heart that I have to leave it. My lip trembles, and this time I let the tears fall. I cry for my home, for Jack and *Äpple* who are missing, but mostly, I cry for my dead parents.

I don't remember standing up and leaving, but I did. I don't remember walking down the wagon road, but I did. I must have passed the remains of Andersson homestead, but I don't remember. It was just another pile of ash. My eyes are red and swollen from crying and from the smoke. My head is pounding and my ears are ringing, but somehow I make it to Grindstone River. I'm standing on the edge of the ravine deciding how to cross. The wagon bridge should be here, but like everything else it is gone.

A short way down river, I can see the lumberyard still ablaze, sheets of flames shooting towards the sky, creating a column of black smoke. That must be what I saw earlier from the wagon road. I could cross the river on the train bridge, but smoke is coming off the trestle. It's not quite on fire, but I don't dare walk across it on foot. My boots would probably melt from the heat. I also don't want to be that close to the fire still burning at the lumberyard. The only way to get to Hinckley is to cross the river on foot. I stumble down the ravine and step into the water which is less than a foot deep and covered in a thick blanket of ash.

Upstream, four bloated bodies lie on the muddy banks. Their

naked bodies are swollen, dark red, and charred. The largest one's arms and legs are bent at strange angles; the fingers are black and bent backwards. The other three bodies are much smaller. They are children, burned black and contorted in grotesque positions. Then, I see the tiny charred baby, and I vomit into the ash-covered water. My chest constricts and suddenly I can't breathe, not from the smoke or the ash, but from the sight of death. So much death. The ungodly sight of dead children forever burned into my memory. I claw my hands into the mud on the other side of the river and climb as fast as I can away from the corpses, gasping for air as I reach the top. I lie on my back on the blackened grass and catch my breath. When the air comes in and out of my lungs freely again, I get up and make my way as fast as I can to the outskirts of Hinckley, tripping over the debris. I can't seem to stay upright for very long, but I don't let that stop me. I have to get away, as far away from the dead children as possible.

I eventually do stop, forced to by a terrible coughing fit. It's so bad that I stop breathing for a moment, and my vision darkens. I kneel down in the ash and dirt, seriously debating if I can stand again. By some miracle, air does enter my lungs. I wipe the spit from my chapped lips and take in my surroundings.

I'm not prepared to see the destruction. The entire city is completely wiped out. My view should be blocked by buildings, but the fire has swallowed them. I can see far off into the horizon; only wisps of smoke obscure my view for miles. Hinckley is gone. In a trance, I walk with no sense of direction into the debris, avoiding the blackened carcasses of horses and cows. The air is thick with the smell of burned hair and flesh. I cover my mouth with my bandaged hand, and my nostrils fill with the smell of ash and smoke. My bandages are completely soiled, and they stink.

Every so often there are charred bodies lying in the street next to the metal skeleton of a carriage or the axle of a horse cart. Some are curled up into balls, their charred hands clutching the ground beneath them, while others stretch out fleshless arms reaching towards something. All portray the agony of their last struggle.

The school building still stands. The brick walls survived the intense heat of the fire, but the roof and anything inside did not. It's a black shell of what it used to be. I can see straight through it, from one window through to the other. A large chunk of the second story is missing, but the smoke stack stands tall. The town hall, which should be right next to the school, is gone. Just a pile of rubble, with the bell laying on its side, charred and black.

A drum pounds inside my head, and I feel dizzy. I push my dirty, bandaged hands to my temples, trying to steady myself. It helps me balance, but the pounding and the ringing in my ears doesn't stop. A cow crosses the street in front of me, walking lazily through the ash. I can't tell if it's real or not. When I walk past the cow, it moves sideways, doubling into two cows, standing right next to each other. I trip over an abandoned suitcase, shake myself off and keep walking.

In the distance the sun reflects light off a large piece of metal. I take one step in that direction, then another. It's something to aim for, something to focus on. I stumble and trip, finding myself yet again, walking on train tracks, but these are twisted and warped. In some places, they look like black snakes reaching up into the sky.

The large piece of metal is a structure, a building, but I don't think I'll reach it. The pain in my head consumes me. It takes so much energy to take one step that I fear I'll fall over in exhaustion, right on these twisted tracks. I focus on one step. Then another and another. Eventually, I enter the building walking underneath the arched entrance. It's a roundhouse because there are rails crossing the gravel floor in every direction.

It's so hard to stay upright, the ground keeps shifting and throwing me off balance. A voice shouts at me, and I turn to the sound. It's a woman. I blink a few times, testing to see if she is real or not. Each time I open my eyes, she is still there, but sometimes she is alone and other times there are two women. Then, they double into four fuzzy shapes. I squint, focusing on their faces. Slowly, they come into focus and pure joy radiates from my core. I know these faces. "Annnna!" I slur, running to her as fast as I possibly can, even though the world keeps swaying and throwing me off balance. "Annnna!" I crash into her, squeezing my arms around her as tight as I can. If I let go, she might disappear.

She folds underneath me, and I am too weak to catch her, so we fall on top of each other onto the gravel. Small hands try to pull me off her, but they can't, so they roll me to one side. Anna props herself up on her elbows next to me. She asks me something, but I'm not sure what she says, so I just smile at her. I'm so happy that she is here with me.

I notice that she has no shoes on. "Where arrrre yourrr shoezzzzz?" I manage to ask before everything goes black.

26

Karl

Sunday, September 2, 1894
Pine City, Minnesota
1 day after

Muffled voices talk to each other near me. My eyes are still closed, but I can hear them. I stretch out my legs and arms; they are so stiff from sleep. The wool blanket that covers my body shifts with my movement. I try to swallow, but it's difficult. My throat is parched, and my lips are cracked.

Finally, I open my eyes and am met with a flood of warm, golden light. My eyelids still ache, but it is far less painful than earlier. I blink a few times to adjust to the glow. The ceiling is high above me, held up by tall, wooden poles and V-shaped rafters. The walls are lined with cast-iron wall mounts, each holding a tall, glass chimney resting on the rim of the lamp burner.

I've seen kerosene lamps like that before, on the walls at Hanson's Opera House, but those walls had ornate wallpaper plastered on them, and these are simple, wooden boards painted white. I remember the fire and the fact that it burned down Hanson's. It's gone. I can't possibly be there.

Someone cries out in pain. The sound echoes and bounces off the walls. I lift my head, which is no easy task since it's wrapped tightly in a cloth bandage. I feel so weak, and my head seems too heavy, but I am able to see more this way. I'm surrounded by people. Men, women, and children are sprawled out on the floor in tidy rows. Each has a blanket covering them, but the tattered clothes, burned skin, and singed hair tell the story of what possibly happened. The fire touched us all in some way. Many of us are sleeping, a few are crying, some are moaning, and I see one man lying wide awake with a vacant look on his blistered face.

Where am I?

Behind me a voice asks, "Karl?"

I adjust my head to see the speaker. It's Mary. "Karl, you're awake," She quickly comes to kneel at my side. Her clothes are filthy, and her hair is frayed. But her face is clean and lacking any blisters or red burns.

I haven't talked to Mary since the day I kissed her in front of the gypsy wagon. My face reddens from embarrassment, and I avert my eyes away from hers. She places her hand on my shoulder, "It's all right. You're safe now."

I follow her arm up to her shoulder and notice the other arm is wrapped in a cloth sling. It's just a ripped piece of clothing, but it's holding her arm close to her chest. My head feels too heavy to hold up, so I lay back down, noticing that I'm wearing a clean shirt that has no rips or holes in it, "Mary, I'm . . . so sorry . . . for the kiss."

"Oh, Karl, of all the things to worry about," she says, shaking her head. "All is forgiven."

"Where am I?"

"Pine City, at the skating rink. The townspeople have converted it into a makeshift hospital to help us."

"Pine City? But . . . How?"

"You collapsed in Hinckley, in the Eastern Minnesota roundhouse. Anna and I were there among the other survivors. We boarded a relief train from Pine City and rode it back here. You were carried onto the train and then, into the rink hospital."

Alarmed, I ask, "Anna? Where's Anna?"

"She's here, sleeping on the women's side. Her feet were hurting her something awful, so Dr. Barnum wrapped them and gave her something to help with the pain."

Hearing that Anna is safe, I calm down, but I still have so many questions. "Mary," I try to speak, but my voice cracks and I cough violently, convulsing on my cot. The bandage underneath my shirt collar rubs against the burns on my neck, and intense pain like a million tiny knives stabbing all at once races across my skin.

"Here," she quickly gets to her feet, "let me find you some water."

I lie as still as possible waiting for the pain to pass. Mary reappears with a cup of water in her hands. She kneels down and gently lifts my head with her free arm. I pull my arm out of the blanket to take the cup from her, but my hand is wrapped in a fresh white bandage.

"Oh!" I exclaim. I had completely forgotten about my burned hands.

"I can help you, Karl," she says. She leans forward and pulls her injured arm away from her body in order to reach me. I lean towards the cup and awkwardly drink from it. Some spills down my chin, but it's cold and refreshing, and it soothes my throat and lips instantly. I finish it quickly and wish I could drink more, but I don't want her to leave again.

She slowly sets my head back down and pulls away. "Mary," I point my bandaged hand to her arm. "What happened?"

She frowns and looks away from me. She chews on her lip for a moment, then starts to speak, "There was a terrible fire. I think it started somewhere south of Pokegama. It caught Anna and me unaware. We had minutes to save ourselves, so we jumped into the well at my home. We stayed there for hours until the air was cool enough to leave." She bows her head and whispers, "My house is gone. Burned to the ground with everything I owned."

Home. The images of my burned-down house flash before my eyes. The piles of ash and the blackened foundation of our barn. Mother's sewing machine.

She continues, "On the train here, I heard men saying that the fire moved quickly through Pokegama and reached Hinckley sometime between three and four in the afternoon. But at the same time, a separate fire started in Mission Creek and moved north. The Pokegama fire and the Mission Creek fire combined in Hinckley. Those men called it a firestorm. It destroyed everything, Karl. Towns are gone. Hinckley, Sandstone, Finlayson, Partridge are all gone. There's nothing left of them."

I close my eyes and shake my head, forcing the horrible images of what I saw in Hinckley to disappear. I have to tell Mary about her home, her childhood home. "Mary, I walked on the wagon road into Hinckley. I passed my home and your parents' home. They're gone."

She stares at my face, and I notice her eyes are filling with tears, "Anything?"

I shake my head. She rubs her eyes, pushing the tears back, "Anna and I walked on the train tracks from Pokegama to Hinckley. Everything on the way was destroyed. We saw cooked animal carcasses," she lowers her voice, "and people."

I clear my throat and whisper, "My *Pappa* . . ." but sudden emotion chokes the words back down.

Mary sobs, "I'm so sorry, Karl."

The tears are freely falling down her cheeks now, "You know already?" I ask.

"Yes, we suspected the worst," she sniffles. "On the train to Pine City, you kept crying out for your father. You were screaming at him to hold on."

Now my eyes are getting blurry, filling with tears.

"It was horrible, Karl. You were so upset, and we couldn't calm you down. Finally, you stopped screaming. I think you exhausted yourself, but you kept repeating over and over, 'He's gone.'"

I close my eyes and force the tears back. I won't fall apart again. Her hand squeezes my arm, "I am so sorry. I loved Svard, too."

I place my bandaged hand on top of hers, "What about your father? I saw him at the mill in the morning."

She nods, "Father is alive. We found him here at the rink hospital shortly after we arrived in Pine City. Mother is here too." She lets out another sob and covers her mouth.

She's not telling me something. "Mary? Tell me."

Her hand is trembling as she wipes the tears from her face. "I don't know the entire story yet, but Father is burned all over his body. He hasn't been able to walk or speak yet. Dr. Barnum discussed moving him to a hospital in Minneapolis as soon as possible. He looks awful, Karl. I can't even recognize him."

I hate to see her like this. "He's strong, Mary. He'll survive."

She nods, but I can tell she is not convinced. I'm not entirely convinced myself, but I can't tell her that. We sit in silence for a moment, the topic of death wearing down on us. I look around the hospital rink again, wondering what horrors each person here experienced. There is a man walking through the rows of people. He stops a few rows down from us and kneels, speaking to the man lying there.

Turning my attention back to Mary, I ask her, "Do you know how many?"

She lets out a long exhale, "How many died? No, we don't know the total number yet. It's too soon. Search parties are out now trying to identify bodies and make the proper burial arrangements. I heard one of the volunteers say that there are still men, women, and children in Sandstone, waiting to be rescued."

"Waiting to be rescued? Why? What day is it?"

"It's still Sunday, but it's very late. It may even be Monday morning. You slept all day, Karl."

Strange because I still feel exhausted. "I'm glad you and Anna are all right and that your parents are alive."

"Yes, I can't believe how lucky we are," she smiles wide, her eyes brimming with tears again, but this time I think she is emotional from gratitude. "I didn't think that we'd find them alive."

My chest tightens. I'm thankful that her parents survived, but a small part of me is bitter. She has two parents, and I have none.

Mary continues, "Mother told us that she was in town at her friend's house yesterday afternoon planning a picnic for Labor Day. After lunch, the dark skies and smoky air alarmed her friend, so she packed a suitcase and insisted Mother come with her on the next train out of town. But you know how stubborn my mother can be," Mary wipes the tears from her cheeks, this time with a steady hand, "she said she wouldn't leave without Father. She helped her friend collect the elderly neighbor, and then they left for the train station. Mother told us that she had planned to go to the lumberyard to get Father after seeing her friend off, but on the way to the depot, they saw the Catholic priest, Father Lawler, running wildly through the street, shouting. He yelled at them to leave all they had and get to the gravel pit."

Without warning, I smell smoke in my nostrils, and the sounds of people screaming in my ears. My eyes dart around the rink hospital, but no one is running. Mary doesn't notice either, and she continues, "I think that's when Mother accepted that a fire was truly coming for Hinckley. Her friend and the neighbor woman dropped the suitcases right there on the sidewalk, and they all ran to the gravel pit."

The screaming in my head stops, but it is replaced by the deafening roar of the fire. I push my bandaged hands on my ears to drown it out. Panic rises in my chest, and I try to sit up and escape, but Mary's sudden laugh breaks my concentration, and I realize that I'm still lying on the ground in the hospital rink. No one else is running.

Mary chuckles, "I don't know what's wrong with me. I shouldn't laugh, but Mother always called it the town's 'three-acre eye sore' yet it ended up saving her life."

I realize that she's speaking of the gravel pit. Years ago the Eastern Minnesota Railroad's work crew dug a thirty-foot hole just east of the tracks to supply gravel for the railroad beds. This summer an underground spring had filled it with three feet of water. When I ran through town yesterday, I almost made it to the gravel pit. It would have been on the other side of the train tracks where I saw that boy and his mother collapse on the tracks. I see them fall again in my mind, and I shake my head trying to forget.

"I saw Father Lawler at the fire line," I tell her. "We were all there —volunteer firefighters, millworkers, Kristoff, too. We tried to stop the fire from entering town."

"Where?" she asks. "Where were you fighting the fire?"

"On the south side of town near Reverend Knudsen's house."

"The south side?" she wonders out loud. A loud groan distracts me from her response, and I look away from her. That man who had been walking down the rows before is now kneeling next to an injured man only two places away from me and putting a salve on his blistered neck.

Mary speculates, "Maybe my father was there too, fighting the fire. Mother found him in the pit after the fire had passed through town, but she doesn't know how he got there."

I turn my attention back to Mary, "We plowed a fire line together at the mill after our lunch break, but I left him to go fight the fire as it approached town. I don't remember seeing him at the fire line. My father stayed at the mill with a small crew to protect it. Maybe your father stayed with him."

Mary's face is serious, "Is that where . . ."

"No," I quickly answer. "I ran from the fire line and found Father at home. We ran to the St. Paul and Duluth tracks to catch the Skalley. It was backing up, and we grabbed the cowcatcher. I held on." I swallow the lump in my throat. "He didn't."

She clears her own throat and continues, "Well, when Father is well enough to speak, he can tell us his story."

Needing to change the subject of our conversation, I declare, "I have to find Kristoff."

"You said he was with you at the fire line?"

"Yes, we fought it for over an hour. Then the hose caught fire, so we all ran back through town."

"Did he run with you to your home?"

I shake my head and look away from her, ashamed that I lost my friend in the chaos.

"So he was in town then?" she asks.

"I don't know."

"I heard a woman say that many of the people in town escaped on an Eastern Minnesota passenger train. It coupled with a northbound freight train at the depot and carried hundreds out of Hinckley. Kristoff may be in Duluth right now."

A bubbling feeling, maybe hope, builds inside me. "Can we find out for certain?"

A man clears his throat above us. I look up and see it's the same man that has been walking the rows. He is tall but stooped over. His hair is parted to the side but pieces are falling across his forehead. His thick, dark mustache is matted with dirt, and he has black soot on his face. His shirt is wrinkled and dirty, and there is dried blood on his sleeve.

"Good evening," he greets me. "It's nice to see that you are awake."

"Doctor," Mary greets him, shuffling to move out of his way.

"Good evening, ma'am," he sets a leather bag down next to Mary. "No, no, please, you can stay. Under normal circumstances, I would recommend you return to the women's ward, but these are not normal circumstances."

"No, they are not," she agrees, folding her legs under her and getting comfortable again.

He kneels down between me and Mary. "My name is Dr. Barnum. May I take a look at your head?"

I slowly rise to my elbows, "My name is Karl Sundvquist."

"Yes," he peels back the bandage on my neck and examines the burns. "That's what my notes say." He picks up a small notepad and scans it quickly. "Laceration on the back of head," he murmurs, "yes, that is wrapped up already. Minor burns on neck and shoulders, smoke-damaged eyes." He stops to yawn, closing his eyes and stretching his neck. Then he continues to scan his notes, "Oh yes, now I remember. You are the boy who broke down on the relief train this morning."

I flinch, embarrassed for something I don't remember doing. "My medical training does not include healing those with shattered reason," he scans my face, "but I can see you are not experiencing any of those previous symptoms."

I can only nod and hope he doesn't think I've gone mad. "What I'm really concerned about are your hands," he gestures towards my bandaged hands, "May I?"

I sit up slowly and lean my back against the wall, but pain shoots through the skin on my shoulder, so I grit my teeth and lean forward a little. The pain passes, and I lift my arms towards the doctor. He starts to unwrap the bandage on my left hand first.

Mary speaks up, "Sir, I was with him on the relief train this morning. I know of the symptoms you speak of, but you have to understand . . . yesterday, Karl saw his father die."

The doctor stops and looks me in the face, "I'm sorry, Karl."

I nod once, then look away. He continues to unwrap the bandage. "I'm afraid everyone in Hinckley has lost a loved one. It's a horrible tragedy."

He lifts my left hand up and closely examines my palm as I tell him, "I have to find my friend."

Doctor Barnum sets down my left hand and starts to unwrap the right hand. Quietly, almost to himself, he says, "I have to find my daughter."

"Your daughter?" Mary asks.

"Kate," he answers. "I let her go to Hinckley yesterday morning to shop for new school clothes with her friends." He stops unwrapping my hand and closes his eyes. "She's thirteen. I thought she would be safe making the trip on her own."

Dr. Barnum doesn't open his eyes and doesn't say anything else. Mary interrupts the silence, "Has anyone seen her?"

He opens his eyes, blinks a few times, and then continues to unwrap my right hand. "No, not yet. My son and I went to Hinckley last night in a handcar to search for her, but we came up empty."

This man is clearly exhausted and concerned for his daughter. I'm surprised that he is here, helping everyone in the middle of the night. He lifts both of my bare hands up to his face and looks at the burns. "Children losing their parents. Parents losing their children. How can one remain hopeful?"

Is he asking me? Because I don't have an answer for him. He sets my hands down in my lap and looks at me, answering his own question, "You look for the helpers. It's only been one day since the fire, and already there are so many helpers. I have faith that someone helped my daughter survive."

I stare back at him but have nothing to say. Instead, I think of those who already helped me get to where I am. The Norwegian man, John Blair, Dr. Codding and the midnight helpers from Duluth, the old woman and Miss McNeil who helped me see, all the helpers that came on the relief train going to Duluth. And whoever helped Mary and Anna carry me to Pine City. All of them chose to help me. But who did I help? Not Kristoff. Not the family in the broken horse buggy. I wasn't even able to help my own father. The only person I was able to help was myself. Then at Skunk Lake, I wallowed in my own grief and self-pity instead of choosing to help others.

"Karl," Dr. Barnum clears his throat, "Your head will heal quickly. In fact, you seem to be more alert and aware of your surroundings already, but I'm afraid your hands will have permanent damage."

My heart rate quickens, "My hands? But they don't even hurt."

"No, I doubt you can feel anything. The skin is burned all the way down to the fatty tissues. Meaning the nerves are damaged. That's why you can't feel the pain. We cleaned the burns with carbolic acid when you arrived in Pine City and dressed them with linseed oil and clean bandages." My brain feels foggy. I stare down at my mangled hands as the doctor continues, "Karl, I don't have all the necessary medical treatments to heal them. They should arrive on a train from St. Paul tomorrow. Once they arrive, I'll clean the..."

He continues to describe the treatment to me, but I can't hear his words anymore. His voice fades into background noise. My attention is on my palms, what's left of them. The skin is gone, burned off from the searing heat of the cowcatcher. The flesh in the middle of each hand appears white and ruined. A thin, papery layer of tissue stretches over the outline of my bones. The edges of the burns, near the base of my fingers and thumbs, are charred black, and swollen, red masses of flesh creep underneath peeled back skin.

It's grotesque. I look up and see Mary staring at them too. Tears silently stream down her face. The doctor puts a salve on my palms, but I feel nothing. He reaches into his bag and retrieves new linen to wrap each hand.

My voice shakes as I ask, "Will I still have the use of my hands?"

"I don't know yet, Karl," he begins to re-wrap them in a fresh linen, "I don't know."

I fall back against the wall. Pain radiates across my shoulder and I hiss through my teeth. What use am I without my hands? For what kind of life did I survive? Despair sinks into my muscles and my bones. My body feels so heavy. I sink to the floor and squeeze my eyes shut.

"Get some rest, Karl," Dr. Barnum gently says. "I will check back on you in the morning. We should have more supplies then." I hear him get to his feet, "Ma'am, your husband needs rest now. You can sleep here if you want, but please let him rest."

"Oh, no, he's not my husband," Mary quickly replies as my eyes fly open. "He's my neighbor. My friend."

"Let me escort you back to the women's side, then." He holds his elbow out for Mary.

"Mary!" I shout up at her. "I forgot to ask about John? Where is he?"

Mary stands up and hooks her uninjured arm in the doctor's. She looks down at me and quietly says, "He did not make it to the well."

27

Anna

Thursday, September 5, 1894
Pine City, Minnesota
4 days after

"You need to eat something, Anna," Mrs. Howard says to me. "What are you hungry for?"

I'm sitting in a wooden chair next to the front window looking at the activity in the street. Men and women are bustling about, going from houses to shops and back again. I can tell the difference between a resident and a visitor. The residents know where they are going and usually have something in their hands, like piles of clothing, sacks of flour, or glass bottles of milk. The visitors walk slower, looking every which way, up and down the street. I expect they are family members looking to see if their loved ones survived and made it to Pine City as refugees.

But the refugees, themselves, are the easiest to identify. They don't hurry between storefronts or search the streets for faces that they recognize. Instead, they wander with nowhere to go and nowhere to be. They were saved, but are now lost. Some sit on the wooden plank sidewalk and stare vacantly into the street. I recognize the look on their faces, the despair in their eyes. It's a familiar look because sometimes I have it too. It's the absence of hope.

Their clothing, like mine, is no longer ripped and burned off, but it's not ours. We may have washed the soot and ash from our faces, but the fire left its mark nonetheless. When the wind blows unfamiliar hats off our heads, we don't flinch. We let the wind carry them down the street. It's a trivial pursuit to chase after a hat when you've had to outrun Hell itself.

Mrs. Howard interrupts my observation of the people in the street by asking if I'm hungry. I'm not. Without taking my attention away from the window, I answer, "I'm not hungry."

She clucks her tongue and says, "You didn't eat anything for breakfast either. You can't just sit at the window all day."

That's not entirely true. I leave the window when I see the man I'm waiting for. But she is partially right, I have been sitting at this window for most of the time since Mary and I were assigned to live with Mrs. Howard. That was Monday evening.

"Anna, you are too skinny as it is," she says. "Please eat."

I'm not too skinny. It's the donated dress that I'm wearing. On Monday morning, Mother, Mary, and I visited the Pine City Town Hall. The building has been converted into the relief headquarters for refugees. That's where I received this dress. It's too big for me, but Mother said it would be inappropriate to go back and exchange it. She said to be grateful for what we have been given, and that I could tailor it once we are settled and have sewing materials again.

Mrs. Howard is a kind woman, and I am grateful she is letting us stay in her home until my family figures out what comes next, but she pesters me about food every day. Still on the subject of eating, she continues talking to me from the kitchen, "And, what am I going to tell your parents when they get back? That you just refused to eat? You must eat, child, or else they will think I have neglected you while they are away. You need to be healthy and strong, so you can take care of your father while he heals."

My chest tightens when she mentions Father. Desperation and a thick suffocating sadness crawls up my throat, threatening to come out in a series of sobs, and stop my breathing altogether, so I close my eyes and push it back down. I have cried so much for my father in the past few days. Seeing him lying there so helpless and deformed on the cot at the rink hospital was one of the hardest things I've ever had to do. He's always been a strong pillar in my life, someone to rely on and look to in times of need. Now he is the vulnerable one, and there's nothing I can do to help him.

When he was at the rink hospital, all I could do was kneel next to him and sob and pray. I begged God to save him. Now I steel myself and focus on the good. Father is in a hospital in Minneapolis getting the care he needs to recover. He left on Tuesday with ten other severely burned victims. Mother was able to go with him, and I'm grateful that he is not alone.

Dr. Barnum and several other men carefully carried Father and the others from the rink hospital to the train. They gently lifted them, still lying in their cots, aboard the train and into the passenger carriage. Mary and I were not allowed to ride with him, but we followed them onto the train to say goodbye.

Father was unconscious the entire time. If he had been awake, he would have made a joke to us about the woman who was lying in the cot right next to him. It was Emma Hammond. Before the fire, Madame Hammond ran a brothel on the east side of Hinckley. Now, burned over most of her 300 pound body, the woman needs similar treatment and care as Father does, but that's not why Father would have made a joke. He would have joked about how near she was to Mother, and how uncomfortable Mother was sitting in between Father and a prostitute.

Madame Hammond does not run a brothel anymore. It's gone just like everything else in our town. I sigh and open my eyes to view the street in front of me. A young man, probably Karl's age, passes by the window. He has a determined look on his face, and his eyes are focused. He must be a resident, but he makes me think of Karl.

When I woke up Monday morning in the rink hospital, I thought of Karl first. I should have felt ashamed to think of him before my family, but I didn't. I care deeply about him, and I wanted to know if he was all right. He was in such a terrible state when he walked into the roundhouse on Sunday, so I was worried. I found his cot on the far side near the wall. He looked so much better than when I left him the night before. I was overjoyed to see his progress after just a few hours. He acknowledged my presence, but he didn't share my enthusiasm. He seemed different, which is understandable. Karl's family is completely gone. My heart aches for him and his loss. His fathers death weighs heavily on me. I miss him too, more than words can express. He was the kindest soul, his eyes crinkling at the corners when he smiled. His absence has already left a void in Karl, and it will take a long time for him to heal.

In all honesty, I have not felt like myself since the day of the fire. I suppose no one who experienced it can say they are the same person. The fire changed everything. John and Svard are dead. All three of our homes are gone. Hinckley is gone. Everything I grew up with, the school, the shops, the train stations. All gone. I even miss the mundane tasks I took for granted. The activities that kept my body busy. Feeding the chickens each morning and collecting eggs. Doing the laundry with Mother. Bringing water to Father from the well.

Now I sit in this chair each day, my leg bouncing up and down waiting to see him. He comes, like clockwork, at the same time each day, and the consistency is comforting. I wish Mary's presence was as consistent. She leaves each morning, but doesn't tell Mrs. Howard or me where she goes. Wherever it is, it must be more important than talking to me. She has not spoken to me since Sunday, the day that she slapped me in the face.

A sudden pain at the top of my skull forces me to my feet. I slip into a pair of donated slippers and pace Mrs. Howard's parlor. This pain is now familiar, but still unpredictable. Sometimes moving around helps. Other times moving makes it worse, and I have to lie down until it passes.

I don't want to do that now. I might not see Mr. Hart, the coordinator of relief activities in Pine City. He dispenses meal tickets to refugees who are not housed by local residents, issues transportation passes to those who ask to leave Pine City and stay with relatives in other towns, and he approves all requisitions for clothing and supplies.

He walks past Mrs. Howard's window close to noon each day on his way to the rink hospital. He counts how many refugees are still there and leaves that many meal tickets for lunch, dinner, and tomorrow's breakfast. The volunteers at the rink hospital bring the meal tickets across the street to the Knights of Pythias Hall where the refugee meals are cooked for the rink hospital patients and the refugees that are living in Robinson Park. I know when Mr. Hart walks past this window, that I have about twenty minutes to get to the rink hospital to help Karl eat lunch. His hands are still bandaged, so he can't feed himself. I helped him on Tuesday and Wednesday, and I plan to do it every day until he can do it himself.

The pain in my head fades to a nagging throb, still present, but easier to ignore. I return to my chair at the window, just in time to see Mr. Hart walk by. He always wears a black bow tie and matching black coat. His beard is so full and thick that it mocks the singed and burned beards of fire survivors, like Dr. Kelsey who will probably be forced to trim his.

I slowly get up, careful not to bring back the headache and find Mrs. Howard in the kitchen stirring a pot on the cookstove. It's a stew, simmering quietly, the smell is filling the room, but it is mixed with the smell of burned wood. I feel the heat from it instantly as I enter the kitchen. It triggers a taste of ash in my mouth, and I feel nauseous. I plug my nose and speak behind my hand, "Mrs. Howard, I'm going to visit Karl at the rink hospital. I'll be back in an hour or so."

She turns to me, a look of sadness on her face and says, "Again, Anna? You are always so sad when you return from seeing him."

"He has no one else," I say.

She walks over to me, rummaging in the pocket of her apron. "Here, then," she says, "stop at Glasgow's and buy yourself and Karl something sweet. Maybe he can get you to eat." She holds out her hand to me and sets coins onto my palm, covering them with my fingers.

"Thank you," I say and walk out of the room before the smell of the woodsmoke makes me sick.

🐦 🐦 🐦

I keep my head down walking through town which seems more crowded today, but before I can wonder why, I walk straight into someone who has stopped suddenly in front of me. My head crashes into his back. The man stumbles forward a few steps, but as I immediately begin to apologize, he turns around slowly and stares at me. Then he rushes forward, and grabs my shoulders, and yells, "Anna! You're alive!" The man has a huge grin on his face, half of which is disfigured from burns, but I still recognize him. It's Jake Barden, Belle and Archie's father.

"Mr. Barden!" I shriek in surprise, cover my mouth, then ask, "Belle? Where's Belle?"

He pulls me into a big, warm hug, "She's alive! They're all alive! Oh, Belle and Archie will be so happy to know I ran into you."

I throw manners to the wayside and wrap my arms around his waist, returning the hug. It feels so good to be embraced and comforted. After a moment, he pulls away, still grinning from ear to ear. It startles me at first to see him smile, I haven't seen a genuine smile like that in days. The expression is contagious though because I feel the corners of my mouth tugging up into a smile as well.

"Is she here?" I ask. "Archie too?"

"No, I boarded them all on the Best-Berry combination train right before the fire hit Hinckley. I just found out the address where they are all staying in Duluth."

"You didn't get on the train too?"

"No, I led our team of horses and a wagon full of our belongings out of town, but the wagon caught fire before I reached the Grindstone, so I had to cut the team loose and run on foot. I jumped up on another wagon full of people, and we escaped Hinckley together. What are the chances, but Charlie was in that wagon too. I recognized him immediately from our dancing party the night before."

"Was his sister Clara there too?" I ask, desperately craving more information about my dear friends. Standing on the sidewalk, we divide the stream of people passing us by, like a boulder splitting a river, but we don't care.

"No, not Clara," he shakes his head. "The man driving the wagon stopped at the wagon bridge, because he thought it would be best to jump in the river and survive in the water. We all stood at the top of the ravine and decided the water was too low to survive, so we ran back to the wagon, but it was on fire. Half of the group ran east, including Charlie. I ran north with the others on the wagon road. We didn't run very far before we found an abandoned wagon on the side of the road next to a swamp full of people, and you will not believe what was in the back."

"What?" I ask.

"Three large barrels full of water! I helped lift the three kids in our group onto the wagon and their mother put them each into a barrel. The other man and I jumped in and huddled next to the woman, but the flames were so close now, I could feel the heat on my back. The fire would have killed us, but the woman opened the trunk that was set next to the barrels. It was full of clothes, so we soaked them in the water and wrapped them all over our bodies and hunkered down. We were surrounded by flames and had nowhere else to go."

"What about the people in the swamp?" I ask.

He starts to speak, but his voice chokes and his eyes tear up. He covers his mouth and closes his eyes. I don't know what to say to him. This is Belle's father, and I am not used to adults being so honest and open with me, so I stay quiet and let him compose himself. People keep walking past us, but I give Mr. Barden time.

"The sounds, Anna," he speaks suddenly, barely louder than a whisper. "I can't get the sounds out of my head. At first it was high-pitched screams, so loud, we could hear them over the roar of the fire. There must have been a hundred of them, maybe more. It sounded like squealing pigs running from the farmer on slaughter day when they know the end is near. Then the screams changed. They were unnatural, twisted and garbled, almost animal like. It lasted so long." His face is as white as a sheet.

"What was it?" I whisper, clutching the extra fabric at my collar.

"The men, women, and children in the swamp. They all burned alive."

I know the swamp he speaks of. It lies between the Grindstone River and my home. It crosses the wagon road, too. In a normal summer, it is full of water and marshy, causing us to walk over sapling logs where the marsh meets the road. With so little rainfall this summer, the swamp was dry. The people who ran to the swamp ran to their deaths.

"After the fire passed, the mother calmed her children while the man and I got out of the wagon and walked to the swamp," Mr. Barden says, looking at me, but his eyes are somewhere else, trapped in a memory. "The scene, Anna, I've never seen something that awful in my entire life. Black, burned bodies, everywhere. As far as we could see. Smoke rising from their corpses." A tear runs down his cheek as he says, "The smell . . . ." He bows his head and takes off his hat. His fingers fidget with the brim as he whispers, "There was no mercy. No mercy at all." He closes his eyes, and two more tears escape. Instinctively, I place my hand on his arm. I have no words of comfort for him. I can't remember any Bible verses to bring him peace, so I leave my hand on his arm, close my eyes, and stand with him on the sidewalk while he remembers. We stand together in silent memory of those who died so terribly in the swamp that day.

I can hear the soft thud of boots against the wooden planks as people continue to pass by. Horses whinny and clomp their hooves on the dirt road next to us. Wheels turn, carrying carts and buggies. Life continues, and it feels unfair that Mr. Barden and I stand here breathing, living while so many of our neighbors are gone. The families in the swamp did nothing to deserve the death they experienced. We did nothing to be rewarded with life.

It reminds me of the stories told in the rink hospital, of the fire's randomness. An ax leaning against a well, its wooden handle still intact while everything around it is burned to a crisp, or how one home was spared but the one next to it is a pile of ash. The ringing cowbell I heard at Pokegama meant that an animal with almost no intelligence at all had survived. How could the fire show mercy to a few yet be so unforgiving to others? I see no pattern and no reason. Is life really this arbitrary? Are our fates unplanned and easily snuffed out by a freak incident of nature?

A boy walks past us, but he stops mid-step and turns back around to stare. He looks unsure, but says, "You're Clara and Charlie's friend." His face looks so familiar, but I can't place him. The man he was following notices that the boy has stopped, so he turns back and places his hand on his shoulder and says, "Come on, Antone."

"Antone," I repeat, finally remembering how I recognize him. "You're Clara and Charlie's younger brother." I remember him from when Clara and Charlie hosted one of our dance parties this summer. Antone was there. He never danced or played games with us, since he is a few years younger, but I remember him in the kitchen helping his mother and outside playing with the neighbor kids.

Mr. Barden's eyes flutter open, and he fixes his gaze on Antone. His mouth falls agape, and he gasps, "You—you were in the wagon too, sitting next to Charlie. I can't believe it. Where's Charlie?"

"Where's Clara?" I ask, afraid to hear the answer.

Antone's eyes show no emotion as he states, "They all died." This time I do cry out, and I don't cover it with my hands. A few people turn to look, but they continue walking.

The man standing next to Antone finally speaks, "No, they all didn't die. Clara is in Duluth." He offers his hand to Mr. Barden and says, "I'm John Tenglund, Antone's uncle. My family and I live in Moorhead. I came as soon as I heard of the fire." Mr. Tenglund puts his hand on Mr. Barden's shoulder and turns him away from Antone and me. He talks in a soft voice, and I can't make out their conversation.

Meanwhile, Antone is still staring at me. I take a step towards him, whispering, "Antone, what happened? What do you mean they all died?"

He blinks at me a few times before answering, "That man was in the wagon with us."

"Mr. Barden?" I ask.

Antone shrugs, but points to Belle's father who is still talking with Mr. Tenglund.

"Yes," I nod. "That's Mr. Barden."

Antone continues and as he speaks, scratching furiously at his chest, "We were going to jump in the river, but Charlie said it was too shallow. Father told us to run to the train tracks. I lost them a couple of times."

"Lost who?"

"Father, Mother, Charlie, and my sister Emily," he answers. "The smoke was so thick and the wind was so strong. My derby hat flew right off my head. I saw it floating in the air, but the middle caught fire and burned away. Only the brim was left."

I try to prompt him, "And then what happened, Antone?"

His eyes glaze over, but he continues, "Then, I heard the train whistle and kept running. Father and Charlie found me and ran with me to the train tracks. There were others running on the tracks with us. I passed a man who was completely on fire." I gasp, but he doesn't acknowledge it. "Then it got really dark. I couldn't see Charlie, but I heard him. He yelled at me to cover my face with my hands, so I did. But then I fell. I don't know what happened next. When I woke up, it was morning. Charlie wasn't too far away from me, but he was dead. He told me to cover my face. Why didn't he cover his?"

"Oh, Charlie," I cry.

Mr. Barden and Mr. Tenglund walk back over to us. Mr. Tenglund gently guides Antone by the shoulder and says to him, "Come along, Antone, we're heading for the train."

As they walk away, Mr. Barden kneels down in front of me, puts a hand on my shoulder and says, "Clara didn't die. She made it to the combination train, the same one I put Belle and Archie on."

Tears still fall down my cheeks as I nod and say, "But, Charlie."

Mr. Barden inhales and exhales deeply, "Charlie and his parents are dead. Antone survived on his own. It's a miracle his uncle found him. He's taking Clara and Antone back to Moorhead."

"Right now?" I ask.

Mr. Barden nods and says, "Yes. Service on the St. Paul and Duluth tracks started again this morning." That must be why there are so many people in Pine City today. He continues, "I'm leaving too. I'm going to collect my family in Duluth, and we'll move to Little Falls."

"Little Falls? I'm never going to see Belle or Archie again, am I? And if Clara moves in with her uncle, then I'll never see her again either." I sob and cover my face.

Mr. Barden hugs me again and says, "I don't know, Anna. I'm not sure of anything, but I am happy you survived, and Belle and Archie will find comfort in that."

I keep crying on his shoulder, but he pulls away and whispers, "I have to go now. The train to Duluth leaves soon, but I don't want to leave you like this. Where are you staying?"

"Mrs. Howard's," I blurt.

"All right, well, you head back to Mrs. Howard's and take care. Give my best to your father. He will find a way to reach out to me," he squeezes my arm as he stands back up and walks away. I don't have the heart to tell him about Father.

28

Karl

Thursday, September 5, 1894
Pine City, Minnesota
4 days after

I stare at the white wall. I've memorized the lines and woodgrain underneath the coat of white paint. It's not very exciting, so I usually drift off to sleep after an hour or two.

My stomach growls. It must be close to the noon meal. That means Anna will be here soon. I am happy that she survived and that I am able to see her every day, but I don't know what my place is with her now. I'm confused, and I don't know what to do next. I wish Father was here to talk to, or even Mr. Andersson.

Anna's presence makes me feel lighter, like I can handle the events that happened on Saturday. I even remember things better when she sits next to me, but she also makes me feel inadequate. She always comes right after the volunteers hand out our meals. I know why she does that, so she can help me eat. She brings the food to my mouth, and it humiliates me. I'm a grown man who needs someone to spoon-feed him his meals like an infant.

I hate feeling helpless, but everyone makes me feel this way, not just Anna. The volunteers make me drink water almost every hour. Dr. Barnum said it will help my hands heal, but it makes me have to

266

pee all the time. Since my hands are bandaged, it's always a struggle in the outhouse. I've even had to ask for help at times.

I'm pathetic. I push my face into the pillow. Everything is upside down. I have nothing left. No family. No home, and no way to rebuild it. That thought has been on my mind all day. Each morning when the volunteers clean and redress my hands, Dr. Barnum looks at them. This morning he told me that the skin is starting to heal. That means I will have to leave the rink hospital soon, but I'm not ready to face the world yet, a world where Father does not exist and where I am a cripple. I'm worthless if I lose the use of my hands, and right now, I still don't have any feeling in them. I can't flex them or grip anything.

Loud steps echo in the rink, interrupting my anguish. Someone is running. To my surprise, the steps get louder, then slow down, and come to a stop beside me. I hear a girl sniffling and turn my head to see Anna kneeling down beside me. She has tears running down her face.

"Anna? What happened?" I try to sit up quickly, but my body feels like it is moving through molasses.

"Oh, Karl," she wipes the tears off her cheeks. "I just ran into Antone, Clara and Charlie's younger brother. He told me that Charlie didn't make it. He died on the Eastern Minnesota train tracks."

She continues to cry, her hands trembling as they wipe away more tears. Her sorrow irritates me. Why did she come to me? I didn't know Charlie very well. We weren't friends. I stretch my head from side to side, hoping to relieve a tightness in my neck, but the movement stretches the blisters on my skin. I hiss through gritted teeth as the pain radiates across my neck.

"And I saw Belle's father too. He told me the most awful thing . . . ."

She can't finish the sentence because she has started to sob into her hands, so hard that she is bending over, the top of her head almost landing in my lap. Her hair is matted and snarly. I wonder why she hasn't washed it since the fire. A few volunteers standing on the other side of the building hear her sobbing and look over at us. I can't tolerate this behavior. Women in the rink hospital sob and wail at all hours of the day, especially in the middle of the night. I don't need to hear it from Anna too.

"I didn't know Charlie." That's all I can think of to say to her.

She continues to cry but gradually the sobs get softer. I look back over to the group of volunteers. Most of them returned to their tasks, but a couple are still staring, saying something to each other. Eventually Anna stops, sits up, and stares at me. She is waiting for me to say something to her, something to make her feel better, but I don't have the words to help her, nor the energy.

She wipes her face again and places a few stray hairs back behind her ears. "I suppose not. He was my age, so maybe you didn't know him. It's just awful to hear about someone so young dying that way."

Her words hit a nerve, and I lose my temper. "Why does age matter? Father died on the train tracks and he was in his forties. Are you going to sob that hard for him?"

Her mouth drops open in surprise. "I did sob for your father, Karl. I just didn't do it in front of you. You know I cared about your Father."

"Well, thank you for sobbing in private. I don't have time for sorrow," I sigh. "He's gone, and being sad about it doesn't help."

Just then, a volunteer walks over and sets down a bowl of stew. Anna looks down at the food and then back at me. She waits a moment, then picks up the spoon and looks at me, "Can I help you?"

I nod, leaning forward as she reaches up to my mouth. "Has the doctor seen you today?" she asks, as she carefully tips the stew into my mouth. She doesn't wait for me to answer as she continues, "I know he mentioned yesterday that you could be discharged soon. Tell me when you have the address, so that I can come to your next place and keep helping you."

She must think I'm useless. I want to crawl into a hole and disappear. I swallow the rest of the stew that's in my mouth and slowly move my body back down on my bed.

"I'm not that hungry today," I say as I turn towards the wall. She doesn't answer me, and I don't give her any more explanation than that. She stays by my bed, silent, for some time until eventually I hear her get up and walk away.

🦢 🦢 🦢

"Excuse me sir," a voice says, waking me from my dream.

I open my eyes and turn to see a young man kneeling down beside me, holding a stack of envelopes against his chest.

"I'm sorry to wake you, but I have to deliver these to everyone in the rink hospital today." I know this young man. His face and voice are familiar. I blink a few times, positive that this must be part of my dream, but he doesn't go away.

"Nathaniel Henderson," I say to him as I prop myself up on my elbows, "you worked at the mill."

He stares at me, and I see recognition flash in his eyes, "Hey, I remember you. Karl, right? You stopped Ivar from kissing that girl in the gypsy wagon."

"That's me, Karl Sundvquist."

"Well, I'll be damned," he says and smiles, but then his eyes travel to my bandaged hands, so I tuck them underneath the blanket wrapped around me. "I am glad to see a face I recognize. One that is breathing, anyway." He sits down on the floor and crosses his legs, "Did you come with us to the fire line?"

"Yes," I answer. "Kristoff Ericksson and I fought it for about an hour until the hose burned up."

"Where did you go after that?"

His sudden friendliness surprises me. Nathaniel and I were not friends before the fire; in fact, I barely knew him. He is a few years older than I, so our paths had not crossed before this summer when I started working at the mill. Even then he was always just around, one of Ivar's crew.

I close my eyes and search my memory. It's a little fuzzy from sleeping, but I start to remember, and tell him, "Kristoff and I ran north through town after the hose started on fire, but we were separated. Then, I . . . I think I made it to the Skalley as it backed up to Skunk Lake."

"Root's train!" he exclaims, cutting me off. "I've heard the story, but I thought all the survivors at Skunk Lake went to Duluth?"

"I didn't. I came back through Hinckley to look for Kristoff."

"And?" His eyebrows rise up on his forehead.

"I didn't find him. I don't know where he is." It's true. It's been four days, and I have had no word of Kristoff's fate or that of his mother who lived in town. But I haven't left the rink hospital yet either.

"Hmm," he scratches the stubble on his chin. "I've been in Hinckley the last few days. Some of us survivors have been dealing with the bodies." I brace myself, ready to hear him tell me that he found Kristoff's body. "Most of the bodies in town, the mill, and the swamp have been accounted for. There are so many that we had to dig trenches instead of graves for such a large burial, and some of the bodies can't be moved that far, so we buried them where we found them."

I don't want him to explain why some bodies couldn't be moved. Thankfully, he doesn't. "Of course, I haven't seen everyone we buried, but I haven't seen or heard of anyone else identifying Kristoff."

I must look hopeful because he continues quickly, "Now, I don't know what that means, Karl, but I thought I should tell you."

All I can do is nod. He isn't telling me bad news, but it doesn't help me in finding Kristoff either. I decide to change the subject, "How did you survive?"

"Well, I was at the fire line for a while, but Jan and I left when we figured it was too late to save those houses. We ran to the Eastern Minnesota depot, figuring we'd catch a train out of town, but along the way, we saw so many kids running around alone. We each picked one up and carried them with us. It slowed us down, but we couldn't leave them. There was a huge crowd at the depot. Everyone was trying to board the combination train. We threw the kids in first, and helped a few others to board. Jan yelled at me that he was going back for the other kids, so I followed him."

Nathaniel grins. "We always did everything together. Anyway, I lost Jan in the smoke. I did find another kid, though, and I carried him to the train. It was pulling out when I tossed him up into an open window."

I didn't save anyone. Nathaniel says he saved the lives of two children. Guilt gnaws at my insides.

Nathaniel continues, "I ran back in town and followed a small crowd to the gravel pit."

I raise my eyebrows. The gravel pit. He survived there with Anna's parents.

"Probably a similar experience to Skunk Lake, having to dunk down all the time to avoid the sheets of flame and the heated air."

I nod in agreement.

He chuckles to himself, "I finally got to rub elbows with some of the town's most distinguished. The mayor, Lee Webster, was there. John Craig, the fire chief galloped in on his horse, and the newspaper editor, Angus Hay was there too. I noticed a couple ministers, but you know me," he smirks, "I don't know their names or denominations."

"Was Jan there?"

The smirk instantly disappears. He fidgets with his envelopes and answers slowly, "No, Jan wasn't in the pit. I found him pretty quickly, though. After the fire, when we all crawled out, I looked for him first. He wasn't too far away."

My heart sinks. I know what he is going to say next.

"His face was burned up pretty bad," he clears his throat and sets the envelopes down on the floor. "But, he had this in his pocket, so I knew it was him."

Nathaniel pulls out a metal flask from his shirt pocket. The initials J. E. H. are engraved on the side. Jan Emil Hrbek. He shakes it, and a liquid swishes inside, before he puts it back in his shirt pocket.

"I'm sorry, Nathaniel. Jan was a good man."

Nathaniel picks up the envelopes off the floor. "He was a good man. Not like that coward Ivar."

"Ivar?"

A darkness flashes on Nathaniel's face, "Oh yes. Ivar, the coward. Remember he was missing from the mill that morning?"

"Yes."

"Well, the night before, we stayed out drinking until midnight. Ivar overslept in the morning and missed the beginning of our shift at the mill." I know that Ivar didn't oversleep because he was hungover. He probably didn't go to work because I broke his nose, and he was embarrassed. I don't mention this to Nathaniel because he has already moved onto the next part of his story. "A friend of mine was putting his family on the two o'clock passenger train before he came down to the fire line to help us, and he saw Ivar boarding it. That coward left town with the women and children."

"Ivar left on a train? Before the fire?" I ask.

"He abandoned us, the mill, our town, to save himself."

I may not have saved anyone on Saturday, but I didn't flee until the last possible moment when the fire was upon us. Ivar fled before it was even near Hinckley. He is a coward. He left his friends to die. I may have lost Kristoff in the chaos, but I didn't abandon him. I came back for him twice. I pull my hands out from under the blanket and stare at the bandages. I am still a better man than Ivar.

Nathaniel threatens, "If he dares to come back here, I swear, I'll tell everyone I know what kind of man he is. I'll drag him out of town if I have to. He doesn't belong here anymore."

I sit up a little straighter, "I'll help you. I might not be able to hold him, but I'll help somehow."

He nods towards my hands, "What happened?"

I clear my throat and tell him, "I burned them holding onto Root's train. Dr. Barnum says the skin will probably take a few more weeks to completely heal, but he's just not sure how much they'll work after that."

"Does it hurt?"

"Not yet. The doctor says it will soon. I've been sleeping a lot lately, maybe from the head wound, but that is pretty much healed up."

"Well, that is good to hear," he says and shuffles through the envelopes in his hands. "These are new housing assignments and meal tickets for the remaining hospital patients. Here is yours."

He sets an envelope with my name on it in my lap. "New housing assignments? They're kicking me out?"

"No, I don't think so. Just a more permanent option until some committee from the State figures out how to administer the relief money to everyone."

"Relief money?"

He nods, "Yes, or so I've heard."

"That's reassuring, I've spent a lot of time worrying about how I will start over with nothing and no means to earn a paycheck."

"It'll take time though. You know how slow the government works. I just received my housing assignment today, and it's been four days since the fire."

"Where have you been staying?"

"Hinckley."

"Really?" I'm shocked. "I didn't think anyone could stay there. I walked through from Skunk Lake to the Eastern Minnesota roundhouse, and it was . . . ."

"Completely destroyed?" He finishes my sentence. "Yeah, it's all gone. Houses are just piles of ash and rubble. The saloons, stores, that's all gone. The depots are gone too. The train tracks were mangled, but the crewmen came right away and started to repair them. Service to Duluth started today, so at least we have that. But, the town? It's gone. The mill is gone too. It burned for a few days, but it's over now. The yard is dotted with huge piles of ash."

I do remember seeing the mill on fire when I passed through on Sunday.

"All the survivors in town and the surrounding area were sent down here, so they cleared out for the most part by Monday morning, but I decided to stay with a few others since I didn't have any injuries or major burns. We've built a small tent city with supplies brought in on handcars. It's hard, but we thought the dead deserved to be buried as fast as possible."

Before the fire, Nathaniel was just another man at the mill, nothing about him stood out to me. Now after hearing about his survival story and his decision to stay and help bury the dead, I think I may have misjudged him.

"The stench, Karl, the stench," his face blanches. "Cooked human flesh rots fast, and the smell is awful. I lived the last few days with a handkerchief tied around my face, but the real problem is the livestock. Animals everywhere, rotting in the street. Horse and ox carcass still lie where they died, and their insides are melting in this heat. Chickens, cats, dogs, you name it. We don't have enough kerosene to burn them all or any lime to help with the smell. It's unbearable."

My stomach twists at the images his words create in my mind.

"Is that why you left this morning?"

"No," he waves me off. "I left to get away from the *excursionists*. The tourists."

"Tourists?"

"Oh yeah, the first trains came this morning full of them. Train loads of passengers, coming for a day trip, an excursion to the ruins of Hinckley. They want to see a burned body or take a souvenir."

"What?" I almost shout in disbelief.

"I saw it with my own eyes, a group of young girls running off the train to gawk at a line of bodies by the tracks. One almost fainted from the sight. Some men came off the train carrying shovels. Shovels! They dug through the ashes looking for anything that didn't burn. Anything that they could bring back home and show their friends."

Rage starts to burn on my cheeks. I imagine a group of well-dressed men and women kicking through the rubble of my home looking for something to take. "Thieves," I hiss through clenched teeth.

"That's why I left. I don't care to see that while I'm digging trenches, throwing in legs and torsos I can't identify."

I shake my head in disgust, both at his horrific experience with the burned bodies, and the fact that people would travel to gawk at someone else's misfortune.

"Almost all of the burials are done now," he continues, "so, I'm going to find work here in Pine City until the winter logging crews head out. This spring, I'll go back to Hinckley and rebuild with my logging paychecks and anything I can get from the State."

Nathaniel sounds so hopeful. I bet he can help me with something that I couldn't ask from Anna. This might be my only chance to get assistance with it. I clear my throat, willing myself to ask him. "Nathaniel, um, my father. He didn't live. I'm not certain where his body is, but . . . I know where he fell."

Emotion chokes my voice, so I pause, forcing my grief down, deep into another locked room. Nathaniel lowers his voice, "I'm sorry, Karl."

I look at his face and his eyes show genuine concern. I lift up my bandaged hands. "I need help finding him, and . . . possibly burying him."

He responds quickly. "I can help with that. I have an idea where we can look first. We might not even need to leave Pine City."

I clear my throat again, thankful to have that over with, "Thank you."

"While I'm here let me open this for you," he says and takes the envelope back from me and tears it open. I didn't even think to ask for help with that since my hands are bandaged.

He rummages inside the envelope, "Yep, meal tickets. These are for new clothes. And, here, your tent number. Looks like you'll be staying in Robinson Park too. My tent number is different, but I bet we're close to each other. Or we can swap tent mates, I doubt some of these men will mind."

"Tent mates?" I ask.

"Yeah, there are four or five in each tent," he responds, pointing to a list of names on the letter. "See, their names are here next to the tent number."

I scan the list of names assigned to my tent, but none look familiar.

Nathaniel stands up and says, "Get some rest while you still have a roof over your head. I'll see you around."

"No, I'm not tired," I say, shaking my head and slowly standing up, "I'm ready to leave now."

29

Karl

Sunday, September 9, 1894
Pine City, Minnesota
8 days after

I stare in disbelief at my hands. They are hideous. The flesh on my palms is leathery and crimson. Two white valleys mark the center of each palm where the metal bar of the cowcatcher burned even deeper to a layer of my skin I don't think was meant to see the light of day. It's white and yellow, and I can see the ridges of tendons like taught ropes underneath. The edges of the burn look different. There are large, angry blisters where the skin was peeled back but has since been removed.

That's where the pain started a couple days ago. It stings like a knife and radiates heat up to my fingers and back around my wrist, but I still can't feel anything inside of my palms. And as hard as I try, through the pain and discomfort, I can't bend my fingers or grip anything. I can't hold a cup, pinch my fingers to pull down my pants, or hold a comb to run through my hair. I've tried, but I fail each time.

I have to look away from my hands, so I lift my head up and stare at the back of another volunteer at the rink hospital. She is gathering cloth bandages on a table nearby, a routine I've grown accustomed to in the days since I moved into Robinson Park. I've returned to the rink hospital each afternoon to have my palms cleaned and bandaged. Each day there are fewer cots on the floor as people clear out to more permanent housing options.

"I'm sorry, Mr. Sundvquist," the volunteer walks up to me, frowning, "but we ran out of linseed oil yesterday. Dr. Barnum has been purchasing most of our supplies out of his own pocket, but since he left for Duluth, we've been on our own. We've had to make due with what we have."

"I understand," I answer. "Did he find Kate? Is that why he's in Duluth?"

"Yes," she answers and smiles wide, "A family friend who lives there sent a telegram to the doctor explaining that he had found Kate and took her back to his house to stay until her family could come. She escaped Hinckley on Best's combination train."

I nod as the woman picks up my hand and inspects the palm. As she examines it, I think of Kristoff. He is still missing. Every day Nathaniel and I visit the town hall and look for his name. Since the fire, the town hall has served as the relief headquarters for fire survivors. Twice a day, a volunteer there nails a piece of paper to the wall with the names of those known to be dead and those known to be alive. We have yet to see Kristoff's name on either list, and I am losing hope that I will have a happy reunion with him like the doctor is experiencing today with his daughter.

"Hmm, it looks clean, but you still need something to lock in the moisture," the woman says to me as she picks up my other hand and looks at the palm. "They both look very dry."

She motions to my neck. I lean down to give her better access since she is quite a bit shorter than me. She lifts my shirt collar and examines my neck and shoulder. "Well, good news for you, these burns seem to be healing very well. And quickly. How is the pain?"

"Very little on my neck and shoulder," I answer, "but the blisters on my hands hurt pretty bad."

"Do you have any feeling on either palm?"

I shake my head, "No, not yet."

She looks up at me, "Can you use your hands at all?"

I grind my teeth together and lie, "Some."

She narrows her eyes at me but doesn't challenge my answer. She turns back to the table behind her, picking up a glass jar with a thick, golden liquid inside. "This is a salve of honey and vinegar. I've been using it on burns my entire life, and it is just as adequate as linseed oil. I think it does a better job at stopping the burn from drying out. My grandmother used it on me and my siblings when we were children, and I use it on my own children."

She doesn't wait for me to consent before slathering a spoonful of the honey salve onto my palms. Instantly, I feel a soothing chill on the blisters around my fingers and wrist, but I don't feel it on my palms. She finishes both hands, and begins to wrap each in a fresh cloth bandage.

"Have you run out of laudanum?" I ask her.

"Almost. I only have two bottles left. I'm saving it for those with more extensive burns."

"Hmm," I calmly respond, but inside my mind starts to race. I can deal with pain and discomfort when my body is busy, but sitting in the park with nothing to do makes time crawl. I don't know if I'll be able to bear the pain . . . and grief. The woman winds the long narrow bandage around my palms. When she finishes, she walks back over to the table and sets down the salve of honey. She returns with a small glass bottle and a small spoon. She uncorks it and measures out a dose for me.

She lifts the spoon to my mouth, and I swallow it quickly. "Same time, tomorrow?" She asks. I nod, and she leaves me to see another man waiting behind me. As I walk past the table, I squeeze the last bottle of laudanum inbetween my bandaged palms and walk away quickly.

Anna

Pine City, Minnesota
8 days after

I'm sitting in the rocking chair near the window holding my arms tightly and shivering violently. My teeth chatter loudly against each other, and water drips from my dress to the floor. The sky is starting to change from a hazy yellow to orange and from orange to pink, and finally pink to red. Smoke drifts heavily down the street in front of my window. Fires flared this afternoon thirty miles away near Mora and Milaca, scaring everyone in Pine City and delaying a scheduled memorial service for the dead.

When Mrs. Howard and I saw people running in the street, we followed them without question. The heavy smoke alone had convinced me that another fire was here. It had come to finish me. I held her hand and dragged her to the banks of the Snake River and waded into the shallows. We were not alone. Many others had also run to the river, in fear that flames would follow the smoke. But fire never came. The smoke cleared, and everyone returned to their homes.

I wasn't so easily convinced that the threat of danger had passed. Mrs. Howard had to drag me from the water, and I reluctantly followed her back to her house. Even now my heart is still pounding in my chest, and I can't slow down my breathing. Tears stream down my cheeks, and memories of the real fire, the one I lived through, race through my mind. Giant flames swallowing the forest. The roaring wind that silenced my screams. The smell of burnt flesh.

"Come, Anna," I jump and let out a small scream when Mrs. Howard speaks behind me, "I made a hot bath for you."

She helps me out of the rocking chair and leads me to the kitchen. A large, wooden tub with steaming water sits in the middle of the room. My body is still trembling, and I can't stop my fingers from shaking when I attempt to unbutton my blouse.

"Here, let me help," Mrs. Howard stands in front of me and starts to unbutton from the top. "It's all right, dear. There is no fire. You are safe."

She helps me undress, and I'm too scared to be embarrassed about my nakedness. She holds my hands and helps me into the tub. The warm water feels wonderful on my skin. I sit down and fold my legs up to fit inside. I hug my knees and rest my chin on them.

Mrs. Howard kneels down next to the tub and uses a small pitcher to drench my hair and back. The shock of the warm water on my head makes me gasp. "I'm sorry, Anna, I should have warned you. It's a little hot. I had my neighbors help me fill it."

"It feels good. I haven't had a hot bath in a long time."

"I thought it was time to wash your hair, and it will help you warm up after what happened this afternoon."

She keeps drenching my head with warm water, and it runs

down my face, rinsing away my tears. Then she starts to use a comb and her fingers to work through the knots and tangles in my hair. She is firm but gentle, holding the hair near my scalp so the comb doesn't tug too painfully. She sprinkles some baking soda onto the knots and works it through with the comb. Mother used to help Mary and me wash our hair like this when we were little. In the middle of winter when we couldn't wash our hair in the river, Mother would heat up water in a tub just like this one and help us wash. She would untie the braids in our hair and then work through the knots, just as Mrs. Howard is doing for me now.

My chest tightens thinking about Mother and Mary. I miss them both so much. And Father too. He lies in a hospital bed so far away, and I have no idea how he is healing. I feel alone, and I can't take it anymore. My chest tightens, my throat constricts, and my shoulders stiffen. The pressure is too much, and I can't hold it in any longer. Sobs escape me, and Mrs. Howard stops combing and holds my head against her chest.

"Shh," she whispers. "Shh, there, there. I'm sorry if I pulled too hard. I can go slower. There's no rush."

I shake my head, wiping tears from my wet face. "It's not that. I just miss my family."

Her face softens, and she returns to combing my hair. "I imagine that you do, but your parents will be back as soon as they are able. And you have your sister. She said that she is meeting us at the memorial service this evening. My neighbor told me they already rescheduled it to a new location, so I hope Mary has heard the news wherever she is."

I nod, agreeing with Mrs. Howard, and wonder where Mary could possibly be.

Karl

Pine City, Minnesota
8 days after

I wake up with a start. Another nightmare about Father. I'm sweating through my clothes, and there is no air movement inside this tent. The heat of summer has yet to pass even though we are well into

September. I don't remember falling asleep, but I should have expected it. I usually doze off after taking laudanum. Sunlight seeps through the open flap at the tent's entrance, but it is a warm red, so it must be close to evening.

I slept through another day, and I groan at my laziness. Father would be disappointed in my lack of motivation. But he's dead, so what does it matter what he would think? I squeeze my eyes shut, but images of Father and the nightmare still linger. For the past three days, my nightmares have been the same, a repeating loop of Father slipping off the cowcatcher and the image of his name on the *death list*.

Dr. Cowan, the county coroner who had lived in Hinckley, is responsible for identifying and registering the dead. Nathaniel worked alongside him in Hinckley in the days after the fire. Dr. Cowan has since moved into the small towns and woods of the fire path. He sends a list of his progress to Pine City, and the volunteers at the relief headquarters post it every day. Everyone calls it the death list.

On Thursday, after Nathaniel and I left the rink hospital, we stood in line to read it. That first time was the hardest. Even now as I sit in my tent, a gnawing sense of dread creeps up my throat, remembering what it felt like standing in line. I was with Father when he fell, but somehow seeing his name on the death list would make it final.

The words are burned in my memory:

Sundvquist, Svard - Age 44; single, found 1 mile north of
Hinckley, near railroad track; identified by a jackknife which
he carried; buried at Hinckley.

I rub my eyes with the backs of my bandaged hands, trying to wipe the image from my mind. Seeing his name on the list meant that Nathaniel and I didn't have to look for his body. A stranger buried him. Feeling light-headed, I slowly sit up on my cot. I think I took too much of that laudanum. I twist my body and stand up, then squeeze between the three other cots. I need to leave the stuffy tent and breathe some fresh air.

Outside, Nathaniel is sitting on one of the many mismatched chairs scattered throughout the park. I'm not sure where the chairs came from, probably donated by families in Pine City. He is puffing on a cigar. As I walk over to him and sit down, he pulls another cigar from his pocket and offers it to me. I shake my head, declining it. We stare at the back of the bandstand and the rows of tents that surround it.

"You slept through all the action," he says to me.

"What action?" I ask.

"The streets filled with smoke and everybody ran out of town screaming. They thought another fire was coming. You really didn't hear anything?"

I shake my head.

"You sleep like a log. Are you coming with me to the memorial service?"

"What memorial service?" I frown, not remembering any service scheduled for today.

He answers, "Some of the town leaders and nearby clergymen are hosting a memorial service tonight at Tierney's Hall and Saloon. The hall is upstairs, above the saloon. It will be long and religious, I'm sure," Nathaniel takes a long drag on his cigar, and exhales the smoke, "But, I'm going for Jan."

I don't remember anything about a memorial service, but I nod. "Yeah, I'll go. We should check the lists again before we go. Anna will probably be at the service."

"Anna, Anna, Anna," Nathaniel teases me, "this girl better be worth all the times that you've made me touch your list. Why do you keep it in your smelly boot?"

Lifting up my left foot, I use the heel of my boot to slide off my right one and answer him, "Because it would fall out of my shirt pocket." Nathaniel picks up the boot and shakes it until a piece of paper falls out. He picks it up and waves it in the air while he plugs his nose with his other hand.

Something wet hits my leg. It's a raindrop, then another. The sky opens up and raindrops fall on us. Nathaniel stands up quickly and puts the piece of paper in his trouser pocket. "Let's go stand in line then. Maybe someone will have a bar of soap, and I can wash my neck."

30

Anna

I sit down quietly next to Mrs. Howard. The hall is almost full, and we are lucky to have found three empty seats. We are probably late on account of me. Mrs. Howard had an awful time with my hair, but it is clean now and braided, even if it is still a little damp.

Mrs. Howard borrowed a dress from her neighbor since mine was still too wet. I like this one much better than my donated one. It is light purple with embroidery on the sleeve cuffs and lapels. The skirt is a little long, but I prefer it this way. My slippers are well hidden under the hemline. The lamps hanging from the ceiling cast a warm glow over the crowd, but I still tug on the shawl that Mrs. Howard loaned to me. A cold, heavy feeling of sadness hangs in the air. Everyone present seems close to tears even though the service has yet to start.

I scan the crowd and see sullen faces, forlorn eyes, bandages, blisters and scars. Broken spirits. It is eerily quiet too. Lacking is the cheerful chatter and small talk normally found in a congregation of this size. Only the familiar coughing and hacking that I have grown accustomed to breaks the silence.

"Good evening," Mary says, appearing on the other side of Mrs.

Howard and sitting down in the last empty chair in our row. "It seems that I got here just in time. It looks like it will be a full room tonight."

A small boy sitting on my left coughs violently, so I look down at him to see if he is all right. The side of his head facing me is scarred and blistered, and he is missing the top part of his ear. I quickly look away, toward the front of the room where Reverend Peter Knudsen, Hinckley's Presbyterian minister, begins reading the Scriptures. He is standing in the front of the room at a small wooden podium. My foot taps nervously on the hardwood floor. The reverend reads a list of those in his congregation who died which causes a few sobs and wails from the crowd. Next, a woman sings a song I do not recognize, and then a man reads a poem. He speaks too softly for me to hear. I applaud with the crowd after each speaker, but it is a formality for me and others around me. Our heavy hearts make our clapping lack any real enthusiasm.

After a local priest reads a sermon to the crowd, a tall man walks up to the podium. His clothing does not look like that of a clergyman, and I am curious who he might be. He has a large mustache, bushy in the middle under his nose, but it narrows on each side and comes to a fine point in the middle of each cheek. His hair is shiny from pomade, parted to the side with a dramatic wave. His suit is tailored. He is not a refugee.

He clears his throat and speaks loudly and clearly, projecting his voice, so everyone can hear him. "Ladies and Gentlemen, I'm J.D. Markham of Rush City. I represent one fourth of the Kelsey-Marham Land Company which owns the town site of Brook Park, which you may only know by its other name, Pokegama. I was not present in Hinckley or the surrounding area on Saturday, September first. But I saw firsthand the terror and destruction of the fire. I led an expedition immediately after the fire to search for survivors in that community. We lost many brave pioneers, but the families that I talked to are committed to return and welcome anyone willing to brave the efforts of repairing and rebuilding. I encourage anyone here who lost their home to return and rebuild. There is plenty of affordable land for sale, all cleared and ready to be plowed. Assistance will be forthcoming from all directions which means a new crop and a new start could await you this spring in Brook Park."

No one in the crowd claps as he steps away from the podium.

Mrs. Howard clucks her tongue, and I steal a glance at Mary. She doesn't acknowledge me, so I return my gaze to the front, tapping my foot harder on the floor.

Another man dressed in long, flowing white robes steps up to the podium. He has a full beard and thin hair on top of his head. He speaks with a deep voice, but his body is relaxed. He is familiar with addressing large crowds.

"I stand before you tonight to give voice to the sympathy which swells up from responsive hearts over the land. This little community, before obscure and scarcely discovered on the map, has for the last week been the nerve center for all the world."

A woman behind me whispers to someone, "That's Bishop Mahlon Gilbert."

"Catholic?" Another voice whispers back.

"No, Episcopal."

I turn my attention back to the Bishop who is continuing his address, "We are often like babes who can only cry out with pain and cannot understand the cause, but then like children we can learn the lesson taught us. These calamities are all a part of God's plans. The great civil war of thirty years ago is an illustration of this, where sacrifice and suffering wrought freedom and a united land. Is it not the first thing we are all taught? That God is greater than all material things. So, when those that built up a material fortune and began to worship it, God answered with one sweep of divine justice. And what is the second thing we are all taught?"

He walks around the podium with his arms spread wide, waiting for an answer from the crowd. When none comes, he continues, "That our hearts will be brought together."

Mrs. Howard nods her head and says prayerfully, "Amen."

Bishop Gilbert speaks louder to reach his message above the murmuring crowd, "You have heard of the great strikes that agitated the country a few weeks ago, arraying man against man, threatening anarchy and social disruption. Like the finger of God this calamity has come and swept away all distinction of rank and class. God used this to cement again the bonds of fraternity which were being rent asunder."

He points his finger to the wall and raises his voice, "I stood last

Monday in the chamber of commerce at St. Paul and saw tears moisten the cheeks of the men who rule the finances of a great city as they responded to the appeals made on behalf of those stricken people. They did not know these woodsmen; they did not know these men of toil; but their hearts were touched by the sufferings of a common humanity."

He points to the ceiling and his voice is full of emotion as he says, "God thus used the grim surgery of fire to heal the wound between rich and poor in our great state."

The Bishop continues his address, but for me his speech fades into the background. I never considered my family to be poor. We always had food on our table, clothing on our backs, and a roof over our heads. I think of my neighbors, my friends, and the families who lived in town. None of us were poor before the fire, so I don't know what wound he is referring to. I would argue that now, after the fire, we are poor, destitute even.

He's also implying that the fire was not random. That God sent the fire to set an example for a higher purpose.

"Powers!" The Bishop's voice cuts through my thoughts and makes me jump in my seat. "Best! Sullivan! Root! Campbell and Blair!" He uncurls a finger for each man's name. "Such heroism will cover a multitude of sins, and I doubt not God will blot out some of their faults for they doubtless had faults, and remember that they nobly did their duty in the time of trial."

He pauses, shaking his head, "The trial seems hard but what matters if it makes you better? Look up and let the sacrifice of friends and loved ones make you nobler and purer." My foot stops mid-tap, raised in the air, frozen in place when I hear the Bishop say the word, sacrifice.

"Last of all, when the grass has grown green over their graves and your hearts' wounds are somewhat healed, let us not forget that God came down in a chariot of fire one day as he did for Elijah of old, to take our better selves up to himself."

Many in the crowd, including Mrs. Howard and Mary, applaud with enthusiasm and inspiration as the Bishop ends his main address. A few even give him a standing ovation. My hands lay heavy on my lap while I think of those now unable to ever stand again.

The service ends with the hymn, "Our Great Redeemer Praise Ye."

When everyone is done singing, we exit slowly and solemnly. I follow Mary and Mrs. Howard downstairs, through the saloon, and into the cool night. The rain, which had wept during the beginning of the memorial service, has since stopped. My muscles are stiff from sitting so long, so I stop and stretch out my back and neck. Most of the attendees scatter into the street, heading to their temporary homes in Pine City. Some have decided to stay and visit with couples and families that they recognize. It could be that they are seeing them for the first time since the fire. Some of the reunions include happy embraces, but most are either crying or comforting those who are mourning in some way.

I follow Mary and Mrs. Howard as they walk down the street talking to each other about the Bishop's address. I don't care to hear their conversation, so I lag behind. A man holding onto the hitching post in front of Pat Conner's Saloon catches my eye. He's leaning onto the post with his forearm and one of his ankles is draped across his standing leg. He is struggling to pull his boot over his heel. I keep staring, wondering why his boot was off in the first place. He has no hat on his head, so the glow from the gaslight inside the saloon casts a golden light on his blond hair. His broad inviting shoulders draw my gaze, and I find myself unable to look away.

Another man finally helps him with his boot. When he finishes, the blond man straightens and my breath catches when I see his face. The facial hair is a new feature, but I know him. "Karl!" I call out, walking up to him as he looks over at me. To my surprise, he grins. I left the rink hospital angry with him on Thursday, and I didn't come back to help him eat until Friday evening, but by that time he had already been discharged, so I didn't know where he went or if he was still in Pine City.

"Anna," he says, smiling. "I was hoping to catch you after the service."

The man who helped Karl with his boot takes the cigar out of his mouth and points it at me, asking, "Is this the girl?"

"Yes," Karl answers. "Anna, this is Nathaniel. We share a tent in Robinson Park."

"Oh, that's where you moved to?" I ask. Mrs. Howard and Mary notice that I stopped following them and turn back around. I wave them over and call out, "I found Karl."

Mary rushes over and exclaims, "Karl, you look so much better."

Karl smiles at Mary and answers, "My head and eyes are completely better. The burns on my back and neck are almost healed too."

Mary nods to his hands and asks, "You took your bandages off. That must be a good sign."

Karl puts his hands in his trouser pockets and shrugs, "I'm starting to feel the blisters now."

Mrs. Howard takes a turn in the conversation by asking, "So, you're the boy that Anna has been worried sick over?"

"Mrs. Howard, I have not been worried sick. He's our neighbor and he's . . ." I was about to say alone, but that doesn't seem like a polite thing to say.

Mary saves me by saying, "He's been our friend since we were children."

Karl is still smiling, so he must not have realized what I was about to say. His tent mate, Nathaniel lifts up his hand and says, "Karl made me dig into his boot for this. It's for you Anna." He's holding a small piece of paper in his hand. He offers it to me, and I take it from him while looking at Karl who isn't smiling anymore.

"What is it?" I ask apprehensively while I unfold it.

Karl clears his throat and says, "Nathaniel and I check the lists at the town hall each day for Kristoff's name. I remembered the names of most of your school friends, so I checked the lists for their names too."

Mary interjects, "Kristoff?"

Karl's eyes flash to her, but he quickly looks at the ground and shakes his head as he says, "Nothing yet."

I look down at the paper and see two scrawled lists, their handwriting jagged and hurried. This isn't Karl's handwriting; I assume his friend wrote them. The first says "Alive: Belle, Clara, Edwin." My heart stops beating as I read the next list which says, "Dead: Charlie, Daniel, Helen." A dull pain between my eyes throbs as I read the second list again. The names don't change, but my vision becomes blurry as tears begin to form. Two more of my friends are dead.

"I'm sorry, Anna," Karl says.

A teardrop falls onto the piece of paper, so I fold it and hold it close to my chest. I look at Karl and say, "Thank you. I have been worried about them for days. I'm glad to learn that Edwin survived. Belle's brother, Archie, is alive too."

Mrs. Howard rubs my back and says, "Girls, I think it is best we get home. It is very late." She turns to Karl and Nathaniel and says, "Good evening, gentlemen." She links her arm through Mary's and offers the other to me. I clasp her inner elbow with one hand and begin walking with them, but stop abruptly as a hand brushes against my free hand.

"Anna, wait," Karl says. My fingertips brush against his palm. The skin feels hot against mine, but the texture shocks me. It is rock hard and jagged. I turn back to him, dropping Mrs. Howard's elbow. My eyes travel up from our hands to his face as he says, "Happy birthday, Anna."

He lowers his head to whisper, "I'm sorry about the other day."

Mrs. Howard grabs my elbow, "Is it your birthday, dear?"

I don't answer her because I'm still looking up at Karl's face and touching his hand. Slowly, I slide my fingers along his palm, feeling the extent of his burns. He flinches when my fingertips reach blisters.

"Is today September ninth?" Mary asks.

"Yes, it is," Mrs. Howard answers. "Oh, Anna, I will make you a cake tomorrow. Now, let's head home." She hooks my arm into hers again and pats my hand as she starts leading me.

"Please come over tomorrow," I say to Karl and point down the street. "Mrs. Howard lives right there."

He nods and puts his hands back into his pockets. To my surprise, Mary hooks my other arm into hers. "Anna, I'm so sorry I forgot your birthday. Please forgive me." It's the first thing she has said to me since the day she slapped me.

"It's all right," I say. "I forgot too." Only Karl remembered.

31

Karl

Monday, September 10, 1894
Pine City, Minnesota
9 days after

I step out of the newspaper office and head back to Robinson Park. I placed an advertisement for any information on Kristoff's whereabouts. The man working there said he could wire it to several other newspapers like *The Duluth News Tribune*, and the *St. Cloud Journal Press* to expand the ad's circulation. Many refugees are staying in both of these cities. I thought that was a good idea, so I agreed. Hopefully, someone reads it with information on Kristoff.

Maybe he will read it himself.

I notice movement near our tent, and see a well-dressed man opening the entrance flap. I quicken my pace. Is he trying to steal from us? What could he possibly think we have? "Excuse me, sir," I shout, waving at him. "Can I help you?"

He straightens at the sound of my voice and looks around. When he sees me, he smiles and waves. "Hello, sir," he greets me as I stand in front of him. "Are you Karl Sundvquist, Svard Sundvquist's son?"

I'm surprised this stranger knows who I am and who my father was, "Yes, sir, I am."

"I'm Robert Saunders," he offers his hand to me. "Lawyer and fellow survivor from Hinckley."

I glance at his outstretched hand and clear my throat, "Um, I shouldn't . . . ." I lift my hand up to him, showing him my palm.

His face pales, and he returns his hand to his side, "I . . . I hope it heals quickly for you."

"Me too," I answer and then ask, "Why are you looking for me?"

"I'm investigating land titles in Hinckley," he says as he lifts a leather briefcase off the ground and wipes away the dirt from the bottom. "Can I have a moment of your time?"

I nod, "Sure. Have a seat. I need to clean my hands, but I can do that while you talk. Give me a minute."

"Of course, of course. Do what you need to," he says as he sits down in one of our mismatched chairs. I open the flap of our tent and go inside to grab the carbolic acid and some cloth bandages that I was given from the rink hospital.

When I come back outside, Mr. Saunders has a piece of paper on his lap. I sit down in the chair next to him and apply some of the acid to my palms. Out of the corner of my eye, I see Mr. Saunders flinch. I still feel nothing in the middle of each hand. I clean the inside of my palms with the edge of the bandage, then gingerly dab acid on the blisters that have reopened. That I do feel. I grit my teeth from the pain, but I refuse to make a sound.

I nod my head towards the paper on his lap as I start to wrap my hand, "What is that?"

Mr. Saunders is staring at my hands, but he looks at the paper quickly and then back to my face, "Yes, of course. This is the reason I came to find you."

He clears his throat and continues, "I'll start at the beginning. Two days after the fire, Governor Nelson made an official relief proclamation issuing a call to all citizens to take immediate actions in securing relief for Hinckley fire survivors. He created The State Fire Relief Commission and appointed several influential men to receive and disburse contributions of money." Mr. Saunders' voice is monotone as if he is reciting this from memory, so clearly, I am not the first refugee he has sought out and talked to.

Mr. Saunders continues, "They held their first meeting on September fifth and appointed Charles Pillsbury as the chairman. You may have already met the secretary of the Commission, Mr. Hart. He set up headquarters here in Pine City." He pauses, waiting for me to answer. I shake my head and finish wrapping my hands. "No? Well, he is a busy man, maybe you will meet him soon. Anyway, Mr. Pillsbury, Mr. Hart, and several other Commission members have already visited Duluth, Pine City, and Hinckley. They established relief centers in each city and assigned local agents to distribute meals, clothing, temporary housing, and transportation passes to survivors."

"I already received my letter with my meal and clothing tickets and my tent assignment," I say and wave my bandaged hand toward our lopsided tent. "That was days ago."

"Well, the next action of the Commission is dispensing more permanent relief."

"Permanent relief?" I ask.

"Yes, in the form of money and building supplies. Each refugee will be registered and interviewed to identify needs and future plans. If you wish to remain in Hinckley, the local relief agent who interviews you will determine the amount necessary to rebuild."

So it's true. This is the relief money that Nathaniel had mentioned to me at the rink hospital when I first saw him. This is what I've been waiting for, and this lawyer even mentioned building materials. I ask, "How much relief money is there for everyone?"

Mr. Saunders' face brightens, "Well, our story has touched the hearts of many here in Minnesota and across the country, even across the world. I don't know the exact amount, but I believe it is somewhere around ninety to ninety-five thousand dollars."

My eyebrows lift. That is a very large amount, but there are also many refugees.

"And that does not include donated goods and services. Believe me, Karl, you will have help putting your life back together. Do you wish to return to Hinckley?"

"I do."

"Splendid. After our conversation, you can go to Hart's headquarters and schedule your interview for later this month."

"This isn't my interview?" I ask, still wondering why Mr. Saunders is here.

"Me? No, I've been appointed by the Commission to investigate land titles. Unfortunately, the complexity of administering permanent relief is multiplied for refugees that owned land before the fire."

"Why would owning land before the fire complicate distributing relief money?"

"Well because everything burned, houses, property, livestock. Everything that established a livelihood for landowners was destroyed, and if the land was mortgaged, then there is now no no means for the owner to make payments."

Without my permission, images of my home as a pile of ash and rubble flash in my mind. I clear my throat, "My father owned the land where my house once stood."

Mr. Saunders lifts up the piece of paper on his lap and offers it to me, "Yes, your father, Svard Sundvquist, did own forty acres, but it was heavily mortgaged by a land company based in St. Paul. In the event of his death, the mortgage falls to his remaining heir, which is you. Other homeowners in similar situations can try to extend the mortgage contract or try to liberalize terms of payment with the land company if they plan to rebuild on the parcel. But in your situation I wouldn't recommend that."

I take the piece of paper from Mr. Saunders, but the words on it mean nothing to me. Neither do the words this lawyer just used: *Heavily mortgaged? Liberalize terms of payment?* Father's signature is on the bottom of the paper, and it sends chills up my spine. My father held this very piece of paper. He read this contract and signed it when I was a child. That was years ago, but he had never told me he was still making payments. I just assumed it was ours since we had lived there for so long. Why did he never mention a mortgage to me? When did he send payments?

Mr. Saunders exhales slowly, "The Commission has decided that any houses built with relief money and supplies should not be built on heavily mortgaged land because the land company who holds the mortgage would absorb that house's value if foreclosure occurs.

My forehead creases with concern, "What are you saying?"

He clears his throat, "You have lost any means to make payments, so foreclosure is the likely outcome."

"Foreclosure?"

"I'm so sorry, but you won't be able to use the building materials or the relief money to rebuild on this land."

All I can do is stare at him. He doesn't realize what he is taking from me.

"Karl, I know it sounds unfair since it is your land, but this is a wise decision from the Commission. They don't want large amounts of aid to go to land companies. They want it to go to refugees. For your situation, the best option, in my opinion, is to let your Father's land go back to the land company if indeed the house, barn, and livestock are gone."

I fold my arms across my chest. "Everything is gone."

He sighs. "You said you want to return to Hinckley?"

I give him a quick nod.

"Well, there are some free or cheap pieces of land to build on. I can help you and your wife find a different parcel. After your interview, you would be able to build a relief house on the new parcel."

"Wife? I don't have a wife."

Mr. Saunders blinks a few times and stares at me. "What?"

"I'm not married."

His eyes widen for a moment, then he scratches his beard. Frowning, he retrieves his leather briefcase and digs inside. He pulls out a few different pieces of paper and scans them.

Finally, he exhales, closes his eyes and says, "Oh, dear. Karl, I have to apologize. I have been working on these land titles nonstop, which is not an excuse, but I seem to have mixed up your land title with a similar one." He opens his eyes and looks at me, "Two separate but similar situations, but in my head, I've combined them into one. In the case of the other land title, the inheriting son is married."

"Does this change my situation?"

Mr. Saunders shakes his head and puts the papers back into his briefcase. "Unfortunately, the Commission probably won't distribute building supplies to single men who did not own a home before the fire."

His words slap me in the face. Suddenly, my neck is burning under my shirt collar, and instinctively, I lift my hands up to my shirt to unbutton it before I remember that I can't grasp the small buttons with my fingers. Panicking, I ask, "What? That can't be true. How am I supposed to restart my life?"

Mr. Saunders covers his mouth and shakes his head again, "I am so sorry, Karl, I shouldn't have given you any false hope. That was very unprofessional of me."

I stand up and pace the area in front of the tent. This is terrible. I thought this Commission would help me rebuild, start my life over. Instead, they are telling me they can't help with my mortgage, and they will not give me building materials.

I will have nothing. No home. No land. No livelihood. No family. Utterly nothing. I stop in my tracks and look down at my freshly bandaged hands. A dark thought enters my mind: I should have let go of the cowcatcher and followed my father in death.

"Wait!" Mr. Saunders exclaims. "Wait, there might be . . . ." He stands up, abruptly from his chair. He looks through more papers and mumbles to himself.

"Yes, here it is," he stares at a piece of paper, reading it silently to himself. "Well, it's a handwritten note in the margin, but worth checking out, nonetheless." He looks up from the paper at me and says, "The State Fire Relief Commission could waive this restriction if a young man has since married and intends to settle down in Hinckley."

I stare back at him, blinking and ask, "Are you saying that I should get married?"

He bends down and puts the paper back into his briefcase, "Legally, I'm not telling you to get married in order to obtain building materials from the Commission."

He returns all the papers to his briefcase, clasps it shut, and starts to walk away. He takes a few steps before turning back to me, "But as a fellow fire survivor, I am suggesting that you look into every possibility to return and rebuild. I do not see the Commission being quick to distribute anything, as it is another branch of a bureaucracy. You have some time."

Signaling the end of the conversation, he bows his head to me. I stand still next to my tent, but my head is spinning. So many thoughts run into each other, one more peculiar than the next. Then, I turn on my heel and run towards Mrs. Howard's house.

After knocking on two front doors which were not Mrs. Howard's, I finally find it. She answers the door, but refuses to let me in. "Yes, Anna is here," she explains, "but I don't know if it is appropriate for you to come calling on her, Karl."

"Please, ma'am, I have news for her," I plead, out of breath from running.

"I should get permission from her parents before I let you in."

"Mrs. Andersson is here?" I ask excitedly. Anna's mother likes me. She would let me in. I wonder if Paul is here too, "Is Mr. Andersson with her?" I crane my neck trying to see inside, but Mrs. Howard moves her body in my way.

"No, she is not. She should arrive tomorrow night from Minneapolis. Her husband is remaining at the hospital for an extended stay."

I don't think Mrs. Howard is going to budge. I wonder if Anna would consider coming to the tents at Robinson Park or if I should stay on this street and wait for her to leave the house. As I'm contemplating what to do next, a small hand appears on Mrs. Howard's shoulder. The woman leans back into the house, and Mary appears at her side.

"Mrs. Howard, may I offer a suggestion? Karl is a family friend, and he was Anna's neighbor before the fire. I would also like to speak with him, so I can be present when he talks to Anna."

Mrs. Howard pauses, inhaling through her nose and says, "I suppose."

She opens the door wider and lets me through into the threshold. She motions to the room next to the front entrance. "Please stay in the parlor. I will be right in the kitchen."

I take off my hat, fumbling with the brim, and nod to her, "Yes ma'am."

She looks at me and Mary, standing in the parlor, before turning away into the kitchen. "I'll fetch Anna."

After she leaves, Mary asks me, "How are your hands today?"

I shrug, "They are healing. Slowly." It's a lie, and she can see right through it. I can't even hold the brim of my hat with my fingertips. I have to press one bandaged hand inside the hat and hold it against my chest with my other hand, but Mary doesn't press me for more details.

She doesn't speak again which makes me think she didn't really need to talk to me. She just wanted me to get past Mrs. Howard. Anna pushes through the kitchen door and walks into the parlor. There is space between all three of us, so we create a triangle in Mrs. Howard's parlor.

Anna smiles as she greets me, "Karl, you made it. Mrs. Howard's cake is in the oven."

Mary asks me, "Do you really have news for Anna, or were you just trying to get inside?"

Anna's eyebrows lift up, "News?"

Mary and Anna are looking at me, but I'm not sure how to jump from birthday cake to a marriage proposal. "Well, um, Anna, I need to talk to you about something." I turn around and look for a hook. There is one by the door, so I walk over and put my hat on it. I don't want to fidget with it anymore. "I talked to a lawyer today about my father's land. It's heavily mortgaged, and I have no way to make payments, so it will likely go back to the land company."

"Oh, Karl, that's awful news," Anna says as she places a hand on her chest. "I'm so sorry to hear that."

"Yes, it is difficult since I was hoping to rebuild on that land. But the lawyer also told me that the State Fire Relief Commission, which is responsible for giving out building materials to refugees, is not distributing housing supplies or offering to build homes for single men that did not own a house before the fire. So even if I could keep my father's land, I'd have no way to build a house on it before winter comes."

"The Commission can't expect you to live in a tent this winter," Mary says.

Anna adds, "No, of course not, there must be another housing option. Do you have anyone else? What about the man you were with last night?"

"Nathaniel?" I ask, feeling like the conversation is getting away from the direction I was hoping it would go. "No, he is likely in a similar situation as me. He is also not married, and he did not own a house before the fire."

"Well, I'm not sure what Mother's plans are since Father is still recovering," Anna says, "but I doubt she would turn you away. I can ask her about it once she arrives from Minneapolis."

I shake my head, "No, I don't want to move in with your mother. Besides, I don't think Mrs. Howard is going to offer me a room or even the floor to sleep on. That's not why I ran here." Both girls look at me, and I have no other option but to just come out with it. "The Commission may waive the housing restriction if the single man has since married . . . since the fire."

They both stare at me for what seems like an eternity, until Mary finally says, "You want to get married, so you can build a house?"

I exhale, "There might not be another way for me to rebuild."

Mary laughs in disbelief, "That is the worst marriage proposal I have ever heard."

"It's just an idea," I snap at her.

"A far-fetched idea if you ask me."

"I'm not asking you. I'm asking Anna. I don't have many options, so this might be the only way to get a roof over my head." I lift my hands up between me and the girls. "There's no way that I can earn enough money for supplies before the season changes, let alone build a house. I need that aid."

Mary crosses her arms in front of her chest but doesn't argue with me.

"You . . . you want to marry me?" Anna asks. "I thought you were angry with me."

I turn towards her, "I don't know why I treated you that way, Anna. I'm sorry, please forgive me."

Mary asks, "What is he talking about?"

Anna ignores her sister's question, "Of course I forgive you, Karl. Please don't push me away again."

"I won't, Anna. I . . . I don't know why I didn't comfort you that day in the rink hospital. After the fire, I . . . I'm all messed up. I'm sorry that I hurt you."

Anna looks down at the floor, "The fire changed me too. I'm so sad and tired all the time." She looks up at me and her eyes glisten with tears, "Three of my friends are dead. Four of them moved away. Your father is gone. Mine may be next."

She begins to cry, and I close the distance between us and embrace her. She leans into me, and I rub her back. "Anna, I'm so sorry that your friends died, but don't worry about your father. He is a strong man; he will survive."

She keeps crying on my chest and talking into my shirt. Her voice is muffled from the fabric, "You don't know that. Nobody does." I hate to see her cry, but she's right. I don't know if her father will survive. Just like I don't know if Kristoff survived. I don't have power over my own life much less over the fates of others.

If I have learned anything from the fire, it's that life is not something a person can control. I always planned to be a shanty boy; for me, there was no other alternative. Kristoff wanted to be a veterinarian; he and his mother even saved money for the schooling. We both worked so hard, thinking we could control our destiny, but the fire taught us otherwise. It consumed without regard to character, faith, morality, class, or strength. Maybe Mary is right. It is a far-fetched idea to attempt to regain control over my life, but a small voice in my head, my Father's voice, says I have to at least try.

Mrs. Howard decides to walk into the parlor at this time and sees me embracing Anna. "What is going on?" she cries, rushing over and pulling us apart.

I step back immediately and allow Mrs. Howard to hold Anna, who is still crying, but not as hard as she was before. Mrs. Howard speaks sternly to me, "It is time for you to leave, Karl."

Mary speaks up, "He was only comforting her, Mrs. Howard."

"Please, leave my house," she repeats.

I nod and walk toward the door, taking my hat off the peg and putting it on my head. I try to grasp the doorknob, but my fingers refuse to bend. Mary walks over and turns the doorknob for me. I'm too embarrassed to say thank you.

As I cross the threshold, I turn around and say, "Anna, what about my question?"

She lifts her head up from Mrs. Howard's chest and wipes tears from her face. "I . . . I need more time."

Mary gasps, "Anna, you're not seriously considering this."

"Give me a few days to think about it, please," Anna says to me, ignoring her sister, again.

I smile at her, "I will come back on Thursday. I can ask your mother if you wish, but I'll be back. Thursday."

32

Anna

Wednesday, September 12, 1894
Pine City, Minnesota
11 days after

Mrs. Howard sets a plate of *lefse* in front of me this morning for breakfast. She sprinkles cinnamon over it before she returns to the cookstove to make more. It smells delicious, but I can only pick at the edges. My stomach is in knots because I can't stop thinking about Karl's proposal. I want to tell Mother about it, and ask for her advice, but first, I need to decide if this is something that I want. I like Karl; that's not the issue, but do I want to be his wife? He has always been my friend, so I want to help him. I think the knot in my stomach is from that pull, that need to offer him my help. I could make him happy if I said yes. He would be able to start his life again. My life would start again as well.

Madame Catrina's words echo in my head, *"Your life will not end, but begin again and turn in a new direction."* That conversation seems like it was years ago, but the accuracy of the gypsy's prediction is at the forefront of my mind. My life did not end in the fire, but is Karl the new direction I should take? Is Karl my new beginning?

Before I can answer myself, Mother walks into the room and looks down at my face and smiles. I smile back at her as she settles beside me at the table, but my smile disappears when I notice her appearance. She doesn't look well. Her skin is ashen and dull, and her hair is limp and falling out of her braids. Her eyes are shadowed, and her usual pluck and energy have disappeared, but what worries me most is the stillness. The constant chatter, humming, or singing is absent. Even last night, when I walked her from the train station to Mrs. Howard's house she spoke very little. When we arrived, a large supper was waiting for us in the kitchen, but Mother only asked where she was sleeping and went straight to bed.

"Good morning," Mrs. Howard says and sets a plate of *lefse* in front of Mother, "how did you sleep?"

"Very well, thank you," Mother replies. "It was such a pleasure to sleep in a bed again. I only had a chair at the hospital, and my sleep was always interrupted by nurses and doctors." She looks down at her breakfast before adding, "And other patients."

"That must have been very difficult," Mrs. Howard replies, "but I'm glad your husband was not alone. How is he?"

"He is alive. The first few days were the hardest. There was little hope that . . . ." She pauses and closes her eyes, saying, "The worst is over. He is awake and healing."

Mrs. Howard steps back to the cookstove, holding her hands in prayer, "Thank God Almighty." She starts making Mary's breakfast.

"Indeed," Mother agrees.

Mary walks into the room and sits down without looking at me. She's upset that I'm even considering Karl's proposal.

Mother smiles and nods at Mary before speaking to Mrs. Howard again, "Thank you so much for taking care of my daughters. I don't have the right words to tell you how much that means to me."

"It is a pleasure," Mrs. Howard answers. "They are wonderful young women. You can all stay for as long as you need."

"That is very kind of you, but we will only be here for a few more days, I expect."

Mary and I share a look of surprise.

"Mother?" Mary and I question together.

"Your uncle came to the hospital to see his brother. Remember, Magnus and his wife Elena?" I remember Uncle Magnus. He looked almost identical to Father, just younger. We haven't seen him for a few years.

"Yes, I remember him," I answer as Mary nods in agreement.

"Well, before he left the hospital, he offered us a place to live. He owns the farmhouse where your father grew up, and there are empty rooms since they don't have children yet."

I ask, "Where is that?"

Mary answers, "Father grew up in Preston along the Root River."

Preston? I am not sure where that is or how far away it could be.

"We can stay there for as long as it takes your father to recover . . . which may be some time." Mother looks down at her untouched food before continuing, "I'll have to find a way to earn money, maybe sewing services or laundry." She says it softly, almost as if she is thinking out loud.

Mrs. Howard sets a plate in front of Mary and says to Mother, "You're lucky to have such a helpful family. The State Fire Relief Commission may also be able to help you with the supplies you need to start your sewing or laundry services."

"That could be very helpful. I'll see what they can offer me before we leave. I will need to ask them for help with transportation as well."

"When will you leave?" Mary asks, taking her first bite.

Mother frowns, looking confused for a moment and answers slowly, "We," she says emphasizing the word, "will leave as soon as possible. I can go to the relief headquarters today and see if they have a timeline for us on aid."

Mary stops chewing for a moment before slowly swallowing. Then she says, "Mother, I'm not moving to Preston."

"What? Of course you are. We all are. We're staying together as a family, Mary."

Mary doesn't look upset, but she slowly shakes her head, "No, I am not moving to Preston."

"Mary. Your father needs you now more than ever. We all need each other."

"I love you, and I love Father," Marys says, "but I am not moving with you to Preston." My eyes widen in shock. Mary has never disagreed with our mother.

"I . . . I don't understand," Mother stammers.

"I was going to wait a couple days before I told you, but I intend to live in St. Paul."

My eyebrows go up in surprise. She wants to move to St. Paul? Why? Mother chuckles to herself, "And where will you live in St. Paul, Mary? On the streets?" She smiles and looks at Mrs. Howard, shaking her head dismissively.

"Mother, I am being quite serious. I've already made all the arrangements."

Mother stops smiling and her face grows serious as she says sternly, "Mary, I will not entertain this. We are all moving together to Preston. This is what your Father and I want, to all be together again."

Mary's soft features turn hard and she glares at Mother. "Together, again?" Suddenly, she pushes against the table, knocking her chair to the floor, as she stands up. Mrs. Howard and I both gasp as the back of the chair crashes against the wooden floorboards. "Now, you want us to all be together again? Now?"

Mother stands up and raises her voice, "That's quite enough, Mary."

Mrs. Howard quietly picks up Mary's chair, turning it right again. Mary whispers an apology to her, but she just shakes her head and waves the apology away. She glances at Mother and says, "I'm going to visit with some friends down the street, Mrs. Andersson. I will be back in a couple hours. Please, make yourself at home. Don't clean up, I will do that when I return."

I feel embarrassed and uncomfortable and so confused. I don't understand why Mary is so angry that Mother wants us to be together. Both of them remain standing as Mrs. Howard walks through the parlor to the front door. As soon as the door shuts, Mother starts again, "Mary, I do not want to hear another word. You will move to Preston with your family. I did not raise a selfish daughter who neglects and disobeys her parents."

Mary's stiff posture softens, and her eyes begin to water. When her lip starts to quiver she looks away from Mother.

"Mary," I softly say, "What arrangements did you make? Is that where you've been this past week?"

She looks down at me and clears her throat, "I've been to St. Paul a few times, to visit John's mother, their family lawyer, and his insurance agent."

A chill runs down my spine when Mary says his name. My mind

races back to my sister's small wedding as I try to remember the faces of everyone who attended. The guests were very one-sided. They mostly consisted of our parents' friends and families from church. I do remember John's mother being there, but she was the only member of his family that attended. I don't recall her much except that she was old, reserved, and very quiet.

"Where did you find money for train tickets?" Mother asks.

"In the first few days, transportation was free for refugees," Mary explains as she quickly wipes her eyes and puts her hands on her hips. She stands straight and speaks clearly, "First, I met with John's mother. It was my duty to tell her in person about her son's death. She was sad, of course, but she is a practical woman. We discussed the issues that needed to be settled due to John's death."

"What issues?" Mother asks.

"Land ownership. Inheritance. My relationship with his family moving forward. I managed to save our marriage certificate and the land title from the house in Pokegama."

"How?" I ask her.

"The carpetbag. There is a clause in the land title about the surviving spouse taking full ownership of the land."

"You own land in Pokegama?" I gasp.

Mother finally sits down in her chair, shaking her head, "But I thought John's mother helped pay for that land. Isn't she a part owner?"

Mary sits down as well and says, "She did help John with a down payment, and the rest was in a mortgage with the land company. I assumed she wanted to discuss terms of repayment, but that wasn't the case. In fact, she made it very clear that she never wanted John to marry me in the first place, and she did not care to see me again after this, so she offered me a deal. Instead of part ownership or repayment, she would give up her rights to the land if I did not touch John's inheritance or bank accounts."

Mother frowns, "That is not a fair deal, Mary. The fire destroyed the logging potential of the land. You can't farm it yourself even after clearing the debris. Do you intend to hire someone to work the land?"

"I foreclosed," she replies. "I have no interest in returning to Pokegama ever again. After Mrs. Larson signed the necessary papers, I went to the land company's office in Rush City. I met with Mr. J. D.

Markham to give him the land back. I explained that I have no way to make the mortgage payments, and Mrs. Larson's lawyer cleared her family's name from the title, so he could not contact her."

Mother puts her head in her hands. "Oh my goodness, Mary. Why did you agree to Mrs. Larson's deal?"

Mary's face darkens and I see her shoulders tense, "I do not want John's money."

"Then how will you live in St. Paul?"

Mary leans back in her chair as she says, "Besides the land title, I also saved our property insurance policy from the fire."

Mother's mouth drops open, "Property insurance? You had property insurance?"

"Yes, we did. John bought it from an agent in St. Paul. His name is Peter Johnson. He travels to logging towns sporadically and tries to sell policies, but I know he has had little luck, which is too bad, considering how much it could have helped people in Hinckley and Pokegama. I will receive a payment of $300 for the damage to the house. That should pay for rent and living expenses until I have my own paycheck."

"Rent?" Mother asks.

Mary nods and says, "The insurance agent, Peter and his wife Valerie, own a couple of houses on their block. They rent rooms out, mostly to factory workers at the Northwest Knitting Company. I've already met with them and secured an empty room. It will be ready in two weeks."

"*Aj!*" Mother exclaims, hiding her face in her hands again. "Mary, you must undo this."

"No, I won't. This is what I want."

"*Själviskt barn,*" Mother snaps at Mary. In addition to calling Mary selfish, I hear her curse in Swedish. She looks over at me, "I guess you and I will leave for Preston in a few days." The tension in the room is overwhelming. Anger radiates from Mother to Mary, like the heat from a flame.

My voice squeaks out a question, "Can Karl come with us?"

"Karl?" Mother turns to me, her face changing to one of sadness. "That poor boy, of course he can." She whips her head back to Mary and snaps, "Anna is not thinking of herself. She is thinking of others in the world and what she can do to help them."

Mary shakes her head. "Karl will not want to go to Preston. He is desperate to return to Hinckley and rebuild." Then she tilts her head to the side, thinking, "But maybe it is best that Mother takes care of him. He was speaking nonsense yesterday. I wonder if he has not fully recovered from his head injuries."

Mother frowns, "Speaking nonsense? Mary, what are you talking about?"

"He was not speaking nonsense," I defend Karl, yelling at Mary. "Is it so hard to believe that someone overlooked you and desires me instead?"

Mother says sternly, "Someone tell me what is going on."

Mary rolls her eyes at me and stands up, pacing the kitchen floor.

Mother pulls my hand out from under the table and whispers, "Anna, please tell me."

I inhale and let it out in one breath, "Karl asked me to marry him yesterday."

"What?" Mother reels back, dropping my hand. "Anna! Does this have to do with his kiss before? Was it more than kissing?"

"No!" My cheeks turn red with embarrassment.

Mary answers for me, "The State Fire Relief Commission will not give him building materials or money to build a house because he is single. He thinks if he gets married, they will give him aid to build a house in Hinckley."

Mother blinks at her for a moment and then pinches the bridge of her nose. She rubs her eyes without saying anything to either of us. Mary is still pacing the room, and I realize that I've been holding my breath. I sigh and then inhale slowly waiting for Mother to say something.

Finally she stops rubbing her eyes, looks at me, and asks, "Karl wants to return to Hinckley?"

"Yes."

"And, he will only be able to do so if he gets married?"

"Yes, I believe so."

"So he would not want to come with us to Preston."

I shrug my shoulders, "I'm not certain. I can ask him."

"Do you want to move back to Hinckley?"

"Mother," Mary says, stopping in her tracks.

Mother ignores her and keeps talking to me, "I would like to talk to Karl. Have you spoken to him since he mentioned this to you?"

"No, I haven't. He said he would come by tomorrow."

"I would like to speak with him before you do," she says. I stare at her, not sure what to say. Does she want me to marry Karl?

"No," Mary slams her hand on the table. "Anna, you can't marry Karl, not like this," she says to me. Then she glares at my mother and points a finger in her face, "And you. You are going to tell her the truth about your involvement in my marriage."

Mother smacks Mary's finger out of her face, "How dare you speak to me like this?"

"Please, stop it. Both of you." I cry, tears streaming down my face. I hate to see them like this.

Mary looks back at me, "Anna, you need to understand what our Mother's advice really means. Then you'll know her true motivations are not to help you. She's the selfish one in this room."

"Mary," Mother shouts.

"Tell her," Mary shouts back. "Tell her everything, so she knows what happens when you arrange a marriage. She already knows about the pregnancy."

Mother looks surprised for a moment. Her eyes dart between Mary and me. Then she sighs and says to me, "Last spring, Mary came to me and told me that she had missed two bleedings in a row and that she was vomiting each morning when she woke up." Mother clears her throat a little then continues, "She was already courting John at the time, so I was not naive. I knew she was with child. Your father and I met with John and . . . strongly prompted him to make a marriage proposal."

She turns back to Mary, "I don't see how that is selfish of me or your father. Did you want to be sent away to raise an illegitimate child on your own?"

"Did John want to marry me?"

Mother bites her lip and looks away from Mary before saying, "No, he did not."

"Tell her how you changed his mind, Mother."

Mother fidgets with her blouse button for a moment, gazing at the table before speaking again, "John agreed to marry your sister if we could guarantee him a small income. That was not a possibility for us, so our conversation seemed to be at a standstill. Your father was about to walk away, so I rectified the situation."

I can feel my heart beating in my ears, but Mother's voice manages to push through the steady pounding. "I told John that I was acquainted with Mrs. Kelsey, wife to one of the Kelsey brothers of the land company in Pokegama. I suggested to him that I could set up a meeting between them because they were looking for a salesman to pitch land titles to folks in St. Paul who might be interested in living on the frontier."

"You lied to him," Mary says, sinking back into her seat.

"No," Mother snaps back. "Lucy did come to our church the month before, and she mentioned that they had plenty of acreage for sale and in need of a good salesman."

Mary scoffs at her, "You were not in a position to arrange business meetings for her husband."

Mother folds her arms across her chest. "Maybe not, but I was only thinking of you. Your future."

Mary's shoulders slump. Her face is full of sorrow as she turns to speak to me, "Even if her intentions were to protect me, Mother forced my marriage to John. She had the chance to walk away, but she didn't. She twisted the truth and tricked him into marrying me. John saw an opportunity for his own personal gain through this arrangement . . . not unlike Karl's motivations."

Now I stand up abruptly and stab my finger in the air toward Mary, "How dare you compare him to John."

Mary throws her hands up in defense, "I'm not saying they are the same person, Anna, but you have to see the similarities. Men have their own plans in their head for success and opportunity. They don't care if they use us to attain their goals. I see that in Karl."

I grind my teeth together, infuriated that she is comparing our friend to that monster. I want to slap her for what she just said, but my arms hang heavy at my sides. Instead, I spit out the words, "Karl would never hurt me the way John hurt you."

Mary flinches, as if I did slap her, and her eyes dart to Mother. I don't care that I shared one of Mary's secrets. I'm glad. Now Mother will understand how awful it is to say that Karl and John are cut from the same cloth. I expect her to demand an explanation. I expect her to be shocked, frightened, or upset, so I'm surprised when she doesn't run to Mary's side; instead, she grabs my arm and tugs on my sleeve.

"Anna," Mother whispers, "How do you know about that?" She turns toward Mary, "Did you tell her?"

Mary shakes her head slowly.

The bottom of my stomach drops out completely, and I sink back into my chair, devastated that Mother is not shocked by what I said because she already knew that John hurt Mary.

"Mother," I choke on the next words, but I have to ask, "How do you know?"

Her face pales and her bottom lip trembles, but Mary answers for her, "She saw it, just like you did, Anna. Mother came to visit me in July, to check on me and see if I was showing yet."

"What?" I turn to Mother.

Mother opens her mouth to speak, but Mary interrupts her, "She arrived at a similar scene to the one you saw. I told her about losing the baby and how John began treating me immediately afterwards." Mary clears her throat and says, "I was hysterical. I begged to come back home with her, to be together again, but she said no. She told me to stay."

My insides twist. I feel gutted. Mother knew about John for over a month and did nothing. She didn't save Mary. She left her to face a monster alone.

"Please, Mary," Mother cries. "I'm so sorry. I do regret leaving you, but I didn't know what else to do."

"You abandoned me," Mary says, "and on the day of the fire . . . John tried to kill me. He put his hands on Anna too. He strangled her until she passed out."

"What?" Mother cries. Her reaction is visceral, caught between a scream and a sob. She clutches her chest, trembling. I hold my breath. Was Mary going to tell Mother everything? "I'm so sorry," Mother gasps, "I didn't know he would do that. Please, forgive me. I didn't think—"

Mary interrupts her with a voice that I've never heard her use before. Her tone has a bite to it, "Twice I listened to your advice, Mother. Twice I made the mistake of trusting you. After you abandoned me, God stepped in. He sent the fire to sweep away the demon that you left me with. This life is a gift, and I will not make the same mistakes again. I will not go with you. You can call me selfish, and you might be right. I am thinking of myself, but I don't care. I won't be obedient to you or anyone else ever again."

A sob escapes me. My family is breaking right in front of my eyes. My heart is breaking along with them. Mother doesn't respond. She can't. She's sobbing into her hands and her shoulders shake. Mary walks around the table and kneels next to me. She speaks over Mother's sobs, "Anna, understand what you are getting into if you say yes to Karl."

I swallow a lump in my throat and whisper, "Karl would never hit me, Mary. I know he wouldn't."

She shakes her head, "No, he's not like John in that way. He's not evil, but if he is proposing a marriage to you, so he can build a house —"

"If I say no to Karl, then he will be homeless," I say as tears run down my cheeks.

She shakes her head, wiping one of my tears away with her thumb, "No, he won't. He will figure out something else. Don't feel obligated to him and don't feel obligated to Mother and Father. They have each other."

My lip quivers, and I hold back my tears as best as I can. Mary leans in and whispers, "We survived, together, without anyone telling us what to do. You can do anything, I've seen it."

She stands up and kisses my forehead before walking behind my chair to Mother. She kneels down on the ground next to her and embraces her. Mother hugs her back, burying her face in Mary's neck. Her voice is muffled as she sobs, "I'm so sorry, Mary."

Mary rubs her back and says, "I forgive you Mother, and I still love you, but you no longer have my trust."

33

Anna

Thursday, September 13, 1894
Pine City, Minnesota
12 days after

I'm back in the chair staring out Mrs. Howard's front window. My foot taps frantically up and down against the wooden floor, and my fist is wound tightly around a folded piece of paper. Karl is coming today. He said he would. Mother, Mrs. Howard, and Mary all sit in silence doing various tasks while I look out the window. At midmorning, Mrs. Howard leaves the house to have tea with her neighbor, but Mother and Mary stay.

Soon Mother complains of a headache. She is reluctant to go lie down in Mrs. Howard's bedroom, but Mary convinces her that she will wake her when Karl arrives. She and Mary have not argued again about St. Paul, so I think Mother has accepted Mary's decision even if she does not agree with it. I wonder if she will be as agreeable with my decision.

I turn away from the window for a moment and see Mary sitting in a rocking chair reading. She must feel my gaze on her because she looks up from her book and locks eyes with me.

She tilts her head to the side and her eyes soften, "Anna . . . I'm proud—"

311

A knock at the door interrupts her sentence, and I jump out of the chair dropping the piece of paper. Mary stands up and sets her book on the rocking chair. She starts for the kitchen, probably to go fetch Mother.

"Mary," I plead to her, rushing towards the front door. "Please, wait." She turns to me with a confused look on her face. "Don't wake Mother. Not yet, anyway. I want a few minutes to speak with Karl alone."

"Alone?"

"Yes, just for a moment."

She frowns, "I don't think that is wise, Anna. I don't want to leave you two alone."

"Five minutes, Mary. That's all I ask. Please, I don't want him to feel ambushed."

She folds her arms across her chest as another knock sounds on the door behind me.

"Please," I beg, holding my breath.

"Five minutes, Anna. No more."

I exhale, "Thank you."

She walks into the kitchen and closes the door behind her before I whip around and quickly open the front door. Karl is standing in front of me, his hand raised like he was just about to knock again.

"Anna," he says, grinning. "May I come in?"

"Yes, please," I say, opening the door wider and letting him cross the threshold. He takes off his hat and hangs it on the peg next to the door. I shut the door behind him and walk into the parlor, feeling him follow behind me.

I motion to the couch against the far wall, but he shakes his head. "No, thank you. I'm fine standing. Is your mother home?"

I nod. "She is, but she's sleeping. She's been plagued by headaches since the fire."

"Oh, I'm sorry to hear that. It's a common symptom from all the smoke exposure."

"Yes. I get them sometimes too."

He nods. We're standing about three feet apart, but the distance feels wider. I know what I have to say to him, but I am not sure how to say it without hurting his feelings. Karl has never been anything but kind to me. Even after the strange scenario he created at the gypsy wagon, he was never cruel. He listened to me when I wanted to speak with him, and he respected my decision to lie for my sister. He protected me and Edwin when we were threatened by Ivar, even though it cost him his shanty boy dream. I know he is a good man, and he would make a loyal husband which makes this even more difficult.

"Karl," I say at the same time that he says my name.

We both smile, easing some of the tension in the room.

He motions his hand toward me, palm up, "Please."

I gaze at his healing wound briefly, then meet his eyes. His eyes shift to his hand and back to me. His expression wavers only for a moment, then he smiles again and tucks his hands into his pockets.

"Karl, the last time you were here, I was quite upset. I leaned into my grief when I should have been listening to your question more intently."

"No, Anna, don't apologize. You've lost a lot of loved ones. Believe me, I understand. Besides, I fumbled my proposal. I thought about our last conversation and realized that I never really proposed to you at all."

"You didn't?"

"No, I mentioned the idea, but you deserve a proper proposal."

"Oh, no, Karl, really, that's not what I meant."

"Anna, please, I want to. You are worthy of a hundred proposals. It's the least I can do."

His compliment makes me pause. The irony of what he just said is not lost on me. Before the fire, I would have swooned at his flattery. I craved the attention that young men gave my sister, the gifts they left at the house for her, and the compliments she received at church. "I don't want a hundred proposals," I say.

Karl smiles awkwardly, "Well, no, of course not. Just one, I suppose." He clears his throat, and I know what he is going to say next, so I stop him.

"I can't marry you."

His eyes widen in shock.

"I'm so sorry Karl. I care about you deeply, but I just can't. I'm too young, and—"

"You aren't too young. My mother was your age when she started courting my father. Your mother was seventeen when she married your father."

"I'm not my mother."

"No, you are not. You're Anna. You've been my neighbor since childhood. You are kind and friendly. You love your family. You stand up for your sister." He nods towards me, "You fidget with your hands when you are nervous."

I look down at my hands, which are indeed moving absently at my waist. I stiffen them and return them to my sides. When I look back at Karl, his face is serious. His eyes burn with intensity. "You're beautiful. You are trustworthy and forgiving. You're not afraid to tell me when I'm acting wrong. Like when I kissed your sister."

My face feels hot, and I know my cheeks are reddening.

"I really thought it was you that day, Anna. I was hoping it was you. It should have been you."

I shake my head, "Karl, that was so long ago. I don't care about that anymore."

He takes two strides towards me and closes the distance between us. His sudden closeness surprises me. I take a step back and look up into his face. "I can't marry you, Karl. I think that I want to—"

His mouth silences me, and he places his hands on my cheeks, tilting my face upwards. His lips are warm and soft, but his hands are rough and calloused. His palms scrape against my skin, and I inhale the scent of fresh cream.

I pull my head back, but he kisses me again, so I place my hands over his and peel them off my face, pushing him back.

"Karl, stop," I whisper. "You're not listening to me." I don't let go of his hands, but he does take a step back. My fingers linger on his palms. The skin is ragged and dry. There are ridges and valleys where the skin was burned off. I turn his palms up and look sadly at the sight. Shiny, red blisters line the burn site. The middle of his palm is a splotchy yellow with veins crisscrossing just beneath the surface.

"Please, let go," he says as he pulls his hands away and takes another step back. The kitchen door opens and Mary walks into the room. My five minutes are over.

"Karl," I plead, "I don't want to hurt your feelings, but I can't marry you right now. Everything has changed so fast. I don't want to make an important decision like this so quickly. I do care about you . . . but I don't want to marry you just so you can rebuild."

I pause for him to respond, but he just stares at me. I'm not getting my message across clearly, so I try again. "If we were to get married, I'd want it to be for a different reason. For, for love."

His eyebrows crease together, "For love?"

"Yes, of course. This is too hurried. Don't you feel rushed? You haven't had time to heal from the fire. I don't think it's wise to—"

Karl laughs loudly, and I jump a little from the volume of his voice. "Heal? I have healed, Anna. This is as good as it's going to be for me." He holds his hands out like an offering exposing his palms and the carnage from the burns.

Mary stares at them before softly saying, "She's sixteen, Karl. She doesn't need to marry anyone. Don't use her as a proxy wife for your loophole."

Karl drops his hands and shakes his head. He looks at me and says, "I really meant what I said when I walked you home the other night. You say everything has changed since the fire, and yes, most of it has. But not that. Not for me."

"Court me, Karl. Proposing to marry me? It's too fast."

He shrugs, "If the outcome will be the same, then why wait?" Then his shoulders slump, like he has given up. "The fire took everything from me. I have nothing left, but I thought maybe I had a chance to gain something back with you. Our marriage would have been for more than just a house. I trusted you to understand that, but I was wrong."

My chest tightens with guilt. He does care about me. I should have known this was for more than just a house. Karl turns around and walks to the front door. He takes his hat off the peg and turns back to us. "I'm sorry I wasted your time today, Anna. Please give your mother my regards."

"Karl, wait," I run to the chair by the window and pick up the piece of paper I was holding onto all morning. I lower my voice when I reach him, "I was trying to tell you earlier, that I think I want to register for high school. I can't do that if I'm married to you."

"High school?" he asks, frowning.

"Yes. I want to be a teacher. The nearest one is in St. Paul, and an opportunity has come up that might allow me to attend. I'll be leaving soon."

"That seems like an important decision you are making very quickly." He has turned my own words against me, but is he wrong? It is a big decision that I have made almost overnight. "Maybe you should take some time to think about it. You don't want to be a hypocrite."

I knew Karl might be upset if I rejected his offer, but the name-calling is out of character for him. He sighs and points to the door, "Please, Anna. I'd like to leave now."

It takes me a second before I remember that he can't open the door for himself, so I grasp the doorknob and twist, pulling the front door open. He crosses the threshold and walks out.

I stand there staring at him, until I remember the piece of paper in my hand. "Karl," I yell after him. He stops in the street and turns around.

"Here," I hold up the piece of paper. "This is the address where I'll be staying in St. Paul. Take it, so we can write to each other."

I follow him into the street and offer the paper over to him. He stares at it for a second then whispers, "If I can't even open the door for myself, what makes you think I can hold a pen."

I look up at him with pity in my eyes. He feels so broken without the use of his hands, and my rejection just made him feel worse.

"Goodbye, Anna," he says and turns around. Tears build in my eyes as he walks away. If he doesn't take this address, he'll have no way to tell me where he moves. I'll have no way to find him.

I won't lose him too. Quickly, I step in front of him and thrust the paper in his shirt pocket. "Just in case," I say; but he doesn't answer. He walks away, and this time I let him go.

34

Karl

Thursday, September 27, 1894
Pine City, Minnesota
26 days after

My foot taps the floor nervously.

"Name?"

"Karl Anders Sundvquist."

"Place of birth?"

"Ryd, Sweden."

"Wife? Any children?"

"No wife. No children."

He doesn't even flinch before continuing, "Deceased family members?"

I swallow a lump in my throat before responding, "Svard Sundvquist was my father. He . . . he died in the fire."

He dips the metal nib of his pen into the bottle of black ink. "Where did you and your father live?"

"North of Hinckley, on the wagon road."

"Were you employed?"

"Yes, by the Brennan Lumber Company."

"I see," he pauses to finish copying my responses on a piece of paper. The scratch of the pen is the only noise in the tent. The man across the table is a stranger. I've never seen him at the relief headquarters before. The table we're sitting at has several stacks of papers held down by rocks.

"Were you able to salvage any property from your home? Including livestock?"

"No."

"And, do you now own the property where you and your father lived?"

"No."

"Do you have any insurance? Assets?"

Again, I answer, "No."

His eyes leave mine and look down at the paper while he writes. The State Fire Relief Commission must have appointed him to help register and interview refugees in Pine City. I wonder if he is as nervous as I am. Does he understand that he is the gatekeeper to my future? His decision dictates the next steps of my life. I'm at his mercy.

He looks up at me, taking a pause from his writing, "We are almost finished, Mr. Sundvquist." I nod, and he continues, "What are your plans now?"

"I'd like to return to Hinckley. Build a house," I say and clear my throat to let him know what I really want, what I need him to approve. "I understand the relief houses supplied by the state will build a sixteen by twenty-four foot single room structure. Are you able to distribute those materials to me?"

The man picks up the stack of papers in front of him and lightly taps them on the table, straightening the stack so that they are all aligned. He sets them back down and flips over the top page.

"Mr. Sundvquist, the Commission has agreed that no refugee will be given aid that makes his situation better than it was before the fire."

"Better?" I almost laugh. "How could my situation be better than before the fire?"

"You did not own a house before the fire."

I stare back at him blankly. He wants me to respond, to agree with him, but I can't. I won't. If I do, then he knows that I've given up. Instead, I decide to ask him about what the lawyer told me.

"What if I've recently gotten engaged? Would that mean my situation calls for more aid?"

He furrows his brows, "What?"

"If I get married soon, would the Commission help me build a house for me and my wife?"

"Of course not," he says thoughtlessly.

I groan and scratch at the facial hair on my chin. All of that with Anna was for nothing. I can't even apologize, either, because she's gone.

The man picks up his pen again, positioning it above the paper. "May I have one or two references from you?"

"References?"

"Yes, references; meaning one or two acquaintances that I may interview on your behalf."

I frown as I ask, "Why would you need to do that?"

"Well, I need to understand your habits and personality. I'd like to distribute some cash to you, but first I need to learn of your character."

His condescending tone infuriates me. He's treating me like I've arrived at his tent without justification. "I'm not a pauper."

He raises one eyebrow slightly, but doesn't answer me right away. A moment passes before he says, "I can give you fifteen dollars, a railroad pass, and," he gestures to my body, "a new set of clothing."

I look down at my clothes. They are dirty and wrinkled, but what does he expect? I live in a tent.

"Please give me the names of two individuals that I can find in Pine City who can vouch for you."

I look back up at him. He is staring at me, waiting for my response, but my mind is blank. Who would speak for me? "Everyone I knew before is gone."

His shoulders and eyebrows lower at the same time. I know that look; it's pity. "Surely, there must be someone you knew, maybe an acquaintance at the sawmill?"

Pain hits me in the middle of my chest, like he just punched me in the heart. "I worked with Kristoff."

"And what is Kristoff's last name?"

"It's . . . It's . . . " I search my memory, but it's foggy. "I don't remember."

"I'll need his full name in order to locate him and interview him."

"That . . . that won't be possible," I can't believe I'm saying this, "Kristoff is dead." It's the first time that I've said it out loud. It's been too long to hope that I will find him alive. He died that day in Hinckley. Someone, somewhere in the rubble of our city found his remains and buried him where he lay or in one of the mass graves. Deep down, I know that's what happened. I have ignored the truth for weeks because I didn't want it to be real. He died alone, and that's probably my fault.

"I'm sorry, Mr. Sundvquist. Is there anyone else?"

I look past him at the back of the tent. I do my best to numb my emotions. After a moment, I give him the only other names I can think of, "Anna Andersson and Mary Larson were my neighbors." He writes the names down. I shift in my seat, ready to leave. He doesn't know that they already left Pine City. He can find that out on his own.

"I'd really like to speak with someone who worked with you. The relief aid is meant to help you find new employment, so I'd like to hear about your work ethic."

My hackles rise, "Do you think I'm lazy?"

He stiffens at my reaction, "No, I don't, but if you don't provide me with a name, I'll find someone from the mill on my own. It will take more time, and that's more time before you receive your aid money."

I grind my teeth together but spit out an answer, "Nathaniel Henderson."

His eyebrows raise, "You are friends with Mr. Henderson?"

"How do you know Nathaniel?"

He scribbles on my paper without answering and then folds his hands in his lap.

"I interviewed his references yesterday, and I've had—"

Suddenly, the flap to the entrance of the tent whips open, and a man rushes forward, almost knocking into my chair. He's still holding the flap open, and a cool autumn breeze flies into the tent, scattering the pile of papers on the table all over the tent.

"Excuse me," the interviewer says, trying to catch the papers as they fly in the air.

"I'm sorry, sir, but there's been a wagon rollover," the man shouts at us. "A man is stuck under the rear wheel. We need help lifting the wagon off of him." He looks frantically at me and the man across the table.

The interviewer hurries over to me and pulls me up from the chair, "We need to hurry," he says and follows the other man who is already running away from the tent.

I lift up my hands and show him my palms. "I can't."

He flinches at the sight of my burns, but lets go of my shirt. "Fine," he says.

He opens the tent entrance and ushers me outside. He starts to run after the other man, but yells over his shoulder, "We're done Mr. Sundviquist. You may leave."

I stand at the entrance of the tent and wait until he rounds the corner of the nearest building and disappears. Then I go back inside.

His papers are are scattered all over the dirt. I kneel down and look for mine. I need to know what he wrote down on the back. My eyes scan several forms that are not my own. I leave them on the ground and continue searching. Finally I find mine. The front includes all the responses to my questions, but when I flip it over to the back, I see the interviewers' notes scrawled at the top. "Neighbors, Anna Andersson and Mary Larson" and "Nathaniel Henderson, good for nothing drunken sot. Assume similar character."

My eyes widen in shock, and my stomach flips over. I scramble to grab more papers on the floor, but my useless hands fumble them. I manage to claw some together and, similar to my own, the front has formal responses to the same set of questions. The back of each has freely-written notes. One says, "He is blowing his cash on liquor and has always been a drunken dead beat." The other says, "She is a strumpet not worthy of consideration." My mind is reeling, but I read another, "Treat him as if he had no insurance." Finally, the last one says, "Gov. Nelson promised that his character is sound."

I let the papers fall from my hands. This isn't an interview to determine a refugee's permanent needs for relief and aid. It's a judgment of their moral character, a registration based on rumors and reputation. A sound outside the tent startles me, and I expect someone to come inside. I hold my breath and freeze, but no one enters. I breathe again and sift through the papers on the ground until I find my own. I will my fingers to bend, and to my surprise, they comply.

As I grasp my registration paper, intense pain shoots through my palm and wrist, and my fingers retract. I hiss through my teeth and hold my hand to my chest, dropping the paper.

Worried that someone might have heard me, I quickly grab my registration paper with the backs of my hands and rush out of the tent. I walk back to Robinson Park with it clutched awkwardly against my chest. Thankfully, no one cares or notices that I stole it. As I approach our tent, Nathaniel comes into view. He's perched on a chair beside a campfire.

"How did it go?" he asks when he sees me.

I throw my registration paper into the fire and sit down next to him.

He chuckles, "That well, huh?"

"It was a waste of my time," I say, staring into the flames. The paper ignites quickly, turns to ash, and floats away.

"That's saying something considering you sleep all day."

I shrug. I'm debating whether or not I should tell him what I read about him when he says, "Only a few more days until we head north to the shanties."

I turn my head to face him, wondering if he misspoke or if he is poking fun at me. He sees my confusion and clarifies, "The winter logging camps. The sawmill burned down, but the Brennan Lumber Company still exists. Lumber cruisers are locating timber right now, just farther north, out of the fire zone."

If I was in a good mood, I'd laugh it off, but I'm not. I'm annoyed that he is being so oblivious. I shake my head and cross my arms, saying, "Have fun. I won't be ready in time."

"What do you mean?" he asks. "It's not like you have anything to pack."

"Really?" I scoff and hold out my palms to him.

"Karl," he turns his whole body in the chair, so he is facing me while he says, "the Company takes care of its employees. If you can walk to the table to eat, the foreman will find work for you in the camps."

I stare at him in disbelief. Slowly lowering my hands, I stammer, "What?"

"There's always a few old jacks at the camps," he comments as he leans back in his chair.

"Old jacks?"

"Yeah, men who are too old or too sick," he points to my hands, "or too injured to work in the woods. Like I said, if they can walk to the table to eat, then they're kept on the payroll."

Something releases inside my chest. I feel so much lighter that I actually stand up from the chair. It feels like my whole body is vibrating with energy and something else. I think it's hope. I look up to the sky which is a beautiful light blue with puffy white clouds slowly blowing in the wind. The air is crisp, but the sun is still warm on my face. The burden I've carried since arriving in Pine City lifts, floating away with the clouds.

I whisper to them, "Thank you."

"Don't thank me," Nathaniel laughs. "That's the way it's always been."

I grin and say, "I'm going to be a shanty boy."

"Of course you are."

I throw my hands up and shout, "I'm going to be a shanty boy!"

A few people on the sidewalk look over at me, but I don't care. I keep grinning from ear to ear.

"Oh, I almost forgot. I found this in our tent," Nathaniel says and stands up next to me. He takes a piece of paper out of his pocket and unfolds it for me. It's the address that Anna stuffed in my shirt pocket.

I lower my hands and stare at it. Then, I ask him, "Can you put it in my boot?"

Epilogue

Present Day
Hinckley, Minnesota

Due to the determination of survivors Hinckley sprang up from the ashes almost overnight. By early October the tent city where Nathaniel stayed while he helped bury the dead had turned into a collection of small frame dwellings. These "Fire Relief Houses" were designed and supplied by the State Fire Relief Commission. The Commission continued to interview and determine refugees' needs into the spring of 1895, providing clothing, food, seed, and tools. By this time, business blocks had taken shape, and the townspeople were optimistic.

That changed when the town's two largest employers decided not to rebuild in Hinckley. James J. Hill, owner of the Eastern Minnesota Railway, decided to move the rail yards and facilities to Sandstone. Thomas Brennan, owner of the Brennan Lumber Company, never rebuilt the sawmill that once dominated Hinckley's landscape. Gone were the summers of boisterous shanty boys throwing money away in the shops and saloons of Hinckley. Without the logging and railroad companies, Hinckley became an area of agriculture.

Life continued, but it was different. For decades, the land was treeless, as seen in many black and white photos from the early twentieth century. Eventually trees grew back, but the once thick evergreen forests that created magical canopies like the one that Anna walked down on her way to Mary's house never returned.

The Golden Age of the American Railroad that thrived before the fire ended a century ago, but vestiges are still present. The Eastern Minnesota train tracks that cut diagonally through Hinckley are still there and are now operated by the Burlington Northern Santa Fe Railway (BNSF). The gravel pit, where a hundred people survived the fire, is now a park with a skating rink and sledding hill.

The St. Paul and Duluth tracks that ran north of Hinckley, the same tracks that Karl and Svard ran on to catch the Skalley, have been converted into a paved bike path—part of the Willard Munger State Trail. A plaque on the bike trail at Skunk Lake marks where three hundred people survived the fire. Running south, the St. Paul and Duluth tracks still exist and are operated by the St. Croix Valley Railroad (SCXY). Now reduced to a short line track, it spans only 36 miles between North Branch and Hinckley where the tracks interchange with BNSF.

The railroad no longer transports passengers between Duluth and St. Paul as it did during its heyday. Nevertheless, if you stand in Robinson Park today, you could witness a black and yellow locomotive chugging by, occasionally halting traffic on Third Avenue as it pulls freight cars to Hinckley. Proudly painted on its side are the crisp yellow letters: "The Skalley Line."

Hinckley's old downtown area, the Hinckley that Karl and Anna once knew, is now a residential neighborhood with modest homes, restaurants, shops, banks, and a grocery store. A large brick school building stands on top of the old school ruins. On the other side of town, across the interstate, new development in the late twentieth century has brought a movie theater, fast food restaurants, gas stations, and the county's largest employer, the Hinckley Grand Casino, which is owned and operated by the Mille Lacs Band of Ojibwe.

Even though Hinckley is now green, lush, and full of life, ghosts from the fire still linger. Street names honor its heroes: Barry, Best, Blair, Root, Stephan, and Sullivan Avenues. Even now, an unassuming red minivan passes the cross streets of Fire Monument Road and Lawler Avenue. Its passengers are unaware that the Catholic priest this avenue is named after was at the fire line and ran through the streets after the hose caught fire. He warned others to run for the gravel pit, saving their lives.

The red minivan turns right onto Old Highway 61 and rolls over the BNSF train tracks, the same spot where Anna waited and wondered why Karl had kissed Mary. Then the minivan turns left into an empty parking lot, its final destination. It is only 9:30 a.m., so the museum is not yet open.

The mother driving the van puts it in park and shuts off the engine. She unbuckles her seatbelt and opens the door. The humid air hits her face like a wall as she steps out. Her two children, a son and daughter, unbuckle themselves and hit the automatic buttons on their respective sides of the van. The large doors open seamlessly, letting out a rush of cool, air-conditioned air. The father in the passenger seat sets down his e-reader on the middle console. He steps outside and looks up at the building in front of him. It's painted light green with darker green trim around the doors and windows. A brown sign above one door says, "Hinckley Fire Museum" but the small white and blue sign in the window is flipped to "CLOSED."

He shuts the van door behind him and puts his hands on his hips, moving from side to side and cracking his back as he stretches. "It's bigger than I thought," he muses to himself. The sun is bright this morning, so he pulls his sunglasses down from the top of his head. He observes his surroundings from behind UV protected lenses.

He's read about the town of Hinckley extensively before this trip, but his interest in this small rural community started in his youth. He has many fond memories of his grandparents sharing the story of their grandparents. Tales of survival, bravery, and of course, walking to and from school in droughts, blizzards, and rainstorms. As an adult, he wants to know what was true and what was exaggerated.

He looks around the front of the van and says to his wife. "Honey, did you know that this is the location of the original train depot?" He's correct, this is the original site of the St. Paul and Duluth depot, where Anna and Belle drank Coca-Cola three days before the fire.

"I didn't know that," she answers. "We still have a few minutes before it opens."

"I'm going to check out the train," the son announces, leaping out of the van. He walks toward the red train car replica on the far side of the parking lot, near a small wooden pavilion with four picnic tables underneath. Disappointment awaits him, though, as he will soon discover that the interior is off-limits.

The rest of the family follows him up the long ramp, while another woman settles at one of the picnic tables. She sips her iced coffee, preparing for her shift at the museum. Since the family can't explore the train car replica, they make their way down to the picnic tables, patiently waiting for the museum to open.

"Good morning," the woman greets them as they take their seats.

The mothers asks, "Are you here to visit the museum too?

"Me? No, I volunteer here," the woman with the coffee says cheerfully. "The collection is fascinating to me, and I love to meet new people. I'm retired, so this is a perfect fit for me."

"We're excited to see the collection too," the father says and waves his hands to his wife and himself. "We've been reading about the Great Hinckley Fire and trying to learn more about what happened."

"Good for you," the woman smiles and politely asks, "And where are you coming from?"

"South Haven, Michigan," the mother responds. "I'm an accountant, and my husband designs custom fire trucks."

The woman nods to the father, "That's impressive. You must have the mind of an engineer."

"I think it's in my blood," he replies. "I'm a fifth generation engineer. In fact, my ancestors survived the fire. That's partly why we're here."

The mother hugs the young girl and says, "Our daughter, Anna, is named after a fire survivor. That's part of why we are here today, to try and learn what she went through."

The woman sets her coffee cup down and asks, "Do you know where she was on that day?"

The father shakes his head and says, "Not exactly, but we know that she survived in a well with her sister."

"She was my great-great-great grandmother," the little girl pipes up, "and she married my daddy."

The adults all laugh together. The father chuckles, "Well, no not exactly."

The mother squeezes her husband's arm, proudly stating to her children, "Your great-great-great grandmother married the man that Dad is named after, sweetie. He was also a fire survivor."

"He survived on Root's train, the one that backed up to Skunk Lake," the father adds. "I think it was called the Skalley back in the day."

"No way," the woman gasps. She is awestruck. Not every day do descendants of fire survivors show up at the museum let alone one that survived on Root's train.

"Yes, he did. I'm his namesake," the father says as he places his hand over his chest. "I'm Karl Sundvquist, named after my great-great grandfather."

Thank you for reading my novel!

Are you interested in the rest of Karl and Anna's story? Join my mailing list to receive an email when I have the release date for book two of The Pine County Chronicles.

Join the mailing list, purchase books, and find out about local author events at:
https://kristinashuey.wordpress.com

Thank you so much!
-Kristina Shuey

ROOT'S ENGINE

The engine that carried the last train load of survivors out of Hinckley during the 1894 fire.
Reprinted by permission of the Minnesota Historical Society

Acknowledgments

This novel would not have been possible without the help of so many people. First and foremost, I am eternally grateful for my parents, Tom and Teri Borich, as well as my in-laws, David and Joanne Shuey. Both sets of grandparents did the bulk of the childcare while I researched the Great Hinckley Fire and wrote *The Day the World Burned*.

A heartfelt thank you to my mom, who also served as my research assistant. She patiently helped me decipher the cursive script on one-hundred-and-thirty-year-old handwritten notes and registration cards. She was also the first person to read my manuscript, and she has always been my biggest cheerleader.

Thank you to Rebekah at the Pine City Library for teaching me how to use the microfilm machine, and for being so patient with my kids when they were not the quietest library patrons. Thank you to Christopher at the Gale Family Library, Margaret at the Pine City Library, Freda at the Hinckley Library, and Ryan at the Borchert Map Library.

I cannot understate the exceptional expertise of my editor, Diane Engelstad. With the sharpest eyes, she meticulously examined each sentence for structure, clarity, comma placement, and word choice. Diane transformed my rough and tumble manuscript into near-perfection. Her quick responses, dry humor, and encouraging support made the editing journey surprisingly painless. I look forward to working with her again, hopefully with fewer shuffles and exclamation points.

The cover art is the creation of Haley McMillan—an incredibly talented artist and author. When she sent me the cover image on my phone, I swear, I stared at it for hours. I am absolutely in love with it.

Thank you to Andrea Borich and Judy Scholin, who contributed to the creation of the maps. Andrea, a rock star mapmaker and all-around adventurer, skillfully transformed my hand-drawn sketches into clear, accurate depictions of the past. I hope readers can feel the weight of history at their fingertips. Judy, Pine City's early history expert, deftly shared her knowledge of the businesses and buildings around Robinson Park before the 1900s—not an easy task since so much has been lost to history (and fire).

I self-published this book with the help and coaching of my aunt and uncle, Judy and Bruce Borich. They have been in the publishing game for almost twenty years, and they were kind enough to share their knowledge with me. Thank you for the e-mails, phone calls, and support.

Thank you, Beth Spinler, for always being my hype-woman. And thank you to the Pine County community and my extended family. Even before publication, I received so much support and encouragement from family, friends, neighbors, businesses, and community members.

Back in the fall of 2020, when I first dreamed up Anna's story, I told my husband, Daniel. Immediately, he responded, "You should write a book about it." I shrugged off his comment and made up some excuse as to why that was not possible. But, Daniel didn't let it go. He said it was a great idea, and that I'm a great writer. He believed in me when I didn't. If you don't have a Daniel, I hope you find one someday.

References

Primary Sources

Akermark, Gudmund Emanuel. *Eld-Cyklonen Eller Hinckley-branden*, 1894. Translated and reprinted as *Eld-Cyklonen or Hinckley Fire*. Askov, Minnesota: American Publishing Company, 1976.

Anderson, Antone A. and Clara Anderson McDermott. *The Hinckley Fire: Stories from the Hinckley Fire Survivors*. New York: Comet Press Books, 1954. Reprinted by Hinckley Fire Centennial Committee, 1993.

Brown, Elton T. *A History of the Great Minnesota Forest Fires*. St. Paul: Brown Bros. Publishers, 1894.

Dougherty, Gorman, McGhee, & O'Brien. Speeches honoring John W. Blair. September 13, 1894. John W. Blair Papers, 1867-1915. Manuscripts (P1788). Minnesota Historical Society, St. Paul, MN.

Hinckley Enterprise. August 29, 1894.

Kelsey, Lucy N. A. *The September Holocaust*. Minneapolis: Alfred Roper Printing Co., Printers. 1894.

Minnesota State Commission for the Relief of Fire Sufferers. Relief Application for Sarah Barry. 1894. Hinckley Fire of 1894. Commission for the Relief of Fire Sufferers. Box 1. Government Records (Minnesota Historical Society, St. Paul, MN).

Minnesota State Commission for the Relief of Fire Sufferers. Relief Application for Adolph Schepstedt. 1894. Hinckley Fire of 1894. Commission for the Relief of Fire Sufferers. Box 1. Government Records (Minnesota Historical Society, St. Paul, MN).

Wilkinson, Rev. William. *Memorials of the Minnesota Forest Fires in the Year 1894*. Minneapolis: Norman E. Wilkinson, 1895.

Secondary Sources

Bell, Mary T. *Cutting Across Time: Logging, Rafting and Milling the Forests of Lake Superior*. Schroeder, Minnesota: The Schroeder Area Historical Society, 1999.

Brown, Daniel James. *Under A Flaming Sky: The Great Hinckley Firestorm of 1894*. Guilford, Connecticut: Lyons Press, 2009.

Cole, Rachel. "Bicycle Catalogs of the 1890s," LIBRARIES | Blog (blog), Northwestern University, June 14, 2018, https://sites.northwestern.edu/northwesternlibrary/2018/06/14/bicycle-catalogs-of-the-1890s/.

Foster, Earl J. & Troolin, Amy. *Images of America: Northern Pine County*. Charleston, South Carolina: Arcadia Publishing, 2011.

Johnson, Nathan. *Images of America: Pine City*. Charleston, South Carolina: Arcadia Publishing, 2009.

Larsen, Lawrence H. *Wall of Flames: The Minnesota Forest Fire of 1894*. Fargo: The North Dakota Institute for Regional Studies, North Dakota State University, 1984.

Lorenz-Meyer, Elizbeth & Wagner O'Brien, Nancy. *Onward Central: The First 150 Years of St. Paul Central High School*. St. Paul, Minnesota: Transforming Central History Committee, 2016. https://central.spps.org/about

Lyseth, Alaina Wolter. *Images of America: Hinckley and the Fire of 1894*. Charleston, South Carolina: Arcadia Publishing, 2014.

Peterson, Clark C. *The Great Hinckley Fire*. Hinckley, Minnesota:

The Hinckley News Incorporated, 1977.

Swenson, Grace Stageberg. *From the Ashes: The Story of the Hinckley Fire of 1894.* Stillwater, Minnesota: The Croixside Press, 1979.

Bible Verse

In chapter 16, Karl remembers a bible verse (Matthew 13:42) that Mrs. Andersson used to read to them as children. The bible Karl remembers from the Andersson's parlor was probably the Gustav Vasa Bible which was first published in Swedish in the 16th century. For this novel, I used the New Living Translation of the Bible because of the vivid imagery emphasized in modern English.

Bishop Mahlon Gilbert's Address

In chapter 30, at the memorial service, many of the phrases that Bishop Gilbert uses are his own words. I found a brief synopsis of his address in William Wilkinson's book, *Memorials of the Minnesota Forest Fires in the Year 1894,* pages 205 - 207. Wilkinson read Gilbert's address in an edition of the St. Paul Pioneer Press.

Photograph

Gale Family Library. *Root's Engine, St. Paul and Duluth Railroad Company, the Engine that Carried the Last Train Load of Survivors Out of Hinckley during the 1894 Fire.* Photograph. *Minnesota Historical Society.* Locator Number: HE6.2N p3.

Song Lyrics

"The Shanty Boy and the Farmer's Son" is a traditional folk song of Minnesota passed down from generation to generation. As such, it was never formally published, and the author is unknown. The lyrics were first printed in June 1893 in *Scribner's Magazine.* I found the lyrics in *The Minnesota Heritage Songbook*, https://mnheritagesongbook.net, compiled and edited by Robert B. Waltz.

Made in the USA
Monee, IL
17 October 2024